SOME OF THE CHARACTERS ON OUR SIDE

LUCIFER DYE—born in Montana, raised in a Shanghai brothel, he's paid $50,000 to corrupt an entire town

VICTOR ORCUTT—mysterious, fanatical, his motto is, "To get better, it must get much worse"

CAROL THACKERTY—cool, erotic, she was first educated by an aunt in only the best private schools, then by her rich customers as a top call girl

THEIR TOWN IS SWANKERTOWN—RICH AND CORRUPT—IT'S ABOUT TO EXPLODE!

The Fools In Town Are On Our Side

Ross Thomas

AVON
PUBLISHERS OF BARD, CAMELOT, DISCUS, EQUINOX AND FLARE BOOKS

AVON BOOKS
A division of
The Hearst Corporation
959 Eighth Avenue
New York, New York 10019

First Avon Printing, May, 1972
Fourth Printing

AVON TRADEMARK REG. U.S. PAT. OFF. AND
FOREIGN COUNTRIES, REGISTERED TRADEMARK—
MARCA REGISTRADA, HECHO EN CHICAGO, U.S.A.

Printed in the U.S.A.

"Hain't we got all the fools in town on our side? And ain't that a big enough majority in any town?"

Mark Twain, *Huckleberry Finn*

Part One

1

The debriefing took ten days in a sealed-off suite in the old section of the Army's Letterman General Hospital on the Presidio in San Francisco and when it was finished, so was my career—if it could be called that.

They were polite enough throughout, perhaps even a bit embarrassed, providing that they felt anything at all, which I doubted, and the embarrassment may have prompted their unusual generosity when it came to the matter of severance pay. It amounted to twenty thousand dollars and, as Carmingler kept saying, it was all tax-free so that really ran it up to the equivalent of twenty-eight or even thirty thousand.

It was Carmingler himself who handed me the new passport along with the certified check drawn on something called the Brookhaven Corporation. He did it quickly, without comment, much in the same manner as he would shoot a crippled horse—a favorite perhaps, and when it was done, that last official act, he even unbent enough to pick up the phone and call a cab. I was almost sure it was the first time he had ever called a cab for anyone other than himself.

"It shouldn't take long," he said.

"I'll wait outside."

"No need for that."

"I think there is."

Carmingler produced his dubious look. He managed that by sticking out his lower lip and frowning at the same time. He would use the same expression even if someone were to tell him it had stopped raining. "There's really no reason to—"

I interrupted. "We're through, aren't we? The loose ends are neatly tied off. The crumbs are all brushed away. It's over." I liked to mix metaphors around Carmingler. It bothered him.

He nodded slowly, produced his pipe, and began to stuff it with that special mixture of his which he got

9

from some tobacco shop in New York. I could never remember the shop's name although he had mentioned it often enough. He kept on nodding while he filled his pipe. "Well, I wouldn't put it quite that way."

"No," I said, "you wouldn't. But I would and that's why I'll wait outside."

Carmingler, who loved horses if he loved anything, which again was doubtful, rose and walked around his desk to where I stood. He must have been forty or even forty-two then, all elbows and knee joints and what I had long felt was a carefully practiced, coltish kind of awkwardness. The flaming hair that stopped just short of being true madder scarlet half-framed his long narrow face, which I think he secretly wanted to resemble a horse. It looked more like a mule. A stubborn one. He held out his hand.

"Good luck to you."

Sweet Christ, I thought, the firm handshake of sad parting. "By God, I appreciate that, Carmingler," I said, giving his hand a brief, hard grasp. "You don't know how much I appreciate it."

"No need for sarcasm," he said stiffly. "No call for that at all."

"Not for that or for anything else," I said.

"I mean it," he said. "Good luck."

"Sure," I said and picked up the new plastic suitcase that failed utterly in its attempt to resemble cordovan. I turned, went through a door, down a hall, and out onto the semicircular drive where a pair of chained-down mortars that had been made in 1859 by some Boston firm called C.A. & Co. guarded the flagpole and the entrance to Letterman General Hospital, established 1898, just in time for the war with Spain. In the distance, there was Russian Hill to look at.

The cab arrived ten minutes later and I placed the bag in the front seat next to the driver. He turned to look at me.

"Where to, buddy?"

"A hotel."

"Which one?"

"I haven't thought about it. What do you suggest?"

He looked at me some more with eyes that were too old for his acolyte's face. "You want high-priced, medium high-priced, or cheap?"

"Medium."

"How about the Sir Francis Drake?"

"Fine."

He let me off at the Sutter Street entrance and the desk clerk gave me a room on the seventeenth floor with a view of the Bay Bridge. I unpacked the new plastic suitcase they had given me and hung the two suits and the topcoat in the closet. I was wearing one of the three new suits, the gray one with the small, muted herringbone weave. It had a vest, as did the other two, and I suspected that Carmingler himself must have chosen them. He always wore vests. And smoked a pipe. And fiddled with his Phi Beta Kappa key.

I had been mildly surprised that everything fitted so well until I remembered that they had my exact measurements on file, had had them, in fact, for eleven years and even required new ones every January 15th on the off-chance that I might have developed a penchant for sauce-soaked noodles and ballooned out by thirty pounds or so, or even grown too fond of the bottle, given up eating, and dropped unhealthfully below my normal 162½ pounds. They always wanted everything exact. Height, 6′ ¼″. Neck, 15¼″. Chest, 41½″. Waist, 32¾″. Arm, right, 34¼″. Arm, left, 34″. Shoe, 10-B with a double-A heel. Hat, 7¼. But they hadn't bought me a hat, just the three suits to replace the gray cotton, pajamalike prison uniform that I had arrived in, plus a top coat and six shirts (all white, oxford cloth, all button-down collars—Carmingler again); six pairs of calf-length socks (all black); one pair of shoes: black, plain-toed, pebble-grained and expensive; six pairs of Jockey shorts; one belt, black alligator, and four ties (awful).

I estimated that it had cost them around seven or eight hundred dollars. Less than a thousand anyhow. If I'd been more important, they might have gone as high as fifteen hundred, but what they had spent accurately reflected my former niche in the hierarchy. It also reflected their fussy conviction that no ex-colleague, regardless of how wretched or ignominious, should be shunted into the real world unless he were properly (if not richly) attired.

The contents of the closet and the bureau were my sole possessions other than the new passport and the check for $20,000. I also owned a renewed aversion, or perhaps only antipathy, toward the word debriefing, but that didn't have any cash value.

After the clothing was stored away I called down to the desk to find out the time and where the nearest bank was and whether it was open. I had no watch. It had been taken from me at the prison, at that damp, sweating, gray stone structure that the British had erected almost a century ago. When I was released after three months, nobody had ever heard of the watch. I hadn't really expected to get it back, but I had asked anyway.

The man at the desk said the nearest bank was just up the street, that it was now 12:36, that the bank was open, and that if I didn't have a watch I could look out the window at an insurance building whose flashing tower sign would tell me not only the time, but also the temperature. I told the man at the desk to send up a bottle of Scotch.

When the sad-fc   ꞏ bellhop handed me the bill for the whisky, I was surprised at its cost.

"It's gone up," I said.

"What hasn't?"

"Talk," I said. "It's still cheap."

I signed the bill, adding a twenty percent tip, which made the bellhop happy, or at least a little less morose. After he left I mixed a drink and stood by the window gazing out over the city with its bridge in the background. It was one of those spectacularly fine days that San Fransisco manages to come up with sometimes in early September: a few quiet clouds, an indulgent sun, and air so sparkling that you know somebody's eventually going to bottle it. I stood there in my room on the seventeenth floor and sipped the Scotch and stared out at what was once touted as America's favorite city. Maybe it still is. I also thought about the future, which seemed to offer less than the past, and about the past, which offered nothing at all. Carmingler had seen to that.

I finished the drink and went in search of the bank, which turned out to be a branch of Wells Fargo. One of its minor officers, a young man with a handlebar mustache, seemed busily idle so I told him I wanted to open a checking account. The mustache jiggled a little at that and I assumed that the jiggle was a smile of welcome or at least acquiescence. A nameplate on his desk said that he was C.D. Littrell and I tried to re-

12

member whether I had ever seen a bank official with a handlebar mustache before and decided that I hadn't except in some old Westerns and then he had usually turned out to be a crook. But this was Wells Fargo and perhaps its traditions encouraged handlebar mustaches.

After I sat down Littrell produced some forms and the forms contained questions to which I would have to think up some answers. I decided to tell the truth when convenient and to lie when it wasn't.

"Your full name?" Littrell said.

"Dye, D-y-e. Lucifer C. Dye." The C stood for Clarence but I saw no sense in mentioning that. Lucifer was bad enough.

"Your address?"

Another good question. "Temporarily the Sir Francis Drake."

The mustache twitched slightly and this time I knew it wasn't a smile. Littrell looked up from his writing and stared at me. I returned his gaze, gravely, I hoped.

"How long do you plan to stay there?" he said, coming down hard on the "there" as if he felt that anyone who stayed at a hotel for an extended period of time was either profligate or flighty. Perhaps both.

"I'm not sure," I said.

"You should let us know as soon as you get a permanent address."

"I'll let you know."

"Your previous address?"

"Hong Kong. You want the street number?"

Littrell shook his head, a little sadly, I thought, and wrote down Hong Kong. He would have been happier had I said Boise or Denver or even East St. Louis.

"Your previous bank?"

"Barclays," I said. "Also in Hong Kong."

"I mean in the States."

"None."

"None at all—ever?" He seemed a little shocked.

"None at all."

This time Littrell did shake his head. I couldn't decide whether it was a gesture of disapproval or commiseration. "Where are you employed, Mr. Dye?" he said, and from his tone I knew he expected the worst.

"Self-employed."

"Your place of business."

"The Sir Francis Drake."

Littrell had given up. He was scribbling hastily now. "What kind of business, Mr. Dye?"

"Export-import."

"The name of your firm?"

"I haven't decided yet."

"I see," Littrell said, a little glumly, and wrote down unemployed. "How much would you like to deposit?"

I could tell that if I said fifty dollars, he would be pleasantly surprised. If I said a hundred, he would be ecstatic.

"Twenty thousand," I said. "No, better make it nineteen thousand, five hundred."

Littrell muttered something to himself which I didn't catch and then pushed two cards over to me. "These are the signature cards. Would you sign them the way that you'll be signing your checks?"

I signed the cards and handed them back along with the certified check for $20,000. Littrell examined the check carefully and for a moment I thought he might even sniff it for some telltale odor. But he went on examining it, knowing it was good and, I thought, hating the fact that it was. He turned it over and looked for the endorsement. There was none. "Would you endorse it, please, Mr. Dye?" I wrote my name for the third time.

"Do you have some identification?"

"Yes," I said. "I have some."

We waited. He was going to have to ask for it. After fifteen seconds or so he sighed and said, "May I see it, please?"

I produced the passport, newly issued, never used, which said that my hair was brown, that my eyes were hazel, that I had been born in 1933 in a place called Moncrief, Montana, and if anyone still cared, I was a businessman. It didn't mention that my slightly crooked teeth had just been cleaned by an Army dentist, a major who wanted desperately to get back into civilian practice.

Littrell accepted the passport, glanced at it, gathered up the forms, and excused himself. He headed for a glass and wood enclosed office a few feet away which barricaded an older man from those who dropped by wanting to borrow money. The older man's head was pinkly bald and his eyes were colored a suspicious blue.

Littrell didn't try to keep his voice down and I easily

overheard the conversation. "A hot shot with a certified twenty thousand," he said. "Regular checking."

The older man looked at the check first, riffled through the forms, and then examined the passport. Carefully. He pursed his lips for a long moment and finally initialed the papers. "It's only money," he said, and I had the feeling that he was saying it for the four-hundredth time that year.

Littrell took the check and the forms, disappeared behind the tellers' cages, and then came back to his desk where, still standing, he counted $500 on to its surface and then counted them again into my hand. He sat down after that, reached into a desk drawer, and produced a checkbook and some deposit forms, which he handed me.

"These checks are only temporary as are the deposit slips," he said. "We'll mail you a supply with your name and address printed on them, if you get a permanent address."

I ignored the "if" and put the checks and deposit slips in my inside jacket pocket. The $500 I folded and casually stuck in my right-hand trouser pocket, which seemed to irritate Littrell. That's probably why I did it—that and because I had no billfold or wallet or anything to put in one other than the $500. No driver's license or credit cards. No snapshots or old letters, not even a pocket calendar from the corner liquor store. The only proof that I was who I said I was rested with my new passport that, with a few exceptions, allowed me to journey to any spot in the world that struck my fancy, providing I could think of one that did which, as a matter of fact, I couldn't.

I said goodbye to Littrell who gave me a final twitch of his mustache. Once outside the bank, I turned right up Sutter Street. I was looking for a jewelry store so that I could buy a watch and it was at least ten minutes before I found one and five minutes before I spotted the man in the brown suit who was tailing me and seven minutes before I came to the pleasant realization that I really didn't give a damn if he followed me to the ends of the earth—which some thoughtful San Franciscans claimed lay just across the bridge in Oakland.

2

It had all begun, the entire mess, or my fall from grace, I suppose it could be called, when they overheaded the instructions by commercial rate from the home office of Minneapolis Mutual, which was located, for some unfathomable reason, in Las Vegas. The message arrived in Hong Kong on May 20th. It was in an antiquated, one-time code that was keyed that week to page 356 of the thirteenth edition of *Bartlett's Familiar Quotations* which turned out to be excerpts from Oliver Goldsmith's *The Deserted Village*. It took me a good half hour to break it down and I felt that any reasonably bright computer could have made it in seconds and, for all I knew, might already have done so. Decoded, the message was still childishly cryptic, as if whoever had sent it clung to a wistful hope that it would be meaningless to anyone but me. Its four words read: Cipher the Village Statesman.

It was one of their more asinine orders, a shade dumber than most, so I tore everything up and flushed it down the toilet. I then called in Joyce Jungroth, my Minnesota-born secretary who after three years still clung to her romantic notions about Hong Kong, had a bad complexion, and always smelled faintly of Noxzema. I handed her the *Bartlett's*.

"Get rid of it," I said.

She sighed and accepted the book. "Don't you ever use dirty novels, something that I could read?"

"You're not supposed to read them; you're supposed to get rid of them."

I suspected that she took the books home to her apartment. Not that it mattered, because the method—inexcusably old-fashioned, out-dated, even juvenile—was used but once or twice a year and always by someone like Carmingler whose inbred distrust of technological innovations caused him to choose kitchen matches over a

16

butane lighter, a bicycle (whenever possible) over a car, and even a knife over a revolver. You couldn't pay Carmingler enough to travel by subway.

By then I had spent ten years in Hong Kong as managing director of an American-owned life insurance company called Minneapolis Mutual. During that time I had personally sold three policies, all straight life. I was running six agents, supposedly insurance salesmen, who worked the Southeast Asian territory. They were fortunate that they didn't have to live on their commissions because their combined efforts over the decade had brought the total number of Minneapolis Mutual policies sold up to an even dozen.

Two of my own three sales, each with a face value of $100,000 had been bought six years previously by a Ford dealer and his wife from Mobile who were on a world tour and suffering from twin cases of diarrhea which proved uncomfortable enough to convince them that they would never see the heart of Dixie again. Arriving in Hong Kong by ship, and determined to complete their tour, they had looked up insurance companies and gratefully spotted Minneapolis Mutual which was, after all, American, even if its headquarters in the States were located a little far up North. Nobody had anticipated drop-in business when they had plunked me into the managing directorship and I still knew next to nothing about insurance. So when the American couple descended on me, checkbook in hand, I had to call in my secretary (not Joyce Jungroth; I had a different one then) who at least knew something about the drill, where the forms were anyway, and she wrote up the policies and dispatched the couple to a doctor, as much for their diarrhea as for the mandatory physicals.

It was the only drop-in business that Minneapolis Mutual's tenth-floor island office on Pedder Street ever got, but it bothered me enough to take out $10,000 worth of straight life on myself that afternoon. I even wrote it up under the amused tutelage of my secretary. But since no one ever came around again, other than the odd office-supply salesman, I let the policy expire after a couple of years.

About the only thing I ever did learn about selling life insurance was that Southeast Asia is a rotten territory.

After Joyce Jungroth left, the copy of *Bartlett's* clutched to her underinflated bosom, I leaned back in my chair, the one with the moulded back that was supposed to correct posture, and pondered the instructions from Las Vegas.

For six months I had been trying to convince a plump, fiftyish Chinese agent that he should double. It had been an odd courtship and for my efforts I had been treated to long recitals of random quotations from Chairman Mao. Nevertheless, Li Teh kept all of the appointments. When he finally ran down, I would murmur something inane such as, "How true," and drop two hundred-dollar bills on the floor or deck or even desk, adding: "Think about it, won't you?" Li always took the money.

I learned eventually that Li Teh had been barely thirty years old when he had entered Hong Kong in late September of 1949, virtually indistinguishable from the swarmy horde of Chinese who sought sanctuary in the colony after Chiang Kai-shek boarded the C-47 called *Mei-ling,* in honor of his redoubtable wife, and skipped to Formosa, remembering to pack along the $200 million (U.S.) gold reserves of the Central Bank of China.

The thing that did distinguish Li Teh from his fellow *pai hua,* or refugees, was capital, a goodly amount in American dollars that Mao's forces had stripped from a money belt found on the dead body of one of the more corrupt members of the Generalissimo's personal staff. It was enough to allow Li to open a camera shop in Kowloon on Nathan Road with a franchise from an East German manufacturer who before World War II had been famous for the quality of the firm's lenses. The shop prospered and Li opened another one on Kimberly Road a few years later, this time specializing in Canons and Nikons from Japan.

From there it was only a short step to Swiss watches (I'd bought one from him), transistor tape recorders, miniature television sets, and transistor radios—anything that hard currency tourists could tote along with them. Had it been his own capital, Li would have been a rich man by the time he was fifty, but his profits were either plowed back into his burgeoning businesses or funneled to Peking where his backers found ready use for the dollars and pounds and francs and marks.

I always thought that Li was a better businessman than he was a spy, although he was that too, dealing in information of all kinds, stealing it when he could, buying it when he couldn't. Once a month he journeyed by train to Peking, a long, hard, uncomfortable trip, bearing a suitcase jammed with as much cash as the profits from his various enterprises would permit. It would have been simpler and more efficient, of course, to have deposited the funds in the Bank of China, but Li also carried along whatever information he had been able to pick up or scrounge and although it was, I understand, welcomed in Peking, it was not met with the same degree of warmth that greeted the hard currency.

Li was a communist and, I suppose, a good one. He once told me that it had all begun in 1938 when as a student he had managed to escape from a Nationalist Army press gang that had roped him to eleven other students. He made his way to Yenan in North China where Mao had located his provisional command post or field headquarters. Although still a teen-ager, Li was obviously bright and, for China, well educated. He had been allowed to live in one of the clean whitewashed caves that was the home of a senior officer who assumed responsibility for Li's military training, party indoctrination, morality, and introduction to espionage techniques and practices. The officer was of middling rank in the communists' intelligence apparatus and as the officer rose, so did Li Teh, until 1949 when they dispatched him to Hong Kong, his even then widening girth encircled by a money belt stuffed with American dollars.

As one of Hong Kong's fairly prominent businessmen, Li had half-convinced his Peking superiors that he should live up to his reputation. They had given him what must have been grudging, reluctant permission, and he drove a Porsche, which he loved, dwelt as a widower in an elegant apartment building not too far from the Bank of China and the Cricket Club, and entertained frequently with a certain amount of grace and even style. He was a member of the Hong Kong Chamber of Commerce, three civic organizations, and one private Chinese club that offered a quite excellent bill of fare. Li did all this with the approval if not the good grace of his superiors, whose tolerance of the high life ran out on the last day of each month when they scrutinized his books to make

19

sure that he wasn't left with a dime that he could call his own.

So Li Teh lived a little too well and as a consequence he was broke. Worse, he was in debt, and moneylenders in Hong Kong are even less forgiving than their loan-sharking colleagues in the States. So I corrupted Li Teh with money. It was what I was paid to do and it was what I knew best. In some circles they even said I was very good at it.

Our last meeting was held in a temporarily vacant godown and we followed the usual script except that Li cut his lecture short by almost six minutes, and even what he did say was delivered in a mechanical, totally uninspired manner. When he was through, he was silent for several long moments. I waited. Finally, in a voice so low that I could scarcely hear it, he said: "Your best price?"

"You name it."

He decided on a moon shot. "Three thousand dollars a month."

I tried to counter. "Hong Kong, of course."

"American."

We were sitting on a couple of empty packing cases. Li Teh leaned back and folded his arms over his bulging belly, which was smoothly cased in a dark green sharkskin suit that must have cost about one hundred and fifty (U.S.) dollars which, in Hong Kong, is a steep price for a suit, even a tailored one. His eyes were half-closed and he sat there, rocking a little, a fat, unlaughing communist Buddha, content in the certainty that he had just set a price which the buyer couldn't possibly afford to turn down. It was an example of supply and demand at its best. Or worst.

"All right," I said. "You've got it—if it's worth it."

"It will be."

"What?"

"Verbal reports twice each month. Nothing in writing."

"Whose?"

"My own."

"And if they're worthless?"

He smiled pleasantly. "Then, Mr. Dye, I seriously doubt that you will pay."

I smiled back. "You've come to know me well."

"Yes, I have, haven't I?"

"When do you plan to return?" I said.

"To Peking?"

"Yes."

"Two weeks from now."

"Good," I said. "That'll give me a chance to obtain clearance."

That troubled Li. To prove it, he arched his eyebrows. "You do not yet have clearance?"

"I never anticipate good news so I didn't ask for it."

"And bad news?" Li said.

"I never anticipate that either."

"Then you must surely live a rather bland existence, Mr. Dye."

I nodded and produced two one hundred-dollar bills and laid them carefully on the packing case which Li was using as a perch. Never once had I handed money to him directly. He ignored the bills.

"In our business, Mr. Li," I said, "a bland existence is sometimes desperately sought."

3

The jewelry store that I found was near Taylor and Bush Streets, about three blocks from the hotel. It was a small shop, and when I tried the door, I found it locked. Inside, I could see a clerk, or perhaps the owner, hurrying toward the door. He unlocked it quickly. The man in the brown suit had stopped three or four doors down, where he made a careful inspection of some hernia trusses and artificial legs that an orthopedic shop had on display.

"I keep it locked now," said the man who opened the door. "I've been robbed three times in the last six months, so I keep it locked now."

"You probably discourage more customers than you do thieves," I said.

"Who cares?" he said. "I'm going bankrupt anyhow. If the punks don't ruin me, the insurance rates will. You know, I remember when this used to be a fairly honest town. Now take a look at it."

He was a thin, short man of about fifty who wore thick-lensed, heavily framed glasses that made his brown eyes pop a little. He looked worn and used up. His thin mouth was an almost lipless, bitter line and his nose kept sniffing as though he could smell his impending economic doom.

"I'd like to see a watch," I said.

"Any special kind?"

"I want an Omega Seamaster, stainless steel, the kind with the calendar thing on it."

"It's a good watch," the man said because he had to say something and he probably felt that there was no sense in wasting salesmanship on someone who had already made up his mind. He darted behind a counter and handed me a watch. It was exactly like the one they had taken from me in the prison, except that this one had a leather strap.

"Do you have one with an expansion bracelet?" I said.

"No, they all come with the strap, but we can put an expansion on for you in a jiffy."

"How much?"

"For the watch or the expansion bracelet?"

"For both."

He told me and it was fifty dollars more than I had paid Li Teh in Hong Kong, but that was what Hong Kong was for, among other things. Cheap watches. "All right," I said. "I'll take it."

"It'll only be a minute or two," the man said, picking up the watch and heading for the rear of the shop where the resident expansion-bracelet expert apparently waited. I turned and looked out the front window. The man in the brown suit stood before it, seemingly transfixed by the display that lay behind the plate glass which was imbedded with thin, gray, metallic strips that would sound an alarm if anyone tried a smash and grab with a brickbat.

"Here we are," the man said, returning a few minutes later with the watch, and as always, I wanted to say "where?" but there seemed to be no sense in it. I paid for the watch, checked to see that it was correctly set, and slipped it on to my left wrist. The shopowner started to put the black case that had contained the watch into a paper sack. I told him to keep it.

"But it contains the guarantee."

"I don't want that either," I said.

Out on the sidewalk I paused for a moment beside the man in the brown suit who still seemed mesmerized by the window display. I looked but could see nothing special other than some watches, several trays of junky rings, and a medium-sized clock with a small sign boasting that it was within three seconds of absolute accuracy. I glanced at my new watch and was vaguely pleased to see that it still kept the right time.

"Fascinating, isn't it?" I said to the man in the brown suit, turned, and started to walk back toward Sutter Street and the Sir Francis Drake.

He was a good tail when he wanted to be. In fact, very good. He made all the right moves, as if he had been making them all his life, but now made them only out of habit, as if he didn't care whether he was spotted or not.

I stopped a few doors from the hotel in front of a bookstore on Sutter Street and inspected the latest crop

23

of best-sellers. Through the diagonally placed window I could read the names of the authors and the titles as well as keep the sidewalk behind me in view through the reflection of the glass. I had heard of some of the authors but only two of the titles, but that's what comes from not reading a newspaper for a hundred days or so. The man in the brown suit was walking toward me rapidly now that it was downhill and the going was easier.

Almost fat, I thought. Overweight by twenty pounds, at least. Perhaps thirty. Around five-ten, probably forty-five or forty-six, but possibly a dissipated forty-two. The brown suit wasn't shabby, just unpressed, and his black shoes needed a shine. The collar of his white shirt was too small and its points stuck up in the air. He wore a blue and purple striped tie and for a moment I wondered if he were color blind. When he was about twenty feet feet from me, I turned and watched him approach. He walked on his heels, bringing them down hard on the sidewalk. If his body was overweight, his face wasn't. It was all planes and angles with a set of dark brown eyebrows that looked as if they should be combed. His hair was brown, too, but dotted with splotches of dirty gray as though certain spots of it had once been shaved and when they grew back, they had grown back a different color. Underneath the fuzzy brows was a set of eyes that regarded me fixedly as he approached. When he drew near enough I could see that one was brown and one was blue and neither of them contained any more warmth that you would find in a slaughterhouse freezer.

He was about three feet away when he stopped and looked me up and down carefully with his two-toned eyes. "Your name's Dye," he said in a quiet, hard tone that made it more like a threat than a statement of fact.

"My name's Dye," I said. "Why the tail job?"

"I wasn't sure it was you until you started back for the hotel. The desk told me you'd gone to the bank, but all I had was a general description. You fitted it pretty well, so I tailed you."

"I noticed," I said.

"You wouldn't have if I'd been trying."

"But you weren't."

"No."

"All right," I said. "What's on your mind?"

24

"I'm with Victor Orcutt," he said, as if that explained everything.

"What's he sell?"

"Nothing."

"Why me?"

He reached into the pocket of his brown suit and brought out a package of Camels. He offered me one. I shook my head no. He lit it with a stainless steel Zippo, inhaled deeply and then blew some smoke up into the air. He seemed to have all the time that there was. He seemed to have almost as much time as I did.

"He didn't think you'd be much interested," the man in the brown suit said.

"In what?"

"An invitation to go see him."

"He's right," I said. "I'm not."

His blue and brown gaze never left my face. "Like I said, he didn't think you'd accept an invitation, so he told me to give you this." He reached into his inside breast pocket and produced a square, buff-colored en. 'ope which he handed to me.

"You could have left it at the desk," I said, pocketing the envelope, not looking at it.

He nodded slightly, but not very much. His heavy, thick chin moved a half-inch down and then up. Twice. "I could have, couldn't I" he said, "except that Victor Orcutt told me to give it to you personally. He gets a little fussy sometimes so I like to do what he says. Makes for harmony, if you know what I mean."

"Only too well," I said.

"Yeah," he said, still memorizing my face with his two-color eyes. "I bet you do at that." Then he turned abruptly and walked on down Sutter Street without a goodbye or even a farewell wave of the hand. I noticed that he still came down hard on his heels.

I didn't open the envelope until I was up in the hotel room. The buff paper could have been made out of fine old linen rags and it crackled richly as I tore the flap open. Inside there was a single sheet of paper, folded once. Centered near its top was the name Victor Orcutt in discreet, squared-off, capitals and small capital letters. There was nothing else on the letterhead. No address, no phone number, no zip code. The name was printed in dark brown ink, the color of old mahogany, and I ran my thumb over the letters to make sure that they were engraved. The hand-written message, also in dark brown ink, was simple, knowing, and even polite:

Dear Mr. Dye,
    I shall be calling on you late this afternoon (shall we say around four?) concerning a matter that should prove of mutual interest. I hope that your brief stay at Letterman General Hospital was both comfortable and rewarding.
                Sincerely,

                Victor Orcutt

The handwriting was calligraphy really and it was so good that it almost made up for its air of affectation. It was a clear, bold hand, straight up and down, without an unnecessary whorl or flourish or serif. It was a studied, strangely economical style and I decided that it must have taken Victor Orcutt a couple of years of hard practice to perfect it.

I tossed the letter onto a table, mixed a drink, and stood by the window to watch the fog roll in and think bad thoughts about Carmingler and his sealed-off suite and his Boy Scout security.

They had chartered a C-130 to fly me the eight thousand miles or so to San Francisco. It had touched down only once on the way, at Honolulu International to refuel, and even then I wasn't allowed off the plane. There had been only two passengers, Carmingler and myself, and it was Carmingler alone who had met me at that gray, crumbling ruin of a prison at midnight when I was released. He wore a hot tweed jacket with leather patches on its sleeves and insisted that there wasn't time for me to change clothes, but that I should wear the pajamalike gray cotton uniform, the same one that I had worn continuously for three months.

Aboard the C-130, I told him: "I've got lice."

"Really?" he said. "Oh, well, I suppose a great many people do. We'll get rid of them for you in a few hours. In the meantime, scratch if you like. I don't mind."

We flew from Honolulu International to Hamilton Air Force Base where a private ambulance waited with its windows carefully blacked out. The ambulance whisked

26

Carmingler and me to Letterman General and I wasn't allowed outside the sealed-off suite except to go to the dentist. According to Carmingler, no one knew that I was at Letterman General. And perhaps no one did, except Victor Orcutt. So much for Carmingler's security measures.

He had talked little on the long flight back, except at Honolulu when we had refueled and he couldn't smoke his pipe. "There's been a bit of a flap, you know," he said.

"How bad?"

"Bad enough, I'm afraid."

"So?"

He took his dead pipe out of his mouth long enough to give me what I assume he thought was a reassuring smile. "We'll get it straightened out. In San Francisco."

"How bad?" I asked again.

Carmingler went through his coltish act. He rose awkwardly, balanced himself on his right foot, and knocked the empty pipe against the heel of his raised left shoe.

"It's bad enough," he said, and his head ducked toward the pipe that he was pounding against his shoe. "Actually, it's about as bad as it could possibly be."

4

I had been waiting for the go-ahead signal on Li Teh for more than a week when the childish message arrived instructing me to Cipher the Village Statesman. Translated, it meant that I was to subject Li to a polygraph or lie detector test. Despite his horror of most things mechanical, especially computers, Carmingler's faith in the polygraph bordered on the mystical. It was the kind of faith that the clergy likes to call deep and abiding.

I decided that it must have been a committee decision. Four or five or even six of them sitting around a table, covering their ruled, yellow legal pads with penciled doodles as they discussed Li Teh and whether he would be worth $3,000 a month to the taxpayers. There would be, of course, the suspicious one, perhaps an old hand, but more likely a new boy trying make a name for himself. He would chew on his pencil's eraser for a while, look worried, and then raise the question as to whether Li could really be trusted. You know. *Really*. After all, if he's agreed to double, couldn't he just as easily triple? Young Masterman might have something there, another of them would say, and cock an eyebrow to show the colors of a true skeptic.

And Carmingler, sitting quietly, sucking on his aged pipe, would toss it out casually, as if he didn't really care, but if they were really worried about Li, the lie machine could clear everything up nicely to the satisfaction of all. If you agree, I'll get a signal off to Dye this afternoon. So they would all nod in agreement, with the exception of Li Teh, unrepresented, who could blow the whole thing with a farewell address delivered in his normal screech and interspersed with a few choice quotations from Chairman Mao. And there would go six months of work out the window or down the drain or even up the spout, depending upon which cliché I felt like using that day. I sighed and picked up the phone and buzzed Joyce Jungroth.

"Put in a call to Shoftstall," I said.

"It might take quite a while," she said. Joyce Jungroth disapproved of the extravagance of overseas calls.

"Just put it through."

She caught the tone of my voice and said, "Yes, sir." She called me sir at least three times a year. While I waited for the call I dialed another number and when Li answered, I said hello in English and then switched to rapid, fluent Mandarin. I know it was fluent because I spoke little else until I was nearly six years old.

"There has been a change in plans," I said.

"They have refused my application?" Li said.

"Not at all. It is only that the underwriters require a careful examination, a simple test, one might say."

"I have heard of such tests," Li said.

I bet you have, I thought. "It is only routine."

"Where will it be held?"

I mentioned that island city-state that lies two thousand miles south of its half-sister, Hong Kong.

"A far distance," Li said. "I am no longer sure that I am even interested in the policy."

"There will be added benefits once you have received the examiner's approval."

"When will the examiner be in attendance?" he asked.

"Tomorrow evening, around nine."

"The place?"

"That is yet to be decided," I said. "However, a message will await you at the airline ticket counter."

There was a brief silence and I could almost hear the abacus that was Li's brain adding up the advantages and subtracting the disadvantages. Finally, he said: "I trust that you, too, will be present."

"It would be remiss if I were not, considering the value of the policy."

Another silence was followed by a soft sigh. "I will make the necessary arrangements," Li said and hung up.

I had stumbled on to Li Teh by accident which, at base, is responsible for most intelligence coups as well as disasters. A Canadian journalist stationed in Peking had once met Li at a cocktail party in Hong Kong. Blessed with an unusual memory for names and faces, the journalist had grown curious when Li had entered the most forbidden government building in Peking, the Forbidden

29

City of forbidden buildings. He waited for two hours for Li to reappear, but when he didn't, the journalist made a note of the date and time. Our Tokyo office kept the Canadian journalist on a small retainer and when he made a routine report to them on Li they had just as routinely forwarded it to me.

I had snooped around until I was positive that Li Teh was an agent and that his personal financial position was not as flush as it seemed. Threats of exposure or an appeal to his concern for the future of mankind would be met with either hostility or giggles, so I decided that immediate financial relief would be the most promising avenue of approach and I traveled up and down it so often that I almost began to think like what I assuredly was not: a life insurance salesman with the solid chance of a quick close on a million dollar annuity.

So now that I had him doubled, I had to fly him two thousand miles and put him through a test of doubtful validity by a machine that probably had been thrown out of whack by the humidity. I remembered my own lie detector test, the one that they'd given me just prior to employment. It was just for the record, they'd said. First, there was the stream of innocuous questions: "Did you drive here this morning? Was the sun shining? Did you eat breakfast?" All yes or no. Then they slipped the shaft in: "Have you ever had a homosexual experience?" I had answered yes.

My answer startled both the technician and the machine. The machine said I was lying and the technician insisted that we run through the whole set of questions five more times, but the machine still said that I lied.

"Look, fella," the technician had said. "The thing says you're lying about the homosexual bit." I remember that everyone was using "bit" that year.

"Then it's wrong. I did have one. I was four and my consenting partner was five and a half."

"Aw, shit," the technician said. "Just say no and let's see what happens."

"Then I'd be lying, wouldn't I?"

"Just say no, fella. For my sake."

I said no and the machine registered nothing, not even a tremor. "Four years old," the technician muttered. "Jesus."

While waiting for the overseas call to go through I

thought about the new help that Carmingler had sent me. I lumped them together as the two smart boys from Illinois, making it Illinoyz for the sake of the rhyme. The first, the so-called polygraph expert, was Lynn Shoftstall from Evanston. The other was John Bourland from Libertyville. Both were recent graduates of what Carmingler referred to as "our new in-service training program" which only meant that you could start them out cheap at the bottom and keep them there until it was determined whether they could hack it as junior-grade spies. I thought of the program as something less than a smashing success.

Carmingler had sent them out to replace two of my former salesmen-agents, a seasoned pair, one of whom had been reassigned to Tokyo, a kind of a promotion, while the other had awakened in Bangkok one impossibly hot afternoon, suffering from a dreadful hangover which, among other things, had caused him to say to hell with it and catch the next plane to Sydney where, some said, he was writing a book. I hoped that it would make him a lot of money.

Bourland was the linguist, fluent in both Thai and Mandarin. Shoftstall, not nearly so keen a language student, in fact, barely proficient, was a mechanical whiz. I was informed that he knew virtually all there was to know about such gadgets as phone taps, room bugging devices, and a host of other miniaturized marvels, most of which were anathema to Carmingler and a mystery to me, although some said that they could prove useful. Shoftstall was rated expert in the use of the polygraph, but it didn't really matter whether he was or not. He had the only polygraph around and supposedly only he could peep into Li Teh's mind by measuring the beat of his pulse, the rate of his breathing, the amount of sweat in his palms, and the flutter of his heart as the lies tripped over themselves in their haste to leave his tongue.

My telephone rang and Joyce Jungroth informed me that my call to Shoftstall had gone through and that he was on the line.

"How's the truth business today?" I said after we said hello.

"Beautiful."

"Tomorrow night," I said.

"On what?"

"It doesn't matter."

31

"Where?"

"The usual place," I said.

"We'll be there."

The usual place was a hotel that had been built a hundred years or so ago when they still built hotels with fine, thick walls. It enjoyed a world-wide reputation and now that it was air-conditioned, it even managed to give the new Hilton some stiff competition.

"Check everything out by nine tomorrow night."

"You want it permanent?" Shoftstall asked. He meant taped.

"Yes," I said.

"Consider it done. By the way," he said, "I've been experimenting with a new kind of—"

"Later," I said and hung up.

Li and I ignored each other on the Philippine Air Lines flight to the island city-state whose Chinese premier, armed with a double first from Cambridge, was still groping for a formula that would make his tiny Republic a viable, thriving, unaligned community. It could scarcely be called a nation.

It wasn't hard for Li and me to ignore each other because Li flew first class while I settled for tourist, or economy, as the going euphemism had it. When we landed I left a note for Li at the airline's counter. It told him where to go and when to be there. I took a taxi to the old hotel and walked up a broad flight of stairs to the second floor where Shoftstall and Bourland had rented a large room.

At twenty-six John Bourland was twenty pounds overweight, which wouldn't have been so bad had it not all settled into a paunch that, because of his small frame, made him look as if he were trying to conceal a soccer ball under his jacket. It was Bourland who answered my knock and greeted me in Mandarin. He still seemed amazed that when he opened his mouth another language might pop out.

"You staying over?" Bourland asked.

"Not if I can help it," I said.

"How are you, Luci?" Shoftstall said from his prone position on the bed. Tall and lean, Shoftstall had once been a second-string guard on a losing Northwestern basketball team and was considered something of a prodigy in the electrical engineering field, although he had had to hire someone else to take his final examinations in history, English, and political science. I tried not to wince at the Luci, but failed. It didn't really matter because Shoftstall didn't notice. He didn't notice much of anything unless it had a wire connected to it.

"Is all your stuff set?" I said.

"We checked everything out at the office. Perfect."

"Who's the pigeon?" Bourland asked.

"Just a man."

"You want me to help with the questioning?" Bourland said. He was pressing too hard, I thought, and once again wondered what they were teaching them these days in that in-service training program. Not enough, it seemed.

"Just help with the gadgets," I said.

Shoftstall swung his long legs over the side of the bed and sat up, stretching and yawning mightily. Our nation's yearning, blue-eyed pride, I remembered from somewhere. Cummings, I decided. Or cummings.

"When's he due?" Shoftstall asked, yawning again.

"Any minute if you can stay awake."

Three minutes later there was a rap on the door and I opened it. Li Teh came in quickly, his eyes darting as he catalogued and classified the occupants, the furniture, and the equipment. "This is Mr. Jones," I said, not trying to be clever, only simple. "My associates."

Li didn't even nod at them. "Let's get on with it," he said in English.

I nodded at Shoftstall, who moved to a writing desk which held the lie detector in its gray metal case. "Would you remove your coat and roll up your sleeves, Mr. Jones?" he said. "Then please sit in this straight chair in front of the desk."

Li removed his coat, folded it neatly, and put it carefully on the bed. He sat in the chair. Gingerly, I thought. Shoftstall bustled around, readying his equipment and giving out with an endless line of chatter which he seemed to think would soothe the obviously nervous Li, but which, in fact, only made him more jittery. Li obviously wished that the American fool would shut up.

I let Shoftstall talk. "The purpose of this machine, Mr. Jones, is simply to establish validity. That's all. Nothing else. It's painless, and there's absolutely no reason to worry—Mr. Dye here will just ask some simple ques-

33

tions to which you can answer either yes or no. That's all. Just yes or no. Before you know it, we'll be through."

Li said nothing. Bourland plugged his tape recorder into the outlet under the desk. Shoftstall continued to chatter away as he affixed the lie detector's attachments to Li's chest, forearm, and palm. "Now if you'll just turn your chair a little this way—to the right," Shoftstall said. "Fine. That's just fine."

"We brought the big Ampex," Bourland said. "I thought you might want the fidelity and its mike will pick up everything."

"Good," I said, not really caring, eager only that the entire sorry scene end itself as soon as possible.

Shoftstall stepped back from Li as if to admire his work. "Okay," he said to Bourland. "You can roll the tape."

Bourland turned a knob on the recorder, made a couple of adjustments, and said, "tape one and rolling. Interview with Mr. Jones," He looked at Shoftstall. "It's rolling."

Shoftstall dropped to his hands and knees and groped for the polygraph's plug that dangled down behind the writing desk. He glanced up at me. "As soon as I plug it in, you can start," he said.

"All right."

He groped again for the electric cord, found it, and plugged it into the wall socket, the same one that powered the Ampex.

The flashes were cobalt blue, I suppose. Whatever the color, they leaped three feet out into the room, twice, and they were accompanied by a series of sputtering, wet-sounding plops. The lights in the room died instantaneously, but it took Li Teh a little longer. He screamed only once. It really wasn't much of a scream; it was more like something that a dying kitten would make.

I groped my way over to Li Teh and held the lighter before his face. His eyes were open but they didn't see the flame. I stood there and stared at him until the lighter burned itself out. Shoftstall and Bourland were moving around, cursing and muttering as they rummaged for their equipment. It seemed that we were there in the dark with the dead man for a long time, but it was really only a matter of minutes before the police began pounding on the door and I moved over to open it before they broke it down.

5

They handed Carmingler the chore of telling me that I was finished. He said so when we were about halfway through the debriefing at Letterman General. I don't think he relished doing it, but then it didn't bother him much either. Nothing did really, unless it was when one of his horses came down with the croup or rale or whatever it is that horses get. He sat there behind a gray metal desk in the bare tan room and fiddled with his Phi Beta Kappa key which most thought came from Princeton, a misconception that Carmingler never discouraged, but which actually came from Louisiana State. There was one thing about Carmingler though: he had shucked his bayou accent.

"It's a pity, of course," he had said. "Especially since it wasn't your fault. Not your fault at all. But I'm sure you appreciate our position." If he had been smoother, or if that course in sensitivity that he had once taken had had any effect, Carmingler would have said *their* position, not ours. I let it pass.

"After they issued the initial denial that none of you belonged to them, well, I'm afraid we got stuck with it."

"You could fix it," I said, again not really caring, but willing to argue a little for the sake of form.

"I'm afraid not."

"You've fixed worse ones."

He frowned and gave up on his Phi Beta Kappa key and started to mess with his pipe. "Not recently," he said.

"What about the other two?" I said.

"What other two?"

"Those two clowns you sent me. Shoftstall and Bourland."

"Oh, yes, of course," Carmingler said, as if I had just recalled two mutual acquaintances who really didn't quite belong in his social set. "The same thing for them although we're not being quite as liberal. Financially, I mean."

35

"Why should you?" I said. "They've only got eighteen months in. I've got eleven years and when I go looking for a job I can't very well tell a prospective employer that I've had amnesia for the past eleven years."

Carmingler had finally got his pipe lighted and he was sucking away on it. "That does present a bit of a problem and if it weren't for all that publicity—"

"My name was never mentioned," I said.

"Of course not. But that insurance company's name was. Minneapolis Mutual. People remember. Possibly we can work something out, a few letters of reference from some firm or other saying that you'd been employed by them. That kind of thing. Let me think about it."

"You do that," I said, and never brought it up again because I knew that there wasn't any use.

Carmingler glanced at his watch. "Well, I suppose that'll wrap it up for today."

"Just one other thing," I said.

"What?"

"I hope those eleven years that I put in were worth it."

"Worth what?"

"Worth that million dollars you spent getting me out of jail."

I thought or perhaps brooded about Carmingler and the past three months of my life as I stood there on the seventeenth floor of the Sir Francis Drake and watched the fog roll in. Even with the windows closed, I could hear the anachronistic clang of the cable cars as they ground their way up and down Powell. The streets were still visible, but the Bay Bridge had disappeared. In a few more minutes the fog would settle down for the evening and all I'd have left to admire would be the insurance company tower whose electric sign informed me that it was 64° outside and 3:59 P.M. both inside and out. I checked my new watch and found that the tower was right.

The brisk knock on my door came at precisely 4:02 P.M., according to the tower sign. I opened the door and he was younger than I'd expected. Much younger.

"Mr. Dye," he said and smiled pleasantly enough. "I'm Victor Orcutt. May we come in?"

I opened the door wider and moved back. "Sure," I

36

said. "Come in. We can either have a party or a rubber of bridge."

There were three of them. First came Victor Orcutt, then the man in the brown suit with the two-tone eyes, and last the honey blonde. She was still several years under thirty and her hair came as close to that shade of honey that bees make from yellow clover as nature or her beauty parlor could get it. She let a small smile play around her full mouth, but her mild brown eyes failed to back it up. They seemed sad, even hurt, but then I hadn't even had a woman glance at me in a hundred days or so, and if I'd stared at her a little longer, I probably could have found anything that I was looking for, even my own private version of the land of Prester John.

Once in the room Orcutt spun around gracefully and waved a hand at the man in the brown suit. "I believe you've met my associate, Homer Necessary. I always delight in introducing him to people because of that *wonderful* surname. Don't you think it's wonderful, Mr. Dye?"

He didn't give me a chance to say what I thought because he kept on talking. "And this is my executive assistant, Miss Carol Thackerty. Miss Thackerty, Mr. Dye." I had nodded at Necessary and now I said how do you do or hello or how are you to Carol Thackerty who merely smiled and looked past me at something more interesting. The radiator perhaps.

Orcutt started to talk some more. "Well, I must say that you look awfully fit for having spent three months in what I understand to be a perfectly *wretched* prison." He moved quickly to the window. Or flitted. "And this view should be simply glorious when the fog's gone." He spun around again and if it weren't for his height, or rather lack of it, I would have been almost sure that at one time or other he'd spent a few years in the chorus line. He had the build, but not the height, not even with the elevator shoes. He stared at me for a moment and then smiled again. "I should confess, Mr. Dye, that I did expect you to be more—well—shall we say, emaciated?"

"We'll say that," I said and turned to Carol Thackerty. "Won't you sit down?"

She managed that fleeting half-smile of hers again and gracefully lowered herself into a chair by the window with

37

a murmured, "Thank you." Her legs were fine, I noticed, long and well moulded. She wore a beige dress that was topped by a tweedy sort of cape-coat and she carried a tan leather bag that looked large enough to be a brief case. It matched her shoes. She had a kind of finishing-school poise and she knew how to sit and wasn't at all worried about what to do with her hands.

"Sit down, Homer," Victor Orcutt said to the man in the brown suit. Necessary looked around and found a chair that he seemed to like and was about to sit in it when Orcutt snapped, "No, not *that one*. Use the couch over there." Necessary's expression didn't change. He seemed not to have heard Orcutt; at least he didn't respond or even look at him, but he did move to the couch.

"Let's see now," Orcutt said, surveying the room with his right forefinger pressed against his lower lip. "I think I will sit—" He looked around some more. "Over there. Yes!" Over there was the seat that Necessary had chosen first.

Even with the elevator shoes Victor Orcutt wasn't much over five foot three and I can't say that I ever saw him walk any place. He glided instead. He wore a dark blue suit which looked as if it might be velvet, but on closer inspection turned out to be cashmere. I had never see a cashmere suit before. An odd jacket perhaps, or an overcoat, but never a suit, especially one that was buttoned up the front with twenty-dollar gold pieces. Six of them. Underneath the suit was a Lord Byron shirt, probably silk, and a carefully knotted cravat as red as ox blood and twice as rich that only a boor would have called a necktie. For shoes he favored black alligator, blunt-toed loafers which boasted buckles that were probably real gold too. I assumed that his drawers were also silk, but I never found out.

He perched on the edge of the chair to make sure that his feet could touch the floor. I bet myself another bottle of Scotch that he wasn't a day over twenty-six, if that. His poise reminded me of an actor's whose ego will never allow him to be offstage. His hair was curly and blond and he wore it long, I suspected, because someone had once told him that it made him look like Byron. He had the same thin nose, sensual mouth, and strong, jutting chin which, for some reason, I decided was made out of glass. He smiled a lot, but it didn't mean anything, and I had the feeling he would smile just like that if a dog got run over. He looked, all in all, a little prissy until you noticed his dark blue eyes which he may have borrowed from the local hangman, if there were one. They were eyes that rightfully belonged to a gunfighter or a pirate or perhaps an astronaut gone slightly mad. They were eyes that valued human life cheaply, including his own, and if he had any intelligence at all, he would be an enemy to respect. I doubted that you could ever count on him as a friend.

"I'm not Jewish," he said in a completely ingenuous manner. "Are you?"

"No," I said.

"Necessary isn't either. And, of course, Miss Thackerty is just *pure* WASP. I do so wish you were Jewish. Even *Italian* would do."

"Sorry," I said. "By the way, I have Scotch, and water to mix it with. If you want anything else, I'll have to call down for it."

"Carol?" Orcutt said.

"Nothing, thank you," she said.

"Homer?"

"Scotch is okay," Necessary said. It was the first time he'd said anything since he arrived.

"*I* would like—let's see now. Yes! *I* would like a Dr. Pepper."

"Dr. Pepper," I murmured and moved to the phone. I got room service and told them to send up a Dr. Pepper, a bucket of ice, four glasses, and some Pall Mall cigarettes. Two packs. I thought that the cigarettes made the order a little more respectable. "Hold on," I said into the phone and turned to the girl. "You sure you wouldn't like something—tea perhaps?"

She smiled again—or almost did. "Why, yes, tea would be nice."

"And a pot of tea with—" I looked at her.

"Lemon," she said.

"With lemon," I said.

"This is *extremely* kind of you, Mr. Dye," Orcutt said as he patted a few curls into place.

"My Southern upbringing," I said as I took a seat on the opposite end of the couch from Necessary.

Orcutt waved his right forefinger at me as if I'd said

something naughty. "You were born in Montana, Mr. Dye. In Moncrief, Montana."

I didn't bother to answer and I suppose it was the girl that kept me from kicking them all out. It had been a long time since I'd been near a woman, more that three months, and Carol Thackerty seemed to be as pleasant a prospect as I could hope to encounter. Carmingler, flushing a little and staring out the window, had once offered to run a whore into Letterman General for me, although he'd said that she was an Army nurse. I'd passed it up, more out of pique than moral squeamishness.

After the bellhop came and left, the one who looked as if he cried whenever they played "Melancholy Baby," I served Carol Thackerty her tea, handed Orcutt a glass of Dr. Pepper, and mixed two Scotches with water for Necessary and myself. They all said thank you, even Necessary.

"Now then," Victor Orcutt said as he wriggled around in his chair to make himself more comfortable. "Let me tell you something about me. I won't tell *all*, of course. No one does that, not even to their very *best* friends. But I will tell you quite a bit because I know you're curious and I just *love* talking about myself, don't you?"

"Not especially," I said, "except when I'm drunk."

"Do you get drunk often?" he said.

"Probably not often enough. It's one of my failings."

"You're *teasing!*" Victor Orcutt said. "I like that. But now let me give you a little personal background and then we'll talk about the proposal."

I was looking at Carol Thackerty. She was looking out the window at either the fog or the insurance company tower. "All right," I said.

"Well, I was born in Los Angeles twenty-six years ago. Not Los Angeles *exactly*. It was actually in the San Fernando valley. You know where that is."

It wasn't a question, so I said nothing.

"Now then, I was graduated—summa cum laude I might add, if you don't think its boasting—from the University of Chicago Law School seven years ago—"

"That would make you nineteen," I said.

"That's right. I was nineteen."

"And summa cum laude."

"He was nineteen," Necessary said. "I checked it out. The laude stuff, too."

"Really, Homer, you don't have to—"

"You want another drink?" I said to Necessary. He drank fast.

"Why not?" he said and handed me his glass.

I got up and went over to the bottle and the ice. "Go on," I said to Orcutt.

"After graduation I went to Europe and studied international law at the Free University in Berlin for a year and was awarded my doctorate degree, again with honors."

"In a year," I said.

"I checked that out, too," Necessary said. "He's a fucking genius."

"I *do* wish you would do something about your language, Homer, especially when a lady is present."

Necessary glanced at Carol Thackerty, who was still staring out the window. He said, "Huh," and took a long swallow of his fresh drink. I followed suit.

"After Berlin," Orcutt went on, "I came back to the States and toyed with several positions that were offered to me at the time."

"He got thirty-two job offers," Necessary said. "None of them for less than thirty grand a year."

Orcutt preened a little at that and forgot about admonishing Necessary. "Well, as I said, I toyed with them, but they really didn't interest me. It was all big corporation law and that can be terribly boring. So for a while I even thought that I might join the Peace Corps, but, well, you know—"

"I know," I said.

"So I simply sat down and made a list of things that I really thought I could become interested in and which, by the way, would enable me to earn a *comfortable* living. Well, I had this list of about twenty things that ranged from undersea exploration to diplomacy. I narrowed that down to just *three* things. You know what they were?"

"I wouldn't even guess."

"The three areas I finally selected were the practice of law, the problems of our metropolitan areas, and politics. Now guess which one I chose."

"Private practice," I said because I had to say something.

Orcutt seemed delighted that I'd guessed wrong and

squirmed pleasurably in his chair. "I *almost* did. Almost. But I decided that I was too young and it would take too long. Not *mentally* too young, mind you, but *chronologically*. It would have prevented me from having the *kind* of clients I would like." When he talked he supplied his own italics, like a bad editorial writer.

"The kind of clients you wanted were the kind with money," I said.

"Precisely."

"What about those thirty-two corporations who wanted to hire you?"

"That's just it. They wanted to *hire* me. They wanted me on their payroll at X number of dollars. It would have been *most* confining."

"What did you choose, politics?"

"No, I chose to become an expert consultant on the problems facing our fair city. Or cities. You know, Mr. Dye, cities are fascinating microcosms of the world we live in. We're destroying them, of course, and they in turn are destroying us. Oh, I don't mean *literally*, although smog and traffic and fire and riots *do* take their toll. But the role of the city has changed *drastically* in the last thirty years—within our lifetimes."

"So have we," I said.

"Quite true. But now we flee the city to the suburbs to regain exactly what the city formerly offered—a sense of community, if you will. A sense of belonging, of having some voice in the affairs of the day. The city at one time offered all this, plus a sense of safety, brought about, quite probably, by what was once called the herd instinct, before the term went out of style. Now if offers nothing of the kind. The city is the enemy. And most of those who still live in it, really don't. They have set up their own private enclaves. Not *neighborhoods,* mind you, but *enclaves* from which they rarely stir—except to go to work, usually in neutral territory, or to another friendly enclave. It's all really quite feudal, if you think about it. People who live in cities are actually afraid to venture into what they quite frankly regard as the enemy camp. Some of this is based on race, some on income, and also on such things as resentment, hate, prejudice, greed, and all the other seven deadly sins. It's really most depressing if one has a liking for what cities have traditionally provided."

"All right," I said, "let's say that our cities are sick and that some of them are almost terminal cases. What cure do you suggest other than faith healing?"

"You're *teasing* again. Oh, I do like that! No, Mr. Dye, I don't propose to cure all of the ills that afflict our metropolitan areas. I specialize. You see, the *fears* of those who continue to live in our cities often prevent them from taking an *active* role in their community. They become apathetic, indifferent, and spend most of their time staring at television or drinking or wondering whether they shouldn't really move to the suburbs—for the children's sake, of course. A climate of such apathy is a *perfect* breeding ground for civic corruption. And that's where Victor Orcutt Associates come in. We cure civic corruption and we're paid handsomely to do it. Of course, all we cure is the symptom, not the disease. But most of our clients cling to the belief that if the symptom disappears, the disease will shortly follow. They're wrong, of course, and sometimes out of sheer deviltry, I tell them that they're wrong, but they usually smile knowingly and thank me for a job well done and then hand over a fat check. Over the last four years, Victor Orcutt Associates have been *moderately* successful."

"What's moderate?" I said.

"Well, we netted a little over four hundred thousand dollars last year and our gross—which included all of our living expenses—was approximately four million dollars."

"Four million two," Carol Thackerty said.

Orcutt shrugged. "Miss Thackerty does have a head for figures. By the way, I met Miss Thackerty and Homer Necessary when I landed my first assignment." He mentioned the name of a city in the Midwest that was about the size of Youngstown, Ohio.

"The mayor's son was a college buddy," Necessary said. "That's how he got his in."

"Well, what are friends for, Homer?" Orcutt said. "Incidentally, Homer was chief of police there, and my first recommendation was that he be fired. You've never *seen* such graft—or perhaps you have, in China."

"Perhaps."

"Well, I *immediately* hired Homer as a consultant. I did it quietly, of course, but I thought to myself, now who would know more about foxes than another fox?"

43

"Maybe a chicken," I said.

"Mr. Dye, you've just *ruined* my favorite allegory."

"Sorry."

"At any rate," Orcutt said, "that city was *absolutely* corrupt. Rotten to the core. To the *very* core. The police sold protection along with football betting cards. They had a burglary ring going. The numbers' racket flourished. The tax assessors could be had for as little as five dollars per five thousand dollar evaluation. Gambling was nearly wide open. Not quite, but nearly. Dope was peddled in the *junior* high schools. The city itself was bankrupt. The city manager was a drunk, *pathetically* inept, and hadn't been paid in nearly three months. Neither had the police, but *they* didn't seem to mind. Prostitution. Well, it was simply awful. Anything the perverted taste wanted, from thirteen-year-old girls—or boys—on up. Shocking. *Really* shocking. And, of course, Miss Thackerty here, then a senior in the local college, was part of the vice ring. She'd even bought a very large motel out on the edge of town."

"Just working her way through college," Necessary said.

Carol Thackerty shifted her gaze from the window to Necessary. She smiled shyly, even sweetly, and in a quiet tone told Necessary to fuck off.

"Swell kid, huh?" Necessary said to me. "Nice, I mean."

"To continue," Orcutt said, ignoring the exchange as if it happened often enough, "we first—Homer and I, that is—turned our attention to the police. Homer had collected enough evidence to fascinate a grand jury, but unfortunately most of it was self-incriminating. We decided we needed something else. Homer came up with the idea. My word, he *should,* I was paying him enough."

"I made more as a chief of police," Necessary said.

"But not honestly, Homer."

"Who cares about how?"

Orcutt shook his head sadly. "*Totally* amoral. But he did have a splendid idea, one that would bring the city's police immediately into line. Of course, we had to enlist Carol's aid, and that took some persuasion, but she finally agreed that cooperating with us would be better than spending a number of months behind bars. I *must* say she cooperated so nicely that I asked her to become my executive assistant. That *was* four years ago, wasn't it, Carol?"

"Four," she said, still staring out the window. I noticed that her teacup was empty.

"Through her cooperation we were able to obtain some rather provocative photographs of most of the police force as they lay, deshabille, shall we say, in the arms of a series of very young ladies."

"What he's saying is that we got pictures of most of the cops shacking up with some of her high school whores," Necessary said. "That's what he means. We mailed prints to them at headquarters. They shaped up real good after that."

"So for a modest fee you brought in honest government, morality, and reform?" I said.

Orcutt smiled that meaningless smile of his, rose and walked over to the ice, put another cube into his glass, and filled it with the remains of the Dr. Pepper. "No, Mr. Dye, we didn't. You see, although the city was in bad condition, it really wasn't bad enough. The majority of the citizens weren't yet ready. They *liked* paying off fifteen-dollar traffic tickets with a dollar bill. They *liked* the close-by gambling and the teen-age prostitutes. They *liked* paying less real estate taxes, if all it took was a small bribe. I'm afraid I misjudged that town. Six months later it was worse than it was when I came. But by then some people from Chicago had moved in. They run the city now. Formerly, its vice and corruption were home-grown products. Now they come from outside and the people are frightened. I can't say that I blame them."

"Did they ask you to give it another go?" I said.

"Yes, they did, as a matter of fact. But I wasn't interested in dying."

"I can understand that."

"But I did gain two things from that experience," Orcutt said slowly, apparently speaking to the Dr. Pepper in his glass. "I acquired the services of Miss Thackerty and Homer. That's one. Secondly, I was able to formulate what I'm vain enough to call Orcutt's First Law. I haven't come up with a second one yet."

"What's the first one?"

"To get better, it must get much worse."

"I'm afraid it's a little familiar."

"Not really. Not when applied to my particular field. And that, I think, brings us to the crux of this meeting, which is how I hope to involve you with Victor Orcutt Associates."

"All right," I said. "How?"

"You first of all should understand, Mr. Dye, that I've spent a *considerable* amount of money investigating your background, experience, capabilities, and even your philosophical leanings."

"I wasn't aware that I had any."

"Oh, but you *do!* You do, *indeed.* A little existentialistic perhaps, but admirably suited for the task at hand. As are your experience and training and educational achievements. With just a few exceptions, you're almost perfect. Now I'll bet no one has ever called you almost perfect before."

"You're right," I said. "They haven't." Not even you, Carmingler, I thought. "Just what do you have in mind?"

"You remember that I asked whether you were Jewish?"

"Yes."

"It would be better if you were. Or Negro or Polish or even Italian. You see, Mr. Dye, I need a scapegoat—a whipping boy, if you prefer. Someone whom the citizens of a particular town can chase to the city limits. A kind of a 'don't let the sun set on your head in this town, boy' thing, if you follow me, but I'm speaking figuratively of course. They wouldn't *actually* do that; it would just be the *tone* of their attitude. A member of a minority group is *so* suited for such a role."

"Maybe they could just dislike me for myself," I said.

"Oh, my, that's *very* good," Orcutt said, and to prove that he meant it he let me see that empty smile of his again. The smile went as quickly as it came and he paused to take a sip of his Dr. Pepper. After that he produced a white handkerchief, Irish linen, I assumed, and patted his lips dry. "Now then," he said, "in return for your services I'm prepared to offer the usual incentive: money."

"What kind of money?" I said.

"The fifty thousand dollar kind."

"That is a nice kind. What do I do to earn it?"

"You perform certain tasks—under my direction of course."

"What tasks?"

"They revolve around Orcutt's First Law, Mr. Dye. What I want you to do is to corrupt me a city."

6

I was born December 5, 1933, the day they repealed prohibition. Although the information surrounding my birth is largely hearsay, most of it came from my father's diaries and I have no reason to suspect that it isn't true. He didn't have enough imagination to make a good liar.

I was the only child of Dr. and Mrs. Clarence Dye, a couple of Texans from Beaumont, who bought a medical practice in Moncrief, Montana, in 1932. Moncrief is the county seat and its population was then around 360. I understand it's dropped some since. The first year in practice, my father earned $986 cash, sixty-two chickens, two sides of beef, several bushels of vegetables in the late spring and summer, and about two hundred quart Mason jars filled with something called chow-chow, pickled beets, string beans, corn and tomatoes. "We've always eaten well," my father wrote.

Unfortunately, at least for my mother, my father was out celebrating repeal the day I was born and when he got back to the house he found himself confronted with a Caesarian. He was drunk, "Godawful drunk," he wrote later, and he never was sure what really happened. Either the scalpel slipped or he forgot to wash his hands and sepsis set in or it may have been that my mother was just one of those women who is destined to die in childbirth. He was never certain because he blacked out during the delivery and when he came to my mother was dead and I was lying well wrapped in a crib that they had bought for me. He'd managed that while out on his feet. The temperature outside, my father wrote, was 11 below zero and a blizzard had started. He wrapped my mother up in a sheet and carried her out to the garage where she froze nicely and stayed that way until the blizzard ended four days later and he could get around to having her buried in Missoula. He never did write why he decided to name me Lucifer.

47

My father really wasn't a very good doctor. He barely passed his pre-med at the University of Texas and the only medical school that he could get into in the twenties was the University of Oklahoma in Oklahoma City and that was by a fluke. Somehow he made it through, working as a theater usher at night at the old Empress on Main Street. He had married my mother by then and she worked in a department store, Rohrbaugh-Brown's it was called then. He made $9 a week; she made $12.

My father interned at St. Anthony's hospital in Oklahoma City and got through that without killing anyone. He had enough sense to realize that he would never be a good doctor and barely a competent one. For a while he thought about becoming a ship's physician, but the competition in 1932 was too stiff. Then he heard about the practice that could be bought for a thousand dollars in Moncrief. He borrowed the money from my mother's parents, who died in a car wreck before he had to pay it back. My father didn't kill anyone in Moncrief either, except my mother.

After she died my father suffered fits of what he diagnosed as "depression and remorse." He drank a lot and scribbled long passages in his diary, alternately blaming himself and me for her death. Ultimately, he accepted all of the blame. But I still remained Lucifer Clarence Dye.

He had hired a sixteen-year-old farm girl to look after me. Her name, I later read, was Betty Maude Christianson and he paid her $3.50 a week plus room and board and whatever pleasure she got from his thrice-weekly visits to her bedroom. Or so he wrote.

It was in the spring of 1934 that he sobered up and began writing the letters. He wrote to the Methodists and the Baptists and the Presbyterians. He sent long letters to the Assembly of God, the Church of the Brethren, the Episcopalians, the Christians and Missionary Alliance, and the Ethical Culture Society. He wrote to the Evangelical Covenant, the Evangelical Free, and the Evangelical and Reformed. He wrote to the Lutherans, the Friends, and the Latter Day Saints. He wrote to the Pentecostal Holiness and the Christian Scientists. Finally, he wrote to the Seventh-Day Adventists and, in desperation, to a Catholic cardinal in St. Louis, I think, offering to "come over to your side."

My father, in a spirit of atonement, had decided to become a medical missionary, preferably in China, and he was offering his services to any organized religion that would accept them. None did, unless you can call Texaco a religion. Through an old college friend whose father was the vice-president in charge of Texaco's overseas operations in Asia, my father was offered a job as company doctor in Shanghai. We sailed from San Francisco on August 19, 1934, aboard the *Midori Maru,* bound for Kobe and Shanghai.

My father and I lived in a company house in the International Settlement on Yuen Ming Road with my *amah,* Pai Shang-wa, a thirty-five-year-old spinster from Canton who spoke Cantonese as well as Mandarin and the harsh Shanghai dialect. She insisted that I learn all three, and when I made a mistake she slapped me, but not very hard. I didn't speak English too well until I was nearly six, and this made it a little difficult to communicate with my father, who spoke no Chinese, not even passable pidgin. We also had two other servants, a cook whose name was Ma Yiu-ha, and a house boy-driver, Fu Ying. I remember that I called him Foo-Foo and sometimes he carried me around the house piggyback.

My father wasn't home much, not that his duties were either arduous or pressing, but he preferred to spend his evenings at either the American Club or the Shanghai Club, which then featured the longest bar in the world. It still does, I understand, except for one in Las Vegas, but that one curves, and the one in Shanghai is straight, which still makes it the longest straight bar in the world.

Up until August 14, 1937, I have only the dim recollections that any child would have who was three years and nine months old. But on that Saturday my father, feeling either expansive or guilty for having neglected his only son, took me to lunch at the Palace Hotel. I remember that we had Shanghai duck and that it was very good and that my father cut up my pieces for me.

I remember, too, that outside the hotel, Nanking Road was packed with people, mostly refugees from Hongkew and other northern areas. Although I didn't know it, Japan had launched its attack on Shanghai the day before, once again demonstrating its preference for beginning

49

wars over the weekend, just as it had done in 1932 and would again do in 1941.

Refugees packed Nanking Road. They were the blind, the sick, the old men carrying old women on their backs, babies in their mothers' arms, and just ordinary people, all sagging with the burdens of whatever they could rescue —pans, chickens, pots, their much-prized blue teacups, and rolls of straw matting. They flowed over Soochow Creek Bridge near the Russian Consulate and fanned out over the Bund and Nanking Road, a half-million persons who snarled traffic and stalled streetcars as they tried to escape the war that was to last almost eight years to the day.

Most of them had given up moving. They huddled at the curb, against walls, on any step they could find. Nanking Road was a refugee camp, a reluctant one which offered neither refuge nor safety.

I recall that we came out of the Palace and stood there for a while, looking at the crowd, as my father probed away at a molar with a toothpick. I held his left hand. Across the street were the Sassoon House and the Cathay Hotel. But they were only a couple of buildings to me at the time. In the distance we could hear the crunch of shells as Chiang's big Northrup bombers tried to knock out the *Idzumo,* the Japanese flagship, a superannuated cruiser that had been built by the British. The Japanese Third Fleet was then in the Whampoa River and its cruisers were shelling the Chinese troops, mostly the crack 87th and 88th Divisions, softening them up for the Japanese infantry which had landed at the mouth of the Whampoa at Wusung. I liked the noise because it sounded like firecrackers.

My father started to say something, but just then the Chinese Air Corps' Northrups came over, heading west, and we both looked up. Some cylindrical things fell out of one of the bombers and glistened in the sun.

The first bomb hit the Cathay Hotel across the street. It blew out all the windows. Another bomb ricocheted off the Cathay and into Nanking Road where it exploded. The blast blew us against the red brick wall of the Palace Hotel. Then another bomb hit the Palace and hurled us back into the street. I found myself lying there in the street, still clutching my father's left hand. There was the hand and the wrist and part of the forearm. And that was all. I couldn't find any more of him as I wandered among the dead, trying not to step into pools of blood or on pieces of flesh. Everybody seemed dead. I walked around, still holding my father's hand so that the end of his forearm dragged in the dirt and blood. It was quiet. Almost the only sound I could hear was my own voice, speaking Mandarin, asking a man without a head, "Have you seen the rest of my father?" I looked around and saw another man's body smeared flat against the red bricks of the Palace Hotel. Some parked cars had caught fire. Streetcar lines were down and tangled like old fishing line. I stumbled over the lower half of a woman's body. There was no top half. I kept asking the dead if they had seen the rest of my father and when they didn't answer I started walking up Nanking Road, the blood squishing in my brown high-topped shoes. I still carried all that was left of my father.

For a block there was nothing but mangled bodies. A dead traffic cop was doubled over the side of his control tower, his eyes open. Flies crawled over them. I passed Honan Road where Nanking Road curves slightly and kept on going through a crowd that gradually came alive and chattered and moaned and screamed. They hadn't been hit. I passed Chekiang Road and the Sincere and Wing On department stores and kept on going. A Sikh policeman stared at me once and then looked quickly away. My *amah* had told me to stay away from the Sikh cops because they were mean. The only ones who were meaner, she said, were the Annamites that the French had brought into their Concession. They call them Vietnamese now. I suppose the Sikh cop looked away because he didn't want to fool with a four-year-old foreigner smeared with his own blood and that of others, dirty, disheveled, and bawling, who stumbled through the crowd, panicky, carrying a man's hand, wrist and forearm against his chest much as he would hold his favorite teddy bear. I remember that after the bombs exploded there was that Godawful silence, so profound that all I could hear was my own voice and the tick of the watch which was still strapped to my father's wrist.

I must have gone two or three streets past the department stores before I saw her. She wore an organdy dress with lots of ruffles and flounces in a style that I later found had been popularized by an American actress called Deanna Durbin. I've yet to see one of her films.

I thought then, and perhaps still do, that the woman in the organdy dress was the most beautiful person in the world. She stood there at the curb, waving a silk parasol, and yelling for someone called Fat Li-san. Her blond hair was capped by a wide-brimmed, floppy hat. Dark green, I remember, a color that almost matched her eyes. Slightly behind her stood a Chinese woman who also yelled for Fat Li-san.

I stumbled over to her and stood there, gazing up at her face, my father's remains clutched tightly to my chest. I bawled. She looked at me, frowned, and gestured that I should go away. When I didn't, but just stood there bawling some more, smeared from top to bottom with blood, she turned and snapped something at the Chinese woman. She spoke French, but I didn't know it then. All I knew was that my cuts and scratches and abrasions hurt, that I was lost, and that I couldn't find the rest of my father.

The Chinese woman came over to me and knelt down and began speaking softly in English. I knew it was English but I couldn't understand very much of it and when she saw that it wasn't working too well, she switched to the Shanghai dialect. That was better. She wanted to know who I was and how I'd gotten hurt and where my parents were. The blond woman in the floppy hat kept waving her parasol and yelling for Fat Li-san. I told the Chinese woman that I was Lucifer Clarence Dye and had she seen my father? The woman in the Deanna Durbin dress moved closer, but not too close. She said something in French to the Chinese woman, who turned out to be her *amah*. The *amah* shook her head, rose, and backed off. The woman with the big floppy green hat grimaced and stretched out her hand.

"*Donnez la moi!*" she said. Or so she told me later. Much later. I didn't understand her then, but the out-stretched hand made things plain enough and I hugged my father's severed forearm, wrist, hand, and watch even closer. I bawled some more, partly because I was one of the 865 wounded by the Chinese Air Corps which bombed its own city and partly because my father was among the 729 who were dead for the same reason.

The woman in the green hat stripped the white glove

from her right hand, snatched all that was left of my father away from me, and started to throw it in the gutter. However, she saw the watch and paused long enough to remove it from the wrist. She was always quite practical. After that, she tossed it into the gutter. A dusty red dog covered with sores nuzzled my father's hand, picked it up in his jaws, and trotted off down the street. The dog seemed to be grinning.

The woman in the floppy hat smiled at me and started to pat me on the head, but thought better of it. My hair was matted with blood. "We go my house," she said in her best pidgin English. I understood that and asked her, this time in Mandarin, if she'd seen my father. I wasn't too familiar with death, not familiar at all really, and I'd have liked to have given my father back his hand and wrist and forearm and watch.

"We go," she said and once more yelled for the missing Fat Li-san. A large maroon 1935 Airflow Chrysler, an automotive abortion that was to be rivaled by the Edsel years later, bulldozed its way to the curb, clipping a rickshaw. Fat Li-san had finally arrived. The woman in the green hat sent him off for some newspapers and when he returned he spread them over the back seat so that I wouldn't bleed all over the mohair. The *amah* got in the front with Fat Li-san and I was guided to the newspapers. The woman in the green hat got in at last. Fat Li-san leaned on the horn and bluffed his way through the jammed traffic.

The blond woman started talking to me. She used a mixture of pidgin English, some of which I got, French (which I didn't understand), and Russian (totally incomprehensible). With the help of some interpretative asides from the *amah* in the Shanghai dialect, I gathered that I could stay at her house until she located my parents; that I was to call her Tante Catherine or Katerine, and that if I were good, she would give me something nice.

Her house was in Nantao, the Old Chinese City with its Confucius Temple and its Willow Teahouse. It was painted a green that matched her hat and her eyes and had a high brick wall across its front which shielded a tiny garden. The house was an unusual (for Shanghai) three stories high, and not more than forty feet wide, and it looked magnificently immense to me. It was furnished with an odd mixture of carved Chinese pieces with lots of dragons' heads and with what passed for modern in the 1930s. I thought it all very beautiful. Tante Katerine called out as we entered the house followed by the *amah*. A number of young women came into the wide reception hall and started to make a fuss over me. One of them was assigned the task of giving me a bath. Another was instructed to buy me some new clothes. Tante Katerine remembered her promise and gave me a piece of candied ginger. There was a peculiarly sweetish, pungent, odor in the air and an old man with a whisp of a white beard shuffled slowly toward the door that led to the garden and the gate and the street. He didn't look at me; he didn't look at anybody. One of the girls took my hand and started pulling me toward the stairs. She was Chinese and I asked her if she had seen my father. She said no. About half of the girls were Chinese and about half were foreign: French, American, White Russian, a couple of big-boned Australians, three Germans from Berlin, and a lone representative from Italy. Rome, as I recall. They were all very nice to me, but it was a year or so later before I fully understood that Tante Katerine, a White Russian late of Manchuria, ran what was generally regarded as the fanciest whorehouse in Shanghai.

7

It took twenty-four hours and an autopsy before the island city-state's police were satisfied that we hadn't murdered Li Teh with some kind of infernal machine. He had died of cardiac arrest—or what was once called heart failure—brought on, so I understand, by severe emotional shock. It could have been the blue flashes that had danced around the room. He probably thought that he was being electrocuted.

I learned later that Shoftstall went stupid and came up with a fanciful story that no one believed. He told them that Li Teh's name was Mr. Jones and that I'd wanted to question him with a lie detector because he'd applied for a $200,000 life insurance policy and I wasn't at all satisfied with the information he'd given on his application. After that, they knocked Shoftstall around for a while, which only made him stubborn. All he would say after the beating was that as an American citizen, he demanded to see a representative of the U.S. Embassy. They threw him back in a cell.

Bourland was a little brighter, but not much. He said that the polygraph examination of Li Teh was merely routine.

"What kind of routine, Mr. Bourland?" one of them asked.

"Why, routine procedure," he said.

They knocked him around until they got tired and then threw him back in a cell, too. He didn't get a chance to call the Embassy either. I later learned all this from Carmingler.

They questioned us separately, of course, and they were good. At least the man who questioned me and who called himself Mr. Tung was good. Quite good. He said that he was from the Ministry of Defense and Security and I found no reason to doubt it.

I spent the first twenty-four hours in solitary. They had taken away my clothes, cigarettes, keys, wallet, and

55

watch. I missed the cigarettes most of all. It really didn't seem to matter much what time it was. They gave me the gray cotton, pajamalike uniform, the one that I was to wear for three months without change. The cell was small, five-feet wide and seven-feet long. It was windowless and contained a straw-stuffed mattress, a bucket that served as a toilet, and a small plastic jug of water. Nothing else. The walls were built of gray, porous stones that were clammy and wet. The floor was concrete. A single forty-watt bulb was screwed into the ceiling. It never went off. The temperature seemed to be in the upper nineties, right alongside the humidity.

I was fed twice before I saw Tung. The first meal was a large bowl of rice with some pieces of unidentifiable fish mixed into it. The second meal was the same and so were all the other meals during the next three months. From long ago experience I choked down anything they gave me and didn't lose a pound. Maybe they're right after all and fish and rice are everything you really need.

The room that Tung questioned me in was on the second floor of the prison that the British had built a hundred years or so before with loving attention to all the details that would make it as uncomfortable as possible. The room had two windows that looked out over the prison yard which was surrounded by walls built of that same gray, porous stone. They must have been at least twenty-five feet high. A number of prisoners were walking around the yard, either by themselves or in twos and threes. I didn't bother to ask if I could join them.

Mr. Tung (I never knew his other names, if he had any), was somewhere in his thirties, short, slim, and dapper. He wore a crisp white shirt with a neatly knotted blue tie and light blue linen slacks that were pressed to perfection. There were four ball-point pens clipped to his shirt pocket, all different colors. His black eyes seemed to snap a little and he had the nervous habit of tugging at his right earlobe when he was trying to phrase a question. He didn't smile much, at least not when talking to me, and we spent quite some time talking.

Two prison guards brought me into the room and then left. I stood before Tung's desk while he carefully looked me over. The room contained only the desk, Tung's chair, and the one that he motioned me to sit in. There was nothing on his desk other than a round tin of Players, the kind that holds fifty cigarettes. He offered me one and I accepted it gratefully.

We sat there smoking for a while and then Tung said, "Well, you blew it, didn't you?" I couldn't place his accent despite the use of the vernacular. It wasn't American and it wasn't British. It was that in between, international brand, the kind that Douglas Fairbanks, Jr. used to speak before he began spending too much time in London.

I shrugged at his question and said nothing. There really wasn't anything to say.

"Too bad about Li Teh," Tung said. "I take it that you didn't know about his heart condition?"

"No."

"He wasn't a bad chap really."

"You knew him?"

"Not too well," Tung said. "He was dickering to open one of his shops here, but I suppose you knew that."

"No."

"Yes. As a matter of fact, he'd recently received a promotion. But I'm sure you did know that."

"No," I said.

Tung looked at me carefully and then took a tin ashtray from a desk drawer and placed it halfway between us. I put some ashes into it.

"Really, Mr. Dye, I almost believe that you are as ignorant as you pretend to be."

"I'm just ignorant," I said.

"Then I'll bring you up to date. Peking promoted Li Teh six weeks ago. He was told to keep his operations going in Hong Kong, but to set up a shop down here and run it on a part-time basis. When it was a going concern, they would send someone down from Peking to take over. In the meantime, he'd commute between here and Hong Kong. He didn't tell you any of this?" Tung tugged at his earlobe again. The right one.

"No," I said.

"I think you're lying," Tung said. "But that's to be expected. At any rate, we approached Li. I confess that our approach was none too subtle. Either he doubled for us, or we'd throw him in jail."

"Why did you think he was an agent?" I said.

Tung smiled a little, but not much. "Why did you?"

There seemed to be nothing to say to that either. Tung,

57

however, was waiting for an answer. I let him wait while a fat, heavy silence spread through the room.

"The premier's most unhappy," he said after a time.

"Really? Why?"

"Because of you, Mr. Dye, and your organization which, I might add, fully lives up to its reputation for bungling. Really remarkable. The premier, of course, is just hopping mad. But I've said that, haven't I?"

"Just what am I charged with?" I said.

"We'll think of something."

"I'm sure."

"You should be. But to return to Li Teh. He told us that he thought you'd go as high as three thousand dollars a month. American. Did you?" When I didn't say anything, Tung continued. "We offered to pay him something. Of course, we could never match your largesse, but we did offer him one thousand dollars a month (our variety) and the promise that he wouldn't go to jail which was, I think you'll agree since you've seen our jail, a rather enticing fringe benefit. And by the way, he told us all about you—how you used to meet in out of the way places in Hong Kong and so forth. Even gave us dates and times."

"He talked a lot," I said.

"We can be rather persuasive."

"I can imagine."

Tung rose and walked over to the window and looked out. He was silent for a time and I thought that he may have been counting the prisoners. With his back still to me, he said, "We're going to ask your people for thirty million dollars."

"You'll never get it," I said and helped myself to another cigarette.

"That's our asking price," he said, turning from the window. "We'll settle for ten cents on the dollar. A million each for you and your two colleagues." He lowered himself into his chair again, reached for one of the cigarettes, and this time he did smile. He had good teeth. "But the money's not really important, of course."

"Of course," I said.

"What we really want is a letter of apology."

"From whom?"

"From your Secretary of State. The premier was thinking of going directly to the White House, but he was dissuaded."

58

"You won't get anything," I said.

"You think not?"

"I think not."

"Well, let's see what we have to offer," Tung said and laid his cigarette in the tin tray so that he could count on the fingers of his right hand. "On the surface, we have the dead body of a Chinese spy; two insurance salesmen from here, and their managing director from Hong Kong. Minneapolis Mutual, isn't it?"

"Minneapolis Mutual," I said.

"That's on the surface. Now beneath the surface we have the following interesting documentation." He was using his fingers to count on again. "One, we have a tape recording of the conversation that took place last night in the hotel between you and your two colleagues, even that part where one of them was reassuring Li Teh that the lie detector wouldn't hurt a bit. That's one. I'll play it for you, if you like."

"No need," I said and swore silently at Shoftstall for not checking the hotel room for bugs.

"Two, we have Peking's file on you, Mr. Dye. Li Teh graciously provided us with a copy. Three, we have your tape recorder and the polygraph machine as exhibits D and E. You and your two colleagues, of course, are exhibits A, B, and C. The Peking dossier on you is, I suppose, exhibit F, which possibly could stand for failure. You did fail, didn't you?"

"I don't think I should count on a Christmas bonus this year."

"Tell me something, Mr. Dye, does your organization, which I'll call Minneapolis Mutual, if you insist, really put that much faith in the efficacy of the polygraph?"

"It would seem so, wouldn't it?"

"And yourself, Mr. Dye?"

I shrugged. "It's company policy."

"A rather strange company and a rather strange policy."

"It's the new management," I said.

Tung rose, tugged at his earlobe, and said, "I really have no more questions. I think I know as much about you as I need to, and even if I did have some questions, I'm sure that your answers would be totally unresponsive unless we used tactics which are far more primitive than the lie detector, but also more—oh, I suppose fruitful is as good a word as any."

I got up, too, and helped myself to another cigarette. "Take the tin," he said. "And here're some matches."

"Thanks," I said. "How about a call to my embassy?"

"You don't really expect me to say yes?"

"No, but I thought I'd ask."

"We'll be in touch with your embassy and also your 'company.'" I could almost see the quotation marks around company.

"When?"

"Soon."

The guards came and took me back to my cell. Four days later, despite what I considered to be strict self-rationing, I ran out of cigarettes and didn't smoke until eighty-five days later when Carmingler bummed a pack for me from the pilot of the C-130 that flew us to San Francisco.

The only visitors that I had during those three months were the guards who brought me my bowls of soggy rice and doubtful fish each day. Once a photographer came to take my picture with an old 4 by 5 Speed Graphic. But that was all. I had nothing to read, nothing to look at, and no one to talk to other than myself.

Since the forty-watt light never went out I didn't know whether it was day or night. They seemed to feed me at erratic times, but I wasn't even sure of that. I came to realize that time indeed is relative and what I thought was an entire day could have been an hour and what I was sure was three hours could well have been fifteen minutes. None of the time that I spent in that cell went quickly. Some of it just dragged by more slowly than the rest.

So I talked to myself and tried to remember stories and novels that I'd read. I rewrote them aloud. I exercised a lot, mostly push-ups and toe-touching and knee-bends and sit-ups and running in place. I wasn't trying to keep in shape. I was trying to grow tired enough to sleep. I slept as much as possible and hoped that I would have nightmares. They gave me something new to think about.

When I wasn't talking aloud or exercising or just sitting there staring at the wall, I searched for lice. My record kill was 126. I counted the dead ones carefully every day and then dumped them into the pail that served as a toilet. The guards emptied it daily, but I was never sure whether they did it in the morning or the evening. For all I knew, they emptied it promptly at midnight.

I didn't shave or bathe for ninety days. I stunk. I couldn't smell it myself, but I could tell that I did from the way that the guards wrinkled their noses when they brought me the food. They seldom looked at me and they never spoke. I tried to remember the *Count of Monte Cristo* and Koestler's *Darkness at Noon,* whose title I had never fully appreciated until now. I tried to remember what they did to keep themselves busy and entertained and even amused. Apparently, I wasn't as resourceful as they. The only thing that really amused me was killing lice.

On the ninetieth day the guards took me back up to Tung's office. He wore tan slacks this time with another white shirt and a black-and-brown striped tie. He was down to three ball-point pens. He didn't offer me a cigarette and he didn't ask me to sit.

"Except for your beard you look well enough, Mr. Dye. A little ripe perhaps, but fit."

"Thanks."

"You'll be released at midnight."

"Tonight?"

"Tonight."

"What time is it now?"

Tung glanced at his watch. "Four thirty-five. P.M., in case you're wondering. They do sometimes, you know."

"I know."

"Everything has worked out most satisfactorily since I last spoke with you in June."

"What month is it now?"

"August. August twenty-fourth to be precise."

"I've been here almost three months."

"Three months exactly. Ninety days."

"You run a rotten jail."

"It's something we picked up from our Colonial friends. You may be interested to learn that it went much the way I predicted it would when we had our first chat. It went better than I predicted, in fact."

"They paid up."

"They did indeed, Mr. Dye. Ten cents on the dollar, just as I said they would. Three million dollars in all. The ramifications are even better than that though—far better. But I think I won't gloat. It's not at all becoming and I'm sure that your people are most anxious to tell you about it themselves."

"They probably can't wait."

"Well, I suppose that's all," Tung said. "A Mr. Carmingler will meet you just outside the prison at midnight. Do you know him?"

"I know him. What about the other two?"

"Oh, you mean Mr. Shoftstall and Mr. Bourland? They were released about an hour ago. I regret that they somehow injured themselves, but photographs of their injuries helped convince your people that they should—uh—cooperate. Mr. Shoftstall and Mr. Bourland are now both in hospital, I understand. Would you like to know which one?"

"Not especially."

Tung nodded as if he understood that perfectly. Perhaps he did. "Well, I've enjoyed our two chats, Mr. Dye; I'm only sorry that we didn't have more of them."

"I'm surprised that we didn't."

"Yes. However, Mr. Shoftstall and Mr. Bourland became most cooperative so we saw no need to disturb you, especially since poor Li Teh had provided us with such extensive documentation on your activities as, shall we say, a China watcher. A felicitous phrase, if ever I heard one. Incidentally, Mr. Dye, while you were our—uh—guest the People's Republic removed the hyphen from Mao Tsetung's name in all their official dispatches. It's now one word. Some seem to place an extraordinary amount of significance on this. Do you?"

"Tremendous. Anything else?"

"No. Nothing I can think of. Is there something that you'd care to mention?"

"I'd like my watch back and I still think you run a rotten jail."

Tung smiled broadly and his teeth were just as nice as they were before. "Yes," he said, "we do manage that quite well, don't we?" He didn't say anything about the watch.

First of all they deloused me. Then I showered for twenty minutes. Following that, I put on a red hospital bathrobe and was shaved, barbered, and stuffed with a four-egg breakfast. After all that I got to sit across the desk from Carmingler, wearing one of my new suits, and watch him use three matches to get his pipe going. He used the wooden kitchen kind that come in cardboard boxes and used to sell for a nickel. They're probably a dime now. Everything else has gone up.

We sat in the office that Letterman General had assigned him, the one in the sealed-off suite that was painted a depressing tan and contained a gray desk and four matching chairs and whose lone window offered a gloomy view of the rear of the hospital's kitchen.

"Okay," I said. "Now that I'm all tidied up and sweet-smelling, you can start."

"Well, to begin with," he said, "it wasn't my idea."

"Whose was it?"

"Mugar's."

"I don't know any Mugar."

"He's new."

"I'm sure he is," I said. "What about the lie detector? Whose idea was that? Mugar's again?"

"They were dead set against Li Teh," Carmingler said and dragged on his pipe. "It was all I could think of."

"Then you're losing your touch. Five years ago you could have thought of a dozen ways, but five years ago you weren't in love with a polygraph."

"They wanted to make sure," he said. "They had to be positive about Li."

"All of them?"

"Most of them."

"How many?" I said.

"There were five of us. Me, Mugar, Reo, Werbin, and Pilalas."

"What side was the Greek on?"

"He was the only one with me. He'd go along, but the other three wouldn't. They were following Mugar."

"How old's Mugar?"

"I don't know; twenty-eight, twenty-nine."

"And he's this year's new boy," I said.

"Very new. But he bought the polygraph."

I sighed and lit another cigarette. My tenth for the morning. "It doesn't matter now. Li's dead. I'm blown all over Asia. I just want to know what happened."

"It was a mess," Carmingler said. "A real fuck-up." Carmingler never swore unless he meant it and when he got through describing what had happened, I could see that he did.

"They thought you were CIA, of course," he said. "That started it."

I nodded. Then Carmingler told me the rest of it. On the perfectly sound theory that the United States' left hand seldom knows what its right big toe is doing, the premier of the island city-state republic decided to make two approaches, one to the State Department and one to the CIA who, they mistakenly thought, employed me. It was their Foreign Minister himself who summoned the local U.S. ambassador and then confronted him with extensive documentation that proved beyond doubt that American agents had been fiddling with his country's affairs. The Foreign Minister demanded a written apology from the U.S. Secretary of State. The U.S. ambassador promptly dispatched copies of the damaging material to Washington where the Secretary of State, new to his job and anxious to please, went through the usual seventh-floor shilly-shallying and then wrote, or had someone write, the letter of apology (an almost unheard of gesture) which promised that the culprits (meaning Shoftstall, Bourland, and me) would be severely disciplined. The Secretary himself was under the impression that we were with CIA. He didn't bother to check.

It was my former prison host, Mr. Tung, who approached the CIA. He made the approach in Djakarta, Carmingler said, and when he demanded the thirty million dollar ransom, they just laughed at him. They didn't check with anyone either; they just laughed. It was the wrong thing to do, of course. Mr. Tung merely smiled back and then hurried across the street (or wherever it was) to the local British MI-6 representative and told him all about how the Americans no longer trusted their English colleagues and were running their own agents on what by gentlemen's agreement, had been considered the private turf of Perfidious Albion. Actually, Carmingler said, the CIA was thinking about it. They just hadn't gotten around to it yet.

"Well, the British got most upset," he said. "They accused the CIA of double-dealing and God knows what else. The CIA just kept on denying that any of you belonged to them. They had no choice, of course."

"There's always a choice," I said.

"Name it."

I could think of a number of things, but I let it pass. Having brought the British in and carefully bruised their already tender sensibilities, Tung then leaked the whole story to the press.

"Made headlines everywhere. Every damned place you could think of, and the British got sore all over again." His pipe had gone out so Carmingler used four matches to light it. He seemed to have forgotten his Phi Beta Kappa key, which I thought was just as well. "So all CIA could do was to deny again that you were one of them. They didn't know about the Secretary's letter. State hadn't bothered to tell them about that. Then the premier himself called a press conference, distributed Xeroxed copies of the letter, and made a feisty little speech that lasted an hour all about how the United States was trying to dominate Asia through a program of subversion and what have you. He even hinted that he might play those tapes for the press—you know, the ones that they got in your hotel room."

"Did he?"

"No. But he said—and he was lying, of course—that we had offered him thirty million dollars in foreign aid to release the three of you, and he said that he had evidence to prove it. Well, he did have that fool letter of apology from the Secretary. That was real enough. The British were still fuming and leaking stuff all over the place, so the press went along. Can't say I blame them really. More headlines, and God, the editorials. *The New York Times* called it a 'tragedy of errors.' *The Washington Post* said it was 'inane chicanery.' And the New York *Daily News* wanted somebody 'horsewhipped.' So the word came down from the White House. Buy them out no matter how much."

"How much was it?" I said.

Carmingler gave me his need to know look. "Oh, they still asked for thirty million, but it was less than that. Much, much less."

"Ten cents on the dollar," I said. "Three million."

Carmingler glared at me suspiciously. "Only six persons in the country are supposed to know that."

"Now you can make it seven."

"Who told you?"

"A wily oriental."

65

The deep flush started at the top of Carmingler's fault-less collar and rose slowly until it reached his temples. It made him look like a traffic light that would never say go again. He sucked away on his pipe and fooled with his Phi Beta Kappa key at the same time, a sure sign that he was upset.

"I assume," he said, spitting the words at me from around his pipe, "that the wily oriental also told you why you were kept in solitary."

I shrugged. "Standard procedure, I suppose."

"You suppose wrong. Has it occurred to you that we could debrief you in Hong Kong just as well as we could in San Francisco? After all, Hong Kong's been your home for the past ten years. You probably have more friends there than you do in the States."

"It crossed my mind," I said, "and since it might make you feel better, I'll ask why—about both the solitary and being hustled back to the States, although I don't mind that. I left nothing in Hong Kong except some cheap suits in my hotel and some equally cheap books. My car was leased and my bank account wasn't over two hundred dollars."

"You were paid enough."

"I'm a spendthrift."

The flush in Carmingler's face had receded. He put his pipe carefully into the ashtray and placed the palms of his hands flat on the table. His elbows jutted out as he leaned toward me. He looked something like a middle-aged turkey who thought he would try to fly just one more time.

"They kept you in solitary and we brought you back here because Li Teh's people have put a price on your head." He enjoyed saying that.

"How much?"

"Enough."

"How much, goddamn it?"

He smiled. "Five thousand dollars. American. At that price you wouldn't live two hours in Hong Kong."

"And here?"

"It doesn't matter here."

I nodded. "Monsters of all kinds shall be destroyed."

"Where's that from?"

"From China," I said. "From Chairman Mao."

66

8

Until I was a little more than eight years old I went to school each afternoon for three hours following lunch. My teachers were prostitutes. I would have liked to have gone to school in the morning, but the ladies were never up.

I learned simple arithmetic (they were all good at that), French, Russian, German, and English—speaking the last, I was told, with a pronounced Australian accent. I also learned a highly garbled version of world history, spiced with tales of high romance and shattered dreams during the impossibly good old days in Berlin, Sydney, Canton, Rome, Marseilles, St. Petersburg, and San Diego. My Chinese also improved, but by the time I was eight I still couldn't read or write my name in any language.

And it wasn't until my seventh birthday that they stopped dressing me in rich brocades and silk. Until then I wore a series of long Mandarin gowns with high collars. My trousers were made of contrasting raw silk and red felt slippers covered my feet. The girls took turns painting my cheeks and plucking my eyebrows and powdering my face until it was chalk white except for two round spots of rouge on either cheek. I was a hell of a sight.

I've never been quite sure why Tante Katerine took me home with her or even kept me around after she did. It may have been some latent maternal instinct, but that's doubtful. More likely, she made one of her usually accurate snap judgments and decided that having an American towel boy in her whorehouse would provide a novelty well worth the cost of my room and board.

Three years later, when I was nearly seven, she told me that the officials at the U.S. Consulate, as well as the Texaco management, assumed that both my father and I had been blown to bits in 1937 by the Nanking Road explosions. A few days after she brought me home with her she had coached one of her American girls—the one from San Diego, Doris, I recall—for an hour or so and then had had her telephone both the Consulate and Texaco.

Posing as an old friend of the Dye family, Doris inquired if the doctor's relatives in the States had been informed of his death and that of his son. She was told that the doctor had no living relatives. She then asked if there were any personal effects and the Texaco man said that there was nothing other than the doctor's medical bag, his clothes and those of his son, and four five-year diaries that the doctor had faithfully kept since he was fourteen years old. Doris somehow talked the Texaco man into sending her the diaries to some poste restante or other under the unlikely pretext that they would be of immense value to the Montana State Historical Society, of whose board of directors she claimed to be chairman. After the diaries arrived, Doris occasionally read me some of the juicier passages. I'm still not sure how Doris knew about the Montana State Historical Society, but it may have been that she had once whored in Helena for a while.

Tante Katerine must have been close to forty in 1939. Her full name, so she said, was Katerine Obrenovitch, and she claimed to be a distant cousin of ex-King Alexander of Serbia, who took over the throne when his father, King Milan, abdicated in 1889. She also said that she had been born in St. Petersburg (she could never bring herself to say Leningrad) and had fled the revolution to Manchuria along with a sizeable bunch of other White Russians. I heard the tale dozens of times. It always had a lot of snow in it and even some wolves chasing a sleigh. Although still a very small child, I knew that most of it was a lie, but it was one that I never grew tired of hearing.

When the Japanese took control of Shanghai on November 8, 1937—except for the International Settlement and the French Concession—Katerine employed every guile she had learned during twenty years of varied experience to determine who was what she, in her cosmopolitan patois, called, "Señor Number One Garçon."

Mr. Number One Boy turned out to be a Japanese major who had been too long in grade, at least in his opinion, and was not at all averse to being bribed with both money and free samples. I remember the major, although I can't recall his real name. The girls referred to him as Major Dogshit. That was close enough and since he didn't understand English, he didn't mind. His preferences in money ran to English pounds and American dollars, which commanded an exorbitant rate of exchange on the black market. He liked his girls in matched sets of twos and threes and when that was over, he liked his opium pipe. If I'd been a little older, he might even have liked me.

Tante Katerine's cultivation of Major Dogshit paid off. Hers was the last foreign-staffed whorehouse in Nantao to close its doors, on Christmas Day, 1941. There were about twenty of them running wide open in 1937, offering not only whores and opium, but also gambling. After 6 P.M. my task was to greet the procession of Chinese quislings, Japanese big shots, and foreign dignitaries who often clogged the narrow street in the cool of the evening, borne by their Pierce-Arrows, Chryslers, Humbers, and the occasional Lincoln-Zephyr V-12, a car that I passionately admired.

The Chinese always arrived with four or five hard-faced bodyguards standing on the running boards. The bodyguards wore big Colt .45 automatics strapped to their bellies and they liked to wave them around a lot. All decked out in my silk and brocade finery, which was topped off by a round hat copied from the one that Johnny used to wear in the old Phillip Morris ads, my eyebrows plucked, my face powdered and painted, but unlipsticked (I drew the line there), I greeted the guests, each in his own language, with florid phrases of welcome. The scripts had been written by Tante Katerine and I'd learned them by rote. One of the Chinese girls taught me what she considered to be the proper bows and flourishes.

I can still remember that the English paean went something like this in my best Australian twang: "May it please your lordship (even a merchant seaman arriving in a rickshaw was a lordship if he had the cash) to accept the poor hospitality of this humble house (flourish and bow and up). Your presence brings great honor to this wretched establishment and we humbly seek to satisfy your every need (leer and flourish and bow and up). We pray that time spent with us will help to banish the great cares that surely accompany your exalted position (flourish and bow and up). This way, sir, if you please."

I could rattle that off by the time I was five and a half in English, French, Chinese, Russian (not much call), Japanese, and German, even if I didn't understand a tenth of what I was saying.

That chore kept me busy from nine until eleven P.M. After that I sometimes prepared a few opium pipes and by midnight I usually had prepared enough so that I fell into my own dopey stupor and had to be undressed and put to bed, where I discovered what pleasant dreams really are. I still don't know why I didn't get hooked.

Occasionally, I accompanied Tante Katerine on shopping sprees in the International Settlement and the French Concession. She liked to show off her figure and her looks, which she kept through rigid dieting, chin straps, massage, and carefully applied makeup. It usually took her two hours at the mirror before she felt she was ready to greet customers. Her hair was still blond in 1939, although she had discarded Deanna Durbin in favour of the ringlets of Jeanette MacDonald. To me she remained the most beautiful person in the world and I remember clutching her hand as we sometimes strolled along the Bund, her silk parasol in her right hand and mine in her left, the devoted *amah,* Yen Chi, trotting along behind us. Tante Katerine nodded and smiled at regular customers if they were alone or with other men and ignored them if they were with their wives or mistresses. She kept up a running commentary to me on the sexual prowess and eccentricities of each which I found educational as well as interesting.

By 1939 the Japanese had taken control of the maritime customs and in the months that followed they absorbed the postal system, the Chinese-run radio stations, the railroads, the telephones, and the telegraph lines. They also clamped down on the press, except for those newspapers that were located in the sacrosanct French Concession and International Settlement. But if the Japanese couldn't influence editorial policy, they could influence the editors themselves and they proceeded to do so in a forthright, graphic manner.

I think it was near the busy junction of the French Concession and the International Settlement. Tante Katerine had taken me shopping with her. I was wearing my Buster Brown suit (the brocades and silks were my working uniform) and was minus the powder and paint. I think she got the idea for the Buster Brown suit from an ancient issue of *The Woman's Home Companion* that had happened to come her way. I'd have preferred corduroy knickers, although I'm still not sure how I knew that they

70

even existed, but I didn't want to hurt her feelings because she thought that my tailored Buster Brown suit would please me immensely.

There was a crowd gathered at the junction, I recall, and Tante Katerine, always curious, used her elbows and parasol to snake us through it until we were on the front row with the rest of the professional gawkers. There were an even dozen objects to admire and I remember she said, "Oh, my dear Mary Mother of God!" grabbed my hand, and plowed our way back through the crowd with Yen Chi following as best she could.

"Who were they?" I asked.

"Men," she said in French. "Very good men."

"What did they do?"

She was grim now. "They wrote the truth, Lucifer. Always remember that. They wrote the truth." Tante Katerine was much given to dramatics.

"Then why," I said, speaking French, which I often did when I had a logical question to ask, "are their heads on poles?" They were really pikes, but I didn't know the difference.

"Because—" she began and then changed the subject. "How would you like a sherbet?"

I forgot about the Chinese newspapermen whose heads the Japanese had chopped off and stuck on pikes for all to see. "Oh, that would be *sehr schön*," the multilingual little bastard said.

I can thank Tante Katerine that by the time I was eight I was a street-wise, cynical little snot, much given to gossip and slander, a toady when it suited my purpose, which it often did, and enough of a ham so that I fully enjoyed my role as whorehouse doorman. The tips that I got from the arriving guests, along with what I rolled the pipe smokers and the drunks for, never taking more than five percent of what they had in their pockets, gave me an income that was equivalent to around fifty to sixty American dollars a week which, at first, I dutifully turned over to Tante Katerine, who said that she was investing it for me. I didn't understand what investing meant, but I did know that I never had a dime, so I started squirreling away about a third of my weekly take. I must have been about seven then and on my eighth birthday, three days before Pearl Harbor, I had stashed away a little more

71

than a thousand dollars in American and British currency. I didn't trust anything else. If Tante Katerine suspected that I was skimming a third of my tips, she never said anything. If she had, I would have denied it. Hotly. I was already an accomplished liar. I think she approved of my rolling the drunks and the pipe smokers as long as I didn't get too greedy, but she never said anything about that either.

Another of my daily tasks after school was to provide an audience for Tante Katerine during the two hours that she took to make up her face. She regaled me with tales of her social life in St. Petersburg before the Bolshevik swine took over and it wasn't until years later that I discovered that most of her plots had been borrowed from some of the more impossible Viennese operettas. As I've said, I didn't believe the stories even then, but I was fascinated by the intrigue, the duels (always over her), the romance, and the vivid descriptions of balls, parties, and court receptions. All in all, it was far better than Mother Goose and quite on a par with the Brothers Grimm.

It was also during these daily two-hour sessions that Tante Katerine tried to provide me with a philosophical approach to life that would steer me around a long list of pitfalls, provide comfort and solace in moments of stress, and possibly keep me out of jail. It was a curious mixture of copybook maxims, borrowed and invented proverbs, and what I later came to regard as pure Katerinisms.

"Never trust a redheaded Mexican," she once said. That one was lost on me because I didn't even know what a Mexican was. My geography had been so neglected that I was quite sure that Berlin was just on the other side of the International Settlement and that San Diego lay a couple of miles farther on. One of the girls had once told me that the world was round like a ball, but that, I reasoned, was obviously a complete fabrication.

Tante Katerine, sitting before her vanity, slapping on creams and unguents, plucking an eyebrow or affixing an earring, would break off one of her more fanciful tales in which all the men were handsome and all the women beautiful, turn those dark green eyes of hers on me, lower her voice until it was almost a high baritone, and say: "Get this straight, my little *Kuppler*, free advice is the worst kind you can buy." Or, "Listen well, *petit ami*, nobody's ever as sad or as happy as they think they are.

72

They're more so." But the one I liked best, because I was never sure that I really had it figured out, was one that she always said at the end of the two-hour operation when she was staring at herself in the mirror and perhaps patting a stray wisp of blond hair into place: "My known vices are my hidden virtues, did you know that, Lucifer?" and I would always say yes, I knew that.

9

After Victor Orcutt got through telling me what he wanted done and how much he was willing to pay me to do it, everyone sat there without speaking while I digested the information, much as if it were a half-dozen oysters that could have been a trifle long from the sea. Homer Necessary cleared his throat once. The fretful cable-car bells clanged and railed against the afternoon traffic. A foghorn moaned twice, as if seeking commiseration, or at least sympathy. I got up and mixed a drink and on the way back to the couch I stopped to look at Orcutt, who seemed fascinated by the tip of his left shoe.

"How'd you get on to me?"

He looked up and smiled that meaningless smile of his. "Do you mean how or why?"

"Both."

"Very well," he said. "I think you should know. First, how. It was through Gerald Vicker. You know him, I believe."

"I know him."

"But you don't like him?"

"It runs a little deeper than that. A mile or so."

"He has quite an organization," Orcutt said. "Expensive, but reliable."

"Then he's changed," I said.

"Really? He came well recommended and he did produce on extremely short notice."

"He recommended me?"

"Highly. But you weren't our *only* candidate. There were three others who were put forth by organizations similar to Mr. Vicker's."

"Who?" I said.

"The candidates?"

"No. The organizations."

"I don't really believe that concerns you, Mr. Dye."

"You don't?"

"No."

I put my drink down on the coffee table and leaned forward, resting my arms on my knees. I stared at Orcutt, who stared back, not in the least perturbed but only curious about what came next, if anything.

"I don't know you," I said. "I only know what you've told me about yourself and that's not much of a recommendation."

"You can check him out," Necessary said.

"I plan to. Maybe I'll be surprised and find that it was just a run of bad luck that got you tied in with Vicker. That could be. But you claim Vicker put my name up for membership in the club. That doesn't flatter me; it scares hell out of me bcause I know the only thing that Vicker would recommend me for is something that he could send flowers to."

"Mr. Dye, I assure you—"

"I'm not finished. Assurances aren't any good, not if Vicker's tied into them. I learned long ago to stay away from people who deal with Vicker. They're usually thieves or even worse, fools. So I'll stay away from you unless you tell me the names of the other three firms that you dealt with. Then I might believe it was just bad luck that got you in with Vicker. But if you don't come up with their names, then we've just run out of things to talk about."

Orcutt was quick. If he hesitated, it wasn't for more than a second. "Chance Tubio. Singapore. Do you know him?"

"He's okay," I said. "Some of his people are a little slimy, but he's okay."

"Eugene Elmelder. Tokyo."

"The biggest," I said, "but stuffy, slow, and very, very proper."

"My impression, too," Orcutt said. "Max von Krapp. Manila."

"The best of the lot. He combines Teutonic thoroughness with a vivid imagination. The von is phoney."

"He was the most expensive," Orcutt said.

"Then he's gone up. How did you get involved with Vicker?"

"He was one of four names suggested by a completely disinterested party."

"Why take Vicker's recommendation—why choose me?"

"There is a time factor, Mr. Dye. None of the other three could recommend *satisfactory* candidates who were immediately available. Vicker could. He named you. It's as simple as that—except for the *frightfully* large retainers that the other three organizations demanded."

I lit a cigarette that I didn't really need and leaned back on the couch. "If you want another drink help yourself," I said to Necessary. He nodded, rose, and crossed over to the bottle.

"Why go looking in the East?" I said to Orcutt. "Local talent must be plentiful. I've heard that Europe's swarming with it."

"I needed someone who could command a certain degree of anonymity in the States. It seemed to me that a person who has lived in the Far East for an extended period of time might well have achieved this. More so than if he'd lived in Europe. But I also listed a number of other qualifications."

"Such as?"

Orcutt waved a hand, his left one. He did it gracefully, I thought. "We were *terribly* frank with all of them," he said. "Naturally, we didn't tell them exactly what the candidate would *do*. Rather, we told them what he should *be*."

"How much checking did you do on the people that you dealt with—Tubio, von Krapp, and the other two?"

"They came *highly* recommended."

"By whom?"

"I simply *cannot* reveal that," Orcutt said and I thought for a moment that he was going to pout.

"Hint."

"All right," he said. "He was a United States Senator. There're a hundred or so of them, so you can take your choice."

"Simple the Wise," I said. "From Idaho."

Necessary snorted, received a glare from Orcutt, and I knew I was right but it hadn't been hard to guess.

"Senator Solomon Simple," I went on. "And if I had a name like that I'd change it to Lucifer Dye. Chairman of the Senate External Security subcommittee. He doesn't trust U.S. intelligence—any of it—and he spends a lot of government money with outfits like the ones you've just done business with. How much did he cost you? I mean he's still on the take, isn't he?"

"I made a small campaign contribution," Orcutt said, his tone swathed in frost. "Perfectly legitimate."

"Perfectly legitimate," Carol Thackerty said from her outpost by the window, "but not so small. He nicked you for ten thousand."

"I refuse to have my—"

I interrupted Orcutt. "You know how he works it, don't you?"

"Who?"

"Senator Simple."

"Mr. Dye, I want you to know that I consider the Senator a personal friend of mine."

"So much the better. You should be interested in his personal welfare. He's chairman of the subcommittee that deals with external security. It was created about three or four years ago—"

"I *know* when it was created, Mr. Dye," Orcutt said.

"After all the ruckus about the CIA's subsidies to labor unions, student organizations, and what have you, including one that never made the papers."

"What one was that?" Necessary said.

"An international garden club."

"Crap," Necessary said.

"But still true," I said. "Well, the Senator became the darling of the Old and the New Left as well as all the ragtag liberals who see something sinister in wiretapping, J. Edgar Hoover, the Bay of Pigs, Guatemala, and whatever it was I was doing when they threw me in jail."

Orcutt squirmed in his chair. Necessary was grinning happily. Carol Thackerty seemed bored by the view through the window.

"Mr. Dye," Orcutt said, "if you're going to sit there and slander Senator Simple like some . . . some carbon copy *William Buckley*—"

"I like Buckley," I said. "I think he's funny. I also think he's right about one percent of the time, although that may be just a little high. But what I think isn't important. I was talking about the Senator."

"It was just getting good," Necessary said.

"Well, Simple the Wise—"

"I *wish* you wouldn't use that name," Orcutt said.

"All right. Senator Simple's subcommittee has contracted with three of the firms that you dealt with to provide him with intelligence reports that mostly concern what's going on in China. If I remember the figures, the contracts are for one million to von Krapp in Manila, two million to Tubio in Singapore, and two and a half million to Elmelder's outfit in Tokyo. They're probably worth it. All of them are good, but they're also profit conscious, which is a polite word for greedy. All of them have branched out into industrial intelligence—or espionage, if you like—and they've made a good thing out of it, especially in Japan. But still, those millions authorized by the subcommittee help meet the payroll. So they got together and decided to put the Senator on *their* payroll. I suppose you could call it a kind of intelligence cartel and the Senator gets X number of dollars deposited in Panama, Zurich, and some other place that I'll think of in a moment. Lichtenstein. The last estimate that I heard had the Senator dragging down about a quarter of a million a year, tax free, of course. If he were to ever balk on renewing their contracts, they'd expose him. So you see, the liberals are right after all. It is a little sinister."

I could see that Orcutt believed me, probably because it was his own kind of a deal. "Your organization knows this?"

"Sure," I said. "But it's my ex-organization."

"Why don't they—"

"Expose him?"

"Yes."

"Why should they? They get the information from the Senator—even before the CIA—as soon as he's milked it for whatever publicity value it has, if any. If it's too hot, he turns it over to them—free. It's usually top-grade stuff, or nearly so. The Senator's content with his quarter of a million a year. The cartel, if you want to call it that, has got a multimillion dollar annuity as long as Simple stays in office. Of course when he comes up for election next year, they'll see to it that some legitimate funds are dumped into his campaign."

"It's all real cozy, isn't it?" Necessary said to me. "I like it. I like it a hell of a lot." He turned to Orcutt. "Couldn't we sort of drop a hint to the Senator and—"

"Shut up, Homer," Orcutt said. "Mr. Dye, you must have had some reason for telling me this. I wouldn't quite classify you as the town gossip."

I nodded. "I had a reason and the reason is Gerald Vicker. If the Senator recommended him to you then I have to assume that Vicker's got his hooks in the Senator. I don't much mind the others. Their information's as good as anybody's and sometimes a hell of a lot better. At least that's what my organization—sorry—ex-organization thought. But Vicker's something else. Vicker and I go back a long way. When did you first get in touch with him?"

Orcutt looked at Carol Thackerty. "August third," she said.

"How much did you pay him?"

"Twelve thousand dollars," she said, turning her head from the window.

"When did you get his first report?"

"August tenth," Orcutt said.

"What was it?"

"A six-page, single-spaced precis of you," he said.

"Detailed?"

"Extremely."

"Did it say where I was at the time?"

"In jail."

"Did it say when I would get out?"

"To the day. It also said that you would be brought back to San Francisco, that you would be debriefed for from ten to twelve days in Letterman General, and that you would then be at liberty—I *think* that was the term he used. In fact, Vicker was most complimentary—even effusive—*except* for one thing."

"What?"

"Well, he said that you might be a little nervous."

"He didn't say nervous. Not Vicker."

"He said chicken," Necessary said and grinned at me. "Are you chicken, Dye?"

I looked at him, studying his brown and blue eyes. The right one was brown; the left one blue. "I don't know," I said. "I suppose we'll just have to find out, won't we?"

Orcutt had been admiring the toes of his shoes again. He looked up quickly. "Does that mean that you've decided to accept my proposition, Mr. Dye?"

"You mean to corrupt you a city?"

Orcutt smiled the only way he knew how. "That was a little rich, wasn't it?"

"A little."

"Corn," Carol Thackerty said. "Pure corn. You can never resist it, can you, Victor?"

"Shut up, Carol," he said. It seemed that Victor Orcutt spent a lot of time telling people to shut up.

"Well, Mr. Dye?" he said.

"If you'll answer a question or two."

"All right."

"What qualifications did you specify other than a certain degree of anonymity?"

"You mean to the four firms that I dealt with?"

"Yes."

Orcutt nodded slowly. "Yes, I can see that you'd be interested in that. I was really *quite* specific. The candidate should be unattached, not too old, possessed of *some* social graces, presentable, and willing to undergo a slight risk. Availability was another consideration, of course, because our lead time is just *slipping* away. He should also have a certain amount of experience in clandestine activities, either for government or for private industry. Preferably he should belong to *some* minority group, but I had to give up on that one. He should have rather deep insight into human nature, be slightly skeptical but not so much that it clouds his judgment, and above all he must be intelligent. Not book-smart, mind you, but quickish, cleverish, sharpish—"

"Shrewdish?" I offered.

"You're *teasing* again. I *do* like that. But to continue. He should also be articulate. Not a salesman, mind you, but sincere and well spoken."

"And you think I'm all that?"

"No one is, Mr. Dye. But you possess a majority of the qualifications. Ones that Homer, Miss Thackerty, and even I lack. You will, shall I say, round out our team. Now that you're virtually one of us, I can tell you about our project."

The city that Victor Orcutt wanted me to corrupt had a population of a little more than two hundred thousand and was located on the Gulf Coast somewhere between Mobile and Galveston. It was called Swankerton but the local wits had long ago changed that to Chancre Town, which, Orcutt said, had some basis of fact.

He went on for quite a while and I half-listened, knowing that a recitation of facts and names and statistics was no substitute for personal appraisal. Necessary was on his fourth Scotch without visible effect and Carol Thackerty, still looking bored, kept her vigil at the window. I

80

liked to look at her. Her profile offered a high calm forehead, a straight nose, not at all thin, just delicate, or some might even say aristocratic. She had a good chin, rounded and firm, which swept gracefully back to her long, slender neck.

Victor Orcutt had stopped talking and was looking at me as if he expected a remark or a question. I decided on a question. "What's the deadline?"

"The first Tuesday in November."

"This year?"

"This year."

"It's not enough. You can't even shake down city hall for the Heart Fund in two months."

"We'll have to," Orcutt said. "There's absolutely no lead time, Mr. Dye. The persons whom I'm dealing with in Swankerton have been dilatory. They now recognize full well that they started late. Very late. That's why I was able to demand my fee and that's why I'm able to offer you fifty thousand dollars for two months' work."

"That's too much money for two months' work," I said. "But I won't argue about it. It just means that I'll have to do something that I don't want to do. Something tricky probably. But the real reason I'm taking it is because Gerald Vicker wants me to. And the only reason he wants me to is because he thinks something nasty might happen to me. So do you, or you wouldn't make the ante so high. Vicker worries me. He worries me enough so that I'll go along until I learn what it's all about."

"This seems to be a long-standing feud between you and Vicker, Mr. Dye," Orcutt said.

"It's more of a vendetta than a feud and it goes back about six years."

"What happened?"

"He used to work for the same people I did. I got him fired."

"Jealousy? Rivalry?"

"No. It was because he killed someone."

"Who?"

"The wrong man."

We talked some more about Swankerton and then Homer Necessary announced that he was hungry. "Just a minute, Homer," Orcutt said and turned to me. "Your decision is firm, Mr. Dye? You will go to Swankerton with us?"

I looked at Orcutt, took a breath, then sighed and said, "When do we leave?"

He rose and clapped his hands together in pleasure. I thought for a moment that he might even do us a little dance. "Tomorrow morning. There's a direct flight, but we still have *so* many things to discuss. You'll join us for dinner?"

"Fine," I said.

"But not here. I just can't *abide* hotel food. Any hotel. Homer, go down and get the car. Carol, call Ernie's and make a reservation for four. A good table, mind you. Do you know Ernie's, Mr. Dye? It's on Montgomery."

I told him no.

"It's marvelous. Simply marvelous."

Victor Orcutt did the ordering and everything was as good as he said it would be. We had the *Tortue au Sherry; Dover Sole Ernie's* with a bottle of *Chablis Bougros; Tournedos Rossini w*ith some more wine, this time *Pommard Les Epenots.* There was a Belgian endive salad followed by a crêpe soufflé, coffee, and cognac. It was all simply marvelous and it only cost Victor Orcutt $162.00.

Orcutt sent Necessary for the car while he headed toward the rear, either to compliment the chef or to pee. That left me with Carol Thackerty. She put a cigarette between her lips and I leaned over to light it.

When she had it going she smiled and said, "I understand that you grew up in a whorehouse."

"That's right."

"Well," she said, "we have that much in common. So did I."

82

10

It must have been in the autumn of 1939 that I first met Gorman Smalldane. I was five then, going on six, and sober, and Gorman Smalldane was thirty-four and a little drunk. It was either a Monday or a Tuesday night, about ten o'clock, and I was at my usual post outside the door of Tante Katerine's joy emporium, waiting to greet customers. There weren't many and I was glad when the taxi drew up and the man in the blue suit jumped out, paid off the driver, and checked the polished brass plate to make sure that this was Number 27. That was all the identification that Tante Katerine's establishment ever had. It was all it needed.

Smalldane pushed through the brick wall's wrought-iron gates, which Tante Katerine claimed came all the way from New Orleans, and made his way towards me, tacking only a little now and then. I was wearing my fancy uniform with the pillbox monkey hat. My face was powdered and painted and for added splendor two of my front teeth were missing.

Smalldane stopped in front of me, all six feet three inches of him. He cocked his blond head to one side and studied me carefully. Then he cocked it to the other side and studied me some more. After that he shook his head in mild disbelief and walked around me to see whether the view was any better from the rear. In front of me once more, he bent from the waist until his face was no more than six inches from mine and I could smell the whiskey. It was Scotch. "Now just what in fuck's name are you supposed to be, little man?" he said.

"The humble greeter of clients, my lordship," I lisped because of my teeth, backed up a step, and bowed. Then I launched into a lisping, Australian-accented, English version of the official welcome with all of its bows and flourishes and leers.

Smalldane stood there listening to it all and shaking his head from side to side. When I was done, he bent down

83

from the waist again and said: "You know what I think you are? I think you are a gap-toothed sissy, that's what."

I gave him the full benefit of my black and white smile, bowed again, and said in Cantonese, "And your mother, drunken pig, was an ancient turtle who coupled with a running dog." I'd picked that one up someplace.

Still bent down, Smalldane smiled and nodded his head as if in full agreement. Then he straightened up, put his hands on his hips, and said softly: "You should guard that dung-coated tongue of yours, my little pimp for poisonous toads, or I will rip it from your mouth and shove it up your rectum where it can flap in the breeze of your own wind." His Cantonese was as good as mine, his imagery more vivid.

He didn't scare me. Nothing scared me then, probably because I was spoiled rotten. But Smalldane did impress me with his size and his brilliant command of the foul invective. I bowed again, quite low, and made a sweeping gesture toward the door. "This way, my lordship, if you please."

"Here you go, sonny," he said and tossed me an American half-dollar.

"A thousand thank yous, kind sir," I said, another archaic phrase that someone had taught me, but which— because of my absent teeth—came out with all the sibilants missing.

Smalldane went through the door and I followed, partly because I was curious, partly because business was slack, but mostly because I wanted the cup of hot cocoa that Yen Chi, Tante Katerine's *amah,* prepared for me nightly.

I was right behind Smalldane when the madame of the house swept into the large entrance hall. She stopped abruptly, her eyes widened, and her hand went to her throat, a dramatic ploy that she copied rather successfully from either Norma Shearer or Kay Francis. I had watched her practice it often enough before her vanity table mirror. But now, for once in her life, she abandoned her pose and ran with arms outstretched toward Smalldane, crying, "Gormy!" at the top of her voice. He wrapped her in an embrace and kissed her for a long time while I watched with clinical interest. That's one thing about being reared in a whorehouse: displays of affection and emotion will never embarrass you.

There were a number of half-sentences and unintelligible phrases such as "you promised to" and "I couldn't get away" and "over two years without" and "long time" and "it's so good to" and all the rest of the things that two persons who are fond of each other say after a long separation. I stood there, probably smirking a little, and watched and listened.

Tante Katerine spotted me then and beckoned. "Lucifer, dear, come. I want you to meet a very good and old friend of mine, Mr. Gorman Smalldane, the famous American radio correspondent. Gorman, this is my ward, Lucifer Dye." She must have looked up "ward" some place because it was the first time I'd ever heard her use it.

"Mr. Smalldane," I said, bowing stiffly, more in the European than the Chinese manner. One of the girls from Berlin had contributed that. Her name was Ilse.

"He's an insufferable little prick, isn't he?" Smalldane said. "Who the hell lets him paint himself up like that?"

"I think it's *sehr aufgeweckt*," she said because nobody in Shanghai then had much use for "cute."

"Looks like you're training him for a job in Sammy Ching's place down on the waterfront—if the Japs haven't closed it yet. Sailors like little pogey bait like him."

"Well, you're wrong, Mr. Gorman Famous Smalldane," Tante Katerine said. "He's just a little boy and he goes to school every day. For three hours."

"Where?"

"Here. We teach him here."

Smalldane grinned and shook his head. "I bet he does learn a lot at that. And all of it useful."

I found the conversation fascinating, doubtless because they were talking about me.

"He can do his multiplication through the twelveses," Tante Katerine said, her English lapsing as her anger rose. "You want to hear him? What's twelve times eleven, Lucifer?"

"One hundred and thirty two," the insufferable little prick said.

"There!" she said triumphantly. "See. I bet you can't do that when you are six."

"I can't do it now," Smalldane said. "I never got past my elevenses."

"He also speaks six languages. Maybe even seven. How

many could you speak when you were his age, Mr. Know-some-all?"

"That's know-it-all," Smalldane said, "and I could barely get by in English, but at least I stayed out of mother's rouge and powder and wore pants, for God's sake, and not her bathrobe."

"Now you don't like his clothes," she said, her voice rising. "Now you're making funny of his clothes. Do you know how much that gown cost? Do you know how many I paid for it? I paid fifteen dollars for it American, that's how many."

"He still looks silly."

"That's not all he's got. He's got four more just as expensive. And he's got fine American clothes too that come from a famous house of fashion."

"Sears, Roebuck?"

"Buster Brown, that's who," she said.

"Jesus," Smalldane said. "I quit. Look, Katie, I didn't come here to argue about some Australian kid that you've taken to raise. It's been more than—"

"I'm not Australian, sir," I said, "I am an American," thus proving that there's a little chauvinism in the best of us.

"You didn't pick that accent up in Pittsburgh, kid."

I stood straight as a plumb line, scrunched my eyes closed, and recited: "I am six years old and my name is Lucifer Clarence Dye and I was born December 5, 1933, in Moncrief, Montana, United States of America, and my father's name was Dr. Clarence Dye and I live at Number Twenty-seven."

"Okay, Lucifer," Smalldane interrupted. "That's fine. I believe you. Relax." He knelt down so that his head was level with mine and I could smell the Scotch again. "Look, tomorrow I'll tell you what we'll do. You'll play hookey—"

"What's hookey?" I said.

"You'll miss school and we'll go down and get you some American clothes and maybe hoist a few at the Shanghai Club." He looked up at Tante Katerine. "Is old Chi Fo's tailor shop still going, you know, near the American School in the French Concession?"

Tante Katerine shrugged to show her indifference. "The American School was closed two years ago, but I assume Chi Fo is still in business."

86

"You mind if I take the kid?"

"Why should I mind? I'm only a poor Russian, exiled from her country to this war-torn land, friendless and alone, who's tried to give a decent home to this poor—"

She was going to the afterburners when Smalldane shot her down. "I don't want to adopt him, goddamn it, Kate, I just want to buy him a pair of corduroy knickers so he can hear them squeak when he walks. It's his birthright. I didn't get any until I was almost eleven and before that I had to wear short pants. God knows what it did to me psychologically. I'm not sure, but maybe it's already too late."

"What do you mean too late?" she said.

"For the kid. Still," he added thoughtfully, "perhaps he could do real fine as a female impersonator."

"Take him!" she yelled. "Buy him anything you want to! Buy him the—the whole Bund!"

"How about it, Lucifer?" Smalldane said, still kneeling in front of me. "Would you like some knickers? The corduroy kind?"

I bowed in the Chinese fashion and then gave him my very best all-American boy gap-toothed grin. "Very much, sir."

"Good," he said, rising. He turned to Tante Katerine. "Does he go to bed now or do you work him on the night shift?"

"Goddamn you, Gorman—" she began, but he whacked her on the rear with the palm of his hand and laughed. It's still the most infectious laugh I've ever heard. Then she laughed and he took her hand and they almost raced upstairs. Neither one of them told me good night. Yen Chi brought me my cocoa and I drank it there in the reception hall and thought about Smalldane and the corduroy knickers and Tante Katerine. I had seen her go upstairs before on rare occasions with special "old friends" and it hadn't bothered me. This time it did. I was only six and didn't realize it at the time, but I had just met not only my first rival, but also my first male friend. Or maybe cobber, since I spoke as if I came from down that way.

Gorman Smalldane had been a twenty-seven-year-old reporter for United Press in 1932 when he met Tante Katerine in Mukden. The Japanese invasion of Manchuria

87

had just begun and Tante Katerine wanted out. With Smalldane's help, she made it to Shanghai where she went into business for herself, found a wealthy Chinese protector or patron, who turned out to be the local version of Lucky Luciano, and opened her sin palace in 1933.

Her sponsor was Du Wei-sung (some spelled it Dou Yen-Seng or even Fu-Seng), a peasant who had started out in the best Horatio Alger tradition as a fruit hawker in the French Concession. Ambitious, tough, and completely ruthless, Du staked out the opium trade as his own private monopoly. He also branched out into gambling, prostitution and the protection racket, operating eventually out of a luxurious high-walled compound in the French Concession.

A self-cured opium addict himself, which indicated his single-mindedness, Du fully appreciated the rich potential that lay within a drug monopoly. He dominated the opium traffic completely after he combined the Red and Green Societies, two rival groups that had started out as secret political fraternities but had degenerated into criminal gangs interested in anything that would turn a quick Shanghai dollar. Before Du merged the rival mobs they spent much of their time shooting each other up on Shanghai's west side.

With a fortune securely based on his opium monopoly, Du diversified further and went into legitimate business. China's *Who's Who* listed him as a director of paper mills, forty banks, cotton mills, and shipping companies. He was also a member of the executive committee of the Chinese Chamber of Commerce and bought himself the managing directorship of Shanghai's leading newspaper, *The China Press,* at one time Shanghai's leading American newspaper.

Du seemed to be as shrewd at public relations as he was at finance. He supported two free hospitals and served as their president; he was the chief angel for a couple of orphanages; he buried beggars free, and even sponsored a model farming community.

He also ran the French Concession and the two thousand French who lived there were content to ignore his shady sidelines as long as he maintained a semblance of law and order. They were so grateful, in fact, that they even elected him to the Concession's governing municipal council.

But perhaps Du's crowning achievement came from his fellow member in the *Ching Pang,* or Green Society. The fellow member's name was Chiang Kai-shek, and he addressed Du as Elder Brother. As a newly converted Methodist, Chiang was understandably concerned about the increasing opium traffic. To control it he created something called the Shanghai Opium Oppression Bureau, which was an offshoot of the Nationalist government's six-year opium suppression program. Only the congenitally naive were surprised when Chiang appointed Du as director of the Shanghai Opium Oppression Bureau. In return for the honor, Du sometimes impounded fifty pounds or so of opium and publicly burned it. Everyone agreed it was a nice gesture. In the meantime, he controlled the opium trade, contributed millions to the Nationalist treasury for the purchase of American fighter planes, and whenever an epidemic or a flood ravaged the land, Du could be counted on for a hefty contribution.

Tante Katerine kicked back twenty percent of her profits to Du's organization and the vice squad never got around to bothering her.

I soon learned that Gorman Smalldane was not the famous radio correspondent that Tante Katerine claimed. After Manchuria, he had continued to work for United Press in Nanking until they transferred him to Hong Kong. From there he went to Ethiopia in 1935 to write about what Mussolini was up to and from there to Spain to cover Franco's side of the Civil War.

In Spain he met H.V. Kaltenborn, who was then broadcasting twice a week for CBS for $50 a broadcast and paying his own expenses. In October of 1937 Kaltenborn came down with a bad case of laryngitis and couldn't go on the air. He offered Smalldane $25 to come to a French border town and do his broadcast for him. Edward R. Murrow, then European manager of CBS, heard it, liked Smalldane's voice, as well as the style and content of his news, and hired him as a stringer.

Smalldane probably knew China as well as any American correspondent. He had been born in Canton in 1905 of Methodist missionary parents, now dead, and had gone to Northwestern—a sound Methodist school—on a scholarship, graduating in 1926. He returned to Shanghai in 1927 and because he was fluent in Chinese he got a job with the then American-run China Press, later transferring to United Press. At thirty-four when I met him, Smalldane still thought of himself as an orphan, which established a bond between us and also indicated something or other about his personality.

His downfall—at least a temporary one—came late in 1939. He had written a series of what he called "goddamned brilliant" features on Shanghai which had received unusually wide play in the U.S. He then came up with the idea of doing an exposé of Du Wei-sung, the opium king, and his connections with Chiang Kai-shek. He spent seven weeks of hard, intensive digging on the three-part series and mailed it to the States. The first one ran, the other two were killed, and UP fired Smalldane, supposedly at the insistence of Chiang himself, who then refused him accreditation to Chungking.

At Tante Katerine's urging, Smalldane gave up his room at the American Club (she paid his considerable tab) and moved to Number 27. He made a couple of broadcasts a month for CBS, sold some harmless free-lance stuff to North American Newspaper Alliance, and once to *Liberty Magazine,* and worked a few rather profitable deals on the black market. If Du Wei-sung knew that Smalldane was living rent-and-board free in one of the whorehouses that he protected, it didn't seem to bother him, and the American got along famously with the Japanese's number one boy, Major Dogshit. But then Smalldane got along famously with everyone most of the time, especially me.

It was a kind of hero worship, I suppose. He got me out of the brocade robe and into corduroy knickers. He taught me how to throw a baseball like a boy instead of a girl. He spent long hours lecturing me on the finer points and intricacies of football, although I'd never seen a game; he demonstrated (often) the making of a proper martini; extolled the merits of Franklin D. Roosevelt and the shortcomings of Wendell Willkie; described the sexual aberrations of Adolf Hitler; explained the fact that the earth was really round after all; and predicted the coming war between the United States and Japan in the Pacific. Of this, Smalldane was completely convinced.

Although Major Dogshit spoke no English and Smalldane spoke no Japanese, they communicated well enough in a mixture of French, Chinese, and graphic sign language. And it was in early November of 1941 that the major, well into his cups, gave Smalldane what could have been the biggest newsbeat in history. The major was paying his last visit to Number 27 and he was maudlin about it. He was distressed that he had to leave his great friend "Smardane" and his little friend "Rucifer." But most distressing of all was that he had to give up his monthly stipend and free samples from Number 27 where, he assured us, he had spent the happiest days of his life. He liked Americans, he said, or at least that's what we thought he said, and he did not want to fight them.

Smalldane asked what part of China he was being transferred to, but Major Dogshit wagged a finger at him and shook his head. Not China, he said. No more China. He was going South—far, far South. He was being assigned to a special force for intensive training. Then he giggled and mumbled something in French about not from the sea, but from the land. After that he passed out and Smalldane got one of the house boys to get him home.

Sitting there in what Tante Katerine referred to as Number 27's "hospitality room," which was really a medium-sized cocktail lounge where customers could look over the merchandise, Smalldane tried to figure it out. He got a map from his room and spread it over the table.

"Dogshit said South," he said.

"Which way is that?" I asked.

"Straight down, you ignorant piece of filth," he said to me in Cantonese.

"How could it be down on the map when it is that way where we now are?" I asked, pointing to my left, and since it was a most logical question, speaking in French.

"What's that say right there?" Smalldane asked, jabbing his finger at the map's compass.

"How should I know?" I said. "I am only eight years old and can neither read nor write."

"Christ, I keep forgetting."

"I can now do my multiplication tables up to fifteen," I said. "You want to know what fifteen times fourteen is? It's two hundred and ten."

"Kate!" Smalldane roared at Tante Katerine who was across the room listening to the marital problems of a minor French official. She excused herself and came over to our table.

"When're you going to teach him to read and write?" he said, jerking a thumb at me.

She shrugged. "He has plenty of time. Perhaps we'll teach him next year. Or the next. You're the expert writer. Why don't you teach him?"

"Goddamn it, I will, starting right now!"

Tante Katerine shrugged and swayed back to her Frenchman and the problems that he was having with his wife. He was a regular customer who came to Number 27 more for advice than for sex.

"Here," Smalldane said to me in a harsh tone. "What's that word?" And he jabbed his forefinger at a dot on the map.

I looked carefully. "It's a dot with a circle around it," I said.

"Not the symbol, my little snot, the word! Don't you even know the goddamned alphabet?"

"I am only a child of eight years and can—"

"Start learning right now," Smalldane said. "That's an S, that's an I, that's an N, and that's a G. Now repeat them."

"S-I-N-G," I said promptly and then yawned on purpose. "There's really not much to it, is there?"

"What does it *spell*, stupid?"

"I have no idea."

"It spells sing. S-I-N-G. Sing."

"Like a song," I said.

"Like Singapore, you toad of a pimp." Then he forgot about his tutorial ambitions and started running his finger down Indo-China. "Look," he said to me because he had no other audience, "the Japs have already got Indo-China and they can jump off to Malaya and hit Singapore from the rear. South, Dogshit said. And I'll bet seventeen dollars and thirty-eight cents that that means Singapore from the land and not from the sea." Smalldane was always betting $17.38 on something. I never knew why.

For the next four weeks he was out all day and half the night trying to confirm his theory. He borrowed money from Tante Katerine to get Japanese officers drunk and to bribe privates and non-coms to tell him what little they knew about troop movements. He spent hours in the Shanghai Club talking to its British members about Malaya and Singapore's defenses. "Impregnable, old boy," he would say to me, mocking their accent. "Absolutely impregnable."

I didn't know when or where he got what he thought was the last piece to his jigsaw, but he got it, and then spent three days writing a two thousand-word story. I still remember its lead. Smalldane read it to me at least six times:

JAPANESE IMPERIAL ARMY WILL INVADE EAST COAST MALAYA EARLY DECEMBER ETSTRIKE THROUGH JUNGLE AT SINGA- PORES UNPROTECTED REAR UNIMPEACH- ABLE SOURCES REVEALED HERE TODAY

"You left out a few words, didn't you?" I said, still completely vague about where Singapore was.

"They'll put them back in in New York," Smalldane said. "You want to go with me to file it?"

"Sure," I said.

We borrowed Tante Katerine's Airflow Chrysler and started to the Press Wireless office. It was the morning of December 8, 1941, and Japanese troops arrested us both before we got halfway there.

11

We flew first class from San Francisco to Swankerton and it was dull and fast as most air travel is now that they keep the jets up around thirty-five thousand or more where you can't see anything.

After dinner the night before, Orcutt had asked us to stop by his suite. He was staying at the Fairmont on California and Mason and the suite probably didn't cost him much more than $125 a day. He told Carol Thackerty to order him a cup of hot chocolate and anything that we wanted. Necessary and I asked for brandy; Carol Thackerty wanted nothing.

Orcutt made some small talk, mostly about Ernie's, while we waited for the drinks to arrive. After they came, he took a sip of his hot chocolate and said, "I like to drink it quickly before that slimy skim forms on top." We waited silently while he drank it in small, rapid sips, much like a bird drinks, except that he didn't have to raise his head to let the chocolate flow down his throat. He said, "Ah," when he finished and I assumed that he had gotten it all down without running into any of the slimy skim that forms on top.

"Now then," he said to me, "there are a few items that I've had prepared in anticipation of your joining us, Mr. Dye."

"You must have been confident," I said.

"Not altogether. It's just that I always like everything *ready*. I simply *detest* last-minute scrambling about doing things that could have been done at a normal pace. Carol, would you please give me Mr. Dye's envelope?"

She reached into her large, almost briefcase-sized purse and took out an oblong manila envelope which she handed to him. Orcutt peeked inside it and then motioned for me to join him on the couch. I took my brandy with me.

"First," he said, "your Social Security card. In case you don't remember, it's your right number." I glanced

94

at the card and Orcutt was correct: it was the right number. "Strange about the Social Security card," he said. "It's almost worthless as identification, but the number itself is becoming increasingly important. It's replaced the individual serial number in the armed forces, in fact. I think it's safe to predict that one of these days—quite soon, really—the number will be used to maintain a full dossier on every citizen of this country. What do you think, Mr. Dye?"

"I wouldn't bet against it," I said.

"No," Orcutt said, "I didn't think you would. Next, here is a driver's license issued by the Commonwealth of Virginia just before they began to require a photograph to be attached to each license. We would have secured a District of Columbia license for you, but there they require *color* photographs on their licenses, which presented an *almost* insurmountable problem."

He handed me the license and I read the information on it. It would expire in six months, but everything was accurate except that it had me living in Alexandria.

"Now here," Orcutt said, "are three credit cards, American Express, Gulf Oil, and Carte Blanche. They're legitimate, so use them wisely." He smiled after he said it to show that it was a joke, but with that smile of his, I couldn't believe him.

"This," he said, handing me another card, "is your Blue Cross and Blue Shield identification card. Also legitimate. We've already paid the premiums. And this is a card from Sibley Hospital in Washington which notes that your blood type is AB. Quite rare, really."

"I know," I said.

"We had the devil's own time getting that one because it was so difficult to learn what your blood type is. We— or I should say Homer—finally got it from the State Department's medical division. He's quite good at things such as that. A real ferret."

"How did State have it?" I said.

"You took a physical there eleven years ago," Necessary said. "Remember it?"

"I do now," I said.

Orcutt poked around in the envelope some more. "And here," he said, "is an Alexandria library card, your voter's registration, and a membership card in the Gaslight Club

95

in Washington. That takes care of your identification problem."

"Why Washington?" I said.

"Because the man who supplies us with several of these items of identification operates from there. If you'd like a totally new identity, complete with an honorable discharge from the army, he'll sell you a package that contains a Social Security number, a driver's license, the aforementioned discharge, a library card, and a voter's registration certificate for one hundred and fifty dollars. Credit cards cost fifty dollars each, but he strongly advises against them. They're too much of a temptation. By the way, your credit cards are issued in the name of Victor Orcutt Associates."

"Very thorough," I said.

"Yes, it is, isn't it?" Orcutt said. "Now here is a cashier's check for five thousand dollars with which you'll open a personal checking account at the First National Bank in Swankerton. And this is a letter of credit from my St. Louis bank. I believe it's for—yes—twenty thousand. I hope you don't have to use all of it, but you may. And since you have nothing to carry these various items in, here's a wallet that should contain five hundred dollars cash." He looked inside and counted rapidly. "Yes, it does." Then he turned to Carol Thackerty and frowned. "I specified pin seal," he said.

"They didn't have any," she said.

Orcutt looked at the wallet with distaste. "I suppose this will do, but it's certainly not what I had in mind, Mr. Dye."

"It's fine," I said and started to put all the cards into their proper compartments.

"I've saved the most important until last," Orcutt said. "It's the culmination of more than a month of intensive work on the part of myself, Miss Thackerty, and Homer." He handed me five folded sheets of what seemed to be ordinary typing paper. When I unfolded them I saw that it was a long list of typewritten names that were divided into two sections and labeled "Advocates" and "Adversaries," which I thought to be a little fancy. The adversaries ran four pages; the advocates only one. After each name were four or five single-spaced lines of biographical data which included such personal information as sexual inclinations and preferences; drinking habits; financial pec-

96

cadilloes; emotional hang-ups; social and political position; chronic illnesses; mental aberrations; family background; educational attainments; current and past professions or businesses; estimated net worth; outstanding loans and debts; youthful indiscretions; and previous arrests, if any.

It was condensed and abbreviated enough to make *Who's Who* seem garrulous. But it was all perfectly readable and I skimmed through it quickly, then folded it and stuffed it away in an inside coat pocket.

"It was a two-man job," I said.

"Why two? Why not six or nine or even twenty?" Orcutt said and permitted me another inspection of his nothing smile.

"First, the information is useful for only two things: coercion or blackmail. A committee doesn't do that. Second, one of them is a doctor; the medical terms give that away. So do the personal physical details. The other one is a trained researcher, probably a newspaperman, but somebody who knows where to look and who has a keen sense of the relevant."

Homer Necessary put his empty brandy glass down and squirmed in his chair. When he couldn't keep quiet any longer, he leaned toward me, his arms resting on his knees. "Maybe we dug it all up by ourselves, Dye. Maybe we just looked here and there, asked around, and then put it down on paper."

"Maybe," I said, "if you had a couple of years, instead of a couple of months. But you didn't."

"You're quite right, Mr. Dye," Orcutt said. "Two persons did compile the information. One is Dr. Warner Colfax. He owns a rather large clinic—the Colfax Clinic, to be precise. In addition to the regular medical services that its sixty-bed hospital provides, it's also a drying-out haven for drunks and narcotics addicts—those who can afford it, at any rate. Then, too, it's a place that the aged can comfortably spend their remaining golden years, providing that they, or their children, can come up with fifteen hundred dollars a month; and it's also a place of comfort and care for those who suffer minor mental aberrations."

"He didn't miss much," I said. "The drunks and the addicts will spill anything for a bottle or a fix and the old folks will reminisce and ramble as long as some-

97

body'll listen. God knows what the psychotics would babble. No doubt Dr. Colfax has access to all records."

"No doubt," Orcutt said. "The newspaperman deserves a more fitting appellation, however. He's actually the editor and publisher of *The Swankerton Advocate* and its evening sister, *The Swankerton News-Calliope*. Odd name for a paper, don't you think?"

"Very," I said. "What's his name?"

"Channing d'Arcy Phetwick, the third. Phetwick is spelled with a p-h, not an f. There's a Channing d'Arcy Phetwick the fourth around, too, but he's turned out to be something of a wastrel. The senior Phetwick also owns a television station which is the local NBC affiliate; a fifty-thousand-watt radio station, also NBC affiliated; a tremendous amount of timberland on the Coosa River in Alabama (pulp for newsprint, of course), a statewide trucking service in which he ships his papers, thus boosting his circulation considerably; numerous valuable downtown and suburban real-estate properties, plus a couple of profitable plantations, I suppose one should call them."

"I assume that Phetwick and Colfax are paying your fee?" I said.

"You assume correctly."

"That list of thumbnail biographies is divided into two parts, the advocates and the adversaries."

"Isn't that precious?" Carol Thackerty said.

"Merely convenient, Carol," Orcutt said.

"Maybe you'd better tell me some more about the town," I said.

"Swankerton has changed tremendously in the past ten years," Orcutt said. "A number of manufacturing concerns, formerly located in the North, have moved here for the usual reasons—tax concessions, cheap, unorganized labor, adequate housing, what have you. About six years ago the Defense Department built an Air Force supply depot there which is, I think, the second or third largest in the country and employs about fifteen thousand persons. Swankerton was formerly a nice quiet town of around one hundred thousand. There was an *established* order, and one would be hard put to cite the sociological difference between the Swankerton of 1915 and the Swankerton of 1960. It grew a little, of course, during those forty-five years, but there was that *established* order. *Certain* people ran *certain* things. This one had the gambling and that one had the Chamber of Commerce. Another one had the prostitution franchise, if you will, and yet another one might have the city council in his hip pocket. It was really quite cozy. Homer has made a thorough study of it and I think we may consider him to be our authority."

Orcutt nodded at Necessary benignly, like a piano teacher encouraging a good but bashful pupil at the annual parents' day recital.

"Like Victor says," Necessary said, "it was all very, very sweet. Everybody had everything staked out—from Coca Cola to moonshine. One guy had the ABC—you know, the bar and liquor licensing office. It cost you anywhere from two to five thousand to get a bar license. Liquor stores came cheaper—about fifteen hundred. The gambling was mostly wide-open blackjack and the county sheriff and the Swankerton police chief split that. They got a ten percent rakeoff and they had guys spotted around who could tell what the nightly take was down to the last nickel. They had a sweet little burglary ring going with the buttons working the lookout for the thieves. That was a sixty-forty split. The cops got the sixty naturally. The whores were all local talent, mostly broads from the sticks. Nothing fancy."

He paused and looked at Orcutt. "If you want me to tell him the rest, I need something to gargle with."

Orcutt looked at Carol Thackerty. "There's a rather good bottle of Scotch in my bedroom, Carol—would you mind?"

She rose, got halfway across the room, and then turned to me. "You, too?" she said.

"No, thanks," I said.

"Do go on, Homer," Orcutt said.

"Well, these new plants and factories start moving in about 1964 and 1965 and they bring a hell of a lot of their top-and-middle-echelon people with them. They all had families and they were used to the kind of schools and stuff that they'd had in Jersey and Connecticut and New York and Pennsylvania. A lot of them were real bright kikes, if you know what I mean."

"Could you *possibly* avoid the anti-Semitic slurs, Homer?" Orcutt said it as if he didn't really think there was much hope.

"I haven't got anything against Jews," Necessary said.

"I just call them kikes. I always have and I probably always will."

"Go on," Orcutt said and sighed.

"Well, *they* start agitating and about that time the niggers start getting riled up and *they* start agitating. You know, all that desegregation stuff. There's a reform movement and about 1965 the reformers put up a slate. Well, hell, they win a few offices—they get the school board for instance. Maybe the county coroner, but not much else. But it scares shit out of the old guard.

"In the meantime, some of the boys over in New Orleans hear about the action in Swankerton, so they start scouting around. And when the government announced that they're going to build an air depot in Swankerton, the New Orleans bunch moves in fast."

"How?" I said.

"Look at it this way," Necessary said. "The town's going to have a floating population for a while—about five thousand skilled construction workers, all spenders. After that there'll be the soldier boys plus the civilian employees. That creates a market—a demand. The New Orleans outfit decides to be the sole supplier."

Carol Thackerty came back in the room with a glass of Scotch and water and handed it to Necessary. "There's no ice," she said.

"That's okay," Necessary said and took a gulp of the drink, wiping his mouth with the back of his hand.

"*Do* continue, Homer," Orcutt said, "and *try* to be as concise as possible."

"What the hell you think I been doing?" Necessary said. "You told me to tell him so I'm telling him and if you think I'm too long-winded, then you tell him yourself."

"You're doing fine," I said.

"Okay," he said. "Okay. I'll just tell it the way it happened. Well, the New Orleans crowd comes in and they land hard. First, they move in on the numbers in Niggertown and take that over. Then they run all the white whores out of town and bring in their own and jack up the prices from fifteen and twenty bucks a lay to thirty-five and forty. They don't bother the nigger whores any. Then they knock over a few blackjack games and the next day drop around selling protection. They spread a lot of juice around—the city council, the mayor,

100

the chief of police, and a few of his buddies all get well, if you know what I mean."

I said that I did and went on listening to Homer Necessary's tale, which for him would now and forever remain in the present tense.

"Finally, they move in on the nightclubs and bars. They bust up a few and then work the protection slam. If the guy hasn't got enough money, they loan it to him at twenty percent a week—or ten percent if they like him real well. If he can't pay, they buy him out for maybe forty cents on the dollar. I mean they really make it legal and everything. Next they get the city council to pass a new ordinance allowing the bars to stay open twenty-four hours a day. They do this because they got three shifts working to build that new air depot and when it's finished the civilians are going to be working three shifts, too."

Necessary stopped for a large gulp of his warm Scotch and water. "Now then," he said, "they finally get the air depot built and then they start hiring the civilian help. Well, the niggers get all upset because not enough of them are being hired. At least that's what they say. So some of their fire-eaters move down from up North and start stirring up the colored people. Then the unions get mad because they still aren't able to organize the runaway plants from up North, although they do all right with the air depot because that's all Federal money. So they finally call a strike at six of the biggest textile plants and then the union guys at the depot walk out in sympathy. I hear it's against the law, but what the hell, they do it anyway."

After that, Necessary said, the city officials turned to the New Orleans crowd to break the strike and also put an end to the mounting pressure from the black population.

"It takes them a week," Necessary said with something akin to admiration. "Just a week. The niggers and the laborskates are getting together, you know—starting to cooperate—so the New Orleans people import a few hard cases from somewhere, up North probably. Well, they knock off a couple of the chief niggers and make it look like it's done by a couple of local rednecks from the union. They leave evidence all around, like a rifle that belongs to one of the rednecks. Well, the chief of police can't do anything but bring the two white guys in. Or have 'em brought in. But on the way four niggers stop the car, take the two white boys out, and blast them deader'n hell. Well, that tears it."

"I would imagine," I said.

"The town gets real ugly," Necessary said, after another swallow. "The whites are scared of the niggers and the niggers are scared of the whites. The strike just peters out and a carload of new nigger agitators from up North can't even round up a crowd big enough to fill an outhouse. So everything settles back to just like it was before with the New Orleans crowd running things nice and smooth."

"At this point, Mr. Dye," Orcutt said, "I suppose you do have some questions."

"Lots of them," I said, "but only a few that won't keep for a while. First of all, the deadline of the first Tuesday in November means an election is coming up, right?"

"Right," Orcutt said.

"Since it's an off-year, that means a local election."

"Yes."

"Those who're paying your fee," I said. "Dr. Colfax and Phetwick the third. I assume that they want to throw the rascals out so that theirs will get in?"

"Precisely."

"And what you want me to do in the next two months is to make this town so corrupt that even the pimps will vote for reform?" I said.

"Most graphic, Mr. Dye," Orcutt said. "Most graphic indeed."

"You're not taking this on a contingency basis are you?"

Orcutt smiled. "I may be young, Mr. Dye, but I am not naive."

"No, I don't think you are. But I'm quite sure that you haven't collected your fee in advance."

"No."

"I've heard of deals like this," I said. "One that comes to mind happened in Germany."

"In Hamelin?" Orcutt said.

"That's right."

"They didn't want to pay off after the man got rid of the rats," he said.

"No. They didn't."

"So he piped their children out of town, I recall," he said.

"Everybody does. You may need something like a pipe."

"What do you suggest?"

I tapped my breast pocket that contained the Xeroxed list. "This list is missing a couple of names," I said.

There was always that about Orcutt. He never needed the simple diagram that came with the do-it-yourself kit. He just smiled again and even managed to put something into it other than nothing.

"You mean the names of Dr. Colfax and Mr. Phetwick?" he said.

"Yes."

"I'm glad you mentioned it," he said. "I really am. It demonstrates your level of awareness. However, while we were negotiating our contract, we also investigated the personal background and history of the two gentlemen in question. We secured some most interesting information."

"Okay," I said. "You've answered my first question. The advocates, I take it, are Dr. Colfax and Phetwick the third and the people they can control through sympathy or blackmail or coercion. Right?"

"Right," Orcutt said.

"My last question—for tonight, at least. The New Orleans adversaries or bunch or crowd. Who runs it?"

"He's on the list under adversaries," Orcutt said.

"I only skimmed it."

"His name is Ramsey Lynch."

I leaned back into the couch and rested my head against its rich green upholstery. For several moments, long ones, I inspected the ceiling, which was painted the color of vanilla ice cream. Finally, I said, "Middle name Montgomery?"

"Lynch's?" Orcutt said.

"Yes."

"I really couldn't say. Homer dug up most of the information on him."

"Then he didn't dig far enough," I said.

"I beg your parlon."

"You should. Ramsey Lynch. That isn't his real name."

Necessary snorted. "He did eighteen months in Atlanta under it and that was a Federal rap."

"I know," I said. "But that still doesn't make it his real name."

"Mr. Dye," Orcutt said, "I'm really not overly fond of melodrama. If you have something to say . . ." He let the sentence die as if it had bored itself to death.

I looked at him. His dark blue eyes were chillier than usual. So was his expression. I examined him carefully for a few moments and could find nothing that I really liked.

"Well?" he said in his own private brand of frozen italics.

"Well," I said, mimicking him for no special reason other than I felt he was being a little pompous for twenty-six. "His name isn't Ramsey Lynch. His name is Montgomery Vicker. He's the brother of Gerald Vicker. You remember Gerald. He's the one you retained in Hong Kong who recommended me. He's the one I got fired because he killed the wrong man."

12

I inherited Gerald Vicker. He came with the desk and the filing cabinets and the stationery and the thirty-six-year-old Memphis secretary (my first one) who finally found romance in the Far East and married a pink gin-faced Volkswagen dealer from Malaysia. He was a widower who, after a few drinks, had once confided that my former secretary was a terrific old girl in the sack. She was the one who taught me how to write up an insurance policy.

It was Carmingler, of course, who finally told me about Vicker only three or four hours before I was to catch a plane to San Francisco and there make a connecting flight to Hong Kong. Carmingler brought up Vicker's name casually, as if he were mentioning a mutual friend who had just changed jobs, got married, or gone to jail. We were sitting in one of those bare offices that Carmingler always seemed to prefer. This one was in the Kansas City Post Office and although I've tried often enough, I still can't remember why we met in Kansas City.

The room was small, with only one window. It held a Federal-green desk and two matching chairs, a black telephone, and a picture of the President. It was during the last days of Eisenhower's administration and the photograph was the one that made him look as if he had actually enjoyed the job.

"You'll be in full control, of course," Carmingler said.

"Vicker was number two under Grimes, wasn't he?"

"Yes, he was. Did a good job of it, too."

"And he'll be number two under me, the new boy?"

"I can see what you're driving at, but there's no need to worry. None at all."

"Then he's not human," I said. Carmingler puffed on his pipe two or three times and then waved it at me for either emphasis or reassurance. "Vicker is all right," he said. "He's one of the old crowd who came with us

105

during the big war, drifted away, and then came back. He's solid."

Carmingler had been either fourteen or fifteen when World War II ended, but he always referred to the OSS as the "old crowd" or "us" or "we." It was one of his minor foibles that I eventually found time to forgive.

"Does Vicker know anything about insurance?" I said.

"No more than you, but your secretary does. Her name's Klett, I believe." He took out a small Leathersmith notebook to make sure. "Francine Klett. Miss."

"Any more surprises?" I said.

Carmingler looked around for an ashtray to knock his pipe out in, but finding none, settled on a metal wastebasket that was filled with paper. For a moment I thought that he wanted to burn down the Post Office.

"This is quite a leg up for you," he said.

"That's been impressed on me often enough."

"Vicker should prove quite useful. He's been out there a long time, knows everyone, and has a quick mind."

"Then why doesn't he have my job?"

Carmingler rubbed the bowl of his pipe against some of the freckles that were sprinkled over his large pink nose which some kindly person had once described to me as distinguished. If that meant it was a nose that you wouldn't soon forget, the kindly person was right. "We thought about that," he finally said when he finished his internal debate about how much to tell me.

"And?"

"We decided that you were the better man for the job."

"That still doesn't tell me anything," I said. "What's the matter with Vicker? Does he drink, gamble, whore around, and talk too much? Or does he just diddle the expense account and stay out late at night?"

Carmingler smiled, displaying his long, wide, strong teeth that helped him to resemble a horse. "No, it's none of that. It's simply that we find him—well—a bit *overly* ambitious."

"Christ," I said. "I bet he has a lean and hungry look, too."

Despite the Phi Beta Kappa key there were some gaping holes in Carmingler's education. He looked surprised for a second and then nodded thoughtfully. "Why, yes, now that you mention it. He does look a bit that way."

106

It was no good from the beginning and both Vicker and I knew it. Age had something to do with it, but not all. He was forty and I was barely twenty-seven. He was patronizing and I was insufficiently deferential. He talked too much, sometimes even brilliantly, but I listened too little. His attention to detail was phenomenal and he resented my cavalier attitude. His Chinese had been painfully acquired and my easy fluency irritated him. He had an opinion about everything in God's world and if I didn't share them, he sulked. He would spend an hour telling me why a Patek Phillippe was better than a Rolex Oyster; or why a Nikon was better than a Leica and how a Canon was the match for both; or why the memory of Mao would be banished in less than a year after his death. He was shrewd, glib, and forgot nothing. He lied beautifully, fretted incessantly, and vaguely alluded to tragic experiences during his stretch with the OSS. He was a walking definition of overweening ambition that I found awful and which I got stuck with until one August day three years and eight months later.

It was the middle of August, around the fifteenth, and Vicker was already at his desk when I arrived at the then fancy, new downtown island offices of Minneapolis Mutual on Pedder Street, which I'd leased just to shut him up. I did balk, however, when he wanted to issue a press release claiming that the reason for our move was a record-shattering jump in business.

He walked into my office carrying his coffee cup, the one with "Vicker" carefully glazed on it in a Chinese ideograph. He liked having his name on things and his shirts, ties, lighter, and cigarette case were all monogrammed. He sat in one of the chairs and propped his feet on my desk, probably because he knew that it irritated me.

"Lucky I was here this morning," he said so that I would have to ask why. I think he sometimes sat up half the night figuring out his morning opener which would cause me to ask about something that I didn't know.

"I'm grateful."

"Might have missed him if I hadn't arrived early."

"You're always early and it's earned you a head start in life's great race." It also gave him the chance to read the mail first, both his and mine.

107

"He wants five thousand," he said.

"Sounds like a bargain."

Vicker lowered his feet, brushed some imaginary lint from the lapel of his burnt orange, raw-silk jacket, put his coffee cup on my desk where it was sure to make a ring, and reached for his silver lighter and cigarette case. He was about my height and about my weight, but I always thought of him as lean and of myself as skinny. He had a smooth, oval face, nicely tanned, and his black hair was thick and straight. He wore it long for the times and it looped down over his high forehead and then back in a style that would become popular years later. His eyes were deep-set and dark brown and he could hold them perfectly steady in the middle of an enormous lie. They also had that cool glow peculiar to persons who will never need glasses. Some commercial airline pilots in their fifties have eyes like that. Vicker's nose was a right triangle and he sported a carefully clipped mustache above thin lips that he sometimes licked around lunch time. His chin was unremarkable in any respect.

When Vicker finished lighting his cigarette and putting his case and lighter back where they belonged, he blew some smoke at his brown and green foulard tie and said, "He's yours, you know."

"I didn't."

"They're on to him," he said.

"All right," I said. "Who?"

"Pai Chung-liang."

"He's not worth five thousand."

"He meant Hong Kong, not U.S."

"He's still not worth it."

"He wants to go to Singapore. He said he has relatives in Singapore."

Pai Chung-liang was a middle-aged man who worked in the Bank of China and occasionally passed us fresh snippets of information of varying authenticity. He swore, for example, that the bank, which serves as Peking's financial arm as well as its Hong Kong diplomatic, espionage, and cultural headquarters, had a cache of 6,129 rifles and carbines, 100,000 rounds of ammunition, 197 cases of grenades, and enough food to withstand a four-month siege. Just who the siege-layers would be, he didn't say. He didn't even guess. But some of his information about

Peking's financial transactions had proved interesting, if not vital, and we paid him enough to make it worth his time.

"What did he do, call?" I said.

"Around eight-fifteen."

"How did he sound?"

Vicker thought for a moment. "Desperate, I'd say. Panicky even."

"How does he know they're on to him?"

"He didn't say. He just said that they are."

Pai was a shy, slight man, short by even Chinese standards, barely over five feet, who liked flowers and figures. We had needed someone inside the bank and Pai was the best I could do. I got to him when his wife became ill and needed the services of an expensive surgeon whom Pai couldn't possibly afford. It was one of those things that you hear about when you're standing around some cocktail party, half-listening to a doctor talk about his rare ones. Mrs. Pai had been one of the rare ones and when the expensive surgeon mentioned that her husband worked for the Bank of China I began to listen in earnest. I employed the usual flimflam to reach Pai. We made a deal. The life of his wife in exchange for whatever information he thought might prove interesting. I think Pai loved his wife very much, even more than he did figures and flowers. He was embarrassingly grateful, even after she died on the operating table under the skilled hands of the noted surgeon, and he wanted to know how he could demonstrate his gratitude. I told him and he readily agreed, partly because he was grateful, partly out of pique at the bank because it had done little about his wife's illness, but mostly because of the 500 Hong Kong dollars that I agreed to pay him each month.

Pai Chung-liang was another living testimony to my skill as a corruptor of civil servants. I wondered how his superiors had found out and even if they had. Perhaps Pai was just bored with Hong Kong and thought that Singapore would be pleasant in late August and if he could get an additional five thousand out of me, it might prove even more pleasant than he had anticipated.

There was the chance, of course, that he was telling the truth and if he were, he would soon be telling them about us. Not that there wasn't much they didn't already know, but we still had to go through the motions of maintaining our tattered cover.

"I'm going to pay him," I said to Vicker.

"You just said he wasn't worth it."

"He's not, but I'm still going to pay him."

"Of course," Vicker said thoughtfully, "it could be a setup."

"I know."

"I never did trust the little bastard."

"That puts him at the bottom of a long list," I said.

The telephone rang then and it was Pai. "Mr. Dye?" he said in his soft, shy voice and I said yes.

"I called earlier this morning."

"Are you on a safe phone?"

"Yes. Very safe. I did not go to my employment this morning."

"I understand," I said.

"I have some vital information."

"About the bank?"

"Yes and no. But they have become suspicious and the information I have is vital to you. Personally."

"And you're asking five thousand dollars?"

"Yes. I would not do so unless I needed it desperately. I must go to Singapore. I have relatives in Singapore."

"That's what I hear."

"Oh, yes. My conversation with Mr. Vicker this morning. He is your trusted colleague, is he not?"

"Yes."

"I see."

"All right, Mr. Pai, where and when do you want to meet?"

He suggested a number on Upper Lascar or Cat Street. We had met there twice before in a gewgaw shop stuffed with carvings, lacquered ware, ceramics of doubtful merit, very bad Ming-type copies of Chinese mustangs, gongs of various sizes, and the inevitable scrolls. The old man who owned the place locked the doors and left whenever we appeared. His hour's absence cost another HK $100.

"Anything else?" I said.

"Only one thing, Mr. Dye. I strongly urge that you come alone."

"Fine," I said.

I hung up and looked at Vicker. "He suggests that I come alone," I said.

Vicker smiled a little, but not very much. "Then I'd better go with you."

"Maybe you'd better."

"How'd he sound to you?" he said.

"Just as you described him: desperate and panicked."

We arrived at the shop a little before ten, which was the agreed-upon time for the meeting. I paid the old man his $100 and he left, leaving the door unlocked on the promise that I would snap it shut after Pai arrived.

"If he's skittish, maybe I'd better get in the back," Vicker said.

There was a rear room, small and stuffy, which the old man used for an occasional nap. It had a six-inch peephole that was shielded by a flimsy see-through of split bamboo.

I stood near the six-hundred-year-old table that the shop owner used for a desk and looked out into Cat Street, which was as packed as usual. I sniffed and thought I could smell opium, but it may have been my imagination, although on Cat Street that wasn't necessarily true. I saw Pai Chung-liang burrowing his way through the crowd. He wore a white linen suit and clutched a plastic briefcase under his arm. He paused at the door of the shop, looked carefully both ways, and then slipped in looking for all the world as if he'd just made off with the factory's weekly payroll. He hadn't been born to the business.

"Mr. Dye," he said. "You are in good health?"

"Excellent."

"It is kind of you to meet at such short notice."

"Time is most valuable to those who suddenly are in short supply," I said, making it all up as I went along.

He nodded, looked around shyly, and then started to say something, probably about the money. Before he had to embarrass himself I handed him an envelope. He didn't even look inside, but instead quickly stuffed it into his briefcase which, I thought, demonstrated a pleasant degree of mutual trust.

"I have some information of a most delicate nature," he said. "I scarcely know how to begin—"

He never got the chance really. The door that I'd forgotten to lock burst open and two chunky Chinese were suddenly in the room. They were mumbling some-

111

thing that I didn't catch. I'm sure Pai Chung-liang never really heard what it was either because Vicker shot him right through the briefcase that he had clutched to his chest. The two chunky types looked at me, saw that I didn't have a gun, and then at Pai who was now sprawled on the floor, his briefcase still tight against his chest. They both produced short-barreled revolvers. One of them waved his gun at me, nudged Pai with his foot, and said finished to his partner. The partner nodded, bent down, and took the briefcase. Neither of them seemed to care much about who'd shot Pai as long as he was dead. They backed to the door and disappeared into the crowd.

I bent over Pai. He wasn't quite dead. He opened his eyes and coughed once. It seemed to hurt him terribly to do so. Then he said in a faint voice, "Mr. Dye, they couldn't have known . . . I'm afraid your Mr. Vicker—" He never did finish what he thought Vicker might have said or done. He coughed and died instead.

Vicker came into the room as I rose. I looked at him. He was nodding a little in that self-satisfied way that he did when things went as he predicted. "A setup," he said. "Just like I—"

"You didn't have to shoot him," I said.

"Christ, he set you up. He was about to finger you. If I hadn't shot him, you'd be on your way to Canton."

"They weren't after me."

"Not after he was dead, they weren't. Not after he couldn't finger you."

It was a poor lie, but Vicker was magnificent. His dark brown eyes didn't flicker and his voice dripped oily gobs of sincerity. "Good God, Dye, even a child could see what he was up to."

"You didn't hear what he said. Just before he died."

"What?"

"He said three things." I decided to do some lying myself. "First, he said that you've sold out. Second, he said that you tipped off the meeting to the opposition. And third, he said that you're through. I agree with him on everything."

"You believe him?" he said in the same, hurt tone that he'd use if I were to disagree with his favorite contention that Marciano could have taken Clay in three rounds.

"He was dying," I said. "Why should he lie?"

"You're not that naive."

"Maybe I am. But then he said something else, too," I said, rather pleased with my own skill as a liar.

"What?"

"He said you made a mistake. I agree with him."

That didn't bother Vicker either. It only caused him to raise an eyebrow. His left one. "What mistake?"

Vicker actually had made a number of mistakes and some of them he couldn't help, such as the fact that I didn't much like him. But there were others. One was the call that he'd made from his office just before we left for the meeting with Pai. After that, the two chunky Chinese showed up. That might be called a coincidental mistake. Then he accused Pai of trying to tumble me to the Chinese Communists who already knew everything they needed to know about me. That could only be called a dumb mistake—one very much unlike Vicker. Almost last was the mistake Vicker made when he shot Pai before the Chinese could tell me what he had on his mind. That, I suppose, could be labeled an irritating mistake. But I wasn't going to tell him about all of them just then—only about the final and worst mistake that he'd made.

"Pai said you shot the wrong man, Gerald," I said. "That was your big mistake. You should have shot me instead."

13

I learned to recite the alphabet and how to write a name in the Bridge House Apartments, which the Japanese had converted into a prison. The alphabet was the usual one, but the name was my new one, William Smalldane, first-born son of the noted American correspondent, Gorman Smalldane.

The Japanese who arrested us on December 8 made Smalldane drive Tante Katerine's Chrysler across Szechwan Road Bridge and into the Bridge House compound, which was located about two blocks from the central post office in the Hongkew section. During the drive Smalldane managed to slip me his two thousand-word story that never got filed. I dropped it on the floorboards and kicked it back under the front seat. They must never have found it. If they had, Smalldane probably would have been executed either as a top-grade spy or a small-time prophet.

There was a crowd of foreigners at Bridge House that morning, some of them half-dressed, all of them a little bewildered. They kept talking about Pearl Harbor, but it meant nothing to me. I was more interested in watching them empty their pockets on to a desk behind which sat two Japanese officers, a captain and a major.

"Get this straight, Lucifer," Smalldane whispered to me. "You're now William Smalldane. My only son. You got that? William Smalldane."

"William Smalldane," I said, reveling a little in the sound of it. Even then I didn't care much for Lucifer. When we got to the major and the captain they made Smalldane empty his pockets. They placed the items in a brown envelope and then demanded that he remove his belt.

"The child," the captain said. "Your son?"

"Yes," Smalldane said.

"He must empty his pockets."

I had quite a nice collection. A half-package of Lucky

114

Strikes; a switchblade knife with a seven-inch blade; an empty spool; four dirty pictures; a lint-flaked piece of candied ginger; a chain to a bathtub stopper; a box of wax matches; an Indian head U.S. penny, dated 1902; a purple Crayola; and a Three Little Pigs and Big Bad Wolf pocket watch which didn't run.

The Japanese captain listed everything, even the ginger, and then sealed it in an official envelope, except for the dirty pictures. He snickered at them and kept two for himself and gave the major the other two.

It was cold in Shanghai and I was wearing my treasured corduroy knickers with thick woolen socks; high-topped brown shoes; a flannel shirt; a wollen sweater; a plaid woolen lumberjack coat; a knitted red cap; and long underwear. Underneath all that I wore the handmade money belt that I had painstakingly fashioned out of an old pillow case. It contained around $1,000 in American and British currency. The money was the proceeds from my drunk-rolling efforts and I always wore it, even to bed.

The Japanese officers produced another form and began asking Smalldane questions about where we were born, nationality, occupation, age, and length of residence in Shanghai. Smalldane answered everything and even volunteered information about his alleged ex-wife, and my new mother, who had died in what he claimed to have been the terrible San Francisco cholera epidemic of 1934. They seemed to believe him.

When they were through asking questions, they made Smalldane sign the form. Then they handed me the pen, but Smalldane took it away from me, shook his head sadly at the Japanese officers, and tapped his forehead in the universal gesture that means not quite bright. The Japanese nodded, almost in sympathy, I thought, and let Smalldane sign the form for me. They did, however, insist on fingerprinting us both.

We were turned over to a couple of Japanese guards who escorted us through a door that led to the ground floor of the former Bridge House Apartments. The ground floor was designed orginally to house small shops, but it had been converted into cells whose thick doors were bolted with chains and locks and bars. The guards directed us to a Japanese sergeant who seemed to be the chief jailer. He sat behind a plain wooden desk. On the wall back of him were lists of what I guessed were names, written in Chinese and several other languages, or so Smalldane later told me.

"By God," he said to me, "they've had it planned for months. All that time I spent digging and nobody even had a smell of this place." He was, forever, the reporter. The jailer told him to shut up.

It was cold and the light was dim in Bridge House. The jailer looked at us carefully and then selected some keys from a bunch that must have weighed six pounds. He motioned for the guards to follow him and they prodded us down the hall to one of the cells. The jailer twisted keys in the two locks, slid back the bolt, undid some chains, and motioned us in. Then he clanged the door behind us. We weren't alone. There were almost three-dozen other persons in the cell, which was eighteen feet long and twelve feet wide. Smalldane grabbed my hand and we managed to find a place near enough to a wall so that we could lean against it.

I counted the persons in the room. There were thirty-three of them, including eleven women. It was a cosmopolitan bunch: English, Americans, Chinese, one Korean, four Canadians, and a redheaded man who claimed to be a Mexican national, but remembering Tante Katerine's admonition, I didn't believe him. The Japanese didn't either.

"Will somebody please tell me just what the hell happened at Pearl Harbor?" Smalldane said.

They told him, those who'd listened to the radio that morning of December 8, 1941, in Shanghai. It was December 7 at Pearl Harbor because of the international dateline. Others had heard that the Japanese had landed on the east coast of Malaya, which both depressed and elated Smalldane. "By God," he said, "if I'd just filed last week I'd've had fifteen job offers today and I could've named the price."

"Would it not present a formidable problem to report a war from the inside of a jail?" I said in my most logical French.

"Why don't you take a nap?" Smalldane said. "A long one."

The meals came twice a day, shoved through a twelve-inch aperture in the cell door. The first meal was a bowl of rice which contained the heads of three dried herrings. It was warm. The second meal was the same, except

116

that it was cold. There was no third meal. Having been reared on much superior fare, I refused to eat the first day. Smalldane shrugged, reached for my bowl, and polished it off, fish heads and all. On the second day and thereafter I ate everything edible and some that was not.

The Japanese started coming for Smalldane after we had been in Bridge House a week. They led him away and when he came back, he came with bruises, and once with a black eye, and once with a tooth missing. A lower one on the left side.

"They think I'm the goddamned Scarlet Pimpernel of Shanghai," he told me and when I said I didn't know who the Scarlet Pimpernel was, he spent the next three or four days reciting the tale and improving on its dialogue. The other prisoners listened intently. They had nothing else to do.

Bridge House Prison had either fifteen or sixteen cells which were solid, windowless walls on three sides. At the front of the cell large wooden bars, about six inches in diameter, were set a couple of inches apart. The door was wood, at least four inches thick, and there was a great deal of clanging and banging of chains and bars whenever it was opened. The sound haunted me for years.

A wooden box in the corner served as a toilet. Whenever the women used it, the men turned their backs or looked the other way. It was emptied by the Chinese prisoners at night. They often argued for the privilege since it at least got them out of the cell.

Because the Hongkew section of Shanghai had been under Japanese military control since 1937, they had had no trouble in keeping Bridge House prison a secret. Before Pearl Harbor, I learned that it had been used to jail those Chinese who disappeared suddenly from either the French Concession or the International Settlement. Two of the Chinese in our cell told Smalldane that they had been there so long that they had forgotten what they were originally charged with.

Smalldane was the only foreigner that I ever knew the Japanese to beat, although the guards smacked the Chinese around regularly, often with one-by-four-inch planks that they liked to break over Chinese heads. Any Chinese head. It seemed to be a favorite form of exercise. We were treated casually enough for the first month, except

117

for Smalldane, and then the word apparently came down and the Japanese got tough. There was absolutely no heat in the Bridge House cells and our only warmth came from huddling close together under thin, lice-infested blankets. Smalldane taught me how to kill lice by cracking them between my fingernails. You couldn't just mash them to death. The Japanese guards laughed about the lice. When they weren't laughing about that, they cackled over a Chinese prisoner whose right leg one of them had jabbed with a bayonet. The wound developed gangrene and the Chinese moaned and screamed a lot before he died.

The new crackdown ruled that prisoners couldn't talk to each other, something that the Japanese didn't enforce too stringently except when they had nothing better to do. But because more prisoners were daily being jammed into the cells, they forced us to sit in rows. That made it easier for them to conduct their head count every four hours. We sat, our knees drawn up to our chests, our heads bowed, facing in the general direction of Tokyo and, I suppose, Hirohito. As punishment, they made us sit Japanese fashion, which didn't bother me too much, but which played hell with the circulation of the older prisoners. After six or seven hours of it, some couldn't walk for days.

They searched each prisoner every two days or so. All but me. For some reason the guards didn't think that a child would conceal anything. It wasn't until we'd been in jail for a month that I told Smalldane about the money belt.

"You have what?" he said, and he must have said it in an incredulous whisper although I no longer remember.

"My money belt."

"How much?" he said.

"What's the British pound worth now?" said the rotten little money changer.

"Damn it, I don't know, make it five dollars a pound."

"Then I have twelve hundred and seventy-five dollars. U.S."

"Jesus," Smalldane muttered and then slumped into a halfway comfortable position so that he could think about what use to make of the windfall.

On Christmas, 1941, Tante Katerine sent us a basket of food containing three roast chickens, cigarettes, brandy, tinned goods, including a plum pudding that she had scrounged somewhere, candy, nuts, and about four-dozen dainty sandwiches filled with pâté de foie gras. One of the Japanese guards pounded on the small opening of the cell door and yelled for the Smardane. When the Smardane made his way to the door, the guard displayed each item in the basket. Then he ripped off a chicken leg and chewed it noisily. Next he tried some of the candy. He liked that, too. Finally, he bit into one of the sandwiches, didn't like the pâté, and spat it out. "Here," he said and shoved the sandwiches at Smalldane, who brought them back to our row.

Smalldane wasn't as interested in eating the sandwiches as he was in examining their filling. On the dozenth one that he opened, he found what he was looking for, a note from Tante Katerine.

"Well, it looks like we have Christmas dinner after all, Lucifer." I shook my head and made a vague kind of gesture that took in the entire cell. We were all scruffy by then, dirty, cold, and incredibly hungry. Most of the prisoners sat or knelt huddled in their filthy blankets, their sunken eyes staring at the pile of sandwiches. The Chinese prisoners were the worst of all because they didn't for a minute believe that they would share in our luck. They looked, then looked away, and then looked back again. They couldn't help themselves.

"Aw, shit," Smalldane said. He took four of the sandwiches and gave me the rest. "Here, Tiny Tim, it's your last chance to play Scrooge."

"Who're they?" I said.

"Go pass out the sandwiches and I'll tell you."

I crawled around the filthy floor, passing out cute little pâté de fois gras sandwiches which had all the crust carefully sliced off. Some said thank you. Others said Merry Christmas or God Bless you. And still others just silently snatched the food from my hand and crammed it into their mouths.

"What's the note from Tante Katerine say?" I asked Smalldane when I crawled back to our row.

"Read it yourself. But, hell, you can't read. She says that a boat's leaving for the States with foreign civilians that are going to be traded for Japanese civilians. You got that?"

I nodded.

"She's trying to juice our way on to that boat. She's gone to the Swiss Embassy, to Wu, to everybody she can think of. It's cost her a packet. She mentioned how much, of course."

I nodded again. "Of course. How much?"

"Six thousand American so far."

"I was impressed, not with the amount so much as with Tante Katerine's willingness to part with a dollar that didn't guarantee her a rapid return of at least eight percent compounded semi-annually. I started to cry. It was the first time I'd cried since I'd been in jail.

"What the fuck's wrong with you?" Smalldane said.

"I want to go home," I said.

"Your home's in the States now, kid."

"I don't know anybody there," I said between sobs. "I want to go home to Number Twenty-seven and Tante Katerine."

Smalldane sighed and patted me on the shoulder. "You can't anymore."

"Why?"

"They closed it down today. That's what Kate says. The whorehouse is no longer your home."

When you're eight years old and in jail and someone tells you that the only home you ever really remember no longer exists, it hits hard. I think I went into shock for a few moments and then I stopped crying and started to bawl—in earnest. Smalldane kept patting away on my shoulder, a little embarrassed. He nodded apologetically at the rest of the prisoners, some of whom nodded back, some sympathetically, some dully. But none complained. Finally, Smalldane got bored with my emotional exhibition, leaned over, and speaking Cantonese, whispered into my ear: "If you don't silence yourself, my cowardly little turtle, I will sell you to the fat Japanese guard for the night. He has offered more than a fair price."

I shut up.

"That's better," Smalldane said. "Now for your education. First the alphabet."

It took me an hour to memorize the alphabet by rote and another hour to learn how to draw William Smalldane with my finger in the dirt and filth of the floor. I didn't know which letter was which, but I could draw it fairly well after an hour.

"That's my new name?"

"That's it," Smalldane said.

"Please, Gorman, could you teach me something else?"

"What?"

"Could you teach me how to draw Lucifer Clarence Dye?"

He smiled at me, a sad kind of a smile, I thought, then nodded and said, "Sure, kid. You might even need it again one of these days."

14

They didn't waste any time. The phone rang in my room in the Sycamore Hotel (Swankerton's Oldest and Finest) before the bellhop got through showing me how the color television set worked. I gave him a dollar and a smile and nodded my goodbye as I picked up the green instrument and said hello.

"Mr. Dye?" It was a woman's voice.

"Yes."

"Would you hold on for Mr. Ramsey Lynch?"

I told her yes and then Lynch was talking, his voice as smooth and as buttery as his brother's, but deeper, more confident, and with much less contentiousness in the tone. It was a good voice for a liar and I automatically assumed that he was one of the best.

"Welcome to Swankerton, Mr. Dye," Lynch said.

"Thank you."

"I understand that you're the man."

"From whom?"

"From here and there."

"That's where, not who."

"Well, Brother Gerald did mention you to me."

"I thought he might."

"He sent his best."

"His best what?"

Lynch chuckled. It was a rich, warm, comfortable sound such as fat men make after they no longer mind being fat. "Regards, of course," he said. "Gerry mentioned that he'd recommended you highly."

"So I heard."

"Surprised?"

"Probably not as much as I should be, but then Gerald was always full of surprises."

Lynch chuckled again, happily. "Even as a kid. Never knew what he'd do next. But the real reason I called is that we're having a little policy meeting this afternoon, and I kind of thought you might like to sit in."

"What kind of policy?"

"Civic policy, Mr. Dye. Seems that there may be sort of a hassle going on during the next couple of months so we thought we'd lay out some ground rules."

"Your ground and your rules," I said.

Lynch thought that was funny, too, but not as much as before, and his chuckle was reduced to three or four sharp, deep barks.

"Well, what do you say?"

"All right. What time?"

"About an hour from now. Around five."

"Where?" I said.

"My place, but don't worry about it. We'll send someone for you. Room eight-nineteen, isn't it?"

I looked at the telephone to make sure. "Eight-nineteen," I said.

"Look forward to it," Lynch said before he said goodbye and we hung up.

I stood there by the phone for a few moments and then picked it up and asked the operator for Victor Orcutt. Carol Thackerty answered in what was called, for God knows what reason, the Eddie Rickenbacker suite. Maybe he had once slept there when they were still calling it the Theodore Bilbo suite.

"Is your room all right?" Orcutt said when he came on.

"It's fine. The chief adversary just called."

"Lynch." He didn't make it a question. He just said Lynch to confirm a fact and to give his mind time to hop around and sort out all of the implications.

"He wants to meet me at five this afternoon. Or maybe they call it evening down here."

"Evening," Orcutt said.

"I agreed."

"Good."

"He said he wants to lay out some ground rules."

"There aren't any," Orcutt said.

"I know. It's probably just a mutual sizing-up session. He said that some others will be there."

"What else?"

"I think Gerald Vicker wants his brother to settle a grudge for him and the brother wants to find out how much trouble that could be."

"That's one," Orcutt said. "Two is he might try to buy you off. How much would that take?"

123

"You're forgetting my loyalty to the old firm."

"You're *teasing* again. I do like that. We'll wait until you get back and then we'll all have dinner together at a simply marvelous place that I know."

"I'll call when I can," I said and hung up, reflecting that I was going to have to watch Orcutt's perfectly marvelous places. Although my taste buds relished the rich fare, my stomach still expected rank fish and gummy rice. When it didn't get the expected, it rebelled, just as it had done twice the night before in San Francisco.

Eight-nineteen in the Sycamore Hotel was a corner room with a view of Marseille Boulevard and Snow Street, the latter being the principal downtown thoroughfare, which I assumed was named after somebody called Snow and not for the weather. I judged the hotel to be at least sixty or seventy years old, built in a vaguely European style so that the floors formed a high hollow square. The corridors on each floor ran around the hollow square, and nothing kept the drunks from tumbling down to the lobby other than waist-level iron railings. The hotel ceiling, nine floors above the lobby, was covered with frosted glass which during the day provided the interior with a soft, filtered light that made the profusion of potted plants look even greener than they were.

It was a well-designed hotel with comfortably furnished, spacious rooms whose high ceilings boasted fans that supplemented the central air-conditioning. Unless you were well bundled up when they were both going full blast, the chances for catching pneumonia must have been excellent. The bath in 819 was large enough to have done for a single room in an ordinary motel, its fixtures were fairly new and even included a bidet. Someone had spent a lot of money and thought on the Sycamore's geriatric care.

I hung up the suits and topcoat that Carmingler had provided, regretting that I would have to buy some new clothing to go with the temperature. I unbuttoned the vest of the suit I was wearing, the blue one with the faint gray stripe, and hung it in the closet.

After that I stood by the window, sipped a drink of cool water and Scotch, and watched the citizens of Swankerton go about their business. Across the street was the First National Bank. Next to it was Elene's Boutique, then Osterman's Bar & Grill which offered fine food, and then a Rexall drugstore, a Kress's five and ten, a five-story department store called Mitchell and Farnes, and another bar and grill called The Easy Alibi, which was a little cute for the main drag.

Down Marseille Boulevard was the Liberty National Bank, twenty-four stories tall and the city's only skyscraper; another department store called Biendorfer's, a pancake and waffle shop, and another drugstore which seemed to be the member of a local chain called Mouton's.

The citizens looked just like their town. There was nothing in their dress or gait or color that would distinguish them from those who lived in Pittsburgh, or Atlanta, or Pierre, South Dakota. Some shuffled, some walked briskly, even in the heat, and some just ambled along as if they had nowhere important to go and nothing much to do when they got there. Although I was eight stories up, the citizens seemed to lack animation. There was none of Hong Kong's squealing vibrancy and I found that I missed it. But then there weren't many places in the States that I'd ever really liked, not the way I'd once loved Shanghai, and there was no real reason why Swankerton should prove an exception.

I turned from the window and tried the most comfortable appearing chair in the room, which was even more restful than it looked. I sank into it and stared at the slowly spinning ceiling fan that made an oily click after every third revolution. I could have thought about what I was doing in Swankerton, but I already knew that. I was there because I had nothing better to do and I wanted to find out why someone was willing to pay me $50,000 to do it. The fee, of course, was exorbitant. Far too high for two months' work unless I was supposed to kill a few persons, but I was no good at that. If I had liked coincidences, I could have puzzled over the one that had Gerald Vicker recommending me to do a job of sorts in a town where his brother was obviously Señor Number One Garçon, as Tante Katerine would have had it. But since it was obviously no coincidence, a phenomenon in which I had little or no faith anyhow, there was no need to puzzle over it any more than one puzzles over being dealt a pat hand. When it comes along, you don't fret about it, you play it.

The phone rang and a man's voice wanted to know if I were Mr. Dye. When I said yes, he said that his name was Robineaux and that Mr. Lynch had told him to wait in the lobby. I said I would be right down and when I got there, Mr. Robineaux turned out to be a tall young man with the posture of a question mark who had some interesting scars on his face that looked as if they had been stitched there by a sewing machine. I followed him out to a Lincoln Continental and he opened the rear door for me. The car was air-conditioned and Mr. Robineaux had nothing much to say until we arrived at a house in a residential section some twenty minutes later. Then he said, "This is it," and got out and opened the door for me.

It was an old residential section of Swankerton where the pines grew tall and when the wind passed through them, they sighed a little, as if bored with their murmured, never-ending conversation about the weather. The house was a large, two-story frame structure with a turret at one end which poked up another story and was crowned by what looked to be a shingled dunce cap. There were screened porches running around both the first and second floors and carefully carved gingerbread scrollwork was nailed onto everything that would support it. It was a large house, perhaps three-quarters of a century old, and far too big for most of today's families. Somehow I expected to spot a discreet sign announcing, in a hesitant manner, that there were rooms for rent providing, of course, that one could furnish proper references.

But there was no sign and I followed Robineaux and his interesting scars up the five steps that led to the screened-in porch. There was a lot of honeysuckle climbing around and its odor competed with that of the lawn's freshly cut Bermuda grass. There were some magnolia trees and some azaleas, too, I noticed, but they weren't in bloom, although they must have been a pleasant enough sight when they were, if one cared for that sort of thing.

Ramsey Lynch opened the door and gave me his hand to shake. He said "It's good to see you" and I said something in reply that was equally meaningless. I knew he was Ramsey Lynch because he looked like his brother, Gerald Vicker, although Lynch was a little younger, but not much. His granite gray hair was long and thick and he wore it looped down and back over his forehead much in the same style that his brother favored. His eyes were steady and clear and somehow I knew that although they must have been in use for close to forty-five or even fifty years they still didn't need glasses. He had Vicker's right-triangle nose and the same thin lips but no mustache. He had three or four unremarkable chins, depending upon how high he held his head. Ramsey Lynch was a very fat man and he made no attempt to disguise it. He wore a pale blue suit of some synthetic fabric, a white shirt, and a dark blue tie. It all looked cool, loosely comfortable, and cheap.

The house was air-conditioned, I was relieved to find, as I followed Lynch into the living room or perhaps parlor. He turned and made a vague little gesture. "This was the parlor. Still is, I suppose. We bought it from two old maid sisters who finally couldn't keep it up and went to a rest home. Everything is just like they left it—except the air-conditioning."

It was a stiff room, filled with spindly chairs made out of dark wood and woven cane. There was a purple sofa, a loveseat, and a grand piano. Dead relatives or friends gazed down from the walls where they were trapped in their oval, glass-covered frames.

"We're meeting in the dining room," Lynch said and opened two sliding doors. Five men sat around an ornately carved table. There was a matching sideboard at the right and a tall, glass-fronted highboy at the left which held a collection of china and colored glassware that, to me, looked Bavarian.

The men were down to shirtsleeves. Three of them smoked cigarettes and from the looks of their ashtrays they had been there for at least two hours.

"This is Lucifer Dye," Lynch said to the men. "You know who he works for and why he's here. So I'll just make the introductions and then we can get on with it." Lynch started at the left hand side of the table and worked his way around it clockwise.

"Fred Merriweather," he said. "Fred's a city councilman and owns a lot of property over in Niggertown. Also has a restaurant on Snow Street, right across from your hotel, called the Easy Alibi. He's up for re-election." I nodded at Merriweather, who had a big-jawed face, stupid blue eyes, and a yellow-toothed smile.

"Next to him is Ancel Carp, who's city tax assessor. We elect him, too, and he's running again. He's also the city surveyor." Carp was around forty-five. He looked as if he spent a lot of time outdoors. His hands were extraordinarily large and they went with the rest of him. When he looked at me, his gray eyes seemed to be calculating my net worth and I felt that he wouldn't be much more than two cents off.

"Now at the end of the table is his honor, the mayor. Pierre Robineaux. We call him Pete and his boy's the one who carried you here."

"Glad to have you with us, Mr. Dye," Robineaux said, bobbing his head at me. He had a high forehead and a long chin, and both of them seemed to be too far removed from his button nose, small eyes, and pursed mouth.

"Next to the mayor is our chief of police, Cal Loambaugh. He's appointed so he doesn't have to worry about running. Not much." The chief was younger than I expected, not more than thirty-five. He was dressed in a neat brown suit and had a tight, controlled look about him, like an alcoholic turning down a drink after he's three days off the sauce. Loambaugh didn't smile or nod. He just looked at me, and there was nothing in his gaze that I could find to like.

"And finally, this is Alex Couturier. He's the executive secretary for the Chamber of Commerce, and belongs to the Lions, Kiwanis, American Legion, VFW, and God knows what else. He's sort of the city's public relations man."

Couturier had one of those professionally friendly faces, loose and relaxed. His mouth seemed to be on the verge of a smile and I decided that it always looked that way. He was a big, bluff-looking man, well-dressed, but not so much that it would offend those who bought their suits at J. C. Penney's. "Good to see you, Dye, good to see you," he said and his voice boomed it all out and I thought it might have been nicer if his eyes had managed to join in on the chorus.

"Well, now, I think that's everybody," Lynch said. "Why don't you sit right down here on my left and we'll get started as soon as the mayor yells at that boy of his to bring us something cool."

The mayor yelled "Booboo," and the younger Robineaux popped his head through the door that must have led to the kitchen.

He said, "What?" and his father told him to bring bourbon and water all around.

After the drinks were served we sat there sipping them and waiting for someone to say something. Lynch was leaning back in his chair, his hands crossed over his belly, his thin lips smiling gently, at peace with himself and, for all I knew, with the world.

"You banging that blonde yet, Dye?" It was Loambaugh, the chief of police, and he didn't look at me when he said it.

"Not yet," I said.

"You know what I'd like to do?" he said softly. I looked at him. With a better barber, he could have posed for an FBI recruiting poster, if they had any.

"What?" I said.

"I'd like to get my head right down there between her legs and then have somebody jump up and down on the back of it. That's what I'd like."

The mayor snuffled and said something that sounded like, "Pshaw." The other three grinned at each other and Lynch barked his fat man's laugh. The chief had set the tone for the meeting. The preliminaries were over. The niceties were dispensed with. Nut-cutting time had arrived. I had seen it done often enough before, usually with more polish and grace, but seldom with such dispatch.

Alex Couturier, the Chamber of Commerce lackey, was up next. "I don't know, chief," he said in an exaggerated drawl, "of a real warm summer evening I wouldn't mind taking it out and letting little old Orcutt have a go at it. Not so much sweating and flopping about. He appears to me like a real tube cleaner. How about that, Mr. Dye? Is that little old boss of yours as good as he sounds like?"

"He probably hasn't had as much time to practice as you have," I said and smiled my boyish grin, the one that I kept in reserve for such events as famine, flood, and afternoon sessions with professional country boys.

There was some more tittering by the mayor, and the rest of them did some honking and har-harring, which I assumed was laughter. There was no humor in any of it and they seemed to be the kind who laughed only at someone else's discomfort, but then that's what a lot of laughter stems from. All except Lynch. His deep chuckle sounded as if he really thought that my remark was funny, but he seemed to always chuckle like that.

It was Fred Merriweather's time at the plate. He rolled his stupid blue eyes and moved his big jaw around as if it were taking a couple of practice swings. Even before he spoke, he'd already lost my vote. "You know, I was just recollecting somebody that reminds me of that Orcutt feller." The city councilman paused and let his jaw ruminate about it for a few more moments. "Name was Sanderson and it was right after the war and he was shoe clerking at Mitchell and Farnes, I think it was."

"It was Mitchell and Farnes all right," the mayor said. "His name was Thad Sanderson and he taught Sunday School at the First Methodist when it was still over on Jasper Street."

"Believe you're right, Pete," Councilman Merriweather said and then rolled his blue eyes at me. "Feller reminded me of your Orcutt. Way he talked and walked and all, but none of us thought anything about it."

"That was way before my time," the police chief said, "but I remember hearing about it."

"Old man Kenbold was chief then," the mayor said.

"Well," the city councilman went on, still rolling his blue eyes at me, "they caught this Sanderson feller fooling around with these two youngsters. Weren't more'n eleven or twelve. Know what happened, Mr. Dye?"

"The chief of police went fishing," I said.

The stupid blue eyes popped a little at that. "How'd you know?"

"I just guessed."

"You're a pretty good guesser, aren't you?" said the current police chief.

"Just fair," I said.

"Maybe you can even guess what happened," the city councilman said.

"Probably. But I'll let you tell me."

Councilman Merriweather moved his jaw up and down again, leaned over the table toward me, and licked his lips with a furry, yellow tongue. Bad liver, I thought. "Well," he said, "a bunch of them caught him right in the act, so to speak, so they cut off his gonads with a dull old Barlow knife, but they didn't want him to bleed to death, so they doctored him up." He paused to snigger

130

a moment. "You know what they doctored him up with? Hot tar, that's what. Hot tar. Feller left town."

I nodded and waited. There was nothing to say.

Ancel Carp, the tax assessor, cracked the knuckles on his huge hands, looked up at the ceiling, and said, "I don't think Mr. Dye's too much interested in our past history. He's probably more interested in the current scene so if we've got anything to say, let's say it."

"Well, Ancel, I suppose that sort of serves it right into my court," Lynch said. "Reason we asked you here, Mr. Dye, is that we're just a little upset. Now this is a fine community. A fine one. And although I've only lived here about seven or eight years, I kind of like to think of myself as an adopted native son."

"That's the way we think of you, Ramsey," the mayor said.

"Thank you, your honor. But to get back to it. We don't get upset unless the town's upset. It's sort of like when the town's constipated, we fart." He paused and took a long drink of his bourbon. I'd barely touched mine.

"Well," Lynch said, "the symptoms started about a couple of months ago when this fella Homer Necessary came into town with his two-toned eyes and started asking around. He didn't come to any of us. He just nosed around asking questions that were sort of personal. We checked him out and found that he used to be a police chief himself up north. And not too honest a one at that, was he, Chief Loambaugh?"

"Crooked," the FBI poster said. "Crooked as cat shit."

"So after about a week or ten days of Necessary, we get your Mr. Orcutt and that girl friend of his, Miss Thackerty. Well, she's all right, but we're kind of country down here and maybe we're just not used to the likes of your Mr. Orcutt, especially if he's messing around with all the wrong people."

"Who're they?" I said.

"Well, let's just say they're not on our side."

"Who is?"

"The folks, Mr. Dye," Lynch said and his tone was no longer genial. "The folks in town are on our side."

"Then what are you worried about?"

"Folks can get foolish if they catch the notion. And

131

with a little investigation, we found out that your Mr. Orcutt was going to try to turn them into fools."

"How?"

"I hear," Lynch said in a gentle voice, "I hear that's where you come in."

I looked at my new watch. "I've been here for half an hour and you haven't said anything yet. You've talked a lot, but it's all been the kind of bullshit that I can hear in any four-table poolhall. You've got five more minutes. That's all."

"My brother said you were a little impatient, Mr. Dye."

"Your brother lies a lot."

"But good. Well, since your time is limited, I'll come to the point. We have some of our people in the other camp, so to speak, who tell us things, and they told us about how Mr. Orcutt was trying to find someone out in Asia who might be useful to him here in Swankerton. So, because Gerald's located out there and all, I spent about a couple of hundred dollars of my own money and called him up, told him the situation, and asked him to do what he could. I think he did real fine."

"By recommending me to Orcutt?"

"Well, he really recommended you to us first, if you know what I mean. He gave us a pretty good rundown on you and we told him to go ahead and recommend you to Mr. Orcutt. He said you're pretty good, Mr. Dye, but that you're awfully unlucky. I'm serious now. Bad luck just seems to dog some people and from what I hear, you're one of them. I mean what happened to your wife and all."

"You can leave that alone," I said.

Lynch nodded sympathetically. "I'm sorry I mentioned it. Really am. But you've had your share of bad luck, Mr. Dye. My brother Gerald seems to think that it'll probably continue. But he made me promise him one thing before he would recommend you to Mr. Orcutt."

"What?"

"Well, Gerald isn't really as superstitious about luck as he lets on. Deep down inside he really feels that people make their own. So he made us promise that we'd make some for you here in Swankerton. You can guess what kind. So you got a choice. We can either make you some bad luck or some good luck, despite what I promised my brother. Now just which one are you going to choose?"

They were all leaning forward a little, staring at me. "How much is the good luck worth?" I said.

"Twenty-five percent more than what Orcutt's paying you, whatever it is."

"And how much is your bad luck going for?" I said.

Lynch shook his head sadly and his chins bobbed alone in funereal time. "Well, Mr. Dye, bad luck is just bad luck. Let's say that the kind you might come by would be about as bad as luck can be."

I rose and looked at each of them, one at a time. "I'll think about it and let you know," I said and then moved to the door, stopping only at the sound of Lynch's voice. I turned and he was twisted around in his chair.

"Don't study about it too long, Mr. Dye," he said. "Neither good nor bad luck'll wait forever."

"You're forgetting one kind," I said.

"What's that, Mr. Dye?"

"Dumb luck—the kind you're going to need."

15

They flew Carmingler, of course, out to Hong Kong to deal with Gerald Vicker and me. I met him at the airport and he seemed none too happy with his assignment.

"I was on leave," he said, rather than hello or how are you. "My first in three years."

"I didn't ask for you."

He grunted at that, but said nothing else until we had picked up his bag and were in my rented Volkswagen. "Where's Vicker?"

"Waiting for you."

"At the office?"

"We flipped a coin to see who'd meet you. I lost."

"I read your report," Carmingler said. "Vicker's, too."

"That was thoughtful."

Carmingler turned to look at me. "I didn't fly out here just to listen to your smart cracks. Vicker writes a better report."

"He has a flair," I said.

"You're in trouble," Carmingler said.

"What about Vicker?"

Carmingler didn't say anything until he had used his usual three or four matches to light his pipe. "He's in trouble, too."

"Who's in deeper?" I said.

Carmingler puffed away on his pipe before answering. I glanced at him and he seemed to look less confident that usual. He looked gloomy. "I don't know," he said finally. "That's why I'm here."

"And when do you decide?"

He looked out the window at a new building that was going up. "Those workmen on the scaffolding," he said. "They're the highest-paid skilled labor in Hong Kong. Did you know that?"

"I live here," I said. "What are you going to do?"

Carmingler slumped down in the seat and put his bony

knees against the dashboard. It didn't look very comfortable, but they weren't my knees. "You know what Star Chamber justice is?"

"Yes."

"Well, that's what you're going to get. Both you and Vicker. I'm judge and jury."

"Old Judge Carmingler," I said. "The hanging judge."

"I didn't ask for this."

"Who did?"

Carmingler looked at me and smiled for the first time. "Vicker. He asked for me."

I said, "Oh."

Carmingler smiled again. Contentedly. "I thought that might cheer you up."

It could have been called a trial, I suppose. Whatever it was, it was held in my office late that afternoon after we sent the secretary home. Carmingler sat behind my desk and Vicker and I sat in front of it. Our Star Chamber judge carefully arranged six sharpened pencils on the desk beside a fresh yellow legal pad. Next he produced his pipe, tobacco pouch, and match box, and placed them within easy reach. He then adopted an expression which he may have thought was his best horse-sense look. He made his face as long as possible, showed both of us his teeth in an impartial manner, and nodded several times as if he were adjusting to some invisible halter. I almost expected to hear him neigh us to order.

"This place been swept recently?" he asked.

"This morning," Vicker said. "I had the consulate's man over."

"Good," Carmingler said and made a note that I was too far away to read upside down. He put the pencil on the pad, leaned back in his chair, and locked his hands behind his head. "Let's begin with the facts—the ones that nobody disputes. Both of you went to the rendezvous with Pai Chung-liang, the chap who worked for the Bank of China. Vicker hid in the back room. Dye stayed in the shop itself. Pai came in, said something to Dye, who handed him an envelope. Then Pai said something else, something that only Dye could hear. About that time the two Chinese busted in. Vicker shot Pai. The two Chinese snatched his briefcase and fled. Dye bent down and Pai either said or did not say something before he died." He looked at both of us. "Is that a fair summation?"

I nodded. So did Vicker.

Carmingler picked his briefcase up from the floor and rested it in his lap. He fished out a single sheet of paper that had some typing on it and placed it on the desk before him. He put the briefcase back on the floor.

"You were issued a side arm," he said to me. "A .38 Smith & Wesson, wasn't it?"

"Yes."

"You still have it?"

"Yes."

"Did you have it the day that Pai was killed?"

"No."

"Where is it now?"

"At home."

"In your hotel?"

"Yes."

"Do you always keep it there?"

"Yes."

"Where?"

"You mean where in the room?"

"That's right."

"In a locked suitcase. The suitcase is in a closet. The closet is also locked. It's a special lock. I'm the only one with a key."

"Why?"

"Do you mean why do I keep it there?"

"Yes."

I shrugged. "It seems safe enough."

"Don't you ever carry it?"

"No."

"Why not?"

"I don't have any use for it."

"Ever?"

"Ever."

Carmingler tapped the single sheet of paper. "It says here that you're very good with a gun. Or used to be. I seem to remember that you were. Why don't you ever carry it?"

"I just don't. I don't need it."

"You still don't think you needed it the day that Pai got shot?"

"No."

"And you don't think that Pai needed shooting?"

"No."

"Why?"

"You've got my report."

"Vicker doesn't have it."

"All right," I said. "I think they were on to Pai. I think they would have shot him that morning if Vicker hadn't saved them the trouble."

"Who tipped them off about your rendezvous with Pai?"

I looked at Vicker. "Ask him."

Carmingler nodded and made another note. I still couldn't read it. He turned to Vicker. He looked at him for several moments and for all I knew he may have been admiring Vicker's suit. It was a new one.

"You carry your side arm, don't you?" he said.

Vicker nodded. "Always."

"Why?"

"It's a tough town."

"Any other reason?"

"I'm in a tough business."

"In a tough town," Carmingler said.

"I think so."

Carmingler looked at the sheet of paper again. "Let's see. Mr. Pai was thirty-nine years old. He liked flowers. He liked figures and his wife. He was a bank clerk. He was just a little over five feet tall and weighed a hundred and twenty-eight pounds. And he didn't carry a gun. So you shot him."

"That's right," Vicker said.

"When?"

"Just after the two with the guns came in."

"Did they have their guns out when they came into the shop or did they start waving them around later—after you'd shot Pai?"

Vicker seemed to think about the question. "They had them out when they came in."

"You're sure?"

"Yes."

Carmingler nodded. "All right. We'll come back to that." He turned to me. "What do you remember? Did they have their guns out when they came in or did they pull them later?"

"They pulled them later. After Pai was shot."

"You're sure?"

"Yes."

He turned back to Vicker. "You say just the opposite—that the two men came into the shop with their guns drawn?"

"Yes."

"So you knew that they were opposition?"

"It was obvious."

"So you shot Pai."

"Yes."

"To keep him from doing what?"

"From fingering Dye."

"What do you mean by that?"

Vicker looked pained. "You know what fingering means, for God's sake. They were on to Pai. He was going to accuse Dye."

"Of what?" Carmingler said and made it sound as if he were deeply interested.

"Of having bribed him to feed Dye information from the bank."

"I see," Carmingler said and made another note.

"How long were you in the back room before Pai came in the shop?" Carmingler asked Vicker.

"Two or three minutes."

"Pai was prompt?"

"Yes."

"Did you have your gun in your hand when he entered or did you wait until the two men came in?"

"I didn't draw it until they came in."

"And you still say that they came in with their guns drawn?"

"Yes."

"They pulled the guns from their pockets on Upper Lascar? Wasn't it crowded as usual?"

Vicker crossed his legs. It was the first thing that he had moved other than his mouth. "It was crowded."

"Doesn't it seem strange that they would pull guns on a crowded street?"

"I didn't think about it."

"I find it very unlikely that they would."

Vicker shrugged. "Maybe they pulled them just as they entered the shop."

"Did you see them do that?"

"No."

"But if they hadn't pulled the guns, then you would

138

have thought they were just a couple of customers?"

"I suppose. Maybe."

"And if they hadn't pulled them, and if you had taken them for a couple of customers, you wouldn't have shot Pai? You would have let him tell Dye what he came to tell?"

Vicker waited before answering that one. Then he said yes.

"All right," Carmingler said, making another note. "Let's suppose, just for the hell of it, that Dye's version is correct. The two men didn't pull their revolvers or automatics or whatever until after you had shot Pai. If that's true, then you couldn't have known that they were the opposition, could you?"

"No."

"And you would have had no reason for shooting Pai? I mean he couldn't have fingered Dye to a couple of strangers?"

"That's right."

Carmingler reached for his briefcase again and produced a sheaf of papers. "This is the Hong Kong Special Branch report on the murder of one Pai Chung-liang. It's quite interesting. They're most thorough people, you know. They interviewed twenty-three persons before they came up with a reliable eyewitness. They then interviewed another fifty-two before they found one who could corroborate his story. Let's see, I'll just paraphrase it for you." Carmingler ran his right forefinger down the first sheet, flipped it over, and then ran it halfway down the second sheet. "Yes, here it is. At about ten o'clock on the morning in question two male foreigners (that's you two) dressed thus and so entered the shop on Upper Lascar . . . then the proprietor left . . . then a Chinese in a white suit carrying a briefcase entered . . . then two other Chinese entered . . . and, yes, here it is, no guns were visible. A few minutes later there was the sound of a single shot and the two Chinese were seen running from the shop carrying a briefcase. They disappeared. That's from the first witness. Another witness, a twelve-year-old boy, actually saw the whole thing. Through the shop's window. He backs up the first witness in full and then swears, or whatever they do here, that the two Chinese gentlemen in question did not pull their guns until after Pai was shot. So . . ." Carmingler put the report back into his briefcase. He put the briefcase on the floor and then smiled at Vicker.

"So," he said again. "We have two witnesses now who swear, or affirm, or whatever it is, that the pair didn't draw their guns until after you shot Pai."

"Who's the other witness besides the twelve-year-old?" Vicker said.

"Dye, of course," Carmingler said.

"Shit," Vicker said.

"So it would seem that you knew who the two gentlemen were before they even produced their guns. It would also seem that you had a very good reason for shooting Pai. I don't suppose you'd care to tell me what it was."

"It's the reason I gave you," Vicker said.

"Yes," Carmingler said. "Well, I think that does it nicely. You're through, Vicker. Don't remove anything from the office. Any personal effects will be sent to you. So will your back pay and leave time, if you have any coming. And by the way, don't try to stir this up in any fashion. Special Branch is still awfully anxious to talk to you and we've had a hell of a time smoothing things over."

Vicker looked at me and then back at Carmingler. "This goes to the review board, fella."

"No, it doesn't," Carmingler said. "Not if you think about it, it doesn't. Those two Chinese gentlemen. The opposition, as we're so fond of calling them. Unless they came in with drawn guns, you couldn't possibly have known who they were. But they didn't. That indicates that you knew who they were and that, I think you'll agree, might lead us all down a rather rocky path. We don't want that, Vicker, and you're lucky that we don't. Very lucky. So don't press."

Vicker frowned, first at Carmingler, then at me, and then back at Carmingler. It was a very sincere frown. His voice was level and low when he spoke. His brown eyes were steady. He lied beautifully. "I thought it was a setup when I shot Pai. I still do. What I think is in my report to you and I don't care how many so-called eyewitnesses Special Branch dug up. Somebody had to be the goat. Someone picked me and then sent you out to give me the news. I don't blame you, Carmingler. You're just the chore boy." He turned to look at me then. "But you're something else, Dye. You're really something. I owe you a lot. I really mean that. I owe you a hell of a lot and one of these days I'll remember to pay it all off." He rose then and headed for the door. He stopped when he was almost there and then his right arm flashed under his coat and a a .38 revolver appeared in his hand, the twin of the Smith & Wesson that I had locked away in a suitcase. He was fast. Too fast for his age. He looked at the gun, smiled slightly, and then walked over and laid it carefully on the desk next to the sharpened pencils. "This belongs under office equipment, I believe," he said, nodded at Carmingler, but not at me, and left.

Carmingler picked up a pencil and poked idly at the revolver. "Nasty things, aren't they?" he said.

"I liked the part about the twelve-year-old boy," I said.

"Yes."

"There wasn't any."

"No?"

"No. It wasn't even Star Chamber. Not even that. It was all laid on before you got here. It was locked in."

"You disagree with the verdict?"

"The method maybe. Not the verdict."

"The means," Carmingler said. "You don't like the means." He picked up his pipe and got it going again. "You don't really believe that we'd leave something like this to chance or whimsy?"

"Why not?" I said. "It would match everything else. Blend right in."

Carmingler nodded and looked out the window. Another new building was going up. Hong Kong was booming. "There're a couple of things I really like about old Vicker," he said.

"What?"

"Well, first of all he lies better than you do."

"Better than anybody."

"Secondly, his reports."

"What about them?"

"Very well written," Carmingler said. "Damned fine reading, in fact. It's a pity that there was hardly a word of truth in any of them."

"Why press about the gun?" I said. "That wasn't necessary."

"Yours?"

"Yes?"

"I was told to."

"You already knew."

141

Carmingler nodded, picked up a pencil again, and used it to shove the short barrel of Vicker's revolver back and forth. "You still don't like these things much, do you?"

"No."

"All because of your wife." It wasn't a question.

"That had a lot to do with it, but you knew that."

"I had to ask."

"Why?" I said.

"They thought you might have gotten over it, but you haven't."

"No."

We sat there in the office for a while, neither of us saying anything. Then Carmingler shoved Vicker's gun over to me with the pencil. "Here," he said, "you can lock this one away with yours. I don't think you'll ever use one again."

"No," I said, "I probably won't."

16

It must have been freezing inside Bridge House prison the day that Captain Toyofuku came for Gorman Smalldane and me. He really didn't come for me, but Smalldane insisted that I be permitted out of the cell for the first time in three months, and Toyofuku simply nodded his agreement. He didn't speak. It was the first decent thing that I had seen any of the Japanese do and I should have noted the date, but all I can remember is that it was some-time in March, 1942.

Escorted by two bundled-up guards, we were led to a small room on the second floor of Bridge House. It was warmer there and Toyofuku motioned us to a couple of chairs. He sat behind a table, stripped off his gloves, and produced a package of cigarettes, offering one to Small-dane.

"How about the kid?" Smalldane said, taking a ciga-rette. "He hasn't had a smoke in three months."

Toyofuku looked at me, shook his head sadly, and of-fered me a cigarette. I accepted it with a grateful sitting-down-type bow.

After we were all lighted up, Toyofuku gazed at Smalldane and said, "You've got a lot of big-shot friends in the States, don't you?" His accent was pure California, which meant that it had about as much regional character as a bowl of cold oatmeal.

Smalldane picked it up. "I'll make two guesses. The first is UCLA. The second is Southern Cal."

"Berkeley," Toyofuku said. "Class of thirty-eight. Your son's too young to smoke."

"That's what I've told him."

"Slap the shit out of him a couple of times and he'll stop. It's not the Japanese way, but it works."

"I'll remember that."

Toyofuku nodded approvingly. "Now let's not go through how I was caught in Japan when the war broke out and was forced into the army. I wasn't. I joined in

1940. I should make major next month. I like it fine and with a few breaks we'll keep a lot of what we've already taken. Not the Philippines necessarily, but maybe Indochina, Malaya, the East Indies, and some of the islands."

"What about China?" Smalldane said.

"Nobody can take China."

"Treason."

"Make the most of it," Toyofuku said and smiled for the first time. "But as I said you've got a lot of big-shot friends in the States. So you're on the list. We were going to shoot you."

"Why?" Smalldane said.

"You wrote nasty things about us in Manchouku in 1932. Then you wrote some more nasty things when you came back in thirty-nine. We've got long memories, but you've got big-shot friends. If we hadn't agreed to put you on the list, then they were going to take one of our bankers off. He's in New York now and we'd very much like him to come home."

"This is the repatriation list?" Smalldane said.

"Right. It's divided into five classifications: diplomatic and consular officials, correspondents, missionaries, Canadians, and Latin Americans. Also some businessmen."

"When do we leave?"

"That presents a problem," Toyofuku said. "I studied business administration at Berkeley. The stock market fascinated me. So did the commodity market. I learned all about hedging."

Smalldane grunted and ground out his cigarette. I still had a couple of puffs left. "How much?"

"Three thousand for you. Two thousand for the kid."

"What about that banker in New York?"

"You could always come down with pneumonia and die. They'd just exchange him for somebody else."

"I haven't got five thousand."

"You can get it. Just write a note." Toyofuku took a pad from a pocket and handed it to Smalldane along with a thick fountain pen. "She's still in good health and prosperous. She married, you know."

Smalldane looked up. "I didn't."

"A Frenchman. She's now a Vichy citizen. Sort of an ally of mine."

Smalldane finished the note and handed it to Toyofuku, who read it and said, "It tugs at the heart strings."

"I gave it my all," Smalldane said.

"You'll sail in two or three months on the *Conte Verde*. It's Italian. The *Gripsholm* will sail out of New York with our people. You'll rendezvous at Lourenço Marques in Portuguese East Africa and trade ships. The *Gripsholm* will take you to New York, the *Conte Verde* will bring our people to Japan. Probably Kobe." He tapped the note that Smalldane had written. "If this works, I'll let her see you off."

"How many bets are you hedging?" Smalldane asked.

"Twenty or so. It's my personal share in the greater co-prosperity sphere."

"I think you think you'll lose."

Toyofuku shrugged. It must have been something he'd learned in San Francisco. Possibly from an Italian girl friend. "If we do, we'll bounce back. And with a hundred thousand bucks I'll be right on the ground floor."

"You know something, Captain?"

"Yes?"

"I'm not really so sure that you could keep anyone off that repatriation list."

Toyofuku picked up the note from the table and offered it back to Smalldane. "Would you like to bet your lives against it?"

Smalldane shook his head. "No, and I don't want to play poker with you either."

Toyofuku smiled for the second time. "I didn't think that you would."

Except for the wide-spread bribing, the International Red Cross handled the whole thing out of Geneva. Only three of us left the cell at Bridge House in late May: Smalldane, me, and the redheaded man who claimed to be a Mexican. They took us to General Hospital, where we were examined by a British doctor. Except for the lice, he complimented us on our health and then gave us a series of inoculations which made me sick. They also gave us some new clothing and Smalldane grinned when I insisted that I be permitted to change mine in complete privacy.

"He's very shy," he said to a nurse.

I wasn't really. I needed the privacy to shift my hoard of dollars and pounds from the lice-infested money belt to the pockets of my new clothing. I distributed it evenly to avoid bulges.

We stayed in the hospital for ten days and then a truck came to take us to the *Conte Verde*. Smalldane was carrying our vaccination certificates and an authorization that allowed us to draw $100 each from the ship's purser for incidental expenses. Before we left for the ship, Smalldane borrowed $10 from me to spend on a wardboy, a born scrounger, who came back an hour later with the order: six pairs of dice.

The *Conte Verde* was one of the better Italian liners that sailed the Pacific route to the Orient and had been caught in Shanghai on December 8. It carried an Italian crew of about 300, and would sail for East Africa with a contingent of Japanese foreign-office officials aboard to make sure that Japan's new allies didn't head straight for San Francisco. None of the Italian crew seemed overly patriotic.

Tante Katerine met us at the dock with a basket of fruit, booze, cigarettes, and her new husband, a wisp of a man, about sixty-five, whom she introduced as M'sieu Gauvreau in French and as Mr. Softstick in English, assuring us that he didn't understand a word.

"He does something in the Vichy government," Tante Katerine said, holding my hand in both of hers, "but nothing in bed." She shrugged, released my hand, and patted her new husband on the cheek. He smiled, delighted at any attention.

"Lucifer's too thin and you owe me eleven thousand dollars," she said to Smalldane. "That Captain Toyofuku was such a nice man, but greedy."

"There's a redheaded Mexican on board," I said.

"Don't trust him," Tante Katerine said automatically. "When do you intend to repay me, Gorm?"

"After the war."

"Yes," she said and smiled sadly. "After the war."

"What are your plans, Kate?" Smalldane said.

"Fatten Lucifer up," she said. "He's far too thin."

"He's been in jail. What are your plans?"

She turned to smile at her husband and to tell him in French that he wouldn't be shivering if he had worn his long underwear as she had suggested. He replied that the weather was too warm and that it made him itch. She said that she had no desire to become a widow and he said that he would wear it from now on even if it did make him itch. It was all very domestic and it was one of

146

those conversations about nothing that somehow become inextricably stuck in memory. It's really the only thing I remember that M. Gauvreau ever said.

"I have no plans, Gorm," Tante Katerine said, turning from her husband. "He talks about returning to France, but he's only dreaming. They have no use for him there. My only plans are to keep alive. As long as he lives, the Japanese will let me alone. Just promise me one thing."

"What?" Smalldane said.

"Take care of Lucifer. Get him safely to America."

"All right."

"See that he brushes his teeth."

"All right."

"Make him change his underwear."

"All right."

"Lucifer."

"Yes, Tante Katerine."

"Look after Gorman."

"Yes, ma'am."

"Don't let him drink too much."

"Yes, ma'am."

"Keep him away from the *poules*. The bad ones at least."

"Yes, ma'am."

She leaned down to kiss me and then fussed with my clothing, straightening it here and there. "I'll miss you, Lucifer. Don't trust that redheaded Mexican. Stay away from him."

"Yes, ma'am."

She turned back to Smalldane. "I don't want to come aboard, Gorm. I don't think I could."

"I know."

He kissed her then. It was a long, friendly, warm, passionate, memorable kiss that I watched with delight. M. Gauvreau turned his head and cleared his throat, but no one paid him any attention.

A harried official from the Swiss Consulate stopped to tell us to get aboard. Tante Katerine backed away from Smalldane, still holding his hands. I think she was doing Ginger Rogers then. "Come back to me, Gorm," she said. "Come back to me in Shanghai."

Smalldane winked at her, gathered her up in his arms again, and then smacked her sharply on the butt. M. Gauvreau hissed in some breath.

147

"We'll both come back, Kate."

She nodded, her right fist to her mouth, a few tears streaming down her cheeks, but not so many that they would ruin her makeup. She waved a little with her left hand as we started up the gangplank. When we were halfway up, Smalldane whispered to me, "Don't ruin her scene. Turn and wave at her and rub your knuckles in your eyes like you're crying."

I turned and waved and knuckled my left eye.

"Gorm!" Tante Katerine shouted.

Smalldane turned. "What?" he yelled.

"Make him change his underwear."

It was the last thing she said, the last time I ever saw her.

We sailed out of Shanghai on June 8, 1942, carrying 1,036 missionaries, both ecclesiastical and medical, nurses, State Department types, correspondents, most of whom Smalldane knew, children, wives, assorted businessmen with varying degrees of influence, a handful of Canadians, two spies (or so Smalldane said), a smuggled kitten, and one redheaded Mexican.

We sailed for Singapore where the Japanese liner *Asama Maru* joined us on June 10. She was carrying North and South Americans from Korea, Japan, and Manchuria. She was just out of Hong Kong, where she had stopped to pick up some more U.S. and Canadian citizens. As soon as we had cleared Singapore and were sailing south toward the Dutch East Indies and the Coral Sea, Smalldane made me his proposition. We spent the next two days going over figures before I agreed to finance the venture that eventually was to launch Smalldane Communications, Inc.

It was a crap game, of course, and when Smalldane got through explaining the odds to me, he made a projection of the profit potential.

"We've got about a thousand persons aboard," he said. "Let's say that three hundred of them are gamblers. When we reach Lourenço Marques the passengers aboard the *Asama Maru* will double up with us on the *Gripsholm*. That'll give us a total of some sixteen hundred passengers. Out of that there should be five hundred hard-nosed gamblers—the kind who'll bet their last dime. Now we

148

know that they've all got the hundred-dollar draw from the purser. So one hundred times five hundred is what?"

"Fifty thousand," I said.

"Jesus Christ," he said. "We're rich."

"But it is still gambling," I said.

"Of course it's gambling."

"In that event one must lose so that the other might win," I said, switching to French to help the logic of my thoughts along.

"Oui, M'sieu Petit Merde," Smalldane said.

"Then I stand the chance to lose my money, and you much face. I would very much like it the other way around."

"The odds," Smalldane said. "Remember the odds. We bet only against the dice. We bank the game. Time is on our side. Sixty to seventy-five days. Maybe three months."

"The risk is great."

"The rewards are greater."

"I don't think—"

"I have been in deep conversation with the redheaded Mexican," Smalldane said in Cantonese. "He is a man of much wealth but strange tastes. He longs for you, but is shy. He has offered me a modest sum to—"

"When do we start the game?" I said.

"Tonight," he said. "I was lying about the Mexican, kid."

"I know," I said. "Already he sleeps with two of the nurses from Hong Kong."

The wire services were the first to fall. AP dropped a little more than $300; UP was good for $275, and INS had only $100 to contribute. Smalldane lent it all back to them on markers at ten percent interest for the remainder of the trip. Collectively, they lost somewhere around $2,000. The doctors and businessmen were next. My job was to return the dice to the proper shooter and quote the odds.

"Two to one no four," I said to a portly physician from New York.

"Hard way, dice," the portly physician said on his knees and bounced them against the bulkhead for a seven. Smalldane gathered up the money. I handed the dice to the next shooter. By the time we arrived in Lourenço Marques on July 23, 1942, the *Conte Verde* crapshooters

149

were broke, we were $21,795 in the black and anxious for the fresh meat aboard the *Asama Maru*.

The Swedish passenger liner *Gripsholm* was already docked at Lourenço Marques when the *Conte Verde* and the *Asama Maru* arrived and docked on either side of her. The crap game was suspended until the new supply of gamblers assembled on the *Gripsholm*. I wandered up to the deck while the rest of the passengers were packing and getting ready to debark. A Japanese boy of about my age was leaning over the rail of the *Gripsholm,* spitting into the water. He looked up, and we stared at each other.

"How's the food on that tub?" he said.

"Lousy," I said. "How's it on yours?"

"Lousy."

He leaned over and spat into the water again. I did the same thing from my rail.

"Where you from?" he said.

"Shanghai. Where you from?"

"New York."

We played spit in the ocean again.

"You American?" he said.

"I don't know," I said. "I guess. You Japanese?"

He nodded slowly and spat one more time. "That's what they tell me," he said.

The crap game started up two days after we left Lourenço Marques bound for Rio, and by the time we had rounded the Cape of Good Hope, the informal gaming firm of Smalldane and Dye was $39,792 ahead. I helped Smalldane count it. When we were finished he looked at me. "Let's quit winners, Lucifer."

"Whatever you say."

"We've got enough."

"What will we do with it?"

"You're going to get an education with yours."

"I am already educated."

"You don't even know how to read and write."

"I am wise in the ways of the world."

"Where'd you learn that one?"

I shrugged. "I heard it some place."

Smalldane shook his head. "Okay, let's agree that you're smart. You can shill a crap game, pimp for a whorehouse, speak six or seven languages, roll drunks, and hustle the rubes. But you can't read or write and you're goddamned well going to school to learn how."

"Will you go too, Gorman?"

"No."

"Why not?"

"I'm too old."

"What will you do?"

"I don't know yet, kid. But I think I've got an idea."

In Rio the FBI agents came aboard and started asking Smalldane how he'd acquired a son since he had never married.

"What do you care?" he said. "The kid's American."

"We've checked your record, Mr. Smalldane. You've never even been engaged."

"So he's a bastard."

There were two of them. One was rather young, somewhere in his twenties. The other was older, thirty-five or so. Both were suspicious.

"If he's not an American citizen, Mr. Smalldane, he can't be permitted to enter the—"

"Tell them, Lucifer."

"My name is William Smalldane. I was born in San Francisco on—"

"For Christ's sake, the real one," Smalldane said.

"Oh," I said. "I am eight years old and my name is Lucifer Clarence Dye and I was born December 5, 1933, in Moncrief, Montana, United States of America, and my father's name was Dr. Clarence Dye and I live at—at—" I stopped.

"He lives with me," Smalldane said. "He's my ward."

"Where are his parents?" the younger man asked.

"Dead."

"This is most irregular," the older man said, and it was the first time I'd heard that phrase. I regret that it wasn't the last.

"Cable Moncrief, Montana, and find out whether there was a Lucifer Clarence Dye born there on December 5, 1933, like the kid says."

"Well, if you'll accept responsibility for him—"

"I'll accept it. Where do I sign?"

"That'll be done in New York," the older one said. "Still, I don't know."

"Hell, he's too dumb to be a spy," Smalldane said. "He can't even read or write."

That was when I made up my mind to go to school.

On the voyage to New York from Rio a couple of the passengers panicked over what they claimed to be Nazi submarines, but nothing happened and we docked in Manhattan on August 26, 1942. There was nobody to meet us.

Once through officialdom's incredible red tape, we took a cab to the Gotham where Smalldane had reserved us a room. He'd won the reservation from a correspondent who had had nothing left to gamble. When we were in the room and the money was in the hotel's safe, Smalldane produced a package wrapped in red paper.

"It's from Kate," he said. "It was in the bottom of that basket of fruit and whisky. She told me to give them to you when we got to New York."

"What are they?"

"Your father's diaries. She wants you to read them."

"But I can't read."

"Kate said for you to learn."

17

Booboo Robineaux drove me back to the hotel from the session with what I suppose could be called Swankerton's city fathers. About halfway there I asked him "Why do they call you Booboo?"

"My friends don't," he said. "Just my father."

"What do your friends call you?"

"Boo."

I thought about asking him how his face had come to be so nicely stitched, but I was afraid that it might turn into a longer story than I really wanted to hear, so I didn't, but instead just thanked him for the lift.

I unlocked the door to my room in the Sycamore and started in. The venetain blinds were down and the drapes were drawn. They hadn't been that way when I left. It was dark. The door opened to my right so I slammed it against the wall, but it didn't hit the wall. It hit someone who grunted. I started backing quickly into the corridor, but I didn't move fast enough. I heard a faint sound like the beginning of a sigh, perhaps a sigh of regret, and something hard smashed into my left shoulder. I kept backing into the corridor and bumped against someone. I turned and it was Homer Necessary who gave me a genial smile.

"Trouble?" he said.

I massaged my shoulder with my right hand. "Trouble," I said. "Two of them."

"Well, now," he said and smiled again. "Which side of the door is the light switch on?"

I thought a moment. "The left. Just inside. There're two of them."

Necessary reached into his right hip pocket and brought out a woven leather blackjack. He thumped it into his left palm. "Well, now," he said again and moved to the door, reached his arm quickly around the jamb, and switched on the room's overhead light. He was fast despite his bulk. He went in low, whirled, and the blackjack started up

153

from near his ankles. I couldn't see it land, but I heard it. It was a wet smack. Necessary turned to his left, still moving quickly, almost sinuously, like an overstuffed snake. Then he stopped, straightened, and grinned at me.

"He doesn't want to get out from behind the door," Necessary said. "You might as well come on in."

I went in. On the floor at my left was the crumpled up body of a man. He wore a yellow velour short-sleeved shirt and tan khaki slacks. He wasn't more than twenty-two or twenty-three and some blood drooled out of the left corner of his mouth. A piece of pipe wrapped in black friction tape lay a few inches from his right hand.

"Just reach over careful-like and close the door," Necessary said. "You might even sort of slam it."

I slammed the door shut. Behind it was another member of what I suppose is the misunderstood generation. He was all of twenty, wore a short-sleeved shirt with a turtleneck, some unsuccessful sideburns, and a panicky look. He carried a nine-inch length of tape-wrapped pipe in his right hand, but he seemed to have forgotten it.

Necessary slapped his blackjack into the palm of his left hand a couple of times. "Just drop it, kid," he said. "Just drop it on to the floor." The youngster looked at the pipe, smiled feebly and a little foolishly, and let the pipe fall to the carpet.

"Now go and sit in that chair over there," he said. The youth moved to the chair that Necessary indicated and lowered himself into it. He still looked panicky.

I bent over the one who lay on the floor. "He's not hurt bad," Necessary said. "I didn't even break his jaw, but he might have a few loose teeth. I got him right along here." I looked up and watched him move his right forefinger along his jaw, just below the left ear.

"You're good," I said to Necessary, rising.

"Uh-huh," he said. "I know." Then he turned to the young man in the chair. "You got a name?"

"Frank. Frank Smith. That's the God's truth. It's Smith."

Necessary returned the blackjack to his hip pocket and slapped Frank Smith across the face. It was a hard, brisk slap. "That's what you get for telling the truth, Frank. You can just let your imagination work on what you're going to get when you start lying."

Not if, I noticed, but when. I lit a cigarette and

154

watched the ex-chief of police operate. I decided that he must have enjoyed his former line of work.

"How much?" Necessary said.

"For what?"

Necessary slapped him again. "Fifty bucks. Each."

"Who? I mean who paid you?"

"I don't know. Just a guy."

That earned him another slap.

Frank Smith's face was red now from both rage and the slaps. "He was just a guy, I tell you. We meet him in Emmett's—"

"What's Emmett's?" Necessary said.

"We shoot pool there, hang around, you know."

Necessary shook his head. "It always starts in a poolhall," he said. "It always starts with just a guy. What did just a guy look like, Frank?"

Frank Smith moved his shoulders up and down a little. "I don't know. Christ, he was about average."

Necessary reached into his hip pocket and took out the blackjack. He did it casually, as if fishing out a pack of cigarettes. Frank Smith tried to ignore it, but failed. It fascinated him.

"I don't want to use this on your arm, Frank." Necessary said. "Right below your shoulder. It'll make it sore. Maybe for weeks. I don't want you to have a sore arm. I don't think you do either, do you?"

"No." It was barely a whisper.

Necessary slapped the blackjack into his left palm again. He had a certain way of doing it so that it made a crackling sound as if he were breaking all the bones in his hand. I wondered what old-time cop he had learned that from.

"He was medium heighth—" Frank Smith pronounced height with a "th" at the end and I couldn't see how he would profit from it if I were to correct him. "Around five foot nine or ten. Weighed maybe hundred and fifty, hundred and sixty. Black hair. He had on a suit, I remember. A tan suit."

"What color were his eyes?"

"I don't know," Frank Smith said. "Shit, I don't remember the color of his eyes."

"You'd be in trouble if you did," Necessary said. "What'd he call himself?"

"He didn't."

155

"No name at all?"

Frank Smith shook his head.

"You ever see him before?"

"No."

"Okay. What'd he say? Everything you can remember."

"Well, he says there's this guy over in eight-nineteen in the Sycamore and this guy owed him some gambling money and won't pay. So he says he'll give us fifty apiece to mess the guy up a little. Then he gives us the key to the room and an envelope to leave with the guy when we get done."

"What else, Frank?"

"Well, he says the guy's out of the hotel right now and we can wait for him in his room. Then he gives us the fifty each and we come on over and start waiting."

"Why you?"

"Huh?"

The "huh" won him another slap. "Why'd he pick you two, Frank?" Necessary said, and his voice was curiously gentle.

Frank Smith didn't seem to find much comfort in the tone. "I don't know—and don't hit me! He seemed to know us. He walked right up to us and called us by name."

"How many times've you been booked, Frank?"

"Three. Maybe four."

"Car theft?"

"Once."

"Assault?"

"Maybe twice."

"D and D?"

"Once."

"What else?"

"Nothing."

"What else, Frank?"

"Nothing. I swear."

"How much time in the joint?"

"Six months." Frank Smith muttered it.

"Car theft?"

"Yeah."

"State?"

"At Mandersfield."

"How old are you?"

"Twenty-one."

"What's your buddy's name?"

"Joe Carson."

"Where'd you meet him, at Mandersfield?"

"Uh-huh."

"What was he in for?"

"Breaking and entry. He done a year."

"How long've you been out?"

"Couple of months."

Joe Carson groaned and I turned around. Necessary didn't bother. Carson moved a little, but it was really only a twitch.

"Either of you on parole?" Necessary said.

"No. We done it all."

"You're lucky."

Joe Carson groaned again and this time Necessary turned to look at him. Then he looked at his watch and nodded in a satisfied way. "Just about right," he said, more to himself than to anyone else. He turned back to Frank Smith. "You got the envelope?"

"Joe's got it," Frank Smith said.

"Well, then, I want you to go over to Joe and get the envelope and hand it to Mr. Dye who you were supposed to give it to in the first place. I also want you to give me the fifty bucks that 'just a guy' gave you and I also want the fifty he gave Joe over there. You got that?"

Frank Smith nodded and moved over to Carson. He took an envelope from Carson's hip pocket, found the fifty dollars, and returned to where Necessary stood. "You want the money?" he said to Necessary.

"That's right."

"Here's Joe's fifty." He handed it over. Then he dug into his own pocket and came up with another wad of bills. "Here's mine." Necessary stuffed them into his own pocket.

"He gets the envelope?" Frank Smith said. He seemed determined to do everything correctly.

"That's right," Necessary said.

"Here," Frank Smith said and handed me the envelope.

"Now drag him out of here before he wakes up and vomits all over the place," Necessary said.

"That's all?"

"That's all, Frank."

"Yessir."

Frank Smith bent over Carson, grasped him under the armpits, and started dragging him toward the door. Carson groaned again. "Can you get the door, mister?" Frank Smith said to me. I held it open while he dragged Carson into the corridor. "What do I do with him now?" he said.

"That's your problem," I said and closed the door.

"How was your meeting?" Necessary said.

I nodded my head as I opened the envelope. "They propositioned me."

"What's it say?"

I handed the single sheet to him. It was printed in penciled block letters. Necessary read it aloud, giving each word the same emphasis as those who aren't accustomed to reading aloud usually do. "Just a sample," he read. "Next time is for keeps." He shook his head. "Amateurs," he said.

"Maybe."

"Pros don't give away second chances."

"I know."

"They may try again and then it won't be a couple of punks."

"Probably not."

"It bother you?"

"Sure it bothers me," I said.

"That's good. I'd be a little worried if it didn't." He sighed deeply. "I guess I'd better stick a little closer."

"You did fine a while ago. Thanks."

"Orcutt sent me down."

"He want something?"

Necessary shook his head. "He just got a hunch. He gets them sometimes. So he got a hunch that I should come down to your room. He was right." He paused a moment. "As usual."

"I'll thank him too."

"We'd better go see him."

"Has he got a drink up there?"

"Sure."

"All right. Let's go."

Necessary started toward the door but paused. "You want I should split the hundred with you?"

"You keep it."

"Half's yours if you want it."

"You earned it," I said.

He started moving toward the door again and again

158

stopped. "What'd they really want with you at that meeting?"

"They wanted to know if I was banging Carol Thackerty yet."

"What'd you tell them?"

"The truth. I said not yet."

18

Major Albert Schiller and I got hit within thirty seconds of each other on April 17, 1953, about halfway up—or down—the Korean hill called Pork Chop which they made a motion picture about some years later. I think it starred Gregory Peck. The major and I could have used him. I was then nineteen years old and a master sergeant, the youngest in the entire United States Army, or so I'd been told. The major was thirty-six which made him, he falsely claimed, the oldest major in the army, and he didn't make lieutenant colonel until shortly before he retired in 1961.

We had stumbled halfway to the top of Pork Chop Hill to set up our equipment at an outpost supposedly held by E Company of the 31st Infantry. The equipment consisted of a battery of loudspeakers similar to those used for public address systems in ball parks, college gymnasiums, and football stadiums. I was to use the speakers to address the CCF from the E-Company outpost. I was to insult the CCF, revile it, even taunt it.

"Hit 'em right in the guts, son," the general had said to me. "Make 'em wonder who's screwing their wives. Make 'em itchy to get home. You know, undermine their morale."

The CCF, whose morale I was supposed to undermine, was of course the Communist Chinese Forces who were more or less ignoring the truce negotiations that were then underway at Panmunjom.

Major Schiller had dreamed up the project all by himself and then went scouting for a Chinese-speaking American. He found me, fresh from the States, in an infantry repple depple and promptly had me transferred to what he fondly called his "little psy-war shop." He somehow had convinced a National Guard general of the merit of his scheme and the general personally had bucked most of Schiller's proposed table of organization through channels. The approval enabled the major to zoom me from private to master sergeant in two weeks. I had a corporal who was a clerk-typist under my command and together we composed all that there was of Major Schiller's little psy-war shop.

On April 15, 1953—or 15 April 53, as the army likes to write it—the major got permission from the general to launch the project that was supposed to undermine Chinese morale to the point where they would lay down their arms and rush back home. But first, the major and I went calling on the general to show off my proficiency in Chinese. "Say something in Chinese, sergeant," the general said, so I smiled and called him the abandoned son of a syphilitic running dog.

"Sure knows it, doesn't he, sir?" Major Schiller said and smiled at me fondly. "Of course, he won't talk that politely to them. He'll talk to them in gutter Chinese that'll hit 'em right where it hurts."

"Right in the guts, son," the general said again.

"Right in the guts, sir," the grizzled young sergeant with the steely eyes replied.

I didn't see any reason to mention that most of the CCF around Pork Chop Hill were probably Mongolians and would understand less than ten percent of what I was saying. I rationalized that they would at least recognize that it was Chinese and probably assume that it wasn't a pep talk. I further rationalized that being a master sergeant in a little psy-war shop was far better than being a replacement rifleman in a line company. Anything was better.

E Company of the 31st Infantry Regiment of the 7th Division had sent back word that the CCF was whooping it up with chants and Mongolian music. The major had convinced the general that it would be a "damned fine spot to give 'em a bit of their own medicine." Major Schiller knew a lot of clichés and used them lavishly.

So we rounded up a squad or so of spare riflemen who were dogging it on sick call, loaded them and the speakers and amplifiers into jeeps, and headed for Pork Chop Hill. When the jeeps could go no farther, we loaded the equipment on to the riflemen's backs. The infantry, I thought at the time, hadn't changed much in the last three thousand years or so.

Major Schiller had found himself a swagger stick some place, probably the only one in Korea other than those employed by the officers of England's two brigades, and he led us up Pork Chop Hill, swishing the swagger stick around and checking every few minutes to see that his .45 Colt automatic hadn't fallen out of its holster.

By the time we were halfway to E Company, it had been overrun by the Chinese and most of its men were either killed, wounded or captured. We no longer needed the loudspeakers and the amplifiers to insult the CCF. A conversational tone would do nicely. Major Schiller summoned his ranking non-coms (both of us) for a strategy conference. The corporal and I agreed that a rapid withdrawal would be expedient. The riflemen abandoned the expensive amplifiers and speakers and joined the discussion. To a man, they backed the major's decision.

It wasn't really a withdrawal. It wasn't even a retreat. It was a rout. I carried a Thompson .45 submachine gun that I'd found along the way. The major had lost his swagger stick and now gestured with his .45, but only after I had made sure that the safety catches were on. We plunged down a deep gully, the major still in the lead. Two Chinese soldiers popped out at us from behind a rock outcropping. The major tried to shoot them with his automatic, but he'd forgotten about the safety catches. I yelled, "Stinking turtles!" in Mandarin at the two Chinese, which they may or may not have understood, but which was enough of a surprise to make them hesitate. As I yelled, I dived for the cover of a rock to the left of the major and fired the Thompson as I went. I didn't hit anything.

The two Chinese were both armed with the highly prized, Soviet-made 7.62mm PPsh 41 burp gun. They must have had them on full automatic because they each fired long bursts at the major and me for at least forty-five seconds. If fully loaded, it meant that they had fired 144 rounds. They were rotten shots, but not all that rotten. One of the 144 rounds ricocheted into my right thigh. Another creased the major's right forearm and made him drop his automatic, which he still hadn't fired. I poked my head around the rock and saw that the Chinese were trying to change magazines, but that they weren't too quick at it, so I killed them both with the Thompson, aiming it low and watching with satisfaction as it climbed up and to the left just as the sergeant at Fort Hood had promised me that it would.

Major Schiller put me in for the Silver Star and got the National Guard general to recommend him for the Distinguished Service Cross, but neither of the medals ever made it past corps headquarters. They did, however, give us a couple of Purple Hearts and then sent us back to recuperate at Brooke General Hospital at Fort Sam Houston in San Antonio.

Major Schiller quickly recovered and landed his usual cushy job, this time in Fort Sam's Public Information Office, where his principal daily task was to issue press releases about the posthumous awarding of medals to the mothers and wives of dead servicemen. The releases were sent to the hometown newspapers and to the San Antonio *Light* and *Express* and they invariably began: "In a brief but stirring ceremony, the Silver Star today was awarded to . . ." It was the same release that the Public Information Office had been using since 1942 and they were used to it. So were the rewrite men on the *Light* and the *Express*.

Schiller had promoted himself a large house on the post not too far from the Snake Hill area of cheap bars at Fort Sam's south end. He lived there with his wife, Ruby, an accomplished legal-engineering secretary who made more money than Schiller, something that never bothered him in the least.

The major looked like a soldier. He was tall, carried himself well, wore his uniform beautifully, and had spent most of World War II in London and Paris on what he called a "sensitive assignment." He had a bachelor's degree from a small college in Pennsylvania and when he was drafted in 1941 he was selling time for a radio station. Before that, he sold Willys cars. When asked about his civilian experience, Schiller always said that he had been "involved" in "radio promotion" and prior to that he had been "involved" in "the management side of the automotive industry."

He had a nose that just missed being a beak, a high, intelligent-looking forehead, thick black hair, a good, thin-lipped smile, and puzzled, blue eyes. He also had boundless enthusiasm for any project at hand, a remarkable ability to forget past failures, and a bad case of satyriasis. He tried to screw anything in skirts and often as not succeeded.

They had decided to discharge me from the army in late May of 1953 despite my lack of points. It was mostly because they didn't know what to do with a nineteen-year-old master sergeant. I had been hanging around the hospital ward, waiting for them to make up their minds, when Schiller dropped by to see me. He came by once or twice a week, usually to borrow ten or twenty until payday. He was always broke.

"Well, I fixed it, son. You go to work next Monday morning."

"I go to work where?"

"In PIO. You're my new civilian assistant. Thirty-six fifty a year. How's that?"

"Lousy."

It didn't faze the major. "Well, it's not too hot to start with, but I can probably jump you a grade or two after a few months."

"In a few months I'll be back in school. I told you that."

Schiller made one of his more expansive gestures with a new swagger stick. He had six of them, his wife later told me. "Well, hell, Lu, take it for the summer. What else have you got to do?"

"What'll I have to do at PIO?"

"Just what I said. You'll be my assistant."

"What do you do?"

Schiller looked around the ward to see whether anyone was listening. They weren't. They were reading Captain Marvel as usual. "Just between you and me and the gatepost, not a hell of a lot, but I have a good time doing it."

"What'll I have to do?" I said again.

"Well, you'll accompany me on my appointed rounds. We check into the office about nine, leave for coffee at ten, then lunch at the officer's club at twelve, back to the office at two. Downtown to the newspapers at two-thirty and then to the Gunther Hotel for a refreshing bottle of Pearl beer and to review the day's activities. How's it sound?"

"Exhausting," I said.

"We have a staff car."

"What else?"

"A WAC driver."

"You screwing her?"

164

"Not any more. She's all yours."

"Thanks."

"But now the piece of resistance." Despite Paris, the major's French was nonexistent.

"What?"

"You live with us."

"With you and Ruby?"

"I've already talked it over with her. Room and board for only seventy-five bucks a month and you supply your own liquor. Or most of it."

"That house only costs you eighty-five."

"Home-cooking, Lu. Ruby's own."

"I'll think about it," I said.

"What else have you got to do until September?"

"I know a guy in New York. I should go see him."

"See him in September. And by the way, there's an added attraction."

"I'm already underwhelmed," I said, stealing a line from somebody. But even a stolen line was wasted on Schiller.

"Weekly poker with the brass. I don't mean captains and lieutenants and light-colonels. The real brass. Nothing less than a bird colonel."

"Except you."

"I'm in public relations," Schiller said, as if that sliced through all social barriers. I don't know, maybe it does.

"I'm an EM," I said. "You know, an enlisted man, the people that the Pentagon designs uniforms for with the nicely padded hips and the carefully narrowed shoulders so that we'll keep on looking ridiculous."

"As of Friday at 1500 hours you will be a civilian and as such outrank any man in the army," Schiller said, and his sincerity was as thick as hot fudge. That was the trouble with Schiller. He was too sincere about everything. His other trouble was that he was a compulsive gambler.

I moved in with the Schillers a week later and Ruby gave me the room with the southeast exposure on the second floor. The Army hadn't yet gotten round to air-conditioning its post houses and I welcomed the breeze at night. San Antonio is hot in May.

Ruby and I got along well enough after I made it clear that I wasn't to be her prime source of information about her husband's philandering. She was a short, slim brunette in her early thirties, quite attractive in an elfish sort of a way, far more intelligent than her husband, and a fine cook. I found her to be excellent company, imagined that she was extraordinary in bed, and thought that Schiller was a fool for chasing his roundheels. I spent quite a few summer nights with Ruby as she manned the nightwatch for the wandering major. We sat there on the screened porch and looked at fire flies and drank while I told her stories about Shanghai. She liked the stories, but I never did develop a taste for Coke and Southern Comfort, which was all that Ruby drank.

Each time that Schiller strayed she would pour her last drink around midnight and say to me, "I'm going to leave that rotten sonofabitch in the morning," and about that time Schiller would turn in the drive with the top down on his 1949 Ford and a story of impossible misadventure that only a child would believe. Sometimes, if he had had enough to drink, he would play the piano and sing songs from the thirties and forties such as "Deep Purple," "I'll Never Smile Again," "Dancing in the Dark," and "Together." He had natural pitch, knew all the words, and his piano playing was, I suppose, enthusiastic. He sang to Ruby, partly to mollify her and partly because she was the only woman available just then. By one o'clock they were on their way upstairs, sometimes arguing bitterly, but by one-fifteen the creaking bed springs either lulled me to sleep or kept me wide awake. It all depended. Ruby never did get around to leaving him in the morning.

I met Colonel Elmore Gay at the fourth weekly poker session that I attended, this one at the house of a two-star general whom I'd taken the week before for $195. They played pot limit and four raises. No wild cards. Check and raise was not only permissible, but expected. It occasionally got hairy and more than once Schiller wrote a bum check. He usually covered them by rushing down to the finance company the next morning to see how much they would lend him on his Ford convertible. When the Ford was already in hock, he borrowed from me.

Colonel Gay played dull, dispassionate poker. The fifth man in the game was a buck general. They were all good, but I found that the one to beat was Colonel Gay. He was thin and tall with extraordinarily wide shoulders, an amused mouth, and questioning dark gray eyes, the kind

166

that always add up the check and count the change. It was his deal and he dealt five-card draw.

"They tell me, Mr. Dye, that you were reared in Shanghai."

"That's right," I said, watching the deck. It was one of a number of things that Smalldane had taught me. "No matter if it's the bishop himself dealing, kid," he'd said. "Keep your eyes on the deck when it's dealt."

"Do you speak Chinese?"

"A little."

He switched to Mandarin. "Then I very much hope that you will join us when the cards are laid out next week. The game is to be held at my house and your presence would honor it."

"One cannot refuse so gracious an invitation," I replied.

"Yes," he said in English, looking at the hand he'd dealt himself, "you do speak it a bit."

"Let's play cards," the two-star general said from around his cigar. "You open, Dye?"

I opened for ten dollars on three tens. Everybody stayed and I filled with a pair of fives. I bet twenty-five into Colonel Gay's one-card draw. He raised me twenty-five, the two-star general called. He had drawn two cards. I folded and Colonel Gay looked at me and smiled. "Four sixes," he said, laying down his hand.

"Beats kings over," the general grumbled.

"Openers, Dye?"

I flipped three cards out in the center of the table. "Tens," I said.

"A lot of persons would have stayed with a full house," Colonel Gay said.

"A lot of persons don't know any better," I said and earned a glare from the two-star general.

"They also tell me," Colonel Gay said, "that you were the youngest master sergeant in the Army."

"So I've heard."

"Why didn't you apply for OCS?"

"That's what I told him," Schiller said.

"I'm not very ambitious, Colonel."

"Pot's light," the two-star general said.

Gay slid two one-dollar chips in. "Sorry."

"Five-card stud," the buck general said.

"Deal," said the general with two stars.

167

"Did you like military life?" Colonel Gay asked me.

"Not much."

"First king bets, Dye," said the two-star general.

"King bets five," I said.

"What are your plans?" Gay asked.

"Go back to school."

"Where?"

"King-jack bets," said the two-star general.

"Another five," I said. "I don't know. Columbia maybe."

Colonel Gay looked at his hole card. He had a seven and a queen showing. "Raise five," he said. I had the kings wired, so I raised him back. Only the one-star general dropped out.

The next round brought me another king and Colonel Gay picked up another queen. I bet twenty-five on the kings and he only called. The rest of them dropped out. Neither of us improved on the final card and I bet twenty-five again. Gay folded.

"A lot of persons would have paid to see my hole card," I said.

"A lot of persons don't know any better," he said. "By the way, here's my address." He gave me a card. "Why don't you drop around early next Friday night. For dinner, say around seven?"

The two generals exchanged glances and smiled faintly. "Why don't you recruit on your own time, Colonel?" the two-star general said.

"We take what we can get where we find it," Gay said.

"Let's play cards," the one-star general said.

We played cards for the rest of the evening and nobody cheated and I won $265, two hundred of which I lent Major Schiller to cover the bum check that he wrote for his losses.

19

Her eyes were lighter than her father's, almost dove gray and just as gentle. She opened the door to my knock and said, "You're Lucifer Dye. I'm Beverly Gay, the colonel's favorite daughter. Please come in."

"Thank you," I said.

She was eighteen then and she wore the standard college-girl's uniform, a sweater, a skirt, and brown loafers, but she wore them better than most. We moved down the hall of the middle-class bungalow in a middle-class San Antonio neighborhood and I admired the way that she walked and the sway of her skirt. "What do you like people to call you, Lu, Lucifer, or Mr. Dye?"

"Sam," I said.

"Is that your middle name?"

"No. It's Clarence."

"Oh."

"That's what I think, too. I would use my initials, but . . ."

"You don't look like an Elsie," she said. "Why Sam?"

"I don't know. I just made it up."

We were in the living room then and it looked as if it had been furnished by a peripatetic world collector who could never say no in the native bazaars. There were spears from East Africa and rugs from the mideast. Woven cane chairs from the Philippines nestled next to American Indian pottery. Chinese scrolls of doubtful merit flanked a tapestry from Iraq. Some of the heavier pieces looked as if they had been manufactured in Berlin during the thirties and they competed grimly with some small knurled tables that may or may not have been early American. Tasseled ottomans from the mideast and gaudy leather poufs from West Africa were scattered about the room for those whose feet were weary. A large Blechstein grand piano crouched in one corner.

"Terrible, isn't it?" she said.

"Well, it's different."

"It belongs to some old friends of the colonel. He's retired from the State Department and they're doing Europe this summer. For the fifteenth time, I think. They let us have the house while Dad gets his treatments at the hospital."

"I didn't know he was ill."

"Schistosomiasis," she said. "It's a blood fluke that he picked up in Burma during the war."

Colonel Gay came in from the hall and smiled at me. "I see you've met the favorite daughter."

"So she claimed," I said, accepting a firm grip from his curiously slender hand.

"She's also my only one. What would you like to drink —martini?"

"Not when I play poker."

He gave me an amused look. "You like to win, don't you?"

"It's better than losing."

"A beer?"

"Fine."

Beverly Gay served us each a beer, but drank nothing herself. She sat on the severe couch with her father. I sat in a leather chair that was all angles and sharp edges.

"I've done some checking on you during the past week," Gay said. "I hope you don't mind."

"If it's already done, there's not much I can do about it. I don't know whether I mind or not."

"I'd mind," Beverly Gay said. "There're too many Paul Prys around as it is."

"She doesn't much care for the Senator from Wisconsin," the colonel said. "What do you think of him?"

"Joe McCarthy? He's a menace."

"Why?"

"I don't like being told what I should be frightened of. I like to find out for myself. Maybe I won't be frightened. Maybe I'll like it."

"Such as a hot stove?"

"That's an oversimplification, Colonel."

"Hah," his daughter said to him and smiled at me. She had a fine smile that came quickly and went slowly, leaving a warm afterglow. I thought that she was less than beautiful, but more than pretty. Appealing perhaps. It may have been her grace and poise and grooming, but that was only part of it. She looked as if she might have been made

170

yesterday, still too new to be shopworn, and incredibly fresh and clean—not clean as the antonym of dirty, but in the sense that a meadowlark's call at dawn is clean—if you've ever been up that early. Her gray eyes as she looked at the colonel seemed solemnly mischievous and her mobile face was seldom in repose. She used only a touch of color on her full, sensitive mouth, and somehow I forgave her for being able to wrinkle her nose like a rabbit.

"My daughter is hopelessly partisan," the colonel said.

"They sometimes make the best cooks."

"What does that mean?" she said.

"I'm not sure."

"Probably that he's hungry."

"You'll eat in fifteen minutes," she said. "Besides, if I left you'd lose half your audience."

Colonel Gay leaned back in the sofa and looked at me quizzically. His wide shoulders made him resemble an inverted isosceles triangle that was loosely hinged in two places.

"What do you intend to do?" he said. "You're surely not going to make a career of working for that charming idiot in PIO?"

"I'm going to school in the fall."

"Where?"

"Columbia, if I can get in."

"To study what?"

"Oriental languages probably."

"Then?"

"Teach."

"That takes a Ph.D., unless you like to starve."

"I have time."

"How many prep schools have you gone to since 1942?" I shrugged. "Eight or nine."

"What happened?"

"I thought you'd been checking."

"Let's say that I'm confirming my research."

"I got kicked out of most of them. Sometimes for gambling. Sometimes for drinking. Sometimes for what they called 'incorrigibility' and sometimes I just walked away."

"Did you learn anything?"

"I learned how to read and write and I lost an Australian accent."

171

"Your parents are dead, aren't they?"

"Yes."

"Were they all private schools?"

"All but the last."

"Who paid your tuition?"

"There was a revocable trust fund that my guardian set up."

"Gorman Smalldane?"

"Yes."

"Is he really your guardian?"

"He is whenever I need one."

"And the rest of the time?"

"I'm on my own. Sometimes I've stayed with Gorman in New York. Once I joined him in Paris for a summer after the war. Once in Athens."

"Do you speak Greek?"

"No."

"How many languages?"

"It used to be six or seven. But it's less now. My Chinese, French, and German are still good. I've forgotten the rest."

"Those were all 'progressive' schools that you attended. I use progressive in quotes."

"Their catalogues didn't."

"Where did you finally get your high school diploma?"

"Reno. Smalldane fixed it up. I dealt blackjack there the summer I was sixteen. He fixed that up, too. Then I took an equivalency test and they put me in the twelfth grade. I finished the year and they gave me a diploma. Gorman flew out from New York for the graduation exercises but we got too drunk to attend."

"Then?"

"Then I went to Montana."

"To school?"

"For a year."

"Where?"

"The University of Montana. At Missoula."

"Why there?"

"I don't know. Maybe because I was born in Montana."

"But you left when you were an infant."

"When I was nine months old."

"And went to Shanghai."

"Where my father got killed by dumb pilot error and

172

where I grew up in a whorehouse. Why all the questions, Colonel, when you know the answers?"

Gay studied me for several seconds as if he were trying to decide something. "Who were your friends when you were growing up? Or playmates, if they're still called that."

"In Shanghai?"

"Yes."

"Whores mostly."

"No children?"

"A few street Arabs."

"And back in the States?"

I shook my head. "No childhood chums, Colonel."

"Not even your classmates?"

"They were children."

"What were you?"

"I don't know. I just wasn't a child anymore."

"Were you always treated as an adult?"

"In Shanghai?"

"Yes."

"I wasn't always treated as an adult, but I was talked to as one. There's a difference."

"And when you got back to the States they tried to talk to you as a child."

"Something like that, but it was too late."

"What about Smalldane?"

I smiled. "I think I've always been a contemporary to him. A fellow orphan. Which says something either about his childishness or my maturity."

The colonel nodded as if satisfied on some important point. He turned to his daughter and smiled. "I think Mr. Dye and I could have another beer without endangering our poker skill."

She rose, started toward the kitchen, and then stopped. "How long do you want it to take, five minutes or ten?"

"Five will do nicely," Gay said.

When she had gone he put his head back on the couch and looked at the ceiling. "You're set on Columbia?"

"I like New York," I said.

"Sometimes I'm in a position to recommend full scholarships for deserving students. Not to Columbia unfortunately."

"Where?"

173

He named a small, rich private school on the Eastern seaboard, not too far from Washington. "Interested?"

"Go on."

"It has an excellent reputation in your field—oriental studies and languages. Even Joe McCarthy thinks so. He's having the chairman of the department hauled up before his committee next week."

"Why?"

"He thinks the man caused us to lose China."

"We never had it to lose," I said. "Nobody did."

"This guy can take care of himself," Gay said. "We're not worried about him. But it's going to destroy some others and we're going to have to replace them. And then we'll have to replace our replacements."

"I'm not following you."

"I didn't expect you to."

"Then what's the point?"

"I want to find out if you're interested in a scholarship. It pays four hundred a month plus all fees and tuition. You can double the four hundred with poker."

"All right," I said. "I'm interested, but I never knew the army to be so generous."

"I didn't mention the army."

"I'll guess again. State Department."

"Hardly."

"That leaves the CIA."

"They're even more frightened of McCarthy than State. They've already started dumping and he hasn't even mentioned them yet."

"Just spell it out, Colonel."

He lit a cigarette and leaned back on the couch so that he had a good view of the ceiling again. "It hasn't got a name really, so we'll just call it Section Two. Okay?"

"What's Section One?"

"There isn't any."

"I see."

"The Section is going to lose some of its best people as replacements for those who McCarthy will get through his witch-hunt. We can't do anything about the witch-hunt. It's got to run its course. All we can do is fill in the gaps that it creates at State and CIA with our own talent. In the meantime, we have to recruit new blood that four, five, or even ten years from now will start recruiting its own replacements. Do you follow me?"

"It's perfectly clear," I said. "The scholarship has strings."

"No," he said. "It doesn't."

"You mean I can collect the four hundred dollars a month, pick up a degree, and then wave goodbye?"

"Or two degrees. Even three."

"And no strings?"

"None," he said.

"How much can you tell me about it?"

"Section Two?"

"Yes."

"Not much. It doesn't exist on paper."

"And it's not CIA?"

"Definitely not. It's what you might call an intelligence bank. When the others run short, they borrow from us."

"Borrow what?"

"Whatever they need."

"When was it set up?"

"In 1945 when we knew China was going."

"You didn't anticipate McCarthy eight years ago."

"No," he said. "We anticipated the reaction, not the person. Some would be blamed and that we could predict fairly well. The individuals, I mean. Somebody, of course, would have to do the blaming and it turned out to be Joe McCarthy. If it hadn't been him, it would have been another. We knew that valuable men would be lost and that they'd have to have replacements. Pure ones, if you follow me."

"I do."

"So we started recruiting them."

"And now that you're lending them out, you need some more."

"We always need more," he said.

"Just for China?"

He shook his head. "For everywhere."

"You're more than a central bank then?"

"Let's just say that we have branch offices in a lot of places."

"And what do they do?"

"Whatever's necessary."

"Who runs it?"

"Section Two?"

"Yes."

"I do."

"Then you're not in the army?"

"I'm on detached service."

"Those two generals we played poker with last week seemed to know what you do."

"No," the colonel said. "They think I'm CIA. I don't discourage it."

"You're telling me a lot."

"Not really."

"All right," I said. "What do I have to do?"

"Nothing. You'll get a letter of acceptance from the university next week."

"And that's all there is to it?"

"That's all. Your check will come every month from a foundation. When you've decided that you've had enough school, somebody'll be around to see you."

"But not until then?" I said.

"No. Anything else?"

"I'd be a fool to say no."

The colonel looked at me thoughtfully. "Yes," he said. "You would be, wouldn't you? But if you were a fool, you'd never have been asked."

20

Beverly Gay and I were married that September in the living room of Major and Mrs. Albert Schiller. Colonel Gay reluctantly gave the bride away and Gorman Small-dane flew in from New York to be best man and to give his legal consent as my guardian. I was still under twenty-one and in Texas the man then had to be of age before he could marry without consent. The woman had to be eighteen. If they had consent, the man could be sixteen, the girl fourteen. They may have changed the law by now, but I doubt it.

I got married because of the usual reason: I was in love with a girl who loved me. The colonel had been a stickler for form. "Goddamn it, Dye, you're going to have to ask for her hand. You're going to have to convince me. She's the only daughter I've got and by Jesus Christ you're going to play by the book."

"My prospects are excellent," I said.

"I know what your prospects are."

"My income is assured for the next several years."

"I know what your income will be down to a dime."

"What about dowry?" I said.

The colonel rose and began to pace the living room that was furnished with the junk of all the world. "I had it all figured out," he said, as if to himself. "Three months with Beverly in San Antonio while I got rid of the bug and then back to work, and you turned up." He spun around. "I'm not sure I want you as a son-in-law."

"I'm not sure that I give a damn what you want."

"It could hurt your career."

"Marrying the boss's daughter? It's the well-known path to success."

"You're both too young," he said, paused, and then smoothed his gray hair back with a thin, hard hand. "No. That's not right either. *You're* not too young. You're too old for her. It's like marrying her off to the town rake."

He turned toward me quickly. "How many girls have you laid?"

"How should I know?" I said. "I never kept score. Did you?"

He ignored the question and paced some more. It was the only time I ever saw him even slightly agitated. He whirled once more and aimed his right forefinger at me like a district attorney who's long on style and short on evidence. "Goddamn it, do you love her?"

"Do you expect me to say no?"

Gay resumed his pacing for a while and then stopped and faced me again. He stood quite still and looked at me carefully, as if he hoped that what he saw wasn't as unsavory as it seemed. When he spoke, his tone was low, soft, and controlled. It sounded almost dangerous. It may have been. "Something might happen to me," he said. "If it does, take care of her. I mean good care. Do you understand?"

"I understand."

"If something happens to me and you're in Section Two by then, get out. If you're not yet in, don't go. Is that clear?"

"Yes."

He raised his voice slightly and nodded toward the dining room. "She's in there, you know. Ear to the keyhole."

"There's no door," I said.

"It didn't go right," he said. "I was lousy as the forbidding father."

Beverly came in from the dining room. "I thought you were fine."

The colonel shook his head. "No, you didn't," he said. "It should have been a Sunday afternoon. All bad domestic scenes should take place on Sunday afternoon, the worst time of the week. Agreements for divorce. Accusations of infidelity. If a husband's going to beat his wife, he should do it on Sunday afternoon." He turned toward me. "You weren't right either. You should have been more nervous."

"What the hell for?" I said.

"Because, goddamnit, I deserve my slice of American banality. I've never had my share."

"It doesn't happen that way," Beverly said.

"I know it doesn't happen that way," the colonel said.

178

"I know that as well as I know that you're not a virgin and probably haven't been one since two weeks after you met the cocksman here."

"Three weeks," she said. "I held out."

"Three weeks. I'd just like something tried and trite, something banal in my own borrowed living room. Something that looks like it stepped out of an ad or MGM. I'm thirsty for the insipid."

"How about a martini?" Beverly said.

"If he wants something insipid, champagne would be better," I said.

The colonel sighed. "We don't have any champagne, we've run out of vermouth, and it's not even Sunday afternoon." He grinned at Beverly. "What the hell," he said. "Just make it a hooker of gin."

It was a small, if not quiet wedding. Ruby cried throughout and Major Schiller pinched Beverly three times, once during the ceremony, which caused her to jump and say "ouch" when she should have been saying, "I, Beverly." The major got a lttle drunk and played the piano and sang. The colonel looked morose throughout while his daughter looked as if she were about to succumb to a fit of giggles. The groom was hungover and testy. Smalldane, twenty or thirty pounds heavier than when I'd seen him last, performed as best man with more gusto than was really necessary, but he seemed to enjoy his role. A fat Army chaplain, a major who claimed to be a Baptist, mumbled the ceremony so that I had to ask him "What?" twice. Afterwards, he drank eleven glasses of champagne and wept a little, perhaps for his own sins as well as for ours.

When it was over the colonel dragged me into the kitchen and produced two items. The first was a set of keys to a new Chevrolet. He did it brusquely, as if embarrassed by his own generosity, or perhaps because he thought he was playing it a shade close to the hearty father. He made up for that with the second item, a .38 Colt automatic. "Keep it handy," he said.

"You mean carry it?"

A pained look spread across his face. It was the look of a man who has just discovered that he has a lout for a son-in-law. "Just handy. Around the house."

I nodded and because I didn't know what to do with it,

I shoved it into a hip pocket and later transferred it to a suitcase.

Gorman Smalldane was equally furtive. He also chose the kitchen, which seemed to be the favorite clandestine meeting place for wedding guests. He took an envelope from his pocket and handed it to me. "Your wedding present," he said.

I thanked him and started to put it into a pocket.

"Go ahead, open it," he said.

I opened it and found a bundle of what seemed to be shares of common stock.

"Two thousand shares," he said.

"Of what?"

"Smalldane Communications, Incorporated. We just went public. First PR outfit in the country to do it. Maybe in the world."

"How's it look?" I said.

"Well, it's not on the big board, of course; it's still over-the-counter, but it started at two and it's only slid to one and a quarter."

"Encouraging, huh?" I said.

"It's the big league, kid. By this time next year, I'll be rich and so will you if you hang on to it. We've got offices opening next month in Paris, London and Rome. They're just desks with telephones now, but they'll look real fine on the letterhead."

"Business is good?" I said.

"Terrific. Everyone who's made more than a million needs a public relations man to get rid of the guilt that the psychiatrists can't root out. If they see something nice about themselves printed in a newspaper or magazine, they really believe it must be true and their consciences are eased. The potential is unlimited."

"Thanks for the shares, Gorm."

"Just hang on to them. They'll hit fifty before you know it."

He paused then and looked over my shoulder at something that seemed to be far away. "When's the last time you heard from Kate?"

"Couple of weeks ago," I said. "She wrote from Hong Kong, giving me some advice about marriage."

"She's dead."

Tante Katerine was too alive to be dead, of course, and it didn't register because Smalldane's words had tripped the switch that brought the automatic denier into operation. It worked for perhaps ten or fifteen seconds before it sputtered to a stop. There must be something else to say besides "no" when you learn of death. I supposed I could have asked "how" or "when," but instead I denied it, as if the denial would prevent me from having to feel anything, at least for a few more seconds.

"I got a cable yesterday. It was a heart attack. I wasn't sure that I should tell you. It's not a very good day for it."

"No," I said. "It isn't, but it's all right—I mean that you told me."

"I knew you'd want to know."

"Yes."

"She wasn't really all that old," he said, as if to himself.

"No, not that way, she wasn't. I suppose I should ask if there's anything I can do."

"Nothing," he said. "What the hell could you do? It's just over. She's dead."

"Okay, Gorman," I said. "She's dead. There's nothing either of us can do."

"Well, hell—there should be something."

"But there isn't."

Smalldane shook his head. "You know," he said, "she was something different—really different. Or the times were."

"Both probably," I said.

"I paid her back that eleven thousand dollars, you know?"

"I know."

"Kate'd tell you to hang on to that stock, kid," he said.

"I'll take her advice." But I didn't. I sold it two years later when it hit twelve and a quarter. It went to sixty-one and a half before it split two for one. The last time I looked, Smalldane Communications, Inc., was hovering somewhere around eighty-three or eighty-four on the American Stock Exchange.

Beverly and I enjoyed each other for the next four years. She turned out to be the one totally unselfish person that I've ever known and I suppose that I took what she had to offer greedily, unable to get enough, fearful that the supply would run out before I was full. It was her love that I took, of course, and in the taking finally discovered that it was unrationed and inexhausti-

181

ble and that I could spare some myself. It required a year or so before I learned what others had known for years and when I did we became impossibly close.

We lived in a small, frame house that I kept threatening to paint a flat black. It was on the edge of the campus, where a portion of what has been described as the silent generation was enrolled. I majored in oriental languages and history; Beverly studied anthropology which, she once said, was the polite way of expressing one's concern for humanity.

Sometimes we would go into Baltimore on weekends, or down to Washington, or up to New York where we could stay free with Smalldane who was becoming impossibly rich as the public relations dodge acquired new tones of respectability. He spent his money, as always, on women, some of whom he even married for as long as a year or so.

The check from the foundation arrived on the first of the month along with the one from the Veterans' Administration, by courtesy of the G.I. Bill of Rights that had been extended to the survivors of Korea by a grateful Congress. The foundation check was my only reminder of the Section Two scholarship. The colonel, working most of the time in Washington, would sometimes disappear for a year or six months and then pop up unexpectedly with the same question:

"He still beating you, Bev?"

As a joke, his infrequent visits made it wear well enough. He never mentioned Section Two and neither did I.

In May of 1957, two weeks before she was to be graduated and I was to be awarded my Master's degree, Beverly announced that she was pregnant. She did so proudly, as if it were something she had done quite alone in defiance of overwhelming odds.

"Well, we tried hard enough," I said.

"But not often enough."

"Any more often and I'd have had to send in a substitute."

"I was going to suggest it once or twice, but—"

"My tender feelings?"

"You are awfully sensitive."

"A weakness."

"Let's celebrate," she said, her gray eyes dancing a

little—or even a lot. "Let's celebrate with louder wine and stronger music."

"I think you've got it backwards."

"It sounds better."

"Where?" I said.

"Where what?"

"Where shall we celebrate?"

She glanced around the room as if seeking something that would help her to decide. Then she looked at me and winked. No nice girl knows how to wink like that. "In bed," she said, "where else?"

We were on our third glass of wine with something by Miles Davis on the record player when the phone rang. For some reason I once liked to answer the phone naked. I don't know why, but I did. I don't anymore. It was a station-to-station call before the time of direct dialing and it was the colonel. He sounded bad and his voice was a harsh, bitter croak.

"Get her out, Dye," he said.

"Where?" I said because I had to make some response.

"That friend of yours—Smalldane. Get her out to him now—they're—" The phone went dead. I hung it up and said to Beverly, "Get dressed."

"Why should I—"

"Just get dressed. It was your old man."

I fumbled through the drawer of the small table that stood next to the bed. I was looking for the .38 automatic that the colonel had given me. I found it, and then I found something to load it with. I had two rounds in the clip when they came in. There was nothing to keep them out. It had been warm and we'd left the front door open with the screen door latched. We did that when it was warm. The screen door latch was only a hook and eye and that hadn't bothered them.

I held the clip in my left hand and the automatic in my right when they came in the bedroom. They came in fast and both wore dark suits and Halloween masks and revolvers. One was several inches shorter than the other. The shorter one waved his revolver at me and then waved it again before I got the idea. I put the automatic and the magazine on the table beside the bed. Beverly pulled the sheet up over her breasts, up to her neck.

She did it slowly. The shorter one held his revolver on me and then nodded at the taller one who slipped his revolver into a coat pocket. He started undoing his belt buckle and the buttons on his fly. Buttons instead of a zipper. He dropped his pants and shorts, blue-and-white striped ones. Then he ripped the sheet away from Beverly. I noticed that he wasn't circumsized. I started to rise, but the shorter one prodded me back with his revolver and used it to turn my head so that I had to watch.

I watched for fifteen minutes or so while the taller one grunted and sweated and clutched and grabbed. When he tired of the front he turned her over and tried it from the rear. When he tired of that he used her mouth. At first, she said, "Don't" several times, but he slapped her across the mouth and after that she didn't say anything. She lay perfectly still and let him rape her. I got to watch her disintegrate, to watch the fear in her eyes grow until it melted away into a kind of resigned madness.

When he was through, he stood up, shook it a couple of times as if he had just taken a pee, and then pulled his trousers back up. He took the revolver from his pocket and turned his head slightly to look at the shorter man whose gun was still pressed against my ear. The shorter man must have nodded because the taller one shot Beverly twice. Once in the right cheek and once through the forehead. It slammed her up against the headboard of the bed. The taller of the two turned his revolver on me. I waited, but the only thing that happened was that the shorter man removed the barrel of his revolver from my ear. He went to the foot of the bed so that I could watch him shoot Beverly in the right breast and stomach. He didn't have to do that, of course. She was already dead. Still wearing their Halloween masks, they backed out of the room. I watched them leave. Neither had made a sound except the taller one, the one who had raped Beverly without taking off his mask. Or shoes. He had grunted a few times. They backed into the living room, and a moment later I heard the screen door slam. Another moment later I heard a car speed away. I looked at what had been Beverly and clinically noted how the right side of her face had been torn away and how white the bone was. There also seemed to be a vast amount of blood.

Carmingler arrived at four that morning after the police had gone and after they had taken Beverly away. I don't remember much about that except the confusion and the noise. Carmingler came in without knocking and I didn't look up until he cleared his throat. He told me who he was and I noticed that he carried a copy of the *Washington Post*.

He was younger then, of course, only twenty-nine or thirty, but he already wore a vest and diddled with his Phi Beta Kappa key. He also smoked a pipe, but was polite enough then to ask if he could light it. He never asked me that again.

"The colonel's dead," he said after he got his pipe going. He never seemed to say anything important until he had lighted the pipe.

I said, "Oh." I wasn't really interested.

"The story's here in the *Post*," he said and tapped the newspaper.

I said nothing.

"The police are calling it suicide. They say he shot himself because of what happened to Beverly."

"But it wasn't," I said, "and he didn't."

"No. We got the police to say that and it took a little doing. Somebody shot him, of course. They tried to get to him through his daughter. They must have told him what was going to happen to her; probably had it timed down to the minute. He was supposed to break. They even let him make that phone call to you so that he could be sure she was home."

"He just sat there and let it happen," I said.

"He couldn't do anything else. There was always the chance that they were bluffing. When it didn't work, they gave up and killed him. Not much point to that, really."

"What about my wife, goddamn it?" I yelled. "What was the point there?"

Carmingler was unruffled. "He might have cracked when they were halfway through. If so, he'd have to talk to her—she'd have to tell him what—well, that's how it happened."

"Who was it?" I said.

"The colonel had been in the East."

"East what?" I said. "East Baltimore?"

"Europe," Carmingler said. "Someone from there probably, but we're not sure."

"You're not sure?"

"No."

"You want a drink?"

"No."

"What the hell do you want?"

"We have to know about you."

"What about me?"

"If you're coming with Section Two?"

I stared at him. "Jesus, you're a cold-blooded shit."

He shrugged. "Not really. We just have to know."

"Why?"

Carmingler made a vague gesture with his pipe. "With the colonel dead, there'll be a shake-up. Top to bottom. The Section's a small, specialized organization. He was counting on you heavily. We want to know if we can."

"Bullshit," I said. "He never counted on anyone in his life except his daughter and she's dead."

"Have it your way," Carmingler said. "But are you in or out? We have to know."

I looked around the room and at the things in it that had once been ours. When they were ours they had looked fine. Now that they were mine they just looked old and worn and used up. I examined the carpet on the floor and noted how shabby it looked. I didn't think about my answer; I just said it. "I'm in."

"Good," Carmingler said. "We'll be in touch."

I looked up as he rose, moved to the door, and paused. "By the way," he said, gesturing toward the chair he'd sat in. "I left the *Post* in case you'd like to read about the colonel."

"You're too kind," I said and kept some of what I felt out of my voice.

"Not at all," he said.

I didn't attend the colonel's funeral, but Carmingler said that a lot of people were there. I wondered who they were. Beverly didn't have much of a funeral. She'd once said that she didn't want one, so it was just a hearse and a limousine from the funeral home that carried Small-dane, Carmingler and me to the cemetery. There was no graveside service either. Some men in blue overalls lowered the casket and I stood there watching for a time, but it seemed to take them forever, so I turned away and

186

walked back to the limousine. Carmingler was still there. He hadn't approached the grave.

The three of us rode back to town in silence. Carmingler got out first. "We'll be in touch," he said, and I said all right.

Smalldane didn't look at him but stared through a window instead. Finally he said, "Fuck it." I nodded and he seemed to understand that I knew what he meant. I don't think that I ever did introduce him to Carmingler.

Part Two

21

Victor Orcutt didn't like my idea and he was telling me why not as we sat there in the living room or parlor of the Rickenbacker Suite on the top floor of the Sycamore Hotel. Only three of us were sitting really, Carol Thackerty, Necessary and I. Orcutt glided about the room, picking up ashtrays and putting them down, straightening pictures that weren't crooked, and talking endlessly.

"They *just* won't believe you," he said for what may have been the fifteenth time. I had lost count.

"They won't or you don't?" I said.

"Oh, I have *perfect* faith in you."

"That's why you've been tearing it to pieces for the past thirty minutes."

"It just won't work," he said.

"Sure it will," Necessary said.

"It's all conjecture," Orcutt said. *"Sheer* conjecture."

"All right," I said. "You get me inside if you've got a better way."

Orcutt walked over to a gold-framed mirror and admired himself for a moment. He patted a stray curl of blond hair into place.

There are those who sneak furtive glances at themselves in every mirror that they pass and most seem afraid of being caught in their act of self-love and admiration. They look quickly and even more quickly look away, either reassured or disappointed. Orcutt liked what he saw and he didn't care who knew it.

"Suppose we do it your way," he said. "What's your first move?"

"I accept their offer for twenty-five percent more than you're paying me."

"They won't believe you."

"But they'll pretend to. They may even pay me some money, which would be something of a novelty."

Orcutt spun around and when he spoke his voice was

small and tight and mean. "Carol, write Mr. Dye a check for twenty thousand dollars."

"No checks," I said.

"Pay him in cash."

"Tonight?" she said.

I shook my head. "Tomorrow."

"Tomorrow *morning*," Orcutt said to her and turned once more to me, smiling as nastily as he could. I thought he did well at it. "Will that be satisfactory?"

"Perfectly."

"After you count your money," he said, "what do you do next?"

"What do *we* do," I said, correcting him only because I knew that he didn't like it.

"Very well. We."

"We establish my bona fides."

"How?"

"We give them something."

"What?" Orcutt said.

"Not what, but who."

"Ah!" he said. Orcutt was with me now. For a time there I thought he'd been slowing down. "A pawn," he said.

"No. More of a knight or a bishop."

"Who?"

"Someone on your list of advocates. Someone important. Preferably someone popular."

"And what do they do with him?"

"They ruin him," I said, "If your conscience bothers you, pick somebody who needs ruining."

Orcutt's eyes were glittering now as he stood before me, his hands jammed deep into the pockets of his yellow silk smoking jacket. "Then what?"

"We—or I—give them somebody else to ruin, again somebody who's closely linked with our side. And again he's got to be well known and well liked."

"Of course," Orcutt murmured. "Of course."

"Lynch and his people will be suspicious the first time. They'll suspect it's a trap; that I'm lying. But the second victim I hand over should establish my reliability. I expect that they'll begin feeding me phony information to feed to you. You'll act on it. Or seem to, but you'll also take countervailing measures. As far as Lynch and friends are concerned, you've swallowed it. I'll be with them, on the inside, passing their spurious information to you and the real stuff from you to them."

"It might work," Orcutt said. "It just might."

"It'll get me inside," I said. "That's all. The Lynch people will never quite believe me, not even after I've helped them ruin a couple of persons. They'll still suspect my—oh, hell, my loyalty, you might say. But they'll play along because they think they're smart enough to spot any cross I might try. I'm betting they're not and all I've got to back that up is eleven years of nasty experience along similar lines."

Orcutt tapped his lower lip with his right forefinger. "You would be, in effect, a double agent."

"No," I said. "I'd be a triple agent and that's the trickiest kind. There aren't many around. Not ones who're pushing forty."

"Triple agent," Orcutt said in a soft low tone and then said it again. He almost seemed to run his tongue over it. "Oh, I *like* that! What do you think, Homer?"

Necessary nodded slowly. "It's good," he said. "Like Dye says, it'll get him inside. What I want to know is who gets set up?"

"You mean whom do we ruin?" Orcutt asked.

Necessary nodded again, even more slowly. "Just so it's not somebody in this room, I don't care."

"You wouldn't care if it were, as long as it's not you," Carol Thackerty said.

Necessary smiled at her coldly. "You're right, sweetheart, so long as it's not me."

Orcutt giggled. "Then whom shall we pick?"

"Not we," I said. "You."

"Ah," Orcutt said and tapped his finger against his lower lip. "I see. They must be prominent, but not so prominent that it will ruin the reform slate's chances, correct?"

"It doesn't matter," I said patiently. "If you do it early enough, it'll be forgotten by election day. It'll be old news. People will be tired of it. They'll want something else."

"Something just as juicy, maybe more so," Necessary said.

"You're right," I said. "And that's why I have to get inside."

"Do you think we can find something like that?"

Orcutt said and started pacing again, silently this time. He straightened another picture, gave himself one more approving glance in the mirror, fiddled with the knot in his tie, and then turned toward me. "This—this—well, whatever it is that you'll look for in the Lynch camp, or manufacture or whatever. Do you have any idea of what it might be?"

"It'll be slimy," Carol Thackerty said.

"The slimier the better," Necessary said and smiled comfortably. It seemed to be his kind of meeting.

"I don't know what shape it'll take," I said. "Not yet."

"And my immediate task is to select two persons of this community to be ruined by Lynch and his associates? Two of our more prominent supporters?"

"That's right."

"What do you mean by ruined?"

"Scandal," I said. "Public ridicule and scorn. Shattered reputations. Jesus, you know what ruined means."

"Yes," he said softly. "Yes, I do. And you want me to select these two persons or families or however it works out?"

"It's your job."

"There should be a number of choices," he said.

"There always are."

"They won't be innocents, of course."

"If they were, you couldn't ruin them."

"It's really a little like playing God, isn't it?"

"I've known some who've grown to like it," I said.

"What is it—power?"

I nodded. "That's part of it."

"It should create quite a stir," Orcutt said.

"You mean stink," Necessary said.

"Yes," Orcutt said and looked at me. "But not as great as the one that you'll create."

"No."

"I trust, Mr. Dye, that you haven't forgotten your ultimate role."

"No," I said. "When it's all over I still get ridden out of town on a rail."

"The citizenry will need a catharsis then—something that will purge them of their emotions, It's all very much like a Greek tragedy, don't you think? Everything is so inevitable."

"Somebody's got to play God, Victor," Carol Thackerty said. "It may as well be you."

Orcutt tugged at his lower lip, frowned, and then brightened. "You know something," he said, "I really think that I'll like it."

"I thought that you might," I said.

I bought Carol Thackerty and Homer Necessary a drink in the Sycamore Hotel's Shadetree Lounge. We had left Victor Orcutt in his suite going over a list of names of persons to ruin. He seemed to enjoy his work.

"How'd you like the way he took the news that his hunch was right and those punks wanted to beat up on you?" Necessary said.

"Disinterested, if not bored," I said and signed the check.

"That's because it didn't happen to him," Carol Thackerty said. "He's only interested in things that touch him personally. Or that inconvenience him."

"If they'd put me in the hospital, he might have been inconvenienced."

"But you weren't, so he dismissed it," she said.

Homer Necessary took a gulp of his Scotch and water, wiped his mouth as usual with the back of his hand, and grinned at me. "Tell me something," he said.

"What?"

"You ever work for somebody that was younger than you before? I mean *that* much younger."

I shook my head. "No."

"Me neither. Christ, I'm almost old enough to be his father and I sit there and he tells me what to do. It's funny. I mean he's smart as hell and all, but it's still kind of funny." He took another gulp of his drink and wiped his mouth again. "Listen," he said and bent over the table toward me. "You know he and me are sitting there talking sometimes and I'll mention something, I mean something that once happened, and suddenly he'll get a blank look on his face like he hasn't got the goddamnedest notion of what I'm talking about. And he doesn't because I'm talking about something that everybody knows about, but something that happened maybe fifteen years ago when he was maybe eleven years old and he just doesn't remember."

"You don't have that trouble with me," Carol Thackerty said.

He looked at her in much the same way that the village wives probably had looked at Hester and her scarlet letter. Necessary had some curious standards. "Hell, you're a broad. Besides you're older than he is."

"Three months older."

"Well," Necessary grumbled, "you act older. You remember things."

"You mean I've read a lot," she said.

"Yeah, you read a lot. Between johns." He paused for another swallow. "But you know what about Orcutt? You tell him something that he doesn't know about and he'll get that funny look on his face and then he'll stop talking about whatever you were talking about and make you tell him everything that you know. I mean, he'll milk you dry and then a couple of weeks later he'll bring it up and use it to make a point to you just like you hadn't told him about it in the first place." Necessary shook his head.

"Any other complaints?"

"I wasn't complaining, Dye. I was just talking about working for somebody who's younger than I am. I never did it before."

"Homer was chief of police at twenty-seven," Carol Thackerty said. "He'll never get over it. He still expects to be the youngest man in the room."

"Like Peter Pan," I said.

"Who?" Necessary said.

"Just somebody else who took a long time to grow up," Carol Thackerty said.

"I don't know him," he said. From his tone it was plain that if Necessary hadn't heard of them, they weren't worth bothering with.

"You want another drink?" I said to Carol Thackerty.

"All right," she said. She was drinking Campari.

"Homer?"

He looked at his watch and shook his head. "I got to go."

"Where?" Carol said.

"I'd better start looking for that 'just a guy.' "

"You need any help?" I said.

He shook his head again. "I'll sort of nose around."

"They know you're doing it," I said.

"You mean Lynch and his crowd?"

"Yes."

"I want them to. You going to see Lynch tomorrow?"

"Yes."

"Ask him about 'just a guy.' "

"I plan to."

"You think Lynch set it up?"

"Maybe," I said.

He rose and leaned over the table, resting his weight on his fists. "There's one thing I'm pretty sure of. Maybe a couple of things."

"What?"

"One is that I'll find out who 'just a guy' is before you do, and two is that Lynch didn't have anything to do with him." He winked one of his eyes at me, the brown one, and left.

Carol Thackerty stared into her fresh drink after Necessary had gone. "We make a lovely crew, don't we?" she said.

"Since you put it that way."

"The crooked ex-cop, the ex-whore, the ex-secret agent —that's what you were, weren't you?"

"That's close enough."

"I should say the cashiered ex-secret agent and the boy wonder boss who's not as swish as he sounds or looks."

"I didn't ask."

"I know," she said.

"You know what?" I said. "That I didn't ask or that he's not swish?"

"Both. He's indifferent to sex. It just doesn't exist for him."

"You found out, I assume?"

"You assume nothing. I just know. As Homer would say, I've had enough johns to know whether they can, can't, or just don't care about it. Orcutt just doesn't care about it."

"That's too bad," I said.

"I don't know," she said. "He may be lucky."

"Do you think he is?"

She stopped staring into her drink and looked at me. "I was wondering how you were going to bring it up."

"Now you know."

"It's not especially innovative."

"I'm not trying."

"You're not interested?"

"I didn't say that."

She blew a thin plume of uninhaled smoke at me. I waved it away. "Well?" she said.

"Well what?"

"Do we romance each other for a while or do we just go up and fall into bed?"

"It's been more than three months. I can skip the romance."

She finished her drink, gathered her large purse into her lap, and said, "Let's go."

"Your room or mine?" I said.

"Mine. I don't like the walk home."

She had a room on the ninth floor, 912. It could have been the twin of mine on the floor below. There was a bed and some chairs and a dresser and a writing table. The floor was carpeted with a synthetic fiber. The pictures on the wall looked synthetic, too. She put her purse on the dresser and looked into the mirror and did something to her hair, something imperceptible that never changes it but which they all do anyway. "How kinky are you?" she said. She could have been asking if I thought that the United Nations had adjourned too early.

"I don't know," I said. "It depends."

"On what?"

"On how you like it."

She turned and leaned against the dresser so that both her pelvis and her breasts arched out, thrusting against the fabric of her dress. She threw her head back slightly and opened her mouth letting her tongue play around her lips. It was an excellent parody of all of those film star pictures of the late fifties and early sixties and she knew it. Then she threw her head back even farther and laughed. I found myself laughing with her for what must have been the first time in more than three months.

Her hands went behind her neck to the fastener and she slipped out of her dress. She left it lying on the floor. Her half-slip followed it. She moved over to me and put her arms around my neck. She ran her tongue over her lips again. "Any fetishes?" she said. "High heels, wet towels, or the like?"

"I'll think of something if you need it," I said, skillfully undoing her bra, pleased that I hadn't lost my touch. She lowered her arms to slip out of the bra and let it fall

198

to the floor in a slow practiced movement. "You like them?" she said, fondling her breasts. She was good.

"Very much."

Her hands went to the zipper on my trousers and then the belt. Then her hands went exploring. As I've said, she was very good. "It feels more like a year than three months," she said and stepped back and slowly slid her bikini panties off. She was about to display the feature attraction and she didn't want to rush it. When they were off, she explored herself there too, her head back again, her mouth slightly open. "You like it?"

"It's fine," I said, the words coming thick and a little phlegmy. "You sure you wouldn't really rather do it yourself?"

She caught my hand and guided it home. Then she started working on my tie and shirt, moving her hips langorously against my exploring hand. The tie came off, then the shirt, and she worked my shorts down to my ankles, where they joined my trousers. "Your shoes," she said and knelt slowly to undo them. She didn't rise for quite a while and when she did we decided to try the bed.

22

Mischief arose early in Swankerton and it was afoot and pounding on my door at seven-thirty the next morning. The pounders were the chief of police, Cal Loambaugh, and Ramsey Lynch himself, with the remains of his breakfast on display between the crevices of his upper teeth. I thought of offering him a toothpick, but merely shuddered instead, averted my eyes, and opened the door wider. They came in.

"I think he was still asleep, chief," Lynch said.

"Just wasting his life away lying in bed like that," Loambaugh said and winked at Lynch. "Of course, that's unless you got something pretty to do your lying with. We're not disturbing anything are we, Mr. Dye?"

"Just my disposition," I said and headed for the phone. I picked it up, got room service and ordered coffee. "You've already had yours, haven't you?" I said to Lynch and Loambaugh. It wasn't polite, but I have yet to be complimented on my morning manners.

"Well, I wouldn't say no to another cup, would you, Cal?" Lynch said.

Cal said he wouldn't say no either so I ordered coffee for four on the chance that somebody else might decide to turn neighborly. If they didn't, I'd drink it myself.

"You don't mind if I get dressed?" I said. I had no pajamas and for a robe I was using the topcoat furnished by Carmingler.

"Take your time," Lynch said. "Cal and I'll just sit here and jaw a while."

"Would you like a toothpick?" I said.

Lynch said, "Huh?" and I said, "Never mind," and headed for the bathroom, taking some fresh clothes with me. I showered, shaved and dressed before the coffee arrived. The Sycamore prided itself on leisurely service. The room-service waiter served the coffee, slopping only a little of it into my saucer. Nor did he neglect the saucers of my two guests. Lynch poured the spilled coffee back into his cup; the chief of police ignored his, while I soaked mine up with a napkin.

"We like to be up and doing in Swankerton," Lynch said after the waiter had gone.

"I noticed," I said.

"I ran into the chief here at the coffee shop so we had breakfast together."

"I've heard a lot of nice things about breakfast at dawn," I said.

"I bet you were sneaking down the hall, carrying your shoes in your hand about dawn, weren't you, Mr. Dye?" the chief of police said, winking at me over the rim of his cup. I winked back and thought that he seemed to have all the makings of a dedicated voyeur. Or he could have been one of those who merely likes to talk about it.

"Well," Lynch said, "since the chief's a bit interested in what your decision's going to be about that little proposition we made you yesterday, and since I'm damned interested, and since the chief already had a piece of business to do with you this morning, we figured we'd drop by together and maybe get everything settled with one visit." Lynch leaned back in his chair and nodded his head in satisfaction over the way he had explained things. His chins bobbed up and down and I noticed that his shirt was too tight around the collar and that a roll of fat oozed down over it. He had on a different suit that morning, a wash and wear cord that fitted him like a tent. Perhaps he hoped to grow into it.

"What business?" I said to Loambaugh.

He put his cup down on the writing desk and leaned forward, his elbows resting on his knees, a concerned look on his face. I had the feeling that he practiced the look at night in the bathroom mirror with the door locked. "We got your friend down in the tank, Mr. Dye."

"What friend?"

"Homer Necessary."

"Have you charged him?"

Loambaugh shook his head. "Maybe yes, maybe no. I thought I'd better talk to you first."

"Why'd they bring him in?"

Loambaugh shrugged. "He was drunk."

"That all?"

"Disorderly."

"What else?"

201

Loambaugh sighed and shook his head in what I interpreted as a regretful manner. "Well, it's pretty hard to ignore resisting arrest."

"Where did all this happen?" I said.

"The Easy Alibi, across the street."

"That belongs to Fred Merriweather," I said. "Your pet city councilman."

"That's right!" Lynch said, trying to work a little astonished recall into his tone, but not doing very well at it. "You met him yesterday."

"What time did they pick Necessary up?" I said to Loambaugh.

He looked up at the ceiling for inspiration. "Midnight or thereabouts."

"What's the leeway?"

"Quarter till, quarter after."

I lit my first cigarette of the day. It tasted good, as only the first one did any more. I'd be smoking my habit the rest of the day. "No buy," I said.

Loambaugh smiled faintly. "Now why'd you say that, Mr. Dye?" He sounded humble, almost hurt.

"It was a roust."

"We don't make it a habit of—"

"You don't roust drunks in this town. I know that. You take them home and pat them on the head and tuck them into bed. You never throw them in the tank unless they're winos with no place else to sleep. When Necessary left me at eleven-fifty last night, he was sober. I've seen him drink and he could have gone on all night and into the morning. But you say he got drunk in twenty-five minutes and I say you're wrong. Chloral hydrate might have worked that fast, but then you couldn't have him on a resisting arrest charge, could you?"

"Well, chief, Mr. Dye seems to have come up with some pretty good points," Lynch said, smiling and bobbing.

"He's been booked," Loambaugh said. "He can post bond and get out or he can sit there and await trial. That night take a week or so. Maybe more."

"How much is his bond?"

"Five hundred."

"Has he got it?"

"He didn't have a dime on him," Loambaugh said with a straight face.

"I want him out of there in fifteen minutes." I said.

Despite his tan, a flush spread up the sides of Loambaugh's neck. It hit his face and raced to his ears, which turned a dark rosy shade. He had that tight, controlled tone back in his voice, the same tone that he'd used when I'd met him the day before. "Nobody," he said, spacing his words, "Nobody tells me how to run my—"

"Shut up and listen, Cal," Lynch said, no longer the jolly fat man. He looked at me and there was nothing jolly in his eyes either. "I don't know what you're used to, Mr. Dye, but folks don't talk to the chief of police in this town like you just did unless they got a mighty good reason. Or some mighty good friends."

"Like you?" I said.

He nodded. "Like me."

"I was in this fine community of yours for less than eight hours before a couple of punks tried to jump me in this room. I thought you might have sent them."

"No."

"All right, you didn't. Somebody else did and Homer Necessary was around to help keep me out of the hospital. I want him around so that he can keep an eye on me and, for that matter, so that I can keep an eye on him. I think you follow me."

Lynch turned to the police chief. "Tell them to get him out of there."

"He's already on the blotter," Loambaugh said.

"Well, now, that's just too goddamned bad, ain't it, Cal? I don't reckon anything can be done if he's already on the blotter. I mean that's just like holy writ engraved in stone. But maybe if you just picked up the phone and told them to hunt around for that old bottle of ink eradicator they just may be able to make that blotter read the way it should rightfully read, and when they're done doing that they can just get one of those fancy, new air-conditioned Ford squad cars and carry Mr. Necessary back to his hotel with your apologies." The phrasing was the phrasing of the South, but the accent was that of Newark. Or Jersey City.

"While they're hunting around for the ink eradicator," I said, "tell them to look behind the rear seat in the squad car. That's probably where they'll find the money that fell out of Necessary's pocket."

"Probably is," Lynch said, nodding agreement. "Probably is at that."

We sat there and listened to Loambaugh call in the new instructions. He did it crisply and no one on the other end of the phone seemed to give him any argument. When he hung up, he didn't look at either of us.

"So, Mr. Dye, that make you any happier?" Lynch said.

"Much," I said.

"About that proposition we made you yesterday. You had enough time to study over it?"

"Quite enough."

"What'd you decide?"

"I'll take it."

"Just like that, huh?"

"Just like that."

"That sure is good news," Lynch said, but without much conviction.

"I hoped you'd like it."

"Well, now," Lynch said again and reached into a coat pocket and brought out a cellophane-wrapped cigar. He examined it carefully, stripped off the cellophane, wadded it into a neat ball, and flipped it at the wastebasket. He missed. He sniffed the cigar and then licked it carefully with a gray-coated tongue. He bit off one end, rose, and walked into the bathroom. I heard him spit the end out into the toilet and then flush it. Back in his chair he searched through four pockets before he found a book of matches. He lit the cigar with one of them and blew out a heady plume of inhaled smoke. I didn't time it, but he must have taken three minutes to light his cigar. Time was cheap that morning.

"Well, now," he said yet again. "You sure didn't take much time in deciding to take us up on our offer."

"You said you were in a hurry."

"I did say that, didn't I? But you know, Mr. Dye, a deal like this is something like courting a gal. You want her to spread her legs for you all right, but if she does it too quick, you start wondering who she spread 'em for half an hour ago. Sort of takes the bloom off the romance, if you know what I mean."

"I don't," I said.

"Uh-huh," he said, which could have meant yes or no or even maybe. "It merely 'pears to me that you're awful

204

anxious to say yes. If you was a gal and I was asking you to marry me and you said yes like that, why I'd maybe suspect you were pregnant and looking for a daddy for your child. You ain't pregnant, are you, Mr. Dye?"

"No," I said.

"Not even a little bit?" he said and laughed his fat man's laugh, which caused him to choke and splutter a bit on some of his cigar smoke.

I smiled, but it was my old joke smile. "Not even a little bit," I said.

Lynch turned to the police chief. "What do you think, Cal?"

"I didn't know I was supposed to. I thought you did all the thinking."

"Why, Cal, you know I value your opinion most highly."

"Shit."

"What do you think?"

Loambaugh looked at me. He took in the black shoes and socks; the new dark green cavalry twill suit; the white shirt, and the terrible tie. He examined my face with its gentle hazel eyes, firm chin, and resolute mouth. He didn't like anything.

"You want to know what I think, huh?" he said to Lynch while still examining me.

"Most certainly do."

"I think he's a fucking plant."

Lynch shook his head and chins up and down several times, not so much in agreement, it seemed, as in appreciation for a frank opinion, succinctly delivered. "That's a real interesting observation, Cal. Real interesting. You care to comment on it, Mr. Dye?"

"Not at all," I said. "He's right."

Lynch threw his head back and whooped. Then he cackled for a while and finally he even slapped a knee. The right one. I wondered if he and his brother, Gerald Vicker, had really shared the same parents. The physical resemblance was apparent, if somewhat bloated, but their personalities had almost nothing in common, unless avarice and malevolent drive can be considered inherited traits.

Lynch stopped whooping and cackling, wiped his eyes for effect, if not for tears, and gave me another chance to inspect the scrambled egg remnants that were tucked away between his teeth. "So you're a plant and you come right out and admit it before God and everybody? That right, Mr. Dye?"

"I wouldn't be worth a damn to you unless I were."

"Explain yourself, sir. Not so much for me, but for Chief Loambaugh here. I think I'm beginning to sort of get the drift of things."

"It's simple," I said. "Victor Orcutt knew I was going to meet with you yesterday. When I got back, I told him about your proposition. It took a while to convince him that I should take it, but he finally agreed."

"Ain't that something, Cal?" Lynch said, again smiling hugely. "You ever hear of anything like that before? Mr. Dye here tells Orcutt about our meeting and then tells *us* that he told him and that Orcutt says to go ahead and join up with us. So what you're really going to do is work for us while Orcutt thinks that you're really working for him."

"That's right," I said.

"Uh-huh," Lynch said. "Brother Gerald said you were a tricky one, Mr. Dye. Mighty tricky."

"I learned a lot from him."

"Bet you did at that. Of course, I never had all of Gerald's advantages. I was sort of the simple one in the family. But it does occur to me that you could really be working for Orcutt and just play like you're working for us."

"That's what Orcutt said, only he thought it might be just the other way around."

Lynch found that really funny. He chortled and snuffled deep down in his belly and nodded his head rhythmically in time with the fist that he pounded against his knee. This time the left one. When he was done he said, "How you expect us to make sure that you're really looking after our best interests, Mr. Dye? By the way, you mind if I call you Lucifer? We're not too much on formality down here."

"Lucifer's fine," I said. "You'll know your best interests are being looked after by what I produce. That'll be your only gauge. I'll provide information and suggestions and that's all. You can check the information out and decide for yourself whether to act on my suggestions. If you don't like what I suggest, you can ignore it."

"What do you think about that, Cal?" Lynch said, turning to the chief of police, who still stared at me as if I were the newest brand of archfiend whose unspeakable speciality was yet to be codified.

"I think he's a fucking liar," Loambaugh said.

"Course he is, Cal. Man has to be *that* in the business he's in. Question is, does he lie for or against us. That's the real nut-knocker, don't you agree, Lucifer?"

"That's it," I said.

"And I suppose it's all based on price."

"You're right again."

"I offered you twenty-five percent more than Orcutt's offering you, didn't I?"

I only nodded.

"I hear he's paying fifty thousand."

"Twenty thousand of it this morning," I said. "You owe me twenty-five thousand."

"You aim to collect from both of us, of course. Can't say I blame you for that."

"No, I didn't think you would."

"Now if we got a little information up within the next few days, you wouldn't mind slipping it to Orcutt, would you, as something you'd sort of wormed out of us, so to speak?"

"That's part of the services," I said. "After I'm retained, of course."

"Wouldn't do it on spec just so we can take a reading on how well you perform?"

"That's a dumb question, if you don't mind my saying so."

Lynch shook his big head glumly. "I suppose it is," he said. "Suppose it is. When can we expect some results?"

"In a few days. Less than a week."

Lynch was silent for almost a minute while he inspected his half-smoked cigar. Then he looked up at me and there was an expression on his face that I'd seen often enough before, but on other faces. It was a mixture of contempt and curiosity and suspicion and a dash of grudging admiration. I'd probably worn it myself when doing a deal with a double agent. Carmingler, I recalled, had often worn it. "We got a deal, Lucifer," Lynch finally said. "It's not one that we have to shake hands on cause I just as soon shake hands with a cottonmouth. But we got a deal."

"No we don't," I said. "Not until I count the money."

"You think you're a pretty hard-nosed son of a bitch, don't you?" Loambaugh said.

"When it comes to getting paid I am."

"We'll get a check up to you this afternoon for twenty-five thousand," Lynch said and rose from his chair. He moved easily for the weight he carried.

I sighed. "No checks. No checks from you and no checks from Orcutt. Cash."

"When do you expect the rest of it?" Lynch said.

"I'll let you know."

"I bet you will," Loambaugh said.

"We'll get it to you in the morning," Lynch said, moving toward the door, hurrying a little as if the air had grown slightly foul. It probably had. Loambaugh followed him.

At the door, Lynch turned and said, "Better bank that money, Lucifer. It's a tempting bundle to leave around loose in a hotel room."

"I intend to," I said. "Any particular bank that you recommend?"

He grinned at me with his breakfast-decorated teeth. "So happens I've got a little interest in the First National across the street and we'd be proud to do business with you."

"Fine."

He paused again, ducked his head, and rubbed the knuckles of his right hand across his nose. It seemed to itch. "By the way, those two punks who tried to bounce you around."

"What about them?"

"I didn't send them."

"Okay."

"Well, if I didn't send them and Orcutt didn't send them, I was just wondering who might have?"

"I don't know," I said.

"Since we're in business together so to speak, maybe we'd better find out."

"Their names were Frank Smith and Joe Carson, or so they said."

Loambaugh nodded. "I know who they are."

"Check 'em out," Lynch said. "We don't want Mr. Dye to have any more trouble or enemies than he needs, do we?"

Loambaugh gave me one of his bleak stares that again classified me as the town horror. "Something tells me that before he leaves Swankerton he's going to have plenty of both."

I couldn't think up much of a rebuttal to that.

23

It was only nine o'clock in Swankerton when I placed the call to New York, which meant that it was ten o'clock there, but that was still too early for Smalldane Communications, Inc. I could hear the firm's receptionist assuring the operator that Mr. Smalldane never arrived before eleven. I left word for him to call.

Carol Thackerty arrived at nine-thirty a few minutes before room service decided that it was time to send up my breakfast now that the eggs and bacon were cool enough to have congealed the grease. The toast wouldn't burn any fingers either.

Carol Thackerty sat in a chair across the room, her legs crossed, her large purse in her lap, and an amused smile on her lips as the waiter lifted up the lids of various silver salvers to let me inspect what the Sycamore's menu fobbed off on the world as "Southern cuisine."

"You forgot the asbestos gloves," I told the waiter.

He said, "Sir?" so I let it pass. He was around fifty with a squeezed-up face, a bad limp, and the look of someone who's realized that he's gone as far as he'll ever go and now wonders why he ever made the effort. He was also white, which the hotel management apparently felt compensated for any laxity in service.

"Heah yo grits," he said and displayed a cold wad of them as if he were showing off the Christmas turkey, "and heah yo aigs and bacon. Toast righchere. I got an extra cup for the lady case she wants some cawfee." He left out a few verbs now and then—to save time, I suppose.

"You shouldn't have run all the way," I said as I signed the check and added an overly generous tip.

"I dint run," he said, and I apologized for accusing him of it.

After he left I asked Carol Thackerty if she would like some coffee and she said that she would so I poured her a cup and served it to her. It was still hot by grace of its sterno burner.

"You look quite pretty this morning," I said as I handed her the cup.

"Thank you," she said, either for the cup or the compliment or both.

"I enjoyed last night," I said, trying to smear some cold butter on some colder toast.

"You're full of compliments."

"Simple courtesy."

"You're not fishing, are you?" she said.

"For what?"

"I just hope you're not leading up to the one that they all like to ask."

"Which one?"

"Did I enjoy it, too?"

"I really don't give a damn," I said. "All I know is that I'd like to try it again."

"When?"

"You have anything against mornings?" I said.

"Not a thing."

I decided that I didn't really want the cold breakfast after all. I took a final sip of the coffee, rose, and walked over to where Carol sat. I remember thinking that I should call her Carol now. She put her coffee cup down and held out her hands to me. I pulled her slowly to her feet. I recall that she still had that faint smile on her face. It was almost quizzical. "No hurry," she said, just before we kissed. "No hurry," I agreed. We tried one of those long, exploratory kisses in which the tongue ventures forth, encounters token resistance that turns quickly into surrender and then into active collaboration. It was a nice girl's kiss after she's decided that she's tired of being nice.

Unlike the night before, we undressed carefully, helping each other when it might prove interesting. There was nothing frenzied about it this time and in bed we stroked and caressed each other with our hands and mouths and words which, if not endearing, were harshly erotic. It went on like that for what seemed to be a long time, her dark red, almost brown nipples taut and erect, her hips thrusting against whatever touched them, sometimes in a smooth and languorous motion, but more often frantic and demanding. And after a look or a moan or a twitch, or whatever it was, we both knew that it was time and I was inside her and she moaned about the ecstasy of it all and we tried to make it last, did make it last, until we

211

damned well couldn't any more and accepted it, with no regrets, and plunged into that final frenzy of oblivion.

There is, of course, always an afterwards and some are far better than others. This one was at first. We lay there in the tumbled sheets, not speaking, just breathing deeply while we each listened to the pound of our pulse. Finally, Carol stirred, rolled over on her side, and ran a fingertip down my chest. "I knew a girl once," she said, "who was terribly afraid of dying until someone told her what death really was."

"What?"

"One long orgasm."

"So she killed herself?"

"No. She just took up parachute jumping, scuba diving, things like that. She'll probably live to be a hundred."

The phone rang and I reached for it. "Is this Mr. Lucifer Dye?" the operator said.

"Just a moment," I said, crossed to the closet, slipped on the topcoat, and came back to the phone. "This is Mr. Dye."

"On your call to New York, we have Mr. Smalldane for you."

There was some more chatter while Smalldane's secretary wanted to make sure that Mr. Dye was on the line and the long distance operator kept assuring her that I was. Smalldane came on in his usual style.

"What do you want with an old fart like me?"

"You're not so old, Gorm," I said.

"I'm sixty-five and don't you ever write?"

"I've been in jail."

"Good or bad?"

"Not bad. Not as bad as Bridge House."

"How long?"

"Three months."

He asked where and I told him.

"What for?"

"I made a mistake."

"You still with the spooks?"

"They fired me."

"Good. You need some money? You want a job?"

"I'm on a job."

"In Swankerton? That's a horseshit town."

"So it seems."

"You know what it hit yesterday. It hit seventy-nine and it's going up again today."

"Don't rub it in."

"I told you to hang on to it. Hell, with that two-for-one split you'd have been worth almost a quarter of a million today."

"I was never intended to be worth a quarter of a million."

Smalldane switched to Cantonese. "Truly, you were destined to collect the wastes of cockroaches and turtles."

"It is unfortunate that old age is too often accompanied by the wisdom of a child."

"Huh," Smalldane said and was silent for a moment. "That's what they seem to think around here. You know what I am now? I'm chairman of the goddamned board. They booted my ass right upstairs. You sure you don't want a job? I think we can use someone in the mailroom."

"Keep it open," I said. "I may need it, but right now I need something else."

"What?"

"You still run that executive check service for your clients?"

"Sure."

"I need a few people checked out. I'll even pay for it."

"You got something going down there that might be fun?"

"I think so."

"You want some help?"

"I just told you what I wanted."

"Shit, I'll take care of that. I mean do you want some sage advice and wise counsel? I'm bored stiff."

"I don't know yet. Maybe."

"I can be there in six hours," Smalldane said.

"How long will it take you to run a check on these names?"

"Forty-eight. We've got the FBI beat by twelve hours, but that's because old man Hoover's not sure that computers are here to stay. There's one thing about him though that I like."

"What?"

"He's older than I am." Smalldane's tone changed. "Okay, Lucifer, just read off the names and I'll get the rundown to you in forty-eight hours. What do you want, a full check?"

"As much as you can get."

"Just read em off."

"You're taping?"

"I'm taping," he said.

"First, Victor Orcutt, Los Angeles. President of Victor Orcutt Associates. Second, Homer Necessary." I spelled it and gave the city where he was formerly the chief of police. "Third, Ramsey Lynch, Swankerton, that's an alias. Real name is Montgomery Vicker. Spent some time in Atlanta. The Federal pen. Fourth, Cal—probably for Calvin—Loambaugh. I'll spell it." After I spelled it, I said. "He's chief of police, Swankerton. Fifth and last, Miss Carol Thackerty, who's from the same city that Necessary's from."

"You son of a bitch," Carol said.

"What's that—what's that? You got a girl there, I can hear her."

"Her name's Carol Thackerty."

"Well, you must have just screwed everything up royal," Smalldane said.

"I'd already done that."

"That's all the names?"

"That's all."

"Forty-eight hours. I can either telex it to our New Orleans office and have somebody fly it over to you or I can call you back."

"Call me back and then we'll decide."

"What do you have down there, Lu, something political?"

"Partly."

"If you want an old fart's help, let me know. I'm bored."

"I will."

"I'll get back to you."

"Fine," I said and hung up.

Carol Thackerty was sitting cross-legged on the bed and smoking a cigarette when I turned to her. She smiled at me, but all it contained were some very white teeth. "The fucking you get's not worth the fucking you get, is it?"

"I've heard that before."

"Most have. Who was that?"

"An old friend."

"So you're checking us out?"

214

"What you really mean is that I'm checking you out. You don't give a damn about the others."

She shrugged and it made her breasts jiggle in an interesting manner. "You almost said that you would."

"That's right."

"You don't trust Orcutt?"

"About as much as he trusts me. He didn't pick my name out of the Yellow Pages."

"I'd be interested in what it will say about me. Have you ever seen one of those government reports that they write about people who they're thinking of hiring?"

"A few," I said.

"They throw in everything. Rumor, speculation, lies, conjecture, intuitive leaps—what have you. They're all neatly typed up on little green-lined forms, although the typing's not always so neat. Sometimes it looks like hunt and peck."

"Where did you see any?"

"I had a friend once who was going after a government job. Federal. It was a presidential appointment. The FBI ran a check on him and this FBI type passed it to someone who passed it to me. Or a copy of it."

"How'd you know it was a green form?"

"I don't remember. He must have told me. But I remember what it said. It's a wonder he got the job. It said he drank too much and played around and owed a lot of money."

"That's called the raw, unevaluated report. It's the FBI speciality. They don't pass judgment, they just go out like a vacuum cleaner and sweep everything up and then dump it out."

"I wonder if they have one on me?"

"Probably."

"Carol Portia Thackerty, twenty-six, born July 22, 1944, daughter of Lieutenant and Mrs. Ernest Thackerty of San Francisco. Lieutenant Thackerty killed in action, June 8, 1944, Omaha Beach. Mother proprietor of a fancy house, Monterrey, California, 1946–1955. Known narcotics user. Died of cancer, July 4, 1955, Monterrey General Hospital. Carol Portia Thackerty educated in private schools. Tuition paid by aunt, Ceil Thackerty, sister of late Lieutenant Thackerty. Aunt died, September, 1961. Niece, Carol Portia Thackerty, worked way through college, first as a call girl, second as owner of small motel

215

specializing in teen-age whores until joining present firm of Victor Orcutt Associates. And that's how a bad girl like me and so forth. Like it?"

"I didn't ask," I said.

"No. There's that about you. You didn't. Why?"

"I don't care."

"You mean that I was a whore or why I did it?"

"I don't care about either. You wanted to go to college. You just didn't want to go the hard way."

"And you think I should have?"

"I don't think anything. You haven't got much of a white slave story, so the only thing I might be curious about is what you studied."

"Home economics," she said, rose, and started to put on her clothes.

I watched her dress. "You'll find that Victor's just what he says he is."

"Probably," I said.

"Then why all the bother?"

"It only took a phone call."

"Why the topcoat?"

"The what?" I said.

"You were naked, but before you'd talk over the phone, you put on a topcoat."

"I never answer the phone naked."

"I like to," she said.

"So did I."

"But you don't anymore?"

"No."

She looked at me for a moment. "I think you're a little weird after all."

"A little," I said.

"Where do you want it, on the dresser?"

"What?"

"Your twenty thousand I got from the bank this morning. By the way, Orcutt wants to see you at noon."

"Okay."

"Well, where do you want the money?"

"On the dresser, honey," I said. "I like to preserve the traditions."

24

They caught a Mutt and Jeff pair in Bonn who they thought might have raped and murdered my wife. It was in January of 1958 and I had just finished the training program that Section Two claimed would equip me to go out into the world and cope with the enemies of the Republic. I could divine a map, shoot a pistol with what everyone agreed was fair accuracy, and even use a knife should the occasion arrive. Not only that, but I could burgle a house or a flat with reasonable competency, defend myself unarmed against the neighborhood bully, and decipher a code or two. There were some other courses which were taught to the five of us who composed the class of '57, and the instructors would usually preface their lectures with the phrase, "This may save your life." But since there were no tests, only an evaluation by a board, I no more listened to the lectures than I did to those that I had endured while in basic infantry training at Camp Hood.

Halfway through the course I received a written evaluation which I suppose was designed to shake me up a little. It noted that I was "inattentive" and "unmotivated," whatever that meant. It didn't bother me. They had spent close to twenty-six thousand dollars sending me to college for four years and they were buying that and my languages, not what I had learned in a six-month course in Maryland. I must have been graduated, if that's the term, at the bottom of my class.

Again it was Carmingler who told me about the pair in Bonn. He wore a greenish-gray tweed suit that day, which emphasized his flaming hair and once more I thought that he must be the world's most conspicuous secret agent. "They fit the description you gave," he said.

"It wasn't much of a description except that one was a little short and the other one was taller than that."

"There are a couple of other things that fit," he said.

"They're East Germans and that's where the colonel had been operating."

"Doing what?" I said.

He ignored the question and didn't even wince as much as usual. Carmingler had been on my evaluation board and in his appraisal had written that I had a "facile mind, but an unfortunately flippant attitude which bodes him ill." Nobody but Carmingler could have written "bodes him ill." He really should have been a major in a proper British regiment seconded to special operations during World War I. It would have made him extremely happy.

"The other thing," he said, "is that the pair removed someone in Bonn who had been working closely with the colonel."

"Removed?"

"Eliminated."

"Killed?"

"Yes, damn it."

"I won't even ask who."

"Good."

"You want me to try to identify them?"

"Yes."

"All right," I said. "When do we leave?"

"Tomorrow."

We flew from Baltimore to what was then still Idlewild and made the long prop flight to Gander and Scotland and London and finally to Cologne. Carmingler read books and documents and otherwise improved his mind during the trip. I stared out the window, drank what was offered, and slept. We didn't talk much.

We were met at the Cologne-Bonn airport by a driver with a black Opel Kapitan. It was one of those wet, nasty January days that the Rhine is so good at producing. The heater didn't work in the Opel and when we finally got to where we were going I was chilled and irritable.

It was an old brick warehouse that somehow had escaped the bombing, probably because it was built just outside of Cologne in a sparsely settled residential area. It hadn't escaped completely, however, and I could see where shell fragments had torn into the brick leaving scars that still looked like pink scabs.

"Ours?" I said.

"Belongs to the British really," Carmingler said.

218

We went up a short flight of concrete steps, through a door, and down a hall that was covered with scuffed green linoleum. The walls were painted a dirty tan and some notices in German about what to do in case of an air raid were still thumbtacked up in several places. Carmingler seemed to have been there before and he walked briskly down the hall as if headed for the executive washroom. He stopped at the door that was half-wood, half frosted-glass, knocked, and opened it before anyone said who is it or come in. He held it open for me and I entered into what once must have been *Herr Direktor*'s office. There was a carpet on the floor and a massive oak desk at one end of the almost square room. There was also a long table with nine or ten chairs around it that could have been used for meetings of the board or the staff. Some photographs of the Rhine decorated the tan walls, along with a calendar whose pages no one had turned since June, 1945. I suppose the British needed the calendar to remind them that they had really won the war.

A man behind the desk rose as we entered and said, "Hullo, Carmingler." They didn't shake hands and Carmingler said, "Dye, Speke," which may have set a record for short introductions.

"Where are they?" Carmingler said.

"In the cellar." Speke was English.

"Did your people do any good?"

Speke nodded his head. "Some, but they both talked a lot of gibberish. Their English is excellent, you know, and they could pass as Americans. Both were P.O.W.s in Mississippi during the war. One even has what I'd venture is a slight southern accent."

Carmingler looked at me and I shook my head. "They never said a word."

"Anything else?" Carmingler said.

Speke looked down at his bare desk as if trying to remember. "We're quite satisfied that they're a team who've been operating out of the GDR since forty-nine or so. They admit that they did for a chap that we had in Hamburg in fifty-three and to a long list of other probables."

"They admit anything else?" Carmingler said.

"Well, they could scarcely deny the Bonn thing after

219

your people caught them in the act—or just after the act, since poor old Basserton was already dead."

"Political?" Carmingler asked, and I noticed that he was shaving his consonants and elongating his vowels more than usual. He always did that around the British.

"No," Speke said, "no we don't think so any more than your people do. They're *professionals* no doubt of that. But their motivation is exclusively money, not politics."

"What about before the war?"

"They both claim that they were petty crooks in Berlin. It could be. They've got the accent and the argot. After they were sent back from the States and demobbed, they say that they drifted into this, although they are a little vague about how one drifts into the assassination profession."

"And despite the necktie they still deny having been back to the States?" Carmingler said.

"What necktie?" I said.

"One of them was wearing a tie with a Hecht Company label on it. The Hecht Company's a Washington department store. We checked the tie out and it can't be more than a year old."

"The one with the tie claims that he traded with a drunken American tourist in a Frankfurt bar," Speke said.

"Who paid them?" Carmingler said.

"The same story they told your people. Some chap in Berlin whom they know only as Willi. They got two thousand marks each plus expenses."

"D'you think you've got everything out of them that you can?"

Speke nodded. "I think so. We've been at them day and night for three weeks."

"Drugs?"

"Your people did. We used—uh—other methods and after a while they talked readily enough."

"But not about Mrs. Dye?"

"Curiously no. They don't seem to mind confessing any number of political assassinations, but they were quite adamant in their denial that they had participated in a rape-murder." He glanced at me. "Sorry."

"It's all right."

"So you're through with them?" Carmingler said.

"Yes. I should think so."

"Dye needs to look at them."

220

"Quite."

We left the office and went down the hall to another door that opened on to a flight of stairs. The stairs led to a bricked cellar with a cement floor that ran underneath the entire length and breadth of the warehouse. At one end was a small room, not more than twelve by twelve. It was much newer than the rest of the building and had been constructed of cement blocks with a metal door that had a small opening covered with heavy iron mesh. Two men sat outside the door in wooden armchairs. They wore coats and sweaters and had an electric three-bar heater which was plugged into the double-socket of a bare bulb that hung overhead.

"Bring them out," Speke said to one of the men, who nodded and rose. He took out a ring of big keys and unlocked the door with two of them and then slid back a heavy iron bar which squeaked and for a moment I was back in Shanghai, in Bridge House, where the sounds had been the same, and I could imagine the apprehension felt by the two inside the cell. They must have known that there never would be any good news again.

Both of the men who guarded the cell were up now. Both had produced revolvers, .38s from the look of them. One stood directly in front of the door while the other pulled it open. Two men dressed in dark suits and sweaters came out. They wore no ties and probably no belts. The laces were gone from their shoes and they had to shuffle to keep them on. One was tall and one was short.

Speke told them what to do in English. "Stand over there," he said, motioning to the brick wall. They shuffled over to the wall and stood facing it. "Turn around," he said. They turned around. I walked over and looked at them.

Mutt, the taller one, was about five-eleven with sloping shoulders and long arms that ended in hairy-backed hands. He had brownish hair and light blue eyes with ordinary brows that ran into each other across a nose that leaned a little to the left. His mouth was small and almost pursed and it didn't go with his big chin and thick neck. He also needed a shave.

Jeff, the shorter one, had long, light blonde hair, almost white, that kept flopping down into blue eyes that were a little piggy and mean. He had a potato nose and red splotches on his cheekbones, light almost invisible eyebrows, and a surprisingly hard slice of a mouth that looked as if it had been drawn with a ruler. He had a sharp chin, a slight build that was probably all gristle, and skinny hands.

"Well?" Carmingler said. He was standing at my elbow.

"They wore masks," I said. "Halloween masks. The rubber kind."

"Their size, their build?" he said.

"Could be."

"The big one. Hairy hands."

"A lot of people have hairy hands," I said.

"You can't make either of them?"

"Drop your pants," I said to the taller one.

He looked at Speke and frowned so I said it again in German and told him to be goddamned quick about it. Speke told him the same thing. The man grumbled something and then undid his fly and dropped his pants so that they lay in what seemed to be a dark puddle about his shoes.

"Your shorts, too," I said.

He didn't like that at all. "What is the meaning of this?" he said.

"I want to look at your cock," I said.

He almost blushed and shot another look of appeal at Speke, who must have played the only friend role with them.

"Drop them." Speke said.

The taller man did blush this time and dropped his shorts. They were blue-and-white striped ones, but a lot of men wore those. I looked at his penis. He wasn't circumsized and it lay there shriveled from cold and fear and embarrassment. I went down on one knee to get a better look at it and he jumped. I rose and stared at the man. "You remember me, don't you?" I said. "You remember how I got to watch you rape my wife and then shoot her one Saturday night?"

He was a good liar, but not good enough. There was a twitch in his left eyelid when I mentioned Saturday because it hadn't been Saturday. It had been Friday. It was only a twitch. "I don't know you," he said. "I have never seen you before."

I turned to Carmingler and Speke. "Are you through with them both?" I said.

222

Carmingler said, "We are," and turned to Speke who shrugged.

"May I use one of those pistols?"

Speke nodded and one of the guards handed me his. It was .38 Smith and Wesson, I noticed. I turned back to the pair and pointed the gun at the smaller one. "You remember me, don't you?" I said.

"No," he said and locked his blue eyes with mine.

"I remember your friend there because of the blue spot on the end of his cock."

The taller one jerked his head forward to look for the blue spot. "There isn't any," he said.

"You got it cured after all."

"I didn't have—" He stopped then.

"I'm going to kill you both, you know," I said.

The taller one must have believed me. He swallowed and began to work his lips around. I knew what he was doing, so I waited. When he had enough saliva he spat at me and it landed on the lapel of my topcoat. He was snarling now "She was rotten sex!" He yelled it in German. The he switched to English and screamed it. "She was a lousy fuck!"

I almost killed him then. I tried to. I remember that my finger was beginning to pull at the trigger and the scene came back of him sprawled across Beverly, his pants and shorts down to his ankles, as he grunted and lunged. I recalled her face and how she looked and what had happened to her eyes. I tried to kill him then, but instead I turned and said, "Ah, shit," and shoved the gun at Speke and hurried for the stairs before any of them could see my face.

We flew back to New York the next day.

25

The friendly folks at Swankerton's First National Bank couldn't have been nicer. Someone smiled pleasantly when I said that I wanted to open a checking account. Someone else beamed when I rented a safety deposit box in which to store the $20,000 in cash delivered to me that morning by Carol Thackerty. A vice-president was absolutely radiant when I showed him the letter of credit from Orcutt's St. Louis bank and for all I knew they were equally charming to those who said they could use a couple of hundred till payday.

I was rich now, I decided. I had more money than I'd had since I was eight years old and a partner in a crap game on the *Gripsholm*. I had $19,500 in San Francisco; $20,000 in a Swankerton safe-deposit box; $5,000 in a checking account for expenses, and the promise of another $25,000 on the way from Ramsey Lynch. I also had $816.59 cash. I thought about retirement and that kept me busy until around eleven o'clock when Homer Necessary called from the lobby and said that he was on his way up.

"You got a drink?" he said as he came in.

"I still have some Scotch."

"That'll do."

I mixed two drinks and handed him his. "No ice," I said.

"I'm used to it."

"How was it?"

"How or why?"

"Both."

Necessary told it quickly in his usually concise manner and once again he placed everything in the present tense. "I leave you last night around ten to twelve and head down the street to a joint called The Easy Alibi. You know it?"

"I've seen it," I said. "A city councilman owns it."

"That figures. I order a drink and I'm sitting there wondering how talkative the barkeep might be when a

224

couple of plainclothes come in, let me look at their badges, and then give me a ride to headquarters. They're new, by the way, the headquarters, I mean, real nice. So they print me and mug me and then they take me into a quiet little room and ask me a few questions."

"About what?"

"About what we've got on who. So I tell em that we haven't got anything on anybody and they ask me again. After a while they get tired of asking and smack me around a little, but not too hard, more like they don't really have their hearts in it. So one of em pulls out a pint and tells me to drink it. What the hell, it's better than getting smacked around so I drink it. Cheap bourbon. Well, I can drink a pint and still move around okay, but they take me down and book me for drunk and disorderly and and resisting arrest. Then they toss me into the tank. It's not so bad—only three drunks in. You oughta see one when they got forty or fifty packed in and most of them are coming down with the d-t's."

"When did they let you go?"

"Maybe an hour ago. One of the trusties comes by and says I must have pull someplace because they're changing the blotter. Trusties know everything. A little later they give everything back, even my money, and send me home in a goddamned squad car."

"Did anyone apologize?"

"No."

"They were supposed to."

"You fixed it?"

"With Lynch. The chief wasn't too happy."

Necessary nodded thoughtfully. "One guy did say something about 'these things happen' and even called me 'mister,' so I guess that's as close as they can bring themselves to an apology."

"It shouldn't happen again," I said.

"You made your deal?"

"Yes."

"They buy it?"

"Only after I told them Orcutt knew that I was doing it and that he's dumb enough to believe that I'll really stick with him instead of switching to them."

Necessary nodded again. "Yeah," he said, "that would make them feel smart." He took a large swallow of his

225

drink, saw that there was only a little left, and finished it. "Only thing is, you might be telling the truth."

"I might," I said.

He flicked his brown and blue eyes over me and there was only indifference in them. "You know something? I bet there're times when you're not sure yourself what side you're on."

"There're times," I said.

"This one of em?"

"I don't think so."

He looked at me again, more carefully this time, and then got up and mixed another drink. He came back to where I sat and looked at me some more.

"They probably made a lot of hard noise about what might happen if you crossed them."

"They mentioned it," I said. "In passing."

"Uh-huh. Well, I'll mention it myself and just give you some advice about not getting too cute unless you want a real unhappy ending."

"You're loyal, huh?"

"To Orcutt?"

"Yes."

Necessary looked into his drink and for a moment he seemed a little embarrassed. Finally he said, "He pays me."

I let it go at that.

Orcutt was cooking lunch for the four of us when we gathered in the Rickenbacker suite at noon after I'd waited in Necessary's room for him to shave, shower and change clothes. There were two chafing dishes bubbling away over lighted cans of Sterno. Several opened bottles of wine stood around as if some of their contents had been splashed into whatever was on the burners. Orcutt was peering into one of the chafing dishes and stirring it with a long wooden spoon. He wore a frilly apron.

"I just don't feel like going out in this heat," he said and followed my gaze down to the apron. "Isn't it ridiculous? But it's the only one that Carol could find. Or so she said."

"It was the only one they had unless I wanted to go traipsing all over town," she said.

"Smells good," Necessary said. "What is it?"

"Chicken livers Orcutt," Carol said. She was sitting in

an armchair and I noticed that she wore a dress different from the one she'd had on that morning.

The hotel (reluctantly, I guessed) had set up near a window a cloth-covered table which held dishes and silverware and glasses. A shallow silver tray contained some green and black olives and I helped myself to one. I also noticed a large green salad.

"You got anything to drink?" Necessary said.

"You'll *simply* have to help yourself, Homer," Orcutt said as he glided between the two chafing dishes, stirring this and poking that.

"Have you got any goddamned ice for a change?" Necessary said to Carol after he found a bottle.

"In the bucket over there," she said.

Orcutt tasted one of the dishes with his wooden spoon. "Now," he said. "Carol, if you and Mr. Dye will bring your plates over, I'll serve while it's still hot. Homer doesn't really care what he eats."

I followed instructions and brought a plate over. Orcutt served Carol and then me. He spooned what looked to be a half-pound of sautéed chicken livers on to my plate and then moved to the second chafing dish. "This is really a kind of paella except that it has a bit more saffron than most people use and also a *tiny* smidgeon more garlic. I hope you like garlic?"

"I love it," I said.

Orcutt waved the spoon. "The wine is over there, so please help yourself."

I helped myself and when we were all settled around the room I tried the chicken livers, which may have been the best I'd ever eaten, but the paella had too much garlic. Everyone complimented Orcutt on his cooking and he beamed for almost five minutes and then remembered to take off the apron.

"Well, I think it's fortunate that I *do* like to cook," he said. "There's only one *decent* restaurant in town and it's not open until six. And there's something else about the South that I've never understood. It doesn't have any *real* delicatessens. I can get by just fine with a proper delicatessen, but there simply aren't any here and no place else in the South unless it's New Orleans or Atlanta. I've also heard that there's one in Montgomery."

"They got some damned good ones in Miami," Necessary said around a mouthful of chicken livers. "They got to because of all the kikes."

"*Really,* Homer," Orcutt said. "Miami isn't the *South.*"

We ate in silence for a while until Orcutt sighed, rose, put his plate on the cloth-covered table, and smoothed the lapels of his double-breasted coat. The coat was one-half of his white-on-white seersucker suit that was set off by a dark blue shirt, a white knit tie, and black-and-white wing-tipped shoes with built-up heels. He was, I decided, a man who took his fashion seriously.

He turned toward me. "Now to business. What happened at your meeting this morning?"

I told him in detail without embellishment or unnecessary footnotes and he listened well, asking only a couple of pertinent questions. When I was done, he said, "You think they really believed you?"

"Not completely. Their faith will increase after I hand over our first victim and when you seem to act on some of their phony information that I'll transmit to you."

Orcutt paced the room and tapped a forefinger against his lower lip. It seemed to help him think. "Oh, by the way," he said, "I understand that someone is checking us out for you."

"An old friend. He's also checking out Ramsey Lynch and the chief of police."

"Good," Orcutt said. "I'm glad you've done that. I'd say it shows that you prefer our side, providing that our references prove satisfactory."

"You can say that," I said. "You can also say that I'm merely suspicious."

"I certainly hope so," Orcutt said. "Now then, I've spent scads of time going over a list of persons who might be sacrificed to enhance your reputation with Lynch and his people. For the purpose of verisimilitude, I've selected a man and a woman, both of whom, as you would say, Mr. Dye, need ruining."

"A woman's good, if she's gone and done something real smelly," Necessary said and then looked around the room as if he expected someone to contradict him. Nobody did.

"We'll start with her then," Orcutt said. "I'll give you a condensed version." He took several four-by-five-inch cards from an inside coat pocket and flipped through them.

Her name, he said, was Mrs. Francine Sobour, widow of Maurice Sobour who had died at seventy-eight six years ago of a heart attack brought on, some said, by the rapacious demands of his bride of six months. Mrs. Sobour was forty-two years old when she married her husband and two months after the wedding he changed his will, disinheriting a number of deserving sons, daughters, grandchildren and charities, and leaving his new wife the entire estate, which was valued at approximately a million dollars. Although Mr. Sobour had no medical history that indicated a heart condition, there had been no autopsy. "We have a sworn statement that she paid the county coroner five thousand dollars cash not to conduct the autopsy."

"Where's the coroner now?" I said.

"Dead," Orcutt said, "but his statement is witnessed and attested to by his wife and two sons, who claim to have been present at the transaction with the Sobour woman."

"Where are they now?" Necessary said.

"In Florida, I think."

"How much the statement cost us?" Necessary said.

"Another five thousand."

"It's not too hot," Necessary said. "What he should have done was perform the autopsy and if he found anything, maybe arsenic, he'd been set for life."

"Which in his case was only three months," Orcutt said. "His car went out of control on a bridge one night and crashed through the guard rail. It was a perfectly clear night."

Necessary grunted suspiciously.

Before she married her late husband, Mrs. Sobour had been the wife of Jean Dupree, last in the line of an old but impecunious Swankerton family. Dupree had been a prominent Catholic layman and a member of a number of the city's civic and social organizations.

"How'd he die?" Necessary said.

"He drank himself to death," Orcutt said.

The Widow Dupree, soon to be the Widow Sobour, was also a great joiner and currently served as co-chairman of the city's United Fund Drive. She was also chairman or president of the Swankerton League of Women Voters and active in the local chapter of the United Daughters of the Confederacy. She belonged to a number of social clubs, had served as an alternate delegate to the 1968

Republican convention in Miami, and was prominent in various Catholic charities and fund-raising drives.

"When her second husband died," Orcutt said, "she became president of the Maurice Sobour Real Estate Company. A year ago she was elected secretary of the Swankerton Clean Government Association which is, of course, nominally the organization that has retained Victor Orcutt Associates."

"What you got on her, Victor?" Necessary said.

"I'm coming to that. Three years ago Mrs. Sobour started a large development of expensive, custom-built homes on some property that was located several miles from Swankerton. Apparently, she sank every cent that she had and could borrow into the venture. Costs skyrocketed, she ran into the usual unexpected delays, there were some zoning problems, and to sum it up she ran out of money."

"So who'd she steal it from?" Necessary wanted to know.

"Homer, your habit of anticipating conclusions could become most irritating," Orcutt said in the sharp tone of one whose punch line has just been ruined by the party buffoon. It didn't bother Necessary.

Orcutt leaned forward and his dark blue eyes seemed to glitter a bit. "Now it really gets delicious," he said, and I decided that he was a born gossip. Some people are. "Mrs. Sobour was desperate for funds. She'd exhausted all sources of credit. In the meantime, a Catholic order of nuns—Sisters of Charity or Mercy or Solace or something like that, I have the name here somewhere—had entrusted her with nearly half a million dollars to invest for them in some land in Florida. Well, she *optioned* the land with a token payment of fifty thousand dollars and used the remainder of the half-million to pay off her debts. The option expires in three months."

Necessary leaned back in his chair and smiled at the ceiling. "That should get her kicked out of the realtor's league or whatever they call it," he said.

"Unless she picks up the option," I said. "Can she?"

"Probably," Orcutt said. "If we do nothing."

"What's the Catholic population in Swankerton?" I said.

"Forty-six percent," Orcutt said.

"Well, the headlines won't be too bad," Carol said. "Reform Movement Secretary Robs Sisters of the Poor."

230

"You have all the necessary documents?" I asked Orcutt. He nodded. "Okay. She'll do for the first ruinee. Old family, prominent Catholic, tied to the reform movement, and caught with her hand in the church poor box. The Catholics might vote for whoever you run in her place out of sympathy—or stubbornness. And the Protestants might vote for him—or her—because they probably hope that the widow's successor will do the same thing to the nuns who, as everybody in the South knows, don't do anything but shack up with the priests and sell their babies to wandering gypsies."

"Now I've never heard *that!*" Orcutt said.

"Common knowledge," Carol said.

"Lynch is going to like it all," Necessary said. "Lynch and his crowd'll like it just fine. Who's next, Victor?"

The next sacrificial lamb was the father of four, a deacon in the First Methodist Church, a well-to-do pharmacist, and one of the Clean Government Association's candidates for the city council. His name was Frank Mouton and he owned a chain of six drugstores that bore his name. "Sale of barbiturates without prescription," Orcutt read from his notes.

"That's not much," Necessary said.

"In wholesale lots, Homer," Orcutt said. "Fifty thousand at a time to the local pushers. It's how he expanded from one drugstore to six."

"How long ago was this?" I said.

"Long enough for the statute of limitations to keep him out of jail, but still recent enough to make a perfectly marvelous scandal."

"How long's the statute of limitations?" I said.

"Five years in the state."

"What about Federal?"

"They probably won't bother."

"Another good headline," Carol Thackerty said. "Prominent Deacon Branded Dope Pusher."

"Well, at least we're ecclesiastically impartial," Orcutt said.

"What was he wholesaling the most of?" Necessary said.

Orcutt looked at his notes. "It seems to have been rather evenly divided between stimulants and depressants. Six years ago he sold a total of more than two hundred thousand capsules of phenobarbital sodium and another hundred thousand of secobarbital sodium. On the stimu-

231

lant side, he disposed of one hundred twenty-five thousand capsules of amphetamine sulfate and one hundred sixty thousand capsules of dextroamphetamine sulfate. I think they're called 'bennies' and 'dexies.' It should have netted him close to one hundred thousand dollars during that one year."

"How good is your source?" I said.

"Unimpeachable, you might say."

"You have solid evidence?" I said.

Orcutt nodded. "Take my word as an attorney, Mr. Dye. It's solid."

"Good. I'll feed Lynch the woman first. A week or ten days later I'll hand him the druggist."

"What are your plans in the meantime?" Orcutt said.

"I thought I'd better take a look at the city."

"You want a guided tour?" Necessary said.

"That sounds good."

Necessary looked at his watch. "What about this afternoon?"

"All right."

Orcutt rose and moved over to a window and stood there for a few moments before he turned with a thoughtful look on his face. "Something just struck me," he said.

"What?" Carol Thackerty said.

He pushed his hands into his trouser pockets, looked at the ceiling, and rocked back and forth a little on his elevated heels. "You know, I don't think that the Deacon Mouton would have made a very good city councilman anyway."

26

Swankerton had the outline of a squatty pear; its fat bottom sprawled along the expensive Gulf Coast beach and then tapered reluctantly north into quiet, middle-income residential areas whose forty and fifty-year-old elms and weeping willows cooled and shaded streets where parking was still no problem. In the warm evenings the owners of the neat houses came home, changed into bermuda shorts, and stood about, gin and tonic in hand, watching their creepy-crawler sprinklers wet down the thick green lawns and wondering whether it wasn't the right time to sell and move to the suburbs, now that the place was looking so nice.

Farther up the pear, just below the neck, the neat homes and green lawns made way for ugly frame houses that once may have been bright green or blue or even yellow, but were now mostly a disappointed gray, ugly as old soldiers. The poor whites lived there, the millhands and the rednecks and their big-boned wives and tow-headed kids. The gray houses weren't really old. Most had been built right after World War II to accommodate the returning warriors and they had been thrown up fast in developments that went by such names as Monterrey Vistas and Vahlmall Gardens and Lakeview Acres. They had been cheaply built and cheaply financed with four percent VA loans and no money down to vets.

But the vets who had lived there right after World War II had long since moved away. The lawns had turned brown and some of the trees had died and the concrete streets with the fancy names were broken. Nearly every block had one or two or three rusting shrines to despair in the form of a '49 Ford with a busted block or a '51 Pontiac with frozen main bearings. Nobody admitted that the shrines even existed because admission implied ownership and it cost fifteen dollars to have them towed away.

The owners and renters here came home after work too, but they didn't change into anything. Those who

worked the day shift just sat around on the shady side of
the house in their plastic-webbed lawn chairs that they
got at the drugstore for a $1.98 each and drank Jax beer
and yelled at their kids.

The gray houses with their composition roofs kept on
going block after block until they ran up against the rail-
road tracks which split Swankerton neatly in two about
halfway up the pear. The tracks, which ran all the way
from Washington to Houston, served as the city's color
line. North of the tracks was black. South was white.

When you crossed the tracks leading north you found
yourself in another enclave of neat houses and emerald
lawns and creepy-crawler sprinklers. It lasted for almost
twelve blocks. The owners here were black and after work
they came home and changed into their bermuda shorts
and stood around, martini in hand, and wondered whether
they should buy their wives a Camaro or one of those new
Javelins. They were Niggertown's affluent, its political
leaders, its doctors and dentists, its morticians, school-
teachers, lawyers, skilled workers, restaurant owners, insurance salesmen, policy men, and the Federal civil servants who worked out at the big Air Force depot.

Past these well-tended houses and still farther up the
neck of the pear spread the rest of Niggertown, a collection of flimsy, gimcrack houses, often duplexes, whose
sides were covered with Permastone or imitation brick
and which often as not leaned crazily at each other. And
on the edge of the city, just before the suburban sprawl
began, was Shacktown, a fully integrated community,
composed of packing-crate hovels, abandoned buses, and
ancient house trailers that hadn't been moved in twenty
years. In Shacktown teeth were bad and bellies were
swollen and eyes were glazed. Those who lived there had
given up everything, but the last luxury to go had been the
comforting awareness of racial identity. But now that
had gone, too, and everyone in Shacktown was almost
colorblind.

The stem of the pear was the Strip, a three-mile-long
double strand of junkyards, motels, gas stations, nightclubs, roadhouses and honkytonks. Interspersed among
these were the franchised food spots, all glass and godawful colors, that hugged the highway to offer fried
chicken and tacos and hamburgers which all tasted the

same but signaled the wearied traveler that a kind of civilization lay just a little way ahead.

The Strip sliced outlying suburbia neatly in two, skirted Shacktown, and when it reached the city limits they called it MacArthur Drive. Desk-top flat and six and eight and even ten lanes wide, it rolled and twisted all the way down from Chicago and St. Louis and Memphis, taking bang-on aim at the Gulf of Mexico. They called it the Strip sometimes but more often just U.S. 97. It was the river that Swankerton had never had, the route of the endless caravan of semis and articulated vans, big as box cars, that growled up hills in low tenth gear and roared down the other side, seventy and eighty miles per hour, black smoke snorting from their diesel stacks and their drivers praying for the goddamned brakes to hold. The teamsters rolled them night and day down the highway that linked the city with the North and the West and they handled more freight in a day than the railroads did in a week. They rolled down from Pittsburgh and Minneapolis and Omaha and Chicago and Detroit and Cleveland, bringing Swankerton what it couldn't grow and what it couldn't make for itself, which was just about everything except textiles and vice.

"The trouble with Swankerton," Homer Necessary said at the end of our two-hour sightseeing tour during which he had served as guide, social commentator, and economic analyst, "is that it ain't got any harbor. They got that nice beach and all those hotels, but there's no river, so there's no harbor. They got that concrete pier that goes out about a mile and the tankers use that some, but that's really why the town never grew as much as it should've. No harbor."

We drove on in silence for a block or so and then he said, "Now I'm gonna show you something else that's wrong with Swankerton. Or right. It all depends on how you look at it."

He headed toward the downtown section, the older part, where the streets that ran east and west were named after such notables as Jefferson, Calhoun, Washington, Lee, Jackson, Stuart, Clay, Forrest, Hampton, Longstreet, Pickett and Early. The streets that ran north and south were numbered. We rolled down Third Street in the blue air-conditioned Impala that Necessary had rented, down to the edge of the commercial and financial districts. He pulled into a parking lot on Clay. "It's about a block from here."

We walked the block and I sweated in my too-heavy suit. We walked past the Texas Chili Parlor and Big Billy's Inn and Emmett's Billiard Parlor where "just a guy" supposedly hung out, past a TV repair shop, and turned into a narrow store front that had a black-and-white sign reading "Books and Movies."

"I've buttered this guy up some," Necessary said as we went in.

Most of the books were paperback and were written by authors with such alliterative names as Norman Norway and Jennifer Jackson and Paula Pale. The covers weren't too well done, but they got their messages across. Often there were two girls of impressive physical proportions who went around in boots and whips and not much else. Sometimes there were two men and one girl or two girls and one man and they all seemed to have large, unmade beds in the background. The paperbacks' titles were about as imaginative as the names of the authors. There was *Red Lust* and *The Longest Whip* and *Broken Dyke* and *Fallen Devil*. The paperbacks took up about three-fourths of the small shop and the rest was given over to magazines that featured extraordinarily well-built muscle boys or nude girls or sometimes both.

"Hello, Croner," Necessary said to the man behind the tall counter that held a cash register.

"You remembered," Croner said and looked first over Necessary's right shoulder and then over his left.

"I remembered," Necessary said.

Croner glanced at his watch. "Should be about fifteen minutes," he said and darted another glance over Necessary's shoulders. I looked this time and found two large, curved mirrors up at the ceiling corners in the rear of the store which gave Croner a view of the entire place.

Croner caught my look and said, "You know what the freaks steal? They steal two, three hundred dollars' worth a week. I sometimes think when they boost it they get more of a jolt, you know what I mean?"

I told him that I did and Necessary said, "This is Lu; he's a friend of mine."

Croner nodded at me and then shot another glance at his mirrors. He had three customers, two well-dressed men of about fifty who browsed through a couple of magazines, one of which was called *Bondage;* I couldn't see the name of the other. The third customer was about eighteen and wore hair down to his shoulders and some pink-and-white pimples on his face. He was moving his lips over some of the words in a paperback.

"So how's business?" Necessary asked and leaned on the counter.

"Compared to what?" Croner said in a bitter tone. His complexion was the color of overcooked rice with dark eyes that reminded me of fat raisins. He was taller than I, almost six-four or six-five, and his thin elbows rested easily on the high counter. He talked out of the left side of his mouth because the right side seemed to be frozen. At least that corner didn't move either up or down, although his dark eyebrows did. They jumped around in constant motion as if compensating for the immobility of his mouth. He had a long neck, extraordinarily long, and his shirt had a collar that was two and a half inches high and a monogram in the place of a breast pocket. I decided that business was good enough for him to afford custom-made shirts.

"Croner here used to write about two thousand bucks' worth of numbers a day until Lynch came to town," Necessary told me. "Now he sells dirty books and rents blue movies. He could still be writing numbers except he thought the dues were too high."

"How much?" I said.

"You'll see in a couple of minutes," Croner said out of the side of his mouth and shot his eyebrows up and down a few times before flicking his glance at the two mirrors.

"Guy across the street in that dry cleaning place writes them now," Necessary said. "Does a nice business. Just watch for a few minutes."

It was a small shop called Jiffy Cleaners and it did seem to be doing a better than fair business. Every two or three minutes a woman or a man would go in, sometimes two and three at a time. They usually came out a minute or so later.

"Now what's wrong with that picture?" Necessary said.

"Not much," I said, "except that they don't carry any clothes in or out."

"Money in, a slip out," Necessary said. "He writes maybe two to three thousand bucks' worth a day. And in about five minutes he'll pay his dues."

We waited five minutes. A uniformed cop sauntered by and entered the dry cleaning shop. He came out forty-five seconds later according to my watch.

"Every day about this time he goes in and collects his five bucks," Croner said. "Except Sunday when he's off. He's off Monday too, but he still comes down for it. I only used to pay him a couple a day. Talk about your god-damned inflation."

"That's an extra thirty a week in take-home pay," I said.

"Thirty shit," Croner said. "He's got another one six blocks down. He drags down at least sixty to seventy a week. Tax free."

"Now watch this," Necessary said. "Should be any minute."

Some more customers without dry cleaning either to be done or to be picked up entered and left the shop. A Ford squad car with Swankerton Police Department on its side double parked in front of Jiffy Cleaners for a minute while one of its uniformed occupants went in and came out. He hadn't dropped by to pick up his other suit either, and the squad car didn't move off until the one who had gone into the shop handed something to the driver.

"They're splitting the weekly take," Croner said. "Three hundred bucks. I used to pay them two hundred."

It was a half hour before something else interesting happened. Two more customers came into Croner's store and the two middle-aged men left after buying a couple of magazines each. The teen-ager with the long hair and the pimples didn't buy anything. The dry cleaning shop across the street continued to do a steady business.

An unmarked green Mercury double parked in front of the cleaning shop. Its single occupant entered the store, remained less than a minute, came out, and drove off.

"He just picked up the monthly take of seventeen hundred bucks for the brass down at headquarters," Croner said. "His name's Toby Marks and he's regular bagman all over town."

"Altogether, that's about three thousand a month," I said.

"About," Croner said. "I figure that guy across the street's working about ten or eleven days a month just for

238

the cops. If he can't cut it and goes out of business, that's too damned bad for him. Somebody else'll open up and pay off and the bastard cops are the only ones who're guaranteed a profit."

"Why pay off the beat cop?" I said. "He's not going to arrest anybody if they're dragging in that much downtown."

Croner gave me a pitying look, which he managed by manipulating his eyebrows. "Why pay off the beat cop, he asks. Well, all he has to do is stand out there for about three hours and the guy inside begins to hurt. Nobody's gonna play numbers at a spot where a cop's holding up the wall."

"How many places like that in town?" Necessary said, mostly for my benefit, I thought.

Croner shrugged his bony shoulders. "I don't know. Maybe a couple of hundred, maybe more. I think they lose count in Niggertown. Last time I figured it out the total monthly payoff to the cops was around maybe half a million a month."

"Nice," Necessary said. "Real nice."

"Why aren't you still writing?" I said.

Croner shot quick looks at his two curved mirrors. "Like your buddy here says, I thought the dues were too high so I quit paying the beat cop. He stood outside my place for four hours a day for two weeks. I went broke. Then the people I banked with got mad and took it away from me and gave it to the guy across the street."

"Seen enough?" Necessry said.

"I think so."

"Thanks, Croner," Necessary said. "I'll be around in a couple of days with a little something for you."

Croner nodded glumly. "You want anything to read?" he said and waved a hand at the racks of books and magazines. "On the house."

Necessary shook his head firmly. "My wife don't like me to read that stuff less I'm home where it'll do her some good. How 'bout you?" he said to me.

"I don't think so," I said.

Croner nodded again, just as glumly as before. "Don't blame you. It's all a bunch of crap. You'd be surprised at who buys it though. Sometimes I think this whole town is full of freaks."

We got the car out of the lot and Necessary drove down Fifth to Forrest and turned left. "How much cash you got on you?" he said.

"About eight hundred."

"That'll get you in."

"Where?"

"I'll show you in a minute." He turned right on Sixth Street and went two more blocks. "Just to your left is the new municipal center and police headquarters where I spent last night," he said.

It was new, about fifteen stories high, and with its parking lot took up most of a city block. It was built of precast concrete slabs and its windows were tinted almost black and recessed a foot or so into the outer wall. The black windows gave it a grim, forbidding air and that was probably the way that they wanted it to look.

"They got the criminal courts in there, too," Necessary said. "The city and county jails are around back."

Across Sixth Street from headquarters were the usual inexpensive restaurants, poolhalls, and bars frequented by those who have good and bad reason to hang agound police headquarters. There was a lawyers' building and a number of signs painted on windows in gold leaf advertising twenty-four-hour bail bond service. The block also had three pawnshops.

Necessary drove into another parking lot and we walked up Sixth Street and turned into the side entrance of a three-story brick building whose ground floor was home to the Bench and Gavel Bar. We walked up a flight of stairs and down a hall that was lined with the offices of bail bondsmen and one-man legal offices. A phone rang occasionally. The sound of electric typewriters was constant. Necessary pushed through a door with no lettering on it. Past the door was a regular reception room with a desk and a chair. Behind the desk sat a young, uniformed policeman who nodded at Necessary and stared at me.

"You gonna try it again, huh?" he said to Necessary.

"Try," Necessary said.

"He okay?" the cop said, nodding at me.

"He's okay," Necessary said.

The cop reached under the desk and a buzzer sounded. We went through another door and into a room whose three windows offered a fine view of police headquarters across Sixth Street. There were two poker tables in the room, six chairs at each, and at least three of the gamblers wore the blue uniforms and the insignia of police lieutenant or captain. There were two chairs open at the far table and Necessary and I sat down next to each other. On my left was a police lieutenant with a small stack of chips in front of him. He nodded at me and I nodded back.

A young man of about thirty with green eyes and crinkly brown hair grinned at Necessary and said, "Well, Chief, you gonna try to get even?"

"I'll take two hundred worth," Necessary said and pushed ten twenties across the table. The man with the green eyes looked at me and said, "How much, friend?"

"Two hundred," I said and gave him four fifties. We played draw for an hour and I won nearly fifty dollars. Necessary lost a hundred. The police lieutenant was the big loser. He dropped nearly a thousand during the hour to a pair of quiet thin men with careful faces whose conversation was limited to "in, out, call, up twenty, or check." Whenever the chips in front of the lieutenant disappeared, he merely looked at the man with the crinkly hair, who shoved another two or three-hundred-dollar stack at him. The lieutenant was a bad player, a compulsive better, and an indifferent bluffer. At four o'clock he looked at his watch, cashed in forty dollars' worth of chips, nodded at me again, rose and left. The two captains at the other table also cashed in and left.

The man with the crinkly hair sighed. "Thank God he doesn't win often," he said to nobody in particular.

"Free ride again, huh?" Necessary said.

"When they win, they win. When they lose, they put it on the tab and the tab's never paid." He looked at Necessary. "Hear you had a little trouble last night."

"Just a misunderstanding," Necessary said.

"Uh-huh," the man with the green eyes and crinkly hair said, "that's what I heard. A misunderstanding."

"Deal," said one of the men with a careful face. We played until five and I lost $125. Necessary was ahead a hundred or so. He shoved his chips in and the man with the crinkly hair cashed them without comment. I tossed him the couple of chips that I had left and he handed me $10.

"Come back," he said, "now that you know the way."

"Thanks," I said. "I will."

A different young policeman was on duty at the desk in the waiting room. He looked at us as we went out but said nothing. Halfway down the stairs, Necessary said. "That's one of the six games that Lynch runs. It starts at nine every morning and runs till about five A.M. The headquarters' brass play free, but they're all pretty bad and don't win much."

When we were on Sixth Street, Necessary paused and said, "You want a drink?"

"Sounds good."

We went into the cool, damp interior of the Bench and Gavel, sat in a booth, and ordered two gin and tonics. Necessary took a long swallow of his and said, "How'd you like the tour?"

"Educational."

"Give you any ideas?"

"A few."

"We only skimmed the surface today," he said.

"What's it look like underneath?"

"It's not the looks so much, it's the smell."

"Pretty bad?"

"It stinks," Necessary said.

"And the more it's stirred, the worse it'll get."

Necessary finished his drink and waved for another one. "You figure on doing a little stirring?"

I nodded. "When I find a long enough spoon."

27

The evening paper, *The News-Calliope*, broke the story a
week later with a screaming, eight-column banner. Skirting the libel laws by a legal pica or so, the publication
charged that Mrs. Francine Sobour, prominent realtor
and secretary of the Swankerton Clean Government Association, had stolen nearly a half million dollars from some
Catholic nuns and had used the funds to get herself out of
a financial hole.

To prove it, the newspaper printed pictures of
Xeroxed copies of various checks and documents that had
been involved in the transaction. There was even a signed,
front-page editorial by the editor and publisher himself,
Channing d'Arcy Phetwick III, calling upon Mrs. Sobour
to resign from the Clean Government Association "until
these damaging and shocking allegations are explained to
the complete satisfaction of concerned citizens, Catholic
and Protestant alike." He forgot to mention those of the
Jewish faith, but that must have been an unintentional
oversight.

The story pushed Washington and Southeast Asia back
to pages four and five. The reform candidate for mayor, a
prissy-looking attorney with rimless glasses, said that he
was "deeply disturbed." The incumbent mayor, Pierre
(Pete) Robineaux, whom I had met at Lynch's Victorian
house, said that it was "shocking, but not surprising," and
Phetwick's paper printed a picture of him saying it with
his tiny mouth agape and his eyes bulging half out of their
sockets. The law firm that handled Mrs. Sobour's affairs
issued a statement that in one paragraph made vague
threats about filing a libel suit and in the next announced
that Mrs. Sobour would "have no comment at present."

The TV stations picked it up, of course, and showed
pictures of the virtually completed luxury development
that Mrs. Sobour was in hock for. They also ran some old
film clips of her which showed a still attractive, dark-
haired woman with a broad smile and a cheery wave.

Some of the Sisters of Solace were also interviewed. They said that they were praying for Mrs. Sobour.

At nine o'clock that night, Mayor Robineaux bought a half hour of political time on all three television stations and used it to attack the Clean Government Association as "the spoiler of Swankerton." He wasn't a very good speaker and since he had preempted two of the top ten TV programs, he probably lost himself a few thousand votes.

It had taken me the entire week to get the information on the Sobour woman to Ramsey Lynch. I gave it to him piecemeal, an item at a time. Some of it was Xeroxed on different machines, some of it I had copied in my own scrawled handwriting on the backs of envelopes, and some of it was verbal stuff that Lynch could check out himself. Orcutt and I spent hours deciding what particular document or scrap of evidence Lynch should get on a particular day and what form it should take. Carol Thackerty had suggested that I use my almost indecipherable handwriting.

Lynch had been like a man who is given a jigsaw puzzle one piece at a time. He had a vague, general idea of its outline, but until I handed him the final damning piece of documentation, the picture had been of interesting composition, but inadequate impact. The final piece brought it all into focus and Lynch said, "Well, I'll be goddamned go to hell, so that's how she did it!"

"She's good," I said.

"Good, my ass, she's damn near perfect. The thing is, she could've paid it all back in three months and nobody'd ever known the difference."

"That's right."

Lynch looked at me carefully. "How'd you get tipped off?"

"I listen a lot," I said. "And I remember what I hear."

"You must have done some sneaking around late at night."

I shook my head. "Early in the morning. Before cock crow."

Lynch grinned and nodded his four or five chins. "That's a good time all right." He tapped the pile of Xeroxed material and scribbled notes with a forefinger. "You know what I'm gonna do with all this?"

"What?"

"I'm gonna get it all typed up neat with extra Xeroxed copies of everything and then I'm gonna wrap it up in a pink ribbon and send it over to old Phetwick at the *Calliope* with a note that says 'for your information.' "

"He'll print it."

"He might sit on it till it's hatched," Lynch said with a dubious look. "He's one of the high muckety-mucks in the Clean Government crowd."

"That's why he'll print it," I said. "That and because he's in the business of selling newspapers. Christ, *The News-Calliope* will be more outraged and hurt than the nuns themselves." I didn't mention that a reporter on the *Calliope* had dug up most of the material on Mrs. Sobour nearly two months before and that Phetwick had locked it away in a safe.

We were in my hotel room at the Sycamore, alone except for Boo Robineaux, the mayor's disenchanted heir, who was reading a copy of *Evergreen*, or at least admiring the pictures.

"Boo," Lynch said, "bring me my bag over here."

Boo rose, not taking his eyes from the magazine, picked up the briefcase, brought it over to Lynch, handed it to him, and went back to his chair without skipping a word. He seemed totally disinterested.

"Got a little something for you," Lynch said, unlocking the briefcase.

"Like money?"

"Like money. Sorry I'm a week late with it, but we wanted a look at the merchandise."

He started taking it out of the briefcase and stacking it on the coffee table. Then he was done and there were ten stacks of brand new fifty-dollar bills.

"Twenty-five grand," he said. "Want to count it?"

I shook my head. "I don't even want to touch it."

"What's the matter? You said cash."

"Tell you what you do," I said. "You put the money back in the briefcase, give it to Boo, and tell him to go across the street to the First National and ask that nice vice-president over there, the one who's so friendly, to change it into used tens, twenties, and just a few old fifties. You wouldn't mind doing that, would you, Lynch?"

Lynch chuckled. "By God, I bet you think it's queer."

"No," I said. "I just think it's new and so are the serial numbers."

Lynch tried to look gravely offended, but it was ruined by the twinkle in his eyes. "There's not much Christian trust in that heart of yours, Brother Dye."

"None at all, Brother Lynch."

We had a drink while Boo Robineaux went across the street to switch the new money for old bills. "What else do you think you might dig up?" Lynch said.

"You just named it," I said. "Something else."

"Just as good."

"Better, I think."

"You're not sure yet?"

"No."

"Well, I'm gonna have something for you to slip your friend Orcutt."

"When?"

"You anxious?"

"I'm supposed to be working for him."

"That's right, I keep getting confused about who you really work for."

"So do I."

"I hope it's nothing you can't straighten out."

"It's not."

"Orcutt pressing you?"

"He keeps asking."

"Next time he does, tell him a couple of days."

"It had better be good."

Lynch smiled comfortably, as if well pleased with life and his place in the scheme of things. "It'll be just dandy," he said.

After I put the $25,000 in old bills in my safe-deposit box, I called an airline just for the hell of it, I told myself, and asked what flights there were from Swankerton to San Francisco and if there was a connecting polar flight from there to Geneva. When she said that there wasn't, I thanked her and lied about how I would make other arrangements out of New York.

I'm still not sure what I would have done if I could have made connections. For a few moments I had been on my way, gone from Swankerton and heading west, the only way to go when flight turns into the final solution. It had happened too quickly, of course. That was most of

246

it, if not all. The body went through its normal functions. It ate and bathed and talked and made love, but the mind still wandered around and waited for the key to turn in the lock and for the thud of the bolt as the guard slid it back. I went over to the mirror and took a good look at the man with the too pale face who only four or five weeks before had been dining on fish and rice and amusing himself by counting the number of lice he killed each day. It wasn't exactly a stranger's face, it was just the face of someone whom I no longer knew very well and whose renewed acquaintance would require too much effort. I waved at him and he of course waved back. It was not a wave of greeting but rather of vague acknowledgment, one that admitted existence, but nothing else.

Gloomy persons like gloomy weather. They like foggy days and rain and sleet. They can understand those and cope with them. But it's on those shiny, bird-singing days that they order up the two-fifths of vodka and take the sleeping pills down from the medicine cabinet, or crawl out on the ledge of the building, or go out to the garage with a length of hose and tape it to the exhaust. I went over to the window and stared down at the girls in their sunglasses and short summer dresses and wished it would rain. I waited five minutes for a bolt of lightning or a thunderclap or at least for a cloud to hide the sun, but when nothing happened I went over to the phone and called Carol Thackerty.

"I'll buy you a drink," I said when she answered.

"I thought you had company."

"He's gone."

"You're supposed to see Orcutt."

"Not for lunch, I hope."

"No. He's having that with Phetwick the third and Dr. Warner Colfax."

"Of the Colfax clinic?"

"The same. You're supposed to give them a report after lunch."

"When will that be?"

"A couple of hours."

"Fine. I'll buy you a drink and lunch."

"Where?"

"My room."

"Shall I bring Homer, and don't say it's not necessary."

"Don't anyway."

"Just a cozy *tête-à-tête* with perhaps a nooner thrown in, right?"

"That did occur to me," I said.

"Me too."

"Fifteen minutes?"

"Make it twenty," she said, "and order my lunch."

"What?"

"Steak tartare with lots of capers."

"And a raw egg?"

"Two," she said.

"Chopped onions?"

"Gobs."

"Well, there's one thing about steak tartare," I said.

"What?"

"If we're busy doing something else, we won't have to worry about it getting cold."

After the drinks, and the wine, and the raw chopped steak, and a most satisfactory midday journey down some heretofore unexplored avenues in sexland, Carol Thackerty and I sat drinking coffee and waiting for my command appearance in the Rickenbacker suite before the crowned heads of Swankerton.

"It's not really your dish, is it?" she said.

"What, sex?"

"No."

"Well, what?"

"This whole Swankerton bamboozle."

"That's a good word."

"It describes it."

"Probably," I said.

"But you don't fit in, do you?"

"I haven't thought about it."

"You're a good liar, but not that good."

"All right, I thought about it. For five minutes just before I called you."

"And what did you decide?"

"Why the hell do I have to decide something? I just thought about it."

"If somebody were setting me up, I'd think about it. Hard."

"I read the enlistment papers carefully," I said.

"You signed on to be tough, huh?"

"Something like that."

"Why?"

"My thinking hasn't got that far yet," I said. "That's tomorrow's episode."

She ground her cigarette out in an ashtray and kept on grinding it even after it was dead. "You're in for a long fall," she said. "I don't think you know how far."

"I've got a fair idea."

"If I had to fall that far, I'd be looking for something to catch me."

"Maybe I'll just bounce."

"No," she said, shaking her head. "You won't bounce. You'll just shatter into a million, billion, trillion pieces."

"That's a lot of pieces."

"I used to say that when I was a kid."

"Why all the sudden concern?" I said.

She looked at me steadily. "Jesus, you ask some dumb questions sometimes."

"Yes," I said, "I suppose I probably do."

28

Channing d'Arcy Phetwick III crossed one bony leg over the other, cleared his throat, and in his old man's faltering tenor said, "What precisely was the reaction of the Lynch person?"

I turned from the window which had a view of the Gulf and said, "He thought Mrs. Sobour was a financial whiz."

Phetwick must have been close to eighty. He occupied one of the three chairs that were drawn up around a coffee table in the Rickenbacker suite. Orcutt and Dr. Colfax sat in the other two. Orcutt in the edge of his so that his feet could touch the floor. Phetwick's voice kept cracking when he spoke, going from tenor to soprano, but each word came out all by itself, freshly minted, and the phrasing of each word was exactly the same. It was a curious way of speaking, something like a talking robot whose voice box needed oiling. Phetwick wore a hearing aid and thick bifocals and the backs of his hands were covered with brown liver spots. He had on a dark suit, almost black, that may have been broadcloth if they still make it, and a high collar, like the one that Herbert Hoover wears in all the history books. His stringy neck was too small for the collar and his flesh hung in gray, flabby folds, as if he had lost a lot of weight.

"Does Lynch believe that I will publish the story?" he said.

"Yes, I think so. He's going to turn the stuff over to you today."

"Excellent. I wrote my signed editorial this morning. It is, I think you will agree when you read it, exceptionally forceful." Phetwick never seemed to use contractions when he spoke. "Now let us get on with the affair of the druggist."

"Dr. Colfax has gone over the information concerning Frank Mouton," Orcutt said. "It appears incontrovertible to him as well as to me and I suggest that Mr. Dye transmit it to Lynch much in the same manner that he transmitted the material on the Sobour woman."

"Mouton is a deacon in my church," Phetwick said to no one in particular. "Pity, I suppose."

Dr. Warner Colfax stirred in his chair at Orcutt's left. He was my idea of what a doctor should look like: his expensive tweed suit was carelessly rumpled, his tie was the wrong shade, and his shirt, while clean enough, was a little too tight at the neck and snug at the belly. His shoes, also expensive, were thoughtlessly cared for, and his blue eyes twinkled merrily behind practical, steel-rimmed glasses. He had a brush mustache, clipped fairly well, but gone to salt and pepper, and a wide sensitive mouth over a strong chin, with gray thinning hair that he brushed just so to cover a bare patch and to reveal that he, too, had a reassuring streak of harmless vanity. Good, gray Dr. Colfax.

"I don't mind if the cocksucker slipped pills to every neurotic old cunt in town," the good gray doctor said in a voice as gritty as ground glass. "But when he started wholesaling to those shitheads, I had a little talk with him."

"To cut yourself in for ten percent, I believe," Phetwick said.

The doctor twinkled his eyes some more. Only his voice kept him from being the lovable rogue. "Prove it," he said with a warm smile and a weasel's snarl.

The old man turned his head to look at the doctor. He turned it slowly and carefully and I almost expected to hear it squeak. "That may not be as difficult as you believe, Warner, should the occasion arise; I am certain that if your participation in the druggist's illegal activities could not be proved, several of your other nefarious adventures would be unable to bear close public scrutiny." Phetwick talked like that—commas, semicolons, and all.

"Don't bang skeletons with me, Channing," the doctor said. "I know where they're all hidden—even yours."

"Fortunately, Mr. Orcutt, Dr. Colfax and I over the years have reached what at one time was popularly described as a Mexican standoff. We could easily ruin each other. Realizing this, we have joined forces, although you may have noticed that a current of animosity runs between us. To be quite frank, we despise each other."

"I think it's perfectly *charming*," Orcutt said and smiled his fake smile to try to show that he really did.

"Yes," Phetwick said slowly and with a trace of doubt, "charming. Let us now return to the druggist Mouton who, sad to say, is also a Clean Government Association candidate for a vacancy on the city council. He can be easily pilloried, true. But if he were to be elected, he would be a most amenable councilman. We sacrifice this virtual certainty so that Mr. Dye can gain the confidence of the Lynch person in the fond but uncertain hope that he will discover information that will be useful to us and conversely damaging to Lynch and his supporters. That is correct, is it not?" He peered at Orcutt through his thick glasses.

"Perfectly," Orcutt said.

"Christ," Dr. Colfax said, "how many times do we have to rake this shit up?"

"As many as necessary, Warner," Phetwick said.

"How bout it, Dye?" the doctor said. "You think you can get something on Lynch's people? And don't fall for that crap about him being an ex-con. Everybody knows that and they all feel soft and gooey inside because they're giving him a second chance."

"There'll be something," I said. "I can't guarantee *quid pro quo*. Nobody can. But there'll be something."

"Something that will turn the stomachs of our voters, I hope," Phetwick said. "Perhaps you have already discovered this, Mr. Dye, but the citizens of Swankerton all seem to have stomachs that are made of cast iron. Nothing really bothers them very much."

"I've noticed." I said.

"I say turn the goods on Mouton over to Dye and let him get on with his job," Dr. Colfax said. "That's what we're paying him for."

"Mr. Phetwick?" Orcutt said.

Phetwick sighed. "I never really cared for Mouton, even though he is a deacon in my church. It is the First Methodist, you know. Will it put him behind bars?"

"Probably not," Orcutt said. "The statute of limitations has run out."

"That's the state statute," Dr. Colfax said. "What about Federal? What about the income-tax boys?"

"That will be up to them, of course," Orcutt said. "It may be that Mouton paid his proper income tax."

"In a pig's ass," the doctor growled.

"It is really not our concern," Phetwick said and sighed

again, so deeply that it made him shudder. "Our concern is to destroy the man and by doing so cast even more of a shadow on the efficacy of the Clean Government Association. It does seem to be a dear price to pay, but if it will help return a semblance of *orderliness* to Swankerton, then I can only agree."

"I have an idea," I said, "which may be an answer to your objections, Mr. Phetwick."

"Then say it, young man, say it."

"I go ahead and turn the information on Mouton over to Lynch. But he doesn't use it to destroy Mouton publicly. Instead, he uses it to blackmail Mouton into informing on the Clean Government Association. Since we have equal leverage, we can force Mouton to channel misleading information to Lynch. We'll supply him with it, of course."

Dr. Colfax slammed a big white fist on his knee. "Now, by God, I like that! That's real shitty!"

Phetwick nodded slowly and carefully. "It does have merit, I agree. However, do you think that Lynch will be able to withstand the temptation? By that I mean if one has the power to destroy another and by doing so achieve measurable gain for oneself, the temptation to destroy is quite often difficult to resist and becomes, in many instances, overriding."

"You should know, Channing," Dr. Colfax said.

"I do know, Warner," Phetwick said. "That is why I mentioned it."

"I might have an answer to that, too," I said. "I'll suggest to Lynch that the information he has on Mouton can be useful in two ways. First, it'll get him inside dope on the Clean Government Association, and if it comes from Mouton, he'll trust it more than if it came from me. But second, I'll suggest that he use the information to force Mouton into making a last minute refutation of the Clean Government Association. You can then counter that, Mr. Channing, with a front-page exposé of Mouton's illegal drug sales."

"By God, Dye, I don't know what the Christ you've been doing up till now, but you sure as hell earned your money today!" It was the good, gruff, gray doctor complimenting me and I started to ask him if he had something for nausea.

"Devilish, Mr. Dye," Phetwick said. "Sound thinking,

253

too. Should have thought of it myself. We first use Mouton to mislead Lynch. When Mouton makes his eleventh-hour attack on the Clean Government Association and embraces the Lynch slate, we expose him as a grubby drug peddler. We thus destroy the validity of his attack on us and at the same time expose Lynch and his people as being foolishly gullible at best, or in cahoots with Mouton at worst. Yes. I like it, probably, I must confess, because of its utter ruthlessness. Are you an utterly ruthless man, Mr. Dye?"

"I don't know," I said.

Phetwick rose from his chair. He did it slowly, helping himself up with the aid of a silver-handled cane. "Come, Warner, you can give me a lift back to my office in that Rolls of yours. We have done enough mischief for today."

Dr. Colfax strode over to me and stuck out his hand. I shook it. There was nothing else to do. Nothing I could think of anyway. "Like your thinking, Dye, by God, I do. You've got the touch."

"Thanks," I said.

"Drop round my office sometime when you're out our way. We'll have a drink."

"Fine," I said.

"Goodbye, Mr. Dye," Phetwick said. "It was reassuring to have met you—probably because I believed that most of my kindred souls were long since dead. Take that as a compliment. It was meant as such."

"I will," I said and wished that I were lying on a deserted beach somewhere with nothing to do but count the waves.

When they were gone Orcutt spun around and pointed a finger at me. "You were just *terribly* good!" he said. "So devious! Now tell me everything that Lynch had to say today."

I told him everything and when I was done he nodded in a satisfied way and said, "What did you think of our two patrons?"

"I think I like Lynch better."

He nodded understandingly. "That old man is simply fantastic, isn't he? One can literally smell the evil coming out of him."

"That doctor friend of his has a nice bedside manner, too."

254

"Oh, he's *terrible!*" Orcutt said. "A real villain. But they both liked you very much."

"That's what bothers me."

Orcutt waved his hand gracefully. "Think of them as chess pieces. I do."

"I'll try," I said.

"Now. Call Necessary's room and tell him to bring the man down."

"What man?"

"He's a photographer. A motion picture cameraman really. Homer has cooked up something that should prove most exciting."

"What?"

"We're going to expose the Swankerton police. And you must inform Lynch, of course."

"Of course."

"Call Necessary and tell him to bring Carol along too. She often has some excellent suggestions."

"It's a fur job," Necessary said.

"How much?" Orcutt asked.

"They might get away with seventy-five, maybe even ninety-thousand worth. They'll fence it for maybe thirty-thousand if they're lucky. More like twenty-five."

The cameraman's name was Arch Soderbell and he was about twenty-five years old, had a fine black beard, smoked Gauloises, and seemed to wear whatever was handy. That afternoon he had on tan chinos, white sneakers, a blue chambray shirt, and dark glasses.

"Are you all set, Mr. Soderbell?" Orcutt said.

"All set," Soderbell said.

"What time, Homer?" Orcutt said.

"They got it planned for around three-thirty tomorrow morning. We'll be there by three to get set up."

"Have you made all the necessary arrangements?"

"Quit worrying, Victor," Necessary said. "You sound like some old maid."

"I'm paid to worry, Homer. Some call it infinite attention to detail and there are others who call *that* genius."

"All right," Necessary said. "You're a genius."

"I want Mr. Dye to go with you."

"Why?" Necessary said. "I don't mind Dye coming along. But it's really a two-man job and we might have to get out of there damned fast."

"It has something to do with Lynch," Orcutt said.

Necessary nodded. "Dye's tipping him off, huh?"

"Not all the way."

"Okay," Necessary said. "I get it." He turned to me. "I'll call you about two unless you want to stay up."

"Call me," I said. "I'll call Lynch from a phone booth."

"When it's too late," Necessary said.

"That's right," I said. "When it's too late."

29

Homer Necessary came back up to my room with me, probably because he knew that I had laid in a new supply of Scotch, and he was thirsty as usual. I ordered up some ice and some coffee for myself while Necessary mixed himself a drink, not waiting for the ice.

"Where'd you find Soderbell?" I said.

"Cleveland," Necessary said. "He was in the army in Vietnam for a year and when he got discharged he went back out there as a civilian free lance. He helped shoot a documentary for some German producer that won an award in Berlin."

"What was he doing in Cleveland?"

"Looking for a job."

"Does he know what he's getting into tonight?"

"Hell, this isn't his first time. He's been flying in and out of here for the last month from New Orleans. Old man Phetwick let us commission him to do a documentary on Swankerton. He's shot some real nice stuff."

"Such as?"

"Well, he sets up inside a delivery truck at noon around a grade school and gets some close-up stuff of kids spending their lunch money on numbers. Now that's not bad, is it?"

"No, that's pretty good."

"Then he sets up just above that dirtybook store we were in and shoots the payoffs of the cops and the customers going in and out across the street without any dry cleaning. Then he rigs a camera up in a briefcase and goes to one of the better cathouses and gets some prominent citizens coming and going. He rigs another one up in a big box, like it was gift-wrapped, you know, and puts it on the front seat of his car and then goes out and gets himself arrested for stop line running and speeding. They arrest him six times in one day and he pays the cops off on the spot with five-dollar bills and gets it all down on film. You can even read their badge numbers. Then he gets some good shots out in Niggertown of cops just standing around on a corner grinning while a pusher takes care of his customers."

"Have you seen any of it?" I asked.

Necessary shook his head. "He's keeping it all in New Orleans. He's made duplicate prints of everything just in case. Oh, yeah, he got one more pretty good shot too—with sound."

"What?" I said.

"Well, Phetwick owns a hell of a lot of property around town, you know, and he owns this small store building that he's going to tear down anyway. It's a three-story building over on Early. The top two floors are vacant and downstairs is a grocery store, one of those mom and pop things, and their lease is about to run out. So I make a deal with them."

"What kind of deal?"

"The old guy has been paying protection to some of Lynch's hard cases. Not much. About twenty-five or thirty a week. We offer him a bundle not to pay the next time they come around and to let Soderbell film and tape it.

"The old guy's afraid he might get beat up, but we tell him not to worry about it, and that we'll stop any rough stuff. Soderbell rigs everything up in the back room, gets his mikes hidden away, and we sit and wait."

"You were with him?"

"I was with him on all of them except when the traffic cops stopped him. I tell the old guy not to pay and sure enough, here they come, a couple of real punks. They call him dad and ask for the weekly premium and all that and the old man says he's not paying. They just smile and open a big jug of Lysol and pour it all over his vegetables. Soderbell gets all that. The old man still won't pay so they get a couple of cans of shaving cream in those aerosol things and squirt it all over the inside of his meat case. Nothing rough yet and Soderbell gets that on film too."

"The conversation, too," I said.

"That too. Then they start getting rough with the old man. They slap him a couple of times and bend his arm a little and he starts yelling. Soderbell wants to go help him, but I tell him to shut up and just keep shooting. Finally, one of them hits too hard and the old man faints or passes out. They open the cash register, take out their thirty dollars or whatever it is, and leave. Soderbell gets it all."

"What happened to the store owner?"

"We send him to Colfax's Hospital, all bills paid Then we give him his bundle and as soon as he gets over his concussion he heads for Florida."

"He recovered?" I said.

"Sure, he recovered," Necessary said. "If I thought they were going to kill him or anything like that, mess him up real bad, I'd of stepped in. But they just mussed him up a little and if I'd done anything about it, then Soderbell'd lost some real fine stuff."

"You're nothing but heart, Homer."

"What the Christ would you have done?"

"I don't know," I said. "Probably have gone for the film instead of the rescue."

Necessary stared at me with his brown and blue eyes and I could find no admiration in them. "You know, Dye, you got something wrong with you inside somewhere. Maybe in your head. You remind me of some tough old cops that I've known who got worried when they couldn't feel about things like they did when they were rookies. It bothered some of them so much that they went out looking for things that'd make 'em feel like they thought they should, and if they didn't get killed doing it, they got preachy. I don't think you feel a hell of a lot about anything or anybody. But you think you should because of all the crap around that says that's the way normal people are. Well, you just as well face it: you ain't normal. You might have been once, but not anymore, so you may as well get used to it."

"I feel I should be taking notes."

Necessary shook his head. "I haven't got much hope for you, Dye. You're the kind who'll keep on playing by somebody else's rules, lose every time, and always wonder why."

"Whose rules do you play by?"

"My own, good buddy, my very own."

"And you never lose?"

Necessary finished his drink. "Sure I lose," he said, "but when I do, at least I know why."

The telephone rang fifteen minutes after Necessary left and it was Gorman Smalldane calling from New York.

"You're five days late," I said.

"And you've got some nice playmates."

"I know."

"You want the good as well as the bad?" Smalldane said.

"Just the bad."

"I'll skim it for you."

"Fine."

"The Thackerty woman's been arrested twice for prostitution. It was nol-prossed both times."

"Anything else?"

"She was Phi Beta Kappa in her junior year."

"Is that supposed to be good or bad?" I said.

"I won't try to influence you."

"Thanks."

"Victor Orcutt," Smalldane said. "No record other than a rather startling academic one. He's a genius."

"If you don't believe it, ask him."

"Like that, huh?"

"Like that."

"Homer Necessary. Now there's a name I like. At twenty-six he was a second-grade detective who busted his own police department wide open. By himself. He nailed every one from the chief on down. He had facts, figures, documents, photographs, and his evidence and testimony helped send thirty-one of his fellow officers to the state penitentiary. The chief himself got five years. The city was so impressed and grateful that it made Necessary its new chief of police at twenty-seven, and for the next fifteen years he—shall we say—prospered. He did everything the old crowd did and added a few new licks of his own."

"Was he fired?"

"They could never nail him. There was a lot of talk about it, but he resigned four years ago to enter what he called 'private industry,' which turned out to be Victor Orcutt Associates. After he resigned, there was another tremendous shake up in the police force, but Necessary was completely absolved."

"He saw to that," I said.

"Ramsey Lynch, born Montgomery Vicker. He's been in and out of trouble since he was sixteen. Born in Newark and at eighteen legally changed his name to Ramsey Lynch at his family's insistence. The family was rather staid and prominent in a mild sort of way. He was on the fringes of the rackets until he took a fall for one of the higher-ups on a narcotics rap and spent eighteen months in Atlanta. After that, they were so grateful that they set him up in New Orleans where he was either Number Two or Number Three boy until he opened up in Swankerton where I understand he's now Number One. The only member of his family who still admits that he's alive is one Gerald Vicker who lives in Hong Kong. They're supposed to be close."

"They are," I said.

"Now the dessert," Smalldane said. "Your chief of police, Calvin Loambaugh. Born in Swankerton and joined the army at nineteen for a three-year hitch. He came out a first lieutenant in the MPs. Served in Germany and there's nothing on him there. He joined the police force in Buffalo and resigned under a cloud."

"What kind of a cloud?"

"Suspected of being a receiver of stolen goods."

"Could they prove it?"

"They could, but they didn't because they had him for something else which they also wanted to forget about."

"What?"

"Two counts of child molestation."

"And they let him off?"

"Buffalo was having a lot of trouble with its cops about that time," Smalldane said. "They didn't need any more."

"What then?"

"Loambaugh joined the Birmingham police just in time for the riots there. He got a couple of commendations and suddenly resigned under yet another cloud, one that really looked like rain."

"Child molestation?" I said.

"Right. Three counts this time. By the way, he's married and has two children of his own."

"Then he came back home," I said.

"Right again, and in a rise that can only be described as meteoric, he was appointed Swankerton's chief of police four years ago, doubtless at the behest of your friend Lynch."

"What does he go for," I said, "little boys or little girls?"
"Both."

"Any concrete evidence?"

"No. All talk, but it was reliable."

"Your service is excellent, Gorm. Send me a bill."

"You think you'll be around to pay it?"

"Why not?"

"Some rumors I heard."

"What about them?"

"They claim that things might get rough in Swankerton."

"Probably."

"I think you need some help."

"From whom?"

"Me."

"This isn't a PR campaign, Gorm. There's no million-dollar budget and no bonus for the cutest press release. I'm not out to win the hearts and minds of men to democracy's side. I'm not even sure that I'm out to win."

"I won't cost you anything," Smalldane said.

"It's not that."

"What is it?"

"I don't know where to fit you in."

"We'll think of a slot."

"I don't think that we—"

"I'll be there at three tomorrow afternoon," he said. "You don't even have to meet me at the airport." Then he hung up.

Homer Necessary called me at two o'clock that morning and wanted to know if I were awake.

"I am now."

"Soderbell's here," he said. "We're leaving in half an hour."

"Where's here?"

"My room."

Twenty minutes later I joined them in Necessary's room. Soderbell was fooling with a Bolex Pro 16mm camera equipped with what looked to be a zoom lens.

"You don't have to carry the lights after all," Necessary said.

"Why?"

"Soderbell's using infra red film. Says he doesn't need lights."

"It's not infra red," Soderbell said. "It's Kodak two-four-eight-five rapid-access retrieval stuff with an ASA of twelve thousand."

"Will it do what it's supposed to?" Necessary said. "I hear that infra red's the best."

"It's got some infra red in it," Soderbell said, and for all I knew he could have been telling the truth. "But with special processing, the film I'm going to use is better."

"Don't get me wrong, but I've heard that the infra red stuff is better," Necessary said.

Soderbell put on the face that he must have used to deal with the enthusiastic amateur. "It's damned good, Homer, but I think my stuff is just a little better for this particular job."

"Well, you're the expert," Necessary said, obviously unconvinced. "Just don't forget that if something goes wrong they're not coming back and pose for retakes."

Soderbell was a patient man. Perhaps most professional photographers are. He lit one of his French cigarettes and blew some of its acrid smoke around the room. "Quit worrying, Homer. The only thing that can go wrong is if we are caught, and if that happens, none of us will have to worry."

The bars were still open at two-thirty in the morning in Swankerton and seemed to be doing a good swing-shift business. We drove down Snow Street in Necessary's rented Impala, turned left onto Fourth, followed that for six blocks, and then turned right onto Forrest. We drove four more blocks until Necessary found a parking place that he seemed to like.

"We walk from here," he said.

We were in Swankerton's wholesale district. The street was lined with long, low brick buildings, most of which had loading docks at their fronts or sides. Rows of silver, red and blue semis, sometimes parked less than six inches from each other, hulking tributes to the teamsters' skill, were backed up to the docks waiting to be unloaded.

In between something called Gulf States Distributors, Inc. and Merriman Liquors (Wholesale Only) was a narrow, frame, three-story house, which sat far back on its fifty-foot lot. We turned into its cracked sidewalk, went up four steps to a small porch with a broken plank, and waited until Necessary unlocked the door. Inside, the house was vacant and smelled as if the door hadn't been opened in years.

By guess and by feel we followed Necessary down a long hall. There was no furniture to bump into.

263

"We turn right and go up the rear stairs," Necessary said.

I reached my hand out and touched Soderbell. "You okay?" he said.

"Fine."

"Step up and turn right again," he said.

I followed slowly, using the bannister and placing both feet on each stair tread.

"Left here," Necessary said from some place up above me. We were in another hall that led toward the rear. Necessary opened a door and a window in the room produced enough light to make a single vague outline of him and Soderbell. I followed them into the room.

"I got three-o-four," Necessary said. "What have you got?"

I looked at the luminous dial on my watch. "About that. Maybe three-o-five."

"What do you think?" Necessary said to Soderbell. The cameraman went to the window and peered out. "That light in the alley will just save us," he said. I moved over to the window and looked out. The frame house was longer than I had thought. Its rear was flush with the alley and the window I stood at had a view of the rear of a firm directly across the alley that was called Bolberg and Son, Wholesale Furriers. There were no windows in the rear of the furrier's building, but there was a sturdy-looking steel door and a corrugated-metal overhead door that was large enough for a good-sized truck to go through.

"Nice, huh?" Necessary said.

"Who owns it?" I said.

"Some guy called Bolberg."

"I mean this house."

"It belongs to Phetwick like almost everything else in town. He just keeps paying taxes on it and waits for the price to rise. I understand it's up to about two thousand dollars now."

"For the house and lot?"

"A front foot," he said. "I think it's on the tax rolls for about five thousand dollars, and that does include the house and lot."

"That light over there's sure as hell going to save us," Soderbell said again, as if to himself. The light that arched over the furrier's metal door was about a hundred watts and was encased in a wire-mesh shield.

"What if they bust it?" Necessary said.

"Then we're shit out of luck," Soderbell said. "Let's break out this window. It's too dirty to shoot through."

"Why not just open it?" Necessary said.

"I tried. It's nailed shut."

"Wait a minute," Necessary said. He took a roll of masking tape from his pocket and started to tape the window in an intricate, cobwebby pattern. He took off his shoe and tapped the window with its heel. It broke and we spent the next few minutes removing pieces of taped glass until Soderbell said he had enough space to shoot through.

We waited five more minutes, until it was 3:20. The lights of a car turned into the alley from its far right end.

"You ready?" Necessary said to Soderbell.

"Always," Soderbell said.

The car rolled down the alley slowly. Spotlights on both sides flashed along the rears of buildings. One of them flicked across the house we were in, but not above the first story. "That's why I said second story," Necessary muttered. "Nobody ever looks up. You can tell 'em till you're purple, but they won't look up."

The car fixed a spotlight on the iron door of the furrier's and kept it there. Soderbell's camera was whirring faintly. The car was black and white and had Swankerton Police Department stenciled on its side along with a nice, official-looking shield. Big white letters on its black top spelled SPD. It slowed, almost to a stop, and then drove on by. The spotlights went out.

"Get its number, boy, get its number," Necessary whispered to Soderbell.

The camera kept on whirring and then stopped. "I got it."

"That's the lookout crew," Necessary said. "They'll cruise around the block from now on."

We waited four or five minutes more until another set of lights approached from the right end of the alley. I looked at my watch. It was almost exactly 3:30 A.M. The car cut its lights when it was slightly past the furrier's steel door. I wasn't sure, but I thought that the car had two occupants. It was a dark color, either blue or black, and it had no markings.

"The thieves," Necessary said.

Whoever was in the car made no move to get out. Another minute went by before yet another set of car lights turned into the alley from the right. Then its headlights went out and the driver used his amber parking lights instead. He switched them on and off in rapid succession four times. The new arrival parked on the other side of the furrier's back door and from where I stood I could see that it was another black-and-white police car. Soderbell's camera whirred some more.

Two men got out of the police car and stood in the pool of light made by the shielded bulb above the metal door.

Soderbell whispered directions to them. "Move, you sonofabitch. Now turn this way and look up just a little . . . a little more, you mother . . . oh, that's fine . . . that's just fine . . . your shield and everything."

The two men who got out of the squad car wore the gray-and-blue summer uniforms of the Swankerton police. They waited by the door until they were joined by two men in dark clothing who had waited in the unmarked car. One of the men carried a small bag. The two policemen took up positions so that they could watch both ends of the alley. The man with the bag handed it to his fellow thief and bent over the door. He turned his head two or three times, and the other man passed him something.

"He's fixing the alarm system," said Necessary, who furnished us with a running commentary on the methodology of the theft. In a few minutes the man in the dark clothes had the door open. His fellow thief went back to the unmarked car, stored the bag away, and opened the trunk.

The two thieves, accompanied by one of the policemen, entered the building. Soderbell got a few shots of the remaining cop as he walked in and out of the circle of light. It was almost another five minutes before the two thieves and the policeman came out, all burdened with armloads of furs. They dumped them into the open trunk of the unmarked car. After that, they made three more similar trips. Soderbell filmed it all, muttering unheard directions to the silent stars of his back-alley drama.

During the thieves' final trip into the warehouse, the policeman on guard moved over to the driver's side of the squad car. He reached in with his left hand and did something else with his right, but we never could see what

266

it was because the car's spotlight blazed on. It blinded Soderbell and transfixed him before the window with his camera aimed directly at the spotlight. He stood there like that until the bullet hit him somewhere in the chest, I thought, and hurled him back into the room a few, wild staggering steps. He fell in a lump, still holding the camera, and in the brief, total silence that followed, I listened to it whir.

The cop must have been nervous because he fired through the window twice more. Then the spotlight went out and I could hear the four of them jabbering in the alley. I was flat against the wall next to the window. Necessary was already bending over Soderbell. He rose quickly and I saw that he had the camera in his hands.

"Let's get out of here," he said, his voice tight, fast and low.

"Do we carry him or drag him?" I said.

"We leave him. Let's go."

I could hear an engine start in the alley. A car trunk lid slammed closed, then two car doors thunked. Tires squealed in high-pitched protest for what seemed to be a long time but could only have been less than a second. Thieves' getaway, I thought. It was an idle, almost lazy thought.

"We can't leave him," I said because it seemed to be the thing to say.

"He's dead, goddamnit," Necessary said and headed for the door. I could think of nothing better to do than follow. We went down the stairs to the long hall much faster than we had come up. I felt or sensed that Necessary turned right instead of left.

"Where the hell you going?" I whispered, a little frantically, I suppose.

"Out the alley entrance. They're around in front by now."

As if to prove it, something large and heavy crashed against the front door of the old house. Something about the size and weight of an archless foot encased in a number eleven shoe. It crashed again as Necessary thrust the camera into my arms and started to fumble with the lock and bolts on the rear door. On the third crash I could hear the front door splinter open. Necessary got the last lock undone and swung the rear door wide. We went through it and down four steps. I stumbled on the last one, almost falling, almost dropping the camera. I recovered and ran after Necessary, who had turned right, heading for the squad car that was still parked in the alley, just beyond the pool of light that came from the bulb above the furrier's still-open door.

Necessary opened the left door of the squad car, reached inside, and came out with the keys. He threw them as far as he could into the darkness. Then he fumbled his hand in again. Once more the spotlight on the driver's side blazed on. I looked up and saw the too-white faces of the cops through the hole in the broken second-story window. They closed their eyes against the glare and I saw why it had been an easy shot for the cop who'd killed Soderbell. It would be hard to miss.

Necessary was off and running down the alley. I followed, the camera cradled in my arms. When we reached the end of the alley, Necessary stopped and peered around the corner. He was breathing even harder than I was, great, harsh, lung-filling pants. That pleased me.

"Let's go," he said or croaked, and we darted across the deserted street, went another block down the alley, only trotting now and barely that. We came out of the alley, turned right, and walked to Necessary's rented car. He opened the trunk and I put the camera inside it.

We pulled out sedately and drove down Forrest at twenty-five miles an hour. A squad car roared by, headed in the opposite direction. Its siren was off, but its red-and-white dome light spun angrily.

Necessary slammed the steering wheel with the palm of his hand. "It just doesn't make any goddamned sense," he said.

"That's probably what Soderbell thought, too, if he had the time."

Necessary glanced at me and shook his head, a little impatiently, I felt. "I wasn't talking about that. I was talking about the cop turning on the spotlight. Christ, I never knew one of them who'd look up even two inches above his head."

I could have said something like "you do now" or "there's always the first time," but I didn't. I just sat there and looked for something that I didn't see.

After a moment or two, Necessary said, "It was a lucky shot. That cop was just lucky." I could have argued that, too, but I didn't. I just sat there and looked some more.

"Funny about Soderbell though," Necessary went on. "He goes all through Vietnam twice and winds up getting shot in some back alley. Makes you think, doesn't it?"

"Yes," I said, "it does that all right." I found what I was looking for and said, "Here's one." Necessary stopped the car beside the lighted telephone booth. I got out, dropped in a dime, and dialed a number. It rang for a long time before someone answered with a gruff hello.

"This is Dye," I said.

"Yeah . . . Yeah," Lynch's sleepy voice said.

"Homer Necessary was up to something tonight. I just found out about it."

"What?" Lynch said and sounded less sleepy.

"I hear that some cops were in on a fur burglary. Homer Necessary got the whole thing down on film. The cops shot somebody. I don't know who yet."

"When'd all this happen?" Lynch said, and his voice was crisp and wide awake now.

"I just heard about it."

"You didn't know about it before?"

"I just heard about it," I said again. "I thought you might want to wake up Loambaugh."

"Shit," Lynch said just before he said goodbye and hung up.

I got back in the car and Necessary said, "What'd he say?"

"He said shit."

Necessary chuckled a little. "Can't say that I blame him," he said. "Can't say that I blame him at all."

30

Necessary and I spent a long, predawn hour with Victor Orcutt in his Rickenbacker suite when we returned to the hotel. Orcutt listened politely while we told him how Soderbell had died. When we were finished he said, "Well, I suppose those things are bound to happen," and never mentioned him again, except indirectly, when he made sure that we had brought back the camera, if not the cameraman.

I spent five minutes telling Orcutt what I thought should be done with the film. He listened attentively, said, "Good. I agree," and then launched a twenty-minute monologue which instructed me how to carry out my suggestion. "You *do* understand?" he said.

"Does that mean do I agree with you?"

"That isn't important," he said. "It merely requires understanding so that you'll be able to function properly."

"Since it was my idea, I understand well enough not to blow it."

"But you don't agree with my method?" he said.

"As you mentioned, that's not important."

Orcutt turned to Necessary. "Homer?"

"Oh, I understand everything just fine," he said, "and I like it even better. I like it so much that I might even have a drink to celebrate."

Carol Thackerty came away from the phone that she'd been using since we arrived. "There's no ice," she said to Necessary, "and your plane will be standing by in fifteen minutes. The lab in New Orleans already has a rough cut of what Soderbell previously filmed. As soon as they process what he shot last night, or rather this morning, they'll make a print and splice it on to the rough cut."

"I don't need any ice," Necessary said and poured himself a drink from a bottle that he'd found on a table near the door. "Did you tell the lab that the new stuff'll need special processing?"

"They know all about it," she said. "Soderbell had

270

already filled them in. They'll be able to deliver a completed rough cut to you by one o'clock this afternoon. The plane will get you back here by two-thirty. You should be able to turn over the rough cut to Dye by three."

"What kind of plane?" said Necessary, the detail stickler.

"A Lear jet."

Necessary finished his drink. "See you around three," he said and left.

I stood up. "I need some sleep," I said.

"Mr. Dye," Orcutt said, also rising, "I dislike to harp on this, but I do very much hope that you will follow my instructions as closely as conditions permit."

"You want it in writing, Orcutt?" I said, the testiness in my voice stronger than I had intended.

"I don't particularly care for that tone."

"Neither do I, but it's the only one I have left at five in the morning. I've had a bad night. I always do when somebody gets killed. It makes me irritable. Even surly."

"It wasn't your fault that——"

"Nothing's ever my fault," I said. "I just do the job I'm paid to do and if somebody dies along the way, well, as you say, those things happen. So quit worrying. I'll do it just the way you told me to and, for all I know, it may work. If it doesn't, you can always fall back on contingency plan R-twenty-three."

"You're teasing again," Orcutt said. "I'm so glad. That means you're in a better humor."

"Ah, Christ," I said and went out the door, slamming it behind me.

I finally went to sleep around six and Ramsey Lynch didn't call until seven-thirty and when I picked up the phone there was no trace of jolly fat man in his voice.

"You'd better get your ass over here," he said.

"I'm busy."

"I'm serious."

"So am I and I'm still busy."

"I might send somebody around for you."

"Who? A pair of those moonlighters who got their pictures taken last night?"

"It's an idea," he said. "They know all about it now,

and if I told them that you were kind of involved in the whole thing, they'd volunteer to go fetch you."

"Do that and you'll never see it."

"Have you got it?"

"I can get it."

"When?"

"This afternoon about three."

"What're you going to do with it?"

"I thought you might like your own private preview before it goes out over the airwaves and into the living rooms of Swankerton."

"You got an idea how to kill it?"

"Maybe. It'll cost a little."

Lynch was silent for a moment and I listened to his heavy breathing. "You bring it out here." He almost managed to make it sound like a polite request.

"Around three or three-thirty. You'll need a 16mm projector."

"I'll get one."

"You'll need something else, too," I said.

"What?"

"Your chief of police."

At three-ten that afternoon, about the time that Gorman Smalldane was supposed to be landing at the airport, I was driving out to Lynch's Victorian home in a newly rented Plymouth Roadrunner which had a hot engine under its hood and a brown, round can of 16mm film on the seat beside its driver whose nerves, some might have said, were shot.

I parked the car at the curb with its bumper about a foot from the driveway so that if a hurried departure were called for, there would be nothing to stand in its path. I put the can of film under my arm, plodded up the brick path to the screened-in porch, and knocked on the door, trying in vain for the confident rap of an aluminum-siding salesman.

Boo Robineaux, His Honor's son, opened the door and took his eyes off a copy of *I.F. Stone's* bi-weekly *Weekly* long enough to say "hello" and "they're in the dining room." He didn't offer to lead the way, but followed instead, still deeply engrossed in the latest machinations of the military-industrial complex. One of these days, I promised myself, I would ask Boo how he'd got those scars on his face.

I opened the sliding doors to the dining room. Lynch was on the right side of the long table; Loambaugh was on the left. At one end of the table rested a 16mm projector. At the other end was a portable screen.

"Howdy, there, Lucifer," Lynch said, once more the professional country boy and jolly fat man, but spreading it on a little thicker than usual. I decided that he was also nervous, just like me. Loambaugh merely nodded and went back to biting his nails.

I said, "Gentlemen," and put the can of film on the projector.

Lynch yelled for Boo, who came in and threaded the film through the projector in an offhand, practiced manner and asked only one question, "Is it sound?"

"Parts of it," I said, and he nodded and adjusted the sound controls.

"When you want it to start, just flip this button," he said to Lynch and then left, closing the sliding doors behind him.

"You seen it?" Loambaugh said to me.

"What the hell difference does that make?" Lynch said. "You want him to give you a goddamned movie review?"

"I just asked, for Christ's sake."

"Well, don't. This ain't the only copy, I suppose?"

"You suppose right," I said.

"Another dumb question," Lynch said. "Do any good to ask you how you got your hands on it?"

"No."

He nodded somberly and said, "Well, we might as well look at it. You want to get the lights?"

I switched the room lights off and Lynch turned on the projector. I found a chair next to him and settled down to watch. It was all there in black and white *cinema vérité* just as Necessary had described it. Even from the rough cut I could see that Soderbell had style. He got a cop picking his nose as he came out of the dry cleaning numbers' joint, zooming right in on the exploring forefinger. You could count the pores and blackheads on the faces of those he had bribed to tear up his traffic tickets. I listened to the rasping tease in the voices of the two punks who had beat up the old man in the grocery store and then watched them spray shaving cream

273

over the cold cuts in the meat case. I watched as the blows landed and listened to the old man scream and stared as he fell behind the cash register. Lynch said nothing during the films, but Loambaugh grunted and cursed every time he recognized a cop. The last episode featured the fur thieves and because I'd been there, I watched with special interest to learn how Soderbell had seen it through the lens of his camera. There was an establishing shot of the alley, dark, gloomy, and deserted, perhaps even forbidding. The first squad car crept along, shining its spotlight on the steel door of the furrier's. The camera followed the car, zooming in close on its number and then cutting to the sign over the door that read Bolberg & Son. He got the entire theft: the cops standing guard while the thieves did for the lock; the cop carrying out armloads of furs and dumping them into the trunk of the car, and finally the cop moving over to the squad car, and reaching inside. Then there was a blinding light for a second or two, and the film racketed through its sprockets and guides, signalling that it was ended. Lynch reached over and switched off the projector. I moved to the room lights and turned them on.

"The guy who filmed it, the cameraman," Lynch said. "He's the one they shot over on Forrest last night, huh?"

"That's right."

"He had a nice style."

"A keen sense of mood," I said.

"There were a few more episodes than I'd been led to believe," Lynch said. "About four more."

"Five really," I said. "I found it a gripping portrayal of the Swankerton Police Department in action."

"Don't ride me, Dye," Loambaugh said. "I'll just tell you once. Don't ride me."

"That's twice already," Lynch said. He pulled a cellophane-wrapped cigar from a pocket and took his usual three minutes to get it lighted. When it was burning to his satisfaction, he blew some smoke at Loambaugh and said, "As a citizen of Swankerton I was shocked by what I've just seen. Shocked. What was your reaction, Chief Loambaugh?"

"Somebody got dumb," he said, "and I'm gonna have their ass by six o'clock tonight."

"That what you going to tell the wire services after this thing goes on TV?" Lynch said.

"What do you mean when it goes on TV? That's why you're juicing him, isn't it?" He jerked a thumb at me. "He's the bright boy. Let him figure out a way to cool it off."

"What happened to Soderbell's body?" I said to Loambaugh.

"It's in the morgue. For autopsy."

"I want it shipped back to his family."

Loambaugh bent toward me and the now familiar flush started rising from his neck. He didn't shout this time. His voice was low and almost toneless. It was far more effective than a shout. "I'm getting goddamned sick of you telling me what to do, buster. I don't care who you got for friends. Don't do it again."

I looked at him for a time and then smiled. "I want his body shipped back to his family. I think they're in Cleveland. I want it escorted back by one of your cops. A lieutenant, at least."

Loambaugh jumped up from his chair and headed around the corner of the table. I assumed that I was the goal line. He got all of two feet before Lynch cracked out his order: "Sit down, Cal, and shut up!"

Loambaugh hesitated, stopped completely, turned and went back to his chair. "Don't ride me," he whispered, not looking at anyone. "Don't do it again."

Lynch's fat round face was wreathed in smoke and smiles now. "I reckon we can take care of that fella's remains okay, Lucifer. No big problem that I can figure. What really concerns me is this little old film we've just seen. Film can lie just like words can. I mean pictures don't always tell the full story. Now if you was taking a picture of a barrel of apples and you had a thousand apples in that barrel and you just picked out six or seven rotten ones and took pictures of those and then showed em to somebody and said, 'Hey, here's what apples look like,' why, they wouldn't really know what a good apple looked like, would they?"

"Jesus, that's vivid," I said. "I never thought of it in just that way."

The wreath of smiles on Lynch's face disappeared and was replaced by a sour, puckered look. "Okay, pal, you came here with a proposition. A deal. Let's have it."

"That was just a rough cut you saw. Wait'll they edit it, throw in some background music, write the narration,

275

and then get somebody like Cronkite or Brinkley to narrate it. Of course, they'd have to interview the chief here. Or if he didn't want to go on, then they'd have to talk about that for a while and about his reasons for being unavailable. Then, too, what you've seen is only what they have on film. They must have a couple of file cabinets of other evidence lying around. Still pictures, sworn statements, witnesses, even victims. They'd all make nice little vignettes that would round out the film—give it breadth and scope and depth, if you follow me."

"How much?" Lynch said.

"I'm getting to that."

"You're sure as hell in no hurry," Loambaugh said.

"Well, after they have the film all put together, with additional facts, a big name voice—what do you think of Gregory Peck?"

"Not much," Lynch said.

"Just an idea. So after they put it all together in a slick, professional, competent manner and give it a catchy title, something like, 'Swankerton's Cops: the Best that Money Can Buy,' well, they'll have no problem giving it —or even selling it—to one of the networks and then you'll have about twenty or thirty million viewers instead of a mere hundred thousand or so here in Swankerton. Think of what the publicity will do for the place. You'll have a special team down here from *Life* the next day plus a couple of dozen other hard-nosed reporters, all specialists in crime and corruption. The state cops will move in. They'll have to, and they'll be falling over the feet of the Justice Department types from Washington. That film, I'd say, can really put Swankerton on the map."

Lynch sat through it all, puffing calmly away on his cigar. Loambaugh listened, at first with a certain amount of affected boredom that changed into interest and then deepened into fascination. By the time I was through he was chewing on his fingernails again.

Lynch sighed and ground his cigar out into an ashtray. It was only half-smoked. "I don't know about Cal over there, Lucifer, but you don't have to paint me any more word pictures. For an old country boy, I got a pretty good imagination. So I'm going to ask you again, how much do they want?"

"They?"

"That's right. They. Them."

"There is no they or them, Lynch. There are no expensive middlemen. I'm what's called the sole source."

"You are, huh?"

"He's a lying sonofabitch," Loambaugh said.

"Well, shit, Cal, we already know *that*." He turned to me again. "I thought you was kind of working for us." He tried to sound a little disappointed, even hurt, but it didn't come out that way. Just petulant.

"Is there anyone else in town who'd have shown you the film?"

"So you're the man?" Lynch said.

I nodded. "That's right; I am."

"Well, Mr. Man, what's your price?"

I coughed once to clear my throat so that I could be sure that my voice wouldn't crack when I named it. I kept my hands flat on the table so that they could be plainly seen, but not their fibrillary tremor. I ignored the sweat that formed in my armpits despite the air-conditioning. I looked at Lynch, but nodded my head toward Loambaugh.

"I want his resignation as chief of police. Today."

Loambaugh hurtled across the table at me, his knees working on the polished surface in a scrambling effort to gain purchase. His hands were around my neck in less than a second and I could smell his Sen-Sen breath and count the veins in his rolling eyes. I brought the heel of my right palm hard against his chin and I heard his teeth click shut. I shot both locked hands up and out through his arms and broke his hold on my neck. Then I hit him again as hard as I could, once with the heel of my left palm just at the base of his nose, and when that straightened him up, I hit him just below the breast bone with my right fist. He was softer than he looked and my fist seemed to sink in several inches and he whoofed and grabbed his middle with both hands, pressing hard. His nose was bleeding now and so was his tongue where he had bitten it when I had knocked his jaws shut. He knelt there on the long table, his head bent as he clutched his stomach and bled all over the polished surface. I leaned back in my chair, pressed my hands flat on the table again, and watched him without much interest. I noticed that the tremor was gone from my hands.

Lynch yelled, "Boo!" and the young man poked his

277

head through the door. He looked at the kneeling figure of Loambaugh on the table, but it wasn't unusual enough to make him change his expression.

"Get Chief Loambaugh a cold, wet towel," Lynch said, "he's had a little accident."

After the blood was mopped from the table and Loambaugh was back in his chair with a towel pressed to his nose, Lynch gave me a genial smile and said, "Well, I reckon that's enough excitement for one afternoon, don't you, Lucifer?"

"Plenty," I said.

"You *were* serious?"

"Completely."

"It's a mighty awesome thing," he said, "asking a man to resign at the peak of his career for the good of the community. It takes a big man to do that. A real big man. You think you're a big enough man to do that, Chief Loambaugh?"

"No resigning, Lynch. You can go fuck yourself."

"Hear that, Lucifer? The chief doesn't much care for your proposition."

"I heard," I said.

"You think this bastard's got something on you?" Loambaugh said to Lynch, his voice muffled by the wet towel. "I got enough on you to send you down for twenty years."

Lynch turned his head slightly and yelled for Boo again. When the young man popped his scarred head through the sliding doors, Lynch said: "Bring us some writing paper and some carbons and a ball-point pen, will you, Boo? Chief Loambaugh here wants to write up something."

When Boo came back he offered the writing materials to Loambaugh, who ignored him. Boo glanced at Lynch, who said, "Just put them down there in front of him. He's busy with his nose right now. He'll get to them directly."

"You know something, Cal?" Lynch said. "I can't recall a day when I've been threatened so much. First old Lucifer here with his film and then you acting uppity and making threats just because it'd be in the best interest of the community if you was to resign. Now when you think it over, you'll just pick up that pen and write out a real nice letter of resignation and sign the original and maybe three or four carbons. You might mention something about personal reasons and other interests. That's always good, isn't it, Lucifer?"

"Usually," I said.

"You want him to say something else?"

"No."

"See how cooperative everybody's being, Cal?"

Loambaugh's nose had quit bleeding and he dropped the bloody towel on the table. "I swear to God I'm not resigning. And the first thing I do when I get back to the office is open the safe and take out some stuff I've been saving. Then I'm going to call in the FBI—that's right, the FBI, Lynch—and they're going to rack you so hard you won't know if you're in Swankerton or Cincinnati." He picked up the writing paper and the carbons and threw them across the table at Lynch. They fluttered in the air, caught a current from the air-conditioner, and floated back in a zig-zag pattern to the table. Lynch waited until the last one had settled to the table before he spoke, and then it was only a mild query.

"Is that a fact?"

"You goddamned right it's a fact. This afternoon, Lynch. This very afternoon, not more than a couple of hours from now."

Lynch got up from his chair and bent over the table. He carefully assembled the papers and the carbons in two neat stacks and slid them back across the table to Loambaugh.

"Write it out, Cal, for your sake," he said in a soft tone.

Loambaugh shoved his chair back and rose. "You can get me fired, you sonofabitch, but you ain't about to get me to resign. Ever. You'll like it back in Atlanta, Lynch. And that's where you're headed sure as shit stinks." He turned to leave.

"Little Timmy Thornton," Lynch said in a low, soft voice that still managed to stop Loambaugh in midstride. "Little Timmy Thornton, five years old, with a torn up rectum where somebody cornholed him."

Loambaugh turned slowly and his face was pale and his hands began to shake. He looked at his hands as if they belonged to somebody else and then rested them on the back of a chair. But the shakes were in his arms now and they seemed to travel up them slowly until they reached his shoulders. He quivered visibly, but seemed unaware of it. His face was no longer white, but almost gray instead, and his eyes were fixed on Lynch in an unblinking stare as if he had just peered into the future and didn't much like what he'd seen.

Lynch wouldn't look at Loambaugh. He gazed at the surface of the table instead, and when he spoke again, his voice was still low and soft as if he were talking to himself and was comfortable doing so. "Well, we've been talking about a lot of threats here this afternoon, haven't we, Cal? So I'm going to talk about something that I thought I'd never have to. I'm going to talk about little Timmy Thornton with his torn asshole and little Beth Mary Farnes, all of six and a half, with her little pussy chewed up so much that they had to take twelve stitches in it, and maybe I should mention little Barbara Wynne-wood, who got it both front and rear and then had all of her upper teeth knocked out because she bit it. Now these are the ones that I got evidence to prove, Cal. I admit that there are a couple of others that are nothing but pure D speculation and rumor, but the ones I mentioned, well, I got the facts and even some nigger witnesses to back them up. Now I suggest you sit yourself down and write out that resignation and then we'll just forget about everything that's been said and done in this room this afternoon."

I watched Loambaugh disintegrate as Lynch spoke. He slumped, caved in really, I suppose, and I wondered if he would ever get his posture back. His eyes glazed, but they never left Lynch, and they seemed to watch the words that came out of the fat man's mouth. He continued to tremble and his mouth opened and his swollen tongue played around his lips, but he didn't seem aware of it. His color went from gray back to pasty white and a couple of red spots appeared high up on his cheekbones. When Lynch stopped talking, Loambaugh looked around warily as if he might have stumbled into the wrong room. Then he pulled out a chair, sat down on it cautiously, like an old man, reached for the paper and carbons, interleaved them in a mechanical fashion, and began to write. His hand still shook and he wrote large, bearing down hard on the paper with the pen. I watched him sign his name. He did it carefully and slowly, as if these were the last times he would ever sign it. All five copies. He put the pen down slowly, pushed the papers toward Lynch, rose, and walked out of the room. He moved blindly, bumped against two chairs, and fumbled with the sliding doors.

Lynch watched Loambaugh leave and when he was gone, the fat man said, "Now, by God, I hated to do that to old Cal." He slipped the carbons from between the sheets of paper and handed me one of the copies. "I'll turn the rest over to the mayor and the city council. You drive a hard bargain, Dye. Mighty hard."

I folded the carbon of the resignation and put it in my pocket. "You haven't heard it all yet."

Lynch turned slowly in his chair until he could face me. He looked as if he expected to chew something that would taste bad. He swallowed once and coughed. "I haven't heard it all?" he said.

"No. There's more."

"You better tell me what it is then, hadn't you?" He was using the same low tone that he had used on Loambaugh. I didn't like it.

"I name the new chief of police."

"You?"

"That's right."

"You name the new chief of police," he said slowly, spacing the words so that he could savor each one. "You."

"Me."

"Well," he said. "Huh. That's really something, isn't it?"

"Yes."

"Part of the whole deal, huh?"

"Part of the deal."

"I suppose you got a candidate?"

"That's right."

"Can I ask who?"

"Sure."

"Who?"

I smiled and tried to make it a reassuring one. I don't think I succeeded. "Who?" Lynch said again.

"Homer Necessary," I said.

31

There were five messages under my door when I returned to room 819 in the Sycamore and all of them urged me to call Mr. Gorman Smalldane. I tossed them into the wastebasket, stretched out on the bed, and made a careful study of the ceiling. In my mind I could still hear the sound of my voice which, in retrospect, had all the warmth of a mechanical duck as it quacked away the afternoon, first with Lynch and Loambaugh, and later, for another hour, with Orcutt, Necessary, and Carol Thackerty. It had taken that long to describe how Homer Necessary would be sworn in as Chief Necessary at a special meeting of the Swankerton City Council come next Friday afternoon, which was three days off.

"You'll receive a hand-delivered letter from the mayor tomorrow offering you the job," I told Necessary.

"How far did you have to bend?" he said.

"Over backwards."

"Be more precise, Mr. Dye, please," Orcutt said.

"I know what he means," Necessary said. "He means I clear it all with Lynch."

"That's right," I said. "You might be able to fix an overtime parking ticket without checking, but that's all."

"Did you have to concede so much?" Orcutt said.

"Once he's chief, I don't think Homer's going to give a damn what I conceded."

"Lynch knows that, of course," Orcutt said.

"Sure. But he still needed the concession. It was a matter of pride. Face. He'll make his own deal with Homer when he thinks it's time. Knowing Lynch, that'll probably be fifteen minutes after the swearing-in ceremony."

"Now that deal's something I really look forward to," Necessary said. "Lynch say anything else?"

"About you?"

"Uh-huh."

"There was one thing."

"What?"

"He said to tell you that you'd have to buy your own uniforms."

That was the day or evening that *The News-Calliope* broke the story on the Widow Sobour. An eight-column banner read: REFORM LEADER BILKED THEM, NUNS CHARGE and old man Phetwick's editorial was also featured on page one in a two-column box bang under the picture of Mayor Pierre (Pete) Robineaux, bug-eyed and gap-mouthed. The photo had a cute little caption line that read: " . . . not surprised . . ." Phetwick's editorial was self-righteous and sonorous, but the news story was well-written, simple, even trenchant. It also left no doubt in anyone's mind that Mrs. Sobour was guilty as hell.

I tossed the paper aside, lay back on the bed, studied the ceiling some more, and tried to decide how I felt about the culmination of my efforts, which that afternoon had helped wreck the lives of a couple of none-too-innocent persons, not to mention their families. I consoled myself with the discovery that while I felt no remorse, neither was there any pride nor any sense of accomplishment, which must have balanced things out in the record book of whoever was bothering to keep score. I wasted some more time wondering if Victor Orcutt ever thought of himself as a spiderlike genius who spun his web of intrigue and coercion only because it served some impossibly lofty ideal, and if he did think of himself as such, whether he realized that his web only caught a few emotional cripples, such as me, whom he apparently liked to have around for company. I had noticed that Orcutt spent very little time by himself and then I wondered if anyone ever called him Vic, decided probably not, but promised myself that I would the next time I saw him. I was thinking some additional, similarly rich thoughts when the phone rang and Carol Thackerty wanted to know if I'd like to take her to dinner.

"I have to see an old friend," I said.

"The one from New York—Gorman Smalldane?"

"You keep busy."

"That's what I'm paid to do," she said. "Smalldane's in room seven-nineteen and he called you four times this afternoon according to my spies at the desk and on the switchboard."

"How's Vic?" I said.

"Who?"

"Orcutt."

"Nobody calls him Vic."

"I didn't think so, but I had to make sure."

"He's fine, if you still want to know. He and Homer are meeting with Phetwick and one of his reporters tonight. The reporter's going to write a profile-type piece on the aging boy wonder who's to be Swankerton's new chief of police. Orcutt and Phetwick are sitting in to make sure that Necessary doesn't mention too many facts."

"I think both of you underrate Homer," I said.

"Victor may; I don't. I don't underrate him for a second."

"That's about how long he'd need."

"If that."

I told her that I would call later to see whether she wanted a nightcap and she said that if it were after twelve not to bother, and I said that I wouldn't, and we hung up. I thought about Carol for a while and decided, or felt, or whatever it was that I did, concluded perhaps, which implies at least a little emotional involvement, that if I needed a temporary entangling alliance, it might as well be with her. It was the nicest thought I had all day.

Because I couldn't postpone it any longer, although I wasn't sure why I'd delayed as long as I had, I picked up the phone and asked for Smalldane's room. When he answered, I said, "Let's have dinner and get a little drunk."

"Why a little?" he said.

"Because I'd only have a little hangover. I can't stand the regular brand anymore."

"You want to come down or do you want me to come up?"

"I'll come down."

I hadn't seen Smalldane in more than ten years and I don't quite know what I expected, but certainly not what opened the door to my knock. Age smooths many by rounding off craggy edges with personal growth which the unkind sometimes call fat. It dehydrates others by squeezing out most of their life juices, leaving nothing but dry husks. The cosmetics of age occasionally dignify a few past all recognition by anyone who knew what clunks they were when young. Age simply ravages some, and Gorman Smalldane was one of those.

When I'd first seen him more than a quarter of a century ago in Tante Katerine's courtyard, he'd been a broad-shouldered man with a nipped-in waist who topped my present 6'—1½" by at least 2". He then had a long mop of light blond hair that always needed a trim and kept falling down over the pale blue eyes that had questioned it all. His mouth, I remembered, had been wide and sardonic and out of it had come some of the world's most infectious laughter.

The hair was gone now except for some white tufts above his ears. His skull was the color of old putty and I seemed to top his height by almost half a foot because of the bent way that he held himself. He had gone to fat in his forties and fifties, which he had then carried well enough, but now the fat was gone too and the skin stretched tight across his face, but raddled around the neck. He must have weighed no more that 125 pounds. Only his eyes remained the same, set a little farther back in their sockets perhaps, but still bright pale blue and as skeptical as ever. So was his voice.

"Well, one of us looks healthy," he said. "Come on in."

I went in and watched him move across the room to the Scotch and the ice bucket. He walked slowly, as if he had to remember how to do it. With his back to me he mixed two drinks and said, "You've seen it before."

"When did you find out?"

"Two months ago. They cut me open and there it was. Big as a grapefruit, they said."

He crossed the room with the drinks and handed me one. "I keep going on booze and pills. I think the pills have opium in them because my dreams have been rather interesting lately. I get to screw some real dolls."

"Well, I won't say how are you."

"That's apparent, isn't it? I never thought I'd be an ugly old man with the eagle pecking away at my liver. They say that I've got a couple of months left. That means a month."

"You still don't like hospitals?" I said.

"That's where they want me so they can stick tubes up every hole they can find. I might last three months that way, but I won't go through the indignity of it all. I don't find life quite that precious."

He eased down into a chair carefully, but it still made him wince.

"Bad?"

"You goddamned right it's bad. Don't ever let them tell you it's not."

"I won't," I said.

He took a long swallow of his drink and then looked at me and grinned with most of his former skepticism. "Now just what the hell are you doing in Swankerton?"

"I'm corrupting it."

"I hear it doesn't need much, but if it does, you ought to be better than a fair hand. After all, you did have a fine upbringing."

"There's that," I said.

"Well, tell me about it."

I told him the entire story, partly because in telling it I brought it into focus, but mostly because I knew that he'd enjoy it and there were few enough things left that he could.

When I'd finished, Smalldane nodded his understanding and held out his empty glass to me. "You mind?"

"Not at all," I said.

I handed him a fresh drink and he said, "That's quite a story. You only left out one thing. Why're you doing it?"

"Lacks motivation, huh?"

"That and an ending."

"I'm doing it because it seemed to be the thing to do at the time."

"That's bullshit and you know it."

"Money," I said.

"More bullshit."

"I can see that we're coming to the stop where the Smalldane Theory gets on."

"I got one."

"I never knew you to run short."

"Born again," he said. "How's that?"

"You could give the one at Delphi some stiff competition."

"A little oracular?"

"A little."

"You should have brought along your chicken entrails."

"I forgot."

"I'll spell it out for you," he said.

"I'll listen."

286

"There were two persons killed that night in Maryland. One of them was Beverly and the other one was you. She may have been luckier because that night you turned into a zombie and, as such, a perfect candidate for the spooks because most of them, at least the ones I've known, have been zombies, too."

"Not all," I said, remembering Beverly's father.

"For example," he said. "That redheaded guy at her funeral, the one you never introduced me to."

"Carmingler," I said.

"He was a zombie. He couldn't have been more than thirty then, but he'd been dead for fifteen years."

"What do you mean dead? Emotionally castrated? Juiceless? Calculating? Cold? Remorseless? Unfeeling? I can go on."

"You don't have to. I can see you've already been turning it over. What I mean is that you're like a vacant house. Nobody lives there."

"Thanks."

"I've seen you among the living just twice, kid. When you were in Shanghai with Kate and me and when you were with Beverly. When they took you away from Kate, that really started it. Beverly stopped it, arrested it probably, and when she died, you went under. Succumbed, if you like the word."

"To what?"

"To zombieism. What had you and Beverly planned to do?"

"I was supposed to go with the spooks. I was on that scholarship of theirs."

"But what were you really going to do?"

"Teach."

"Why didn't you?"

"After Beverly died? There wasn't any point."

"That's why I said born again. You can't go back to that time with Beverly so now you're trying to go back as far as you remember, to Shanghai—back to the whores and the pimps and the crooks who surrounded you then during the only other time in your life you were really happy. Now how's that for penetrating insight?"

"I still think that you were once a good reporter, Gorm."

"The funny thing is—" He stopped and coughed. I hadn't heard him cough before, but if I had heard him without

287

seeing him, perhaps through a thin hotel wall at three in the morning, I would have known he was dying. It was that kind of a cough, the kind that wrenches the whole body, twists it, and sounds like a long series of small, harsh explosions.

He straightened up, used his handkerchief to wipe his lips, and then shook his head. His face had turned a dangerous-looking bright pink. "Not lung cancer," he said. "Just a side effect of its cousin. Where was I in the lecture?"

"Something was funny," I said.

"It is funny. You want to hear it?"

"Sure."

"What you're doing down here and why. The funny thing is that it might work. Lucifer Dye might rise to live again."

We talked through dinner, which we had in Smalldane's room. We got a little drunk, but not very. I had a steak; he had a bowl of oyster stew. We both had a quantity of Scotch.

"I lied to you over the phone the other day," he said.

"How'd you lie?"

"I said I wanted in on this deal just for kicks. I didn't really. I can't do you a damned bit of good. I'm washed up and the pain's too bad. There are four other guys and one woman that I'm going to see in the next week and then I'll go back to New York and sit around and wait for it. If I get tired of that, I might speed things up."

"It's that bad?"

"It will be in another week or ten days. There won't be any funeral."

"All right."

"You need some money?" he said.

"No."

"I'll leave you some anyhow. I got plenty. I got it from zombies like you. They'd spend twenty or thirty years hustling for it and then discover that they weren't immortal after all, so they'd come to me."

"For what?"

"For a slice of immortality. So somebody would remember their name ten years after they were dead. I'd set them up a foundation, have a couple of books ghostwritten for them, maybe have them endow a chair at some university. And then I'd present the bill and to a man they thought it was the best money they'd ever spent."

I switched to Mandarin. "The master said: 'The noble man hates to end his days and leave his name undistinguished.' "

"The *Analects*," Smalldane said.

"Book Five, Number nineteen."

"Substitute rich for noble and you have one of the secrets of my success. There's only one thing more that I really want to do and I think, Lucifer, by God, you've given me the opportunity."

"Delighted," I said.

"I saw a picture show a long time ago."

"So did I. I sometimes think I spent my entire adolescence in picture shows. Carol does, too."

"Carol who?"

"Thackerty," I said. "The girl you checked on."

"The one I saw had Ned Sparks in it," Smalldane said. "You remember Ned Sparks?"

"Never had the pleasure."

"Well, he had a long sad, bloodhound face and a deep voice and a cigar. So this gal and her Negro mammy were running this restaurant where the Negro mammy made the best pancakes in the world from her secret recipe. I think it was secret. Anyway, Ned Sparks comes in and orders some pancakes. He's so impressed that he offers to make their fortune with just two words."

"What was his cut?"

"That isn't important. Say ten percent."

"Okay."

Smalldane took another swallow of Scotch. "Well, he did it in just two words. You want to know what they were?"

"What?"

"Box it."

"The pancake mixture?"

"Right."

"He stole that from Coca-Cola," I said. "The guy there said, 'Bottle it.' "

"Well, this was supposed to be something like Aunt Jemimah."

"And everybody got rich?" I said.

"Sure."

"And happy?"

"Of course."

"And that's your ambition, to make me rich and happy?"

"In two words, just like Ned Sparks. Right here in Swankerton."

"They call it Chancre Town."

"Don't blame them."

"And you've got two words for me?"

Smalldane nodded. "Two words."

"Maybe I'd better get something and write them down."

"You'll remember. Maybe."

"I'll try."

"Ready?"

I nodded.

He spaced them carefully. "Take," he said, "over."

"The whole town?"

"The whole town."

"By God, Smalldane, that's brilliant, that's what it is."

"I think so, too."

"You think I could?"

"That's the only way you're going to get out of it."

"All right, I'll do it." On that much Scotch, anything was possible.

"You've made an old man happy. Now get out of here so I can get some sleep."

I rose, a little unsteadily, and headed for the door. Smalldane followed, tacking a bit, much as he had done the first night that I'd seen him coming up the path in Tante Katerine's garden. I turned at the door.

"Just like Ned Sparks," he said.

"Two words."

He pulled himself up so that he stood straight and taller than I. It required an effort that apparently caused considerable pain. Suddenly, he seemed completely sober. He held out his hand and I took it and was surprised at how thin it was.

"This is the real goodbye, kid, I'm leaving in the morning. Early."

"All right."

"That crap I was talking earlier. That zombie crap. Forget it."

I nodded.

"And those two words. Forget them, too. It might be

fun, but you'd never make it. You're not put together that way."

"All right."

He held on to my hand and looked at me for a long time, his eyes steady and for once almost gentle. He nodded after his inspection. "You're not quite dead after all, are you?"

"Not quite."

He grinned then and released my hand. "Well, that'll leave one of us around anyway."

32

I bought a new suit to go to Homer Necessary's swearing-in ceremony. It was a dark blue poplin that cost all of sixty dollars plus tax at Biendorfer's department store across the street from the Sycamore Hotel. I bought two others of the same material, one tan and the other gray.

The ceremony was held in the City Council chamber, which was on the seventh floor of the same new municipal building that housed Police Headquarters. Attendance was by invitation only and I went alone. Lynch had stubbornly refused to invite either Orcutt or Carol Thackerty.

The City Council was a seven-man body that sat at a long oval walnut table, the Lynch crowd on one side, the opposition on the other, and the popeyed mayor at the end near the door. Lynch himself sat in a spectator's chair that was only a few feet from the far end of the table and gave Mayor Robineaux something reassuring to look at. Three tiers of chairs ran around three sides of the room and during the City Council's regular meetings were used to seat witnesses, reporters, city officials and employees, and citizens who just wanted to kill a dull afternoon. If Lynch's chair had been any closer to the table, it would have occupied the spot usually reserved for a city manager, except that Swankerton didn't have one and, as far as I could see, didn't need one as long as Lynch was around.

The three television stations were represented, as were five or six radio stations. The two newspapers had sent reporters and photographers. There was a handful of ranking police officials and one of them was the captain who had been playing poker a few afternoons before at the table next to Necessary and me.

The seven city councilmen were already in their seats when I arrived. The three who composed what passed for the loyal opposition were middle-aged, mild-mannered men who smiled a lot, wore sensible suits, and favored rimless glasses. The four who belonged to Lynch's crowd seemed heavier and jowlier, liked cigars, and twisted around in their chairs to wave at friends and acquaintances. Fred Merriweather, big-jawed and stupid-eyed and owner of The Easy Alibi bar, covered all bets and even waved at me. I waved back. He was the only one on the council whom I knew.

All of the ones that I had met that first day in Lynch's house were in the room, with the exception of Cal Loambaugh. Ancel Carp, the city tax assessor and surveyor, sat next to Lynch, looking as outdoorsy as ever. On the other side of Lynch was Alex Couturier, executive secretary of the Chamber of Commerce, who wore a big, pleased smile on his face, but that meant nothing because he never wore anything else.

Channing d'Arcy Phetwick III crept in with the aid of his cane, surveyed the room through his thick-lensed glasses, spotted me and came over and sat down at my left. "I understand this was all your idea, Mr. Dye," he whispered. Before I could say that it wasn't quite all mine, he whispered, "Splendid. Perfectly splendid."

Homer Necessary sat in the first row of the tier of seats directly behind the mayor and I found myself wondering if he had called his wife about his new job.

Mayor Pierre (Pete) Robineaux picked up a gavel and tapped it apologetically against the table. The councilmen quit waving their arms and gossiping. The small crowd did the usual amount of coughing and throat-clearing. The mayor said, "This special session of the Swankerton City Council is now convened. Good to see y'all. Our first order of business is the resignation of Calvin Loambaugh as chief of police. I've sent you all copies of it, so we can dispense with its reading. Is there any discussion?"

He waited, but nobody said anything. After almost a full minute Fred Merriweather stuck up a big hand and said, "I move we accept it." Somebody else seconded the motion, the mayor called for the ayes and then for the nays, and Cal Loambaugh was out of a job.

"Now before we go into the second order of business I'd like to make a few personal remarks, if nobody objects," the mayor said. Nobody did, so he said, "Chief Loambaugh's resignation came as a surprise to all of us, I know. Now my first thought was, where in the world are we gonna find somebody of high calibre, competence, and experience to take his place, and then how in the good Lord's name, if we do find a man like that, are we gonna find enough money to pay him?" He waited for his laugh and he got it.

"Well, the good Lord smiled down on us. That's all I can say. Because right after I got the bad news about Chief Loambaugh's resignation, I got some good news. I learned that there was a man right here in Swankerton on private business who's generally acknowledged as one of the top law enforcement officers in the whole United States. And not only that, but I learned that although he was mighty successful in private industry, he just might be interested in getting back into his first love." That brought a titter from the press, if from no one else.

"Well, sir, I didn't let any grass grow under my feet, so to speak. I contacted this man and asked him to come see me and when he did, I laid my cards on the table. We talked man to man and heart to heart. We discussed Swankerton's law-and-order problems and I liked what he had to say. Now this man knows police work. He should because he was chief of police of a city larger than Swankerton when he was twenty-seven years old. Think about that. Twenty-seven. Course, he's a bit older now, but still in his prime. We talked money, too, and I don't mind telling you that I was downright embarrassed when I had to tell him what we could offer. I bet I even blushed some. Well, he said he understood our problems, but he also said that he's a great one for merit increases. So I took the bull by the horns and said I'm going to offer you the job as chief of police, providing the City Council will go along, of course, and what's more I'm going to recommend that we raise the salary of that job up to fifteen thousand dollars a year where it should be. So now I formally recommend to you, the City Council of the City of Swankerton, that we hereby employ Mr. Homer Fairbanks Necessary as chief of police. The meeting is now open for discussion."

Fred Merriweather was the first to stick up a hand. "Your honor, do you think we might ask Mr. Necessary some questions?"

"That's why he's here, Fred," Robineaux said. He turned in his chair and beckoned at Necessary. "Mr. Necessary, you might be more comfortable sitting up here by me."

Necessary rose, walked over to the chair that the

mayor had indicated, and settled himself into it. He wore the easy, attentive expression of an expert about to be questioned by amateurs. I decided that it wasn't the first time that Homer Necessary had appeared before a board of inquiry.

Merriweather leaned forward in his chair. "Mr. Necessary, why did you leave police work?"

"To make money."

"And have you?"

"Yes. I have."

"May I ask how much your present salary is?"

"You can ask, but I won't answer. I think that is privileged information and I have high respect for the privacy of the individual."

"Could I safely say that your present salary is higher— much higher—than what you'd earn as Swankerton's chief of police?"

"Yes."

"I know I'm interested in the answer to my next question and I guess most of us are. What I'd like to know is if you're making a real good living now, then why do you want to get back into something that doesn't pay half or even a third as much?" Merriweather looked around the table at his fellow councilmen. A couple of them nodded. "Now that's what I'd like to hear from you."

Necessary didn't hesitate. "Because I know police work, because I'm good at it, and because I like it. It's my profession. I'm a cop, and without bragging, I think I'm a good one. I also think the salaries paid policemen are a disgrace and if I'm appointed Swankerton's chief of police, then you're going to get sick of seeing me right in this room arguing for higher pay for police and that means from the newest rookie right on up to the top, and the top includes the chief of police." It was a small joke and it got a small laugh.

There were some more questions, perfunctory ones, which Necessary answered with short paragraphs or shorter sentences. When he thought a single word would do, it did. The last question came from Merriweather and I suspected that Lynch had told him to ask it.

"If you're appointed chief, Mr. Necessary, what changes do you foresee under your administration?"

"None."

"None?"

"That's right. You asked what I foresee. I don't foresee any changes. I don't condemn or condone what's gone before because I haven't studied it. When I have made a thorough study of it and get to know the men, there'll be some changes, but I'm not prepared to say right now what they'll be. But there is *one* thing that's got to be made clear. If I think changes are needed, administrative changes, then I'll make them. I plan to run the Swankerton Police Department. If you don't want me to run it the way I see fit, then you'd better find somebody else. I intend to run an honest, efficient department. Lawabiding citizens will like it. The only ones who won't are the crooks and the thieves."

It was the longest answer he had given yet and when he finished they voted to give him the job. The mayor swore him in and the city clerk held the Bible. When Necessary said the final "so help me God" there was a ripple of applause and then the mayor asked him to say a few words.

Necessary stood at the end of the table near Robineaux and looked down its length to the man who sat several feet removed in space, if not in power, from its far end. He stared at Ramsey Lynch. Necessary cleared his throat, acknowledged the mayor and the distinguished guests, and still staring straight at Lynch delivered a close version of what Carol Thackerty had written for him: "I really appreciate your confidence and trust. While I'm police chief, I'll be police chief in fact, as well as in name. I'm beholden to none and I'll never become so. I promise you only this: an efficient, honest, police force dedicated to the preservation of law and order and the maintenance of justice. I'll bow neither to influence nor pressure from any source regardless of its office or power. I'd now like to perform my first official act and announce the appointment of a special investigator who will also serve as assistant to the chief of police. He is a man of talent, dedication, experience, and total honesty. He happens to be in the room now and I wish to introduce him. Mr. Lucifer Dye," The television cameras panned until they found me and I stood up, a little awkwardly, I hoped, and let them all look at me. There were a few smiles of greeting and encouragement from those who didn't know any better. I nodded, sat back down, and glanced at Lynch. He was staring at me and it was difficult to read the expression on his face, but there was nothing that said, "best of luck in your new job."

The mayor asked for a motion to adjourn, got it along with a second, and all of the councilmen crowded around Necessary to congratulate him. The ranking police officials gathered at one side of the room, talking among themselves and shooting glances at Necessary. None of them seemed quite sure what to do or where to go.

Phetwick turned to me and said, "Congratulations, Mr. Dye."

"Thank you."

"A most interesting maneuver," he said. "I must say that I look forward to the events of the next few weeks with what only can be described as keen anticipation."

I told him that I hoped he wouldn't be disappointed. We both left the tier of seats and moved toward the small crowd that was still formed around Necessary. A young policeman hurried into the council room, looked around as if he wanted to tell someone something important, but couldn't decide who it should be. He finally settled on the mayor and whispered into his ear. The mayor popped his eyes and gaped his mouth at the news. He then shook his head and looked more indecisive than usual. He burrowed into the crowd, got Necessary by the arm, and drew him to one side. I moved over to where they stood, but Lynch beat me there. He didn't miss much.

"Terrible news, Mr. Necessary—I mean Chief. This is just terrible news." He drew the uniformed policeman into the small circle. "Now tell him just what you told me," the mayor said.

"It's Chief Loambaugh," the young man said as if that explained everything. He waited until someone asked what about Chief Loambaugh and I got the feeling that the young man would never make sergeant.

"He shot them," the young man said.

"Who?" Necessary said.

"His two kids."

"Dead?"

"Yessir."

"When?"

"His wife too."

"When?" Necessary said again.

"About thirty minutes ago or an hour ago. Around then."

Necessary sighed and then smiled at the young man. "Just tell it," he said in a curiously reassuring voice. "Just start where you want to and tell it."

The young man took a deep breath. "He shot his two kids and his wife and they're all dead and he is too because he shot himself three times in the—" He stopped while he searched his mind for a word. "In the *groin*."

"Jesus!" Lynch said and turned to Necessary. "Could he do that?" he demanded. "Could he shoot himself three times?"

Necessary kept on with his role in the play. "Who're you, mister?"

Mayor Robineaux rushed in as the reporters began crowding around, sensing something had happened, something that needed telling. "I don't think you two've ever met," the mayor said. "Mr. Lynch here is one of our— our—" He stumbled in his search for a word or phrase that would describe Lynch. He finally settled on, "our civic leaders."

Necessary nodded to show the mayor that he understood what a civic leader was. "Well, that's fine," he said and turned to leave.

"You didn't answer my question," Lynch said and put a large, fat hand on Necessary's shoulder. Swankerton's new chief of police stopped quite still and then turned, not with the hand, but away from it, so that Lynch either had to remove it or trot around in a circle after Necessary. He dropped the hand.

"What question?" Necessary said after he had turned fully around.

"I think it sounds fishy. Shooting himself three times."

"You think it might not be suicide, huh?" Necessary said and examined Lynch as if for the first time. He took in the tentlike suit and the ill-fitting white shirt and the stained tie and the big round face that wore its best smile, the one that didn't show too many teeth. Necessary studied it all with his blue and brown eyes and nodded slightly, as if confirming some long-held suspicion.

"That's right," Lynch said, returning the stare. "I think that maybe it might not be suicide."

Necessary cocked his head slightly to one side and nodded again, as if he were giving Lynch's comment a great deal of serious thought. Finally he said, "And what makes you believe I give a goddamn what you think, mister?"

He said it loudly enough so that the reporters could make a note of it, turned and walked rapidly from the city council chamber, still coming down hard on his heels, as the newly appointed assistant to the chief of police hurried after him.

Part Three

33

Carol slept while I dressed, quickly as always, but more quietly than usual. I could dress quietly now because my clothing was hung neatly on hangers or the backs of chairs and I no longer had to make a muttering search for an odd sock or the missing tie. The neatly hung clothes indicated the stage that we had reached by the first week in October. We no longer left them on the floor in what Carol called rumpled piles of passion. Instead we undressed in stages, taking our time, talking and perhaps drinking a final Scotch and water, comfortable in our knowledge that passion would arrive on schedule, or perhaps a few minutes early, but that there was no hurry. In fact we enjoyed each other's company and I'm still not sure which of us was more surprised at the discovery.

I was buttoning my button-down collar when Carol rolled over in the bed, opened her eyes, gazed at the ceiling, and said, "If I go out that door, Vincent, I'm never coming back. Never."

"There was a woman here to see you this afternoon, Countess," I said. "An old woman. She said that she was . . . your mother."

"That medical degree doesn't give you the right to play God, doctor," she said and then yawned as prettily as anyone can. "Okay, I'm awake. Where's the coffee?"

"Roger should be knocking on the door any minute, which will make him only twenty minutes late."

"He's improving," she said.

The knock came three minutes later and I opened the door for Roger, the defeated room waiter. He smiled grumpily, if that can be done, and said, "Right on time this morning, huh, Mr. Dye?"

"On the dot," I said.

"How you, Miz Thackerty?"

"Fine, Roger."

"Gonna be a nice day," he said, pouring the coffee. "Shouldn't get no more than ninety, maybe ninety-two."

"In October," I said.

"Nice day."

I signed the check and added his usual dollar tip. He looked at it glumly and said, "Might rain later though."

"Thanks, Roger," I said.

"Might even storm," he said, moving toward the door. "Even some talk about a hurricane, but that weatherman's a liar." He took another quick peek at Carol, but found nothing interesting, mumbled something else about the weather or the state of the world, and left.

I handed Carol her coffee. "You should walk around naked for him just once," I said.

"Not really. If I did he'd have nothing to anticipate. An occasional glimpse of breast and thigh keeps him stimulated and interested."

I finished my coffee and put the cup down. "Who am I this morning? It's slipped my mind."

"You're Special Investigator Dye from nine until ten," she said.

"Him, huh?" He's the one who always thinks he should have known what lay behind the sealed tomb's door."

"His reports are good, too," she said. "They all begin, 'Chief Homer Necessary and his faithful assistant, Lucifer Dye, moved cautiously through the fog-shrouded night.' From ten-thirty this morning until eleven-thirty you're back being Triple Agent Lucifer Dye. You meet Lynch at his place. At noon you revert to your original role as Orcutt's number one skulk."

"What's a skulk?"

"It's what Orcutt wants to meet with at noon in his suite."

"He likes meetings," I said.

"He needs his audience."

I leaned over the bed and kissed her. "I'll see you at noon."

"After it was over—really over," she said, "I never actually believed that I would come back here to Venice."

"I've never once asked for your love, Myra," I said. "Only for your respect." It was a harmless enough way to say goodbye.

I only needed a glance to tell what he was and who had sent him. He stood in the center of my room, his hands carefully in sight, but well balanced on the balls of his feet

304

in case I tried to throw him out before he said what he had come to say. I nodded at him and tossed my room key on the dresser.

"How's Carmingler?" I said.

"Fine."

I pointed at the bathroom door. "I'm going in there and shower and shave and probably take a shit. I'll be fifteen minutes. You can make yourself useful in the meantime by ordering up some coffee. I've only had one cup this morning and I'd like some more. Okay?"

"All right," he said.

He was still standing in the center of the room when I came out, but he now held a cup and saucer. I went over to the dresser and poured myself a cup. Then I sat in the room's most comfortable chair and looked at him.

"You know what somebody else and I call you?" I said.

"What?"

"We call you 'just a guy.'"

He nodded as if he didn't care what I called him. He was young, probably around twenty-eight or twenty-nine, wore a sleepy expression and a faint smile, as if he thought I was just a little quaint or old-fashioned. Maybe I was.

"I'll make two guesses," I said.

"Yes."

"You sent a couple of punks up here about a month ago to see how nervous I was. That's one guess. The second one is that your name is Mugar and that you're Section Two's young man of the year."

He walked to the dresser and put his cup down. He moved well and had a deft way of pouring a cup of coffee. He drank it black, I noticed. He turned and looked at me, taking his time. His ash blond hair fitted his head like a bathing cap except for a few curly locks that wandered part way down his forehead. It gave him a slightly tousled look that must have cost him fifteen minutes before the mirror each morning with comb and brush.

The rest of him was regular enough, about five-eleven, a hundred and sixty pounds, regular features except for his dark hazel eyes, which I thought were a little too confident for his age, but I may have been jealous.

"Carmingler wants you to pack it in," he said. It was his first complete sentence and it came out Eastern Seaboard from somewhere south of Boston and north of Baltimore.

"All right," I said and watched his reaction with pleasure. He started slightly, but recovered well enough.

"You'll do it then?" he said.

"I'll take the third flight out. If Carmingler had said, 'please,' I'd take the first one."

"They told me to expect some smart answers."

"Anything else?"

"He wants you out of here next week. Friday."

"And you're to see to it?"

"That's right. I'm to see to it."

"He wanted me out a month ago and you made a half-hearted attempt that didn't work. Why wait till now to try again?"

"The first was just a precautionary move," he said. "Now we're certain."

"Carmingler's never been certain of anything," I said.

"He is of this."

"You've waited long enough for it so I'll say what?"

"Gerald Vicker."

"Old Gerald."

"He's got to Senator Simon."

"That's not quite news," I said.

"It will be when Simon makes his speech next Friday."

"You're a born tease, aren't you?"

"You want it all?"

"Most of it anyway."

"All right. Vicker got to Senator Simon and told him all about the Li Teh fiasco and how you'd spent three months in jail. The Senator's not too happy with Section Two anyway, but I won't go into the reasons unless you insist."

"I don't."

"So now he's going to make a speech on the Senate floor about the Li Teh thing and about how Section Two is messing in domestic politics where it's not supposed to be. And you're the goat. That's bad enough, of course, but Simon's also working with a top magazine that's going to run a muckraker's delight on you and this crew you're working with here in Swankerton."

"They've got two sources, I'd say. Gerald Vicker and his brother, Ramsey Lynch."

"That's right."

"Carmingler's worried about his appropriations," I said.

"That and he just doesn't like publicity."

"Well, you can tell him that I think he's got a real problem."

"You've got until Friday," he said.

"Your name *is* Mugar, isn't it?"

"Franz Mugar."

"If I don't bow out by Friday, what happens then, Franz?"

"You'll bow out one way or another."

"A promise, I take it?"

"If you like. If you don't, it's a threat."

"What about my associates?"

"A little scummy, aren't they?"

"Not for me, but then I bet you and I don't travel in the same crowd. I know Carmingler doesn't."

"We don't care about them," Mugar said. "We just don't want anything of ours around that can tie us into this mess when it breaks."

"And I'm the anything?"

"That's right."

"And if I don't go quietly, then I'll go however you decide's best?"

"That's right," Mugar said again.

"I don't like threats. They make me nervous."

"You should take something for it."

I rose, walked over to the phone, and picked it up. "Chief Necessary's room, please."

Mugar stared at me. I beckoned him over to the phone. "I'll hold it so you can hear," I said. He moved over so that he could hear.

When Necessary came on I said, "How much room do we have in that new jail of ours?"

"Plenty," Necessary said.

"There's somebody in town who calls himself Franz Mugar. I think he's our old friend 'just a guy.' "

"You want to cool him off?"

"I think so."

"You want it legal and all?"

"No."

"We can keep him a while on one thing or another. Where is he?"

"Right here in my room."

"Will he stay put until I send somebody around?"

307

"I don't know," I said. "I'll ask him."

Mugar was backing toward the door. "You sonofabitch," he said.

"I don't think so, Homer," I said.

Necessary chuckled. "Well, tell him we'll pick him up inside a couple of hours or so."

"I'll see what he says," I said and told Necessary that I'd ride to headquarters with him. He said he was leaving in fifteen minutes and I said that would be fine. I hung up the phone and turned toward Mugar who was at the door, his hand on the knob, a look of angry disbelief in his eyes.

"You'd do it, wouldn't you?" he said.

"You can call Carmingler and he'll have you out in an hour, but then we'd have you back in another hour. It can go on for quite a while. In and out two or three or four times a day. Of course, you could sue, couldn't you?"

"You've had it, Dye. I swear you have."

"Tell you what I'll do," I said. "I'll give you an hour to get the first plane out of Swankerton. After that, well—"

Mugar shook his head slowly from side to side. "You *are* through, Dye. You just don't know how through you are."

"You are catching that plane, aren't you?"

"Sure. Sure, I'm catching the plane, and when it lands and I get through doing what I'm going to do, maybe I'll even have time to feel a little sorry for you. Maybe. But I don't really think so."

"You know," I said in what I hoped was a thoughtful tone, "there is one thing you can do for me when you see Carmingler."

"On top of everything else that I'm going to do," he said, a little of his confidence coming back.

"That's right. On top of everything else."

"What?"

"Tell Carmingler I said that if he's still set on it, and can't spare the experienced help, he'd better come himself."

"That's all?" Mugar said.

"That's all. You won't forget, will you?"

"No," he said, still keeping most of the bitterness out of his voice, "I won't forget."

"I didn't think that you would."

34

The second thing that Homer Necessary did after he was sworn in as chief of police was to order a specially equipped Chrysler Imperial which had arrived only a few days before. It was black, not much longer than a pocket battleship, and had a hotted-up engine with a four-barrel carburetor to make it go fast. In its air-conditioned rear, where we now were, it had leather upholstery, a TV set, a telephone, a bar of sorts, an AM-FM radio, a police radio, and a sawed-off shotgun which went by the euphemism of riot weapon. Necessary's driver was Sergeant Lester Krone, the sponsor of a local hot-rod club whose members called themselves the Leaping Lepers. Sergeant Krone was fond of the car's red light and siren and used them at his discretion, which meant most of the time. Necessary didn't seem to mind.

"What happened to your friend?" Necessary said.

"You mean 'just a guy'?"

"Yeah."

"He left town."

Necessary grinned. "You roust him?"

"He might call it that."

"Was he bad news?"

"Bad enough. I'll tell you about it at noon when we meet with Orcutt and after I see your friend Mr. Lynch."

Necessary pushed a button that rolled the glass up between us and Sergeant Krone. "Old Lynch is getting antsy."

"I know," I said. "He called you three times yesterday for a meeting. He wants to know what the hell you're up to."

"His weekly take's down," Necessary said and smiled comfortably.

"By about three-fourths, he claims."

"That's about right."

"He's getting pressure from New Orleans."

309

"He'll be getting some more after our meeting this morning."

"More reorganization?" I said.

"The last one."

"Who?"

"Henderson."

"He's vice squad," I said.

"That's right, he is, isn't he?"

Necessary liked me to be present when, in his words, he "rattled the box and shook 'em up." The sessions never lasted more than twenty minutes, were highly educational, often emotional, and those who had been summoned often left white-faced and visibly shaken.

"New uniform?" I said.

Necessary looked down and ran his hand over the blue summer-weight worsted uniform's gold buttons. "Yeah, three of them came yesterday. What do you think?"

"Becoming. It matches your left eye."

"You want one?"

"Not unless it has a Sam Browne belt."

"We can put in a special order."

"Let me think about it," I said.

Necessary's office on the twelfth floor of the new municipal building was richly carpeted, contained a large desk and some comfortable chairs, two flags on standards, the stars and bars of the Confederacy, and the stars and stripes of the U.S.A., a country to which Swankerton's allegiance was nominally pledged. The room also had a small bar, an autographed photograph of the mayor, and an unsigned one of the President. Through the black-tinted windows there was a gloomy view of the Gulf of Mexico.

Necessary had quickly recruited himself a staff of young, able persons who handled the paperwork and left him free for "standing at the window and nodding yes or no," as he put it. His secretary was a young Negro girl whose appointment had stirred up considerable comment, none of it favorable, and when anyone even vaguely alluded to it, Necessary would smile, slip into his best mushmouth drawl, which wasn't bad, and say, "I sho wouldn't have hired her either if she wasn't my wife's youngest sister."

Captain Warren Gamaliel Henderson was born in Ohio the year that they elected his partial namesake President. His family moved to Swankerton the following year in 1921, switched quickly to the Democratic party, and started calling their youngest son by his initials.

Now somewhere past his fiftieth birthday, W.G. had run the Swankerton vice squad for a dozen profitable years and it had rubbed off on him. He was a big man with a red, rubbery face and neatly cropped, thick gray hair. His nose was purpling at its blunt tip and there were networks of deep lines at the corners of his eyes that had all the warmth of old pieces of slate. His big bony chin, freshly barbered, underscored a stubborn mouth that seemed frozen halfway between a smirk and a snarl. He also had gaunt, sunken cheeks whose insides he liked to suck on when he was thinking. He didn't carry any spare fat that I could see and his uniform had cost him more than the city paid him in two weeks. He looked exactly what he was: tough, mean and nasty, and none of it bothered Homer Necessary in the least.

"Time we had a little private talk," Necessary said, leaning back in his high-topped executive chair.

"I like private talks in private," Henderson said and stared at me.

"You mean my special assistant bothers you?"

"If that's what you call him."

"I call him Mr. Dye and I have a lot of confidence in his judgment and I think you should too."

"Whatever you say, boss."

It was a bleak and wintry smile that Necessary gave Henderson. "Mr. Dye calls me Chief Necessary, Captain Henderson, and I think you'd better call me that, too."

"Whatever you say, Chief Necessary."

"How long have you been head of the vice squad?"

"Twelve years."

"Now that's a long time, isn't it?"

"I like it."

"I'm sure you do," Necessary said, "but didn't you ever get just a little sick of all those whores and the pimps and the fags and the rest of the lot?"

"It's my job," Henderson said. "I never thought about getting sick of it."

"Well, maybe you're a little sick of it, but just don't know it."

"You got a complaint?"

"I don't know if you'd call it a complaint or not," Necessary said and turned to me. "You got those figures, Mr. Dye?"

"Right here, Chief Necessary," I said, the way an up-and-coming special assistant should say it.

"Read off some of the highlights for Captain Henderson. These are statistics, Captain, that tell how our crime rate's going. They only deal with the past month. Go ahead, Mr. Dye."

"Armed robbery, up seventeen percent," I read. "Auto theft, up twenty-one percent; homicide, up sixteen percent; assault, up twenty-seven percent; extortion, up nine percent, and what's generally called vice, down four percent. These are only percentages as compared with the previous month's figures."

"Vice down four percent," Necessary said. "And everything else up. You seem to be keeping on top of things, Captain."

"I do my job," he said.

"Now I've had talks with just about every ranking officer in headquarters except you and they've all agreed to cooperate one-hundred percent and I think these figures reflect that cooperation. Our crime rate's up about fourteen percent and I call that progress, don't you?"

"No."

"That a fact?" Necessary said. "Well, I thought that everybody thought that getting at the truth was progress and that's just what these figures are, Captain Henderson. The truth. All except yours."

"You calling me a liar?" Henderson demanded, his tone thick and phlegmy.

"That's right, I am. You've been lying about the number of vice violations and if you want me to prove it, I will. That's why the crime rate's gone up. The rest of the squads have quit lying, all except yours. They're reporting *actual* figures—or near actual. I expect they're still fudging a little, but that's to be expected. But Jesus Christ, mister, you're giving yours six coats of whitewash."

"I report the figures as they're given to me," Henderson said.

"Sure you do. Now correct me if I'm wrong, but I think I've got some more figures down pretty good. A fag can buy himself off for fifty bucks. A whore, ten. Gambling's fifteen for each player and a hundred for the house. A pimp's not good for much more'n fifty and a disorderly house will bring a hundred. I can go on."

"I don't know anything about it," Henderson said.

"You're surprised?"

"Yes."

"Shocked?"

"Sure."

"You've heard of the Sarber Hotel?"

"I've heard of it."

"You know it's a wide-open whorehouse?"

"No."

"Did you know that a police private, Benjamin A. Dassinger, badge number two-four-nine-eight is regularly on duty there from seven P.M. till three A.M. to keep order and to make sure the customers pay up? You know that?"

"No," Henderson said, "I didn't know that."

"For a vice cop you don't know a hell of a lot, do you, Captain?"

"I do my job."

"Well, if you do, maybe you know that the Sarber Hotel is owned by one Mary Helen Henderson and this Mary Helen Henderson is the wife of Warren Gamaliel Henderson who happens to be a captain in the Swankerton Police Department. Now, goddamn it, tell me you didn't know that?"

Henderson said nothing and sucked on the insides of his cheeks.

"There's a crap game that's been running in this town for seven years. It used to float, but it doesn't anymore. It's the oldest crap game in town and it's open every night from nine till two on the second floor of a bakery at two-forty-nine North Ninth Street. You know about that?"

"No."

"Well, that's funny, since the guy that runs it says he pays you five hundred a week to let him alone and, God knows, that's cheap because it's a hell of a big game and it draws the high rollers from as far away as Hot Springs and Memphis, but you wouldn't know about that either, would you?"

"No," Henderson said and sucked on his cheeks some more.

"The last count I got was that there are thirteen regu-

313

lar table-stakes poker games going on in town with an off-duty patrolman playing doorkeeper at each one. That's on this side of the tracks. God knows what goes on in Niggertown, but you don't know anything about those thirteen games or about the three hundred dollars-a-week payoff that each of them makes, do you?"

"No."

"You ever heard of John Frazee, Milton Sournaugh, Joseph Minitelli, Kelly Farmer, or Jules Goreaux?"

"No," Henderson said.

"Well, they say they all know you and that they've been shaking down fags and pimps and whores for you, some of them for as long as three years. They work on a percentage, they tell me; they get twenty-five and you get seventy-five. What you got to say about that?"

"Nothing."

"What do you kick back to Lynch? I hear it's up around two-thirds now."

"I don't know anything about kickback," Henderson said. "I just do my job."

Necessary leaned back in his chair and stretched and yawned. "How long would it take to draw up charges against Captain Henderson here, Mr. Dye?"

"A few hours," I said.

"What do you think?"

"Perhaps you might take into consideration his claim that he was only doing his job."

"That's a thought," Necessary said. He leaned over his desk toward Henderson and nodded in a confidential, you-can-tell-me manner. "How much you really knocking down a year, Henderson? Sixty? Seventy-five?"

"I don't knock down anything," Henderson said.

"You think I should bring you up on charges?"

"That's up to you, *Chief* Necessary."

"It sure is, isn't it? Probably get your wife, too, for running a whorehouse, come to think of it. Be a real mess, but you could probably get off with—oh, say—five years, maybe ten."

Henderson cracked then. Not much, really; just enough. He looked down at his shoes. That was all. "What do you want?" he said dully.

"A list," Necessary said. "Break it all down, where it comes from, who gets it, and how much. And I want your name at the bottom of it. I want it on my desk by five o'clock tonight."

"All right," Henderson said.

"I want your resignation, too."

Henderson looked up quickly and his mouth opened, but no words came out. "Undated," Necessary said, and Henderson closed his mouth.

"What do you think, Mr. Dye?"

"Well, he can't stay in vice. As you said, he seems a little sick of it."

Necessary nodded judiciously. "He sure does, doesn't he. You got any suggestions?"

"There's always the Missing Persons' Bureau," I said.

Henderson looked at me, and if he was afraid of Necessary, he wasn't of me. The snarl came back to his mouth. "There ain't any Missing Persons' Bureau."

Necessary smiled. "There'll be one tomorrow and you'll be in charge of it. How much help you think he needs, Mr. Dye?"

"At least one man," I said.

"Maybe a rookie?" Necessary said.

"A rookie could learn a lot from Captain Henderson."

Henderson rose slowly from his chair and half-turned toward the door. "Sit down, Henderson," Necessary snapped. "I'll tell you when you're dismissed." Henderson sat down again.

"You don't have to make a dash for the phone," Necessary said. "Lynch'll have a full report on this from Mr. Dye inside of an hour. And don't get any funny ideas about appealing either. You're in real bad trouble, buster, and the only thing that's keeping you out of the state pen is me, so don't forget it. Is that clear?"

"Yes," Henderson said.

"Yes, what?"

"Yes, sir, Chief Necessary."

"Take off."

"Yes, sir."

He didn't hurry to the door. He seemed too tired to hurry.

"That was the last one," Necessary said, going down a list on his desk.

"At least he didn't get down on his knees and beg like Purcell did," I said.

315

"I'm gonna transfer Purcell to head up the vice squad," Necessary said.

"Jesus Christ."

"We've sort of shuffled them around this last month," Necessary said happily. "None of them knows whether to shit or go blind. They're scared to take their payoffs. Christ, I've had some punks even call me at the hotel at night and ask me who they should pay."

"What did you tell them?"

"Sit tight and don't worry. That the lid's off."

"I hear that the word's getting around," I said.

Necessary nodded. "It doesn't take long. Listen to this. It's a list of what Lieutenant Ferkaire calls 'distinguished arrivals.' He's that young cop outside there."

"I know who he is," I said.

"Listen to this. These are just the ones who've flown in during the past three days. Edouardo (Sweet Eddie) Puranelli, Cleveland; Frank (Jimmy Twoshoes) Schoemeister, Chicago; Arturo (Tex) Turango, Dallas; the Onealo brothers, Roscoe and Ralph from Kansas City; Nicholas (Nick the Nigger) Jones from Miami; and a whole delegation from New Orleans. They came to see Lynch."

"What are the rest of them doing?"

"Looking around. Taking a market survey. Sizing things up. The word's got out that Lynch has slipped. The New Orleans crowd knows goddamn well something's slipped and I hear they're unhappy about it."

I rose and moved toward the door. "I'll go see him."

"Lynch?"

"Yes."

"Give him my best."

"He'll want a meeting."

"What do you think?"

"Let's see what happens this morning."

"Okay," Necessary said.

I paused at the door. "Is Lieutenant Ferkaire still keeping a check on arrivals?"

Necessary nodded.

"You might tell him to keep an eye out for one."

"What's he look like?"

"Tall, redheaded, and wears a pipe and Phi Beta Kappa key."

316

"Name?"

"Carmingler." Necessary made a note of it.

"Hard case?"

I nodded. "About as hard as they come."

35

Two unfriendly strangers met me at the door of Lynch's Victorian house. About the only difference between them was that one was bald and the other wasn't. The bald one stood squarely in the doorway while the one with hair took up a protective flanking position. Neither of them said anything. They stood there and looked at me and their expressions made it clear that they didn't want any today, no matter what it was.

"Where's Boo?" I said.

"Who's Boo?" the baldheaded one said.

"The mayor's son."

"We don't know any mayor."

"Tell Lynch I'm here."

"Tell him who's here?"

"Dye. Lucifer Dye."

"Lucifer Dye," the bald one said slowly, as if he couldn't decide whether he cared for its sound. "We don't know you either, do we, Shorty?"

Shorty was close to five-eleven so something else must have earned him the nickname, but there was no point in dwelling on it. "I never knew nobody named Dye or Lucifer either," Shorty said. "Where'd you get a name like Lucifer?"

"Out of a book," I said. "A dirty one."

"And you want to see Lynch?" the baldheaded one said.

"No," I said. "He wants to see me."

They thought about that for a moment until they got it sorted out. "I'll go see," Shorty said and left. I stood there on the screened porch with the man with the bald head. We had nothing further to say to each other so I admired his dark green double-breasted suit, his squared-off black shoes, and his green-and-black polka dotted tie. A bumblebee had fought its way through the screen and buzzed about the porch. When we got tired of admiring each other, we watched the bee.

"They ain't supposed to fly," he said. "I read somewhere that the guys who design airplanes say bumblebees ain't built right for flying."

We pondered the mystery of it all until Shorty came back. "This way," he said. The baldheaded man took two steps backward so that I could enter. He waved a hand in the direction of the dining room. They didn't seem to want me behind them.

Ramsey Lynch looked as if he hadn't been getting enough sleep. His eyes were bloodshot and had dark smears under them. He wore an ice cream suit that made him look fatter then he was. He didn't smile when I came in, but I hadn't expected him to. Three of them sat at the far end of a table. Lynch wasn't in the center; he was on the left side. The man on the right side wore glasses and had an open attaché case before him. The man in the center stared at me and I thought that he had the oily eyes of an unhappy lizard.

"Sit down, Dye," Lynch said, so I sat at the opposite end of the table, near the sliding doors. Neither Shorty nor the baldheaded man had followed me into the room.

"So you're what we paid twenty-five thou for," the man in the center said, and from his tone I could tell that he didn't think I was much of a bargain.

"Twenty-five thousand so far," I said. "The final bill is for sixty."

"You know me—who I am?" he said.

I knew, but he didn't wait for my answer.

"I'm Luccarella."

"From New Orleans," I said.

"You've heard of me, huh?" He didn't seem to care one way or another.

"Giuseppe Luccarella," I said, "or Joe Lucky."

"That Joe Lucky's newspaper stuff," he said. "Nobody calls me Joe Lucky, but if they did, I wouldn't mind. I don't care about things like that anymore. You wanta call me Joe Lucky, go ahead."

"I'll call you Mr. Luccarella," I said.

He shrugged. "This is my lawyer, Mr. Samuels."

I nodded at the lawyer and he nodded back and said, "Mr. Dye."

Luccarella leaned over the table, resting his elbows on it. He had a narrow, crimped face that looked as if it had been squeezed so hard that his lizard eyes and gray teeth threatened to pop out of his skull. His skin had an unhealthy yellowish tinge to it, as if he had just suffered a bad bout with jaundice. The deep lines in his face, especially his forehead, said that he was somewhere past fifty, but his hair was still thick and black and glossy and he wore it long. He looked like a man who worried a lot.

"Lynch works for me," he said. He had that New Orleans Rampart Street accent that borders on Brooklynese and makes works come out close to woiks and for sound like fah. "You work for Lynch, so that means you work for me, right?"

"I don't work for anybody," I said. "Particularly Lynch."

"He pays you, don't he?"

"He pays me a fee in exchange for information. I don't work for him. We'd better get that straight at the start."

"Possibly Mr. Dye would prefer the word retained," the lawyer said in that smooth, conciliatory tone that the expensive ones seem to be born with.

Luccarella gestured impatiently. "Works, retained, who the hell cares? All I know is that since Lynch's been paying you this town's gone to hell."

"Well, it's not quite that bad," Lynch said.

"I say it's gone to hell and when receipts are down sixty-five percent I don't know what it's done if it hasn't gone to hell."

"Sixty-eight percent, Mr. Luccarella," the lawyer said.

"It'll be even worse next week," I said.

Luccarella frowned. "What do you mean worse?"

"Necessary busted Henderson down to the Missing Persons' Bureau."

"There isn't any Missing Persons' Bureau," Lynch said.

I smiled. "There is now."

"What was Henderson?" Luccarella said.

"Vice squad."

Luccarella threw up his hands and flopped back into his chair. "That's the fucking end!" he yelled. He turned on Lynch and the fat man seemed to cower in his chair as if afraid of being struck. "You can't even keep a line on a goddamned vice-squad cop! What are you doing to me, Lynch? I hand you the sweetest setup in ten states and you just sit around and piss it away. What are you doing it to me for?"

Before Lynch could answer, I said, "You might have some competition, too, but I suppose Lynch has already told you about that."

Luccarella pulled himself together with a visible effort. "I shouldn't do that," he said in an apologetic tone. "I shouldn't fly off the handle like that. My analyst tells me that it's inner-directed rage that should be channeled into something constructive. So that's what I'm gonna do. No, Mr. Dye, Lynch hasn't told me about any competition. Lynch doesn't seem to know what's going on anymore. He seems to have let things sort of slide. Ever since that tame police chief of his shot hisself, Lynch seems to be sort of out of it, you know what I mean?"

"I've tried to keep him informed," I said.

Lynch glared at me, but said nothing. "Sure you have," Luccarella said. "I bet you've kept him right up to date, but maybe you can sort of bring me up to date, if you don't mind too much?" He was trying to be very polite and constructive and perhaps the tight grip that he had on his end of the table helped.

"By competition I mean that Swankerton's got some visitors. Chief Necessary says that they're making a market survey and he seems to think that they might move in. Or try to."

Luccarella squeezed his eyes shut. "Who?" he said. Then he said it again without opening his eyes.

"I think I remember most of them," I said. "Jimmy Twoshoes of Chicago is one. The Onealo brothers, Roscoe and Ralph out of Kansas City. Nick the Nigger from Miami. Tex Turango, Dallas. A guy named Puranelli from Cleveland."

"Sweet Eddie," Luccarella said, his eyes still tightly closed.

"You didn't tell me none of this," Lynch said.

"I just found out."

Luccarella opened his eyes and looked at me. "I want things back the way they were, Mr. Dye. I want things nice and calm and peaceful. I want to know how much that will cost me." He gripped his end of the table so hard that his knuckles turned white. "You notice I'm being constructive."

"Your analyst would like it," I said.

"He's an interesting guy. I had a lot of the worries and that's why I went to him. I still have the worries, but I

321

don't mind them so much now. He said that most people have got the worries, but when they find out that they got them, then they can live with them. He said worrying about having the worries is what really gets you down. So you see why I don't want to have any of the worries over here in Swankerton."

"I understand," I said.

"That's good. That's real good. So how much is it gonna cost me?"

I leaned back in my chair and smiled at Luccarella. I hoped it was a friendly one, the kind that wouldn't worry him. "Chief Necessary said he would be willing to meet Friday to discuss things."

Luccarella shook his head. "I have to be at my analyst Friday. What about today?"

"No chance today. Tomorrow's a possibility."

"Set it up with Lynch."

I shook my head. "As you said earlier, Lynch has sort of lost touch."

Luccarella smiled for the first time, a big, buck-toothed smile. He even chuckled. Then he looked at Lynch and chuckled some more. It was turning into his kind of a meeting after all.

"You agree with him, Lynch?" he said. "You agree that you've sort of lost touch?"

Lynch looked at me and moved his head slowly from side to side as if he could see seven chess moves ahead to the end of a game that he couldn't possibly win. The lawyer looked a little embarrassed and busied himself with some papers. Luccarella chuckled some more. I smiled at Lynch. Everyone knew what was coming, but only Lucca-realla seemed to have any relish for it. Perhaps I did too, but I'm still not sure.

"I asked you something," Luccarella said.

"You asked me if I thought I've lost touch," Lynch said, still looking at me.

"That's what I asked you."

"I've only made one mistake, Joe, and you're about to make the same one. I haven't lost touch. I just made that one mistake."

"Sometimes one mistake's one too many," Luccarella said, looked around for confirmation, and got it from Samuels, the lawyer, who nodded automatically.

"The only mistake I made," Lynch said, "was to believe

322

one word that lying sonofabitch down there at the other end of the table ever said."

"I told you I was a liar," I said.

"Yeah," Lynch said. "You did. And I believed that, too."

"So your price is gonna cost me Lynch, huh?" Luccarealla said to me.

"That's right."

"What else?"

"I name his successor."

"What about this new chief of police, what's his name—Necessary?"

"What about him?"

"What's he gonna cost me?"

"I don't know," I said. "He sets his own price."

"He'll probably come high."

"Probably."

"But all you want to do is name Lynch's successor?"

"That's right."

"When?"

"Tomorrow."

Luccarella nodded. "What time?"

"Ten o'clock. My room in the Sycamore."

Luccarella shook his head. "My room. It's six twenty two."

"Your room," I said.

"You'll bring Necessary?"

"I won't bring him; he'll come with me."

Luccarella turned to Lynch. "There's a plane out of here this afternoon for New Orleans. Be on it. Just make sure you hand all the records over to Samuels."

Lynch didn't argue. He nodded his understanding and then in a mild tone said, "You're making a goddamned bad mistake, Joe."

"At least I'm making it and not letting somebody do it for me."

"I'm not fixing to dispute that," Lynch said. "I'm just saying that if you try to make a deal with him, you're gonna regret it to your dying day."

"You don't think I'm smart enough to do a deal with him?"

"I'm wasting my breath," Lynch said.

"No. I want to know. You don't think I'm smart enough, do you?"

"Being smart don't have anything to do with it. I've skinned lots of guys smarter than Dye is, twice as smart, and so have you, but like I said, smart has got nothing to do with it."

"What's got to do with it?" Luccarella said.

Lynch stared at me some more. "I'll tell you what it is. He's a loser who doesn't expect to win. You don't have to worry about losers who think they'll win because that always gives you the edge. But you haven't got any edge on the loser who'll play by your rules and not give a damn if he wins or loses or breaks even. He doesn't really give a damn if he even plays, so that means that you never hold the edge on him and it means that you never really win. And that matters to you, but it don't to him, so that puts you in the hole, I don't care what happens."

Luccarella nodded after Lynch finished and slumped back into his chair as if winded. "You know what my analyst would call that?" he said. "My analyst would call that insight."

"Or projection," I said.

"You got an analyst, Mr. Dye?" Luccarella asked in a hopeful tone, as if he wanted to compare notes.

"No."

"What do you think of what Lynch said?"

"Not much."

"But you do want something, despite what he said. You want to name his successor, like you said."

"That's right."

"I can tell you who it's gonna be," Lynch said.

"You want to let him guess?" Luccarella said. "After all, it's his own successor."

"I don't care," I said.

"Okay, who?" Luccarella said.

Lynch stared at me again. He seemed to find something about me fascinating. "It's gonna be you, isn't it, Dye?"

"That's right," I said. "It's going to be me."

36

"What do you think you should call yourself at this particular point in time, Mr. Dye?" Victor Orcutt asked. "Are you Swankerton's vice lord apparent? Or would vice lord designate be more appropriate?"

Four of us had just lunched on some more of Orcutt's homecooking, thin slices of veal swimming in a thick sauce whose principal ingredients seemed to have been sour cream and a heavy Marsala that I thought had been too sweet. I had eaten all of mine anyway.

"Either one," I said.

Orcutt flitted over to the coffee and poured himself another cup. He wore a blue blazer with gold buttons, striped blue-and-white trousers, white buck shoes with red rubber soles, and another Lord Byron shirt, whose open neck was partially filled by a carelessly knotted narrow paisley scarf. He looked all of twenty-two.

"The only thing that disturbs me is Senator Simon's speech," he said as he glided back to his chair by the window that looked out over the Gulf.

"What about that magazine piece?" Homer Necessary said. "What's that thing got, about nine million circulation?"

"Six," Carol said.

"You know, Mr. Dye, you were right," Orcutt said. "I really did place too much trust in Gerald Vicker. This grudge he has against you seems almost pathological."

"His brother doesn't like me much either," I said.

Orcutt almost bounced up and down on the seat of his chair. "Oh, I would have given *anything* to have seen Lynch this morning! You give excellent reports, Mr. Dye, but you never include all the little spicy details. You're really not much of a gossip, you know."

"Sorry."

"No matter. It just means that we're going to have to move our schedule back—or is it up? I never could get that straight."

"Back," Carol said.

"Up," Necessary said.

"Never mind." Orcutt said. "What we hoped and planned would happen will now have to happen earlier than we had hoped and planned. All right?" He didn't wait for a vote. "Senator Simon will speak Friday after next, that's ten days from now, and the main thrust of his speech will charge that Mr. Dye's former employers are now engaged in domestic politics and Swankerton will be his proof. Data on this and other details relating to Mr. Dye's past activities were furnished the senator by Gerald Vicker and his brother, Ramsey Lynch. Am I correct so far?"

"So far," I said.

"Good. Meanwhile that awful magazine—I simply never *could* read it, especially its editorials—will publish an article buttressing and embellishing the senator's speech. It also will appear a week from Friday. It will not only attack Mr. Dye and his former employers, but it will also carry an account of Victor Orcutt Associates' involvement here in Swankerton. Incidentally, Homer, have you heard of any of the magazine's writers or photographers being in town?"

Necessary nodded. "They're around, but they've been working with Lynch."

"Isn't it strange that they haven't called any of us?"

"No," I said.

"Why?"

"Because they'll put together what they think is a story, and at the last minute ask what we think of it. They've still got time to do that."

Orcutt made a church of his hands, and then a steeple, and then opened them up to look at the people. He was thinking. I wondered how much faster he thought than I did. "You know," he said, "it's really quite simple."

"What?" Necessary asked.

"We're going to apply Orcutt's First Law."

"To get better, it must get much worse," I said.

"You *remembered!*" he said. "I'm so delighted!"

"You were going to tell us how simple it was," Necessary said.

So Orcutt told us and as he said, it was simple, but then a broken neck can also be described as a simple fracture.

Homer Necessary made two calls before we went back to his twelfth-floor office. Carol Thackerty was on the other phone that Orcutt had had installed in the Rickenbacker Suite and when I went out the door I heard her setting up a conference call between Swankerton, Washington, and New York.

While we waited for the elevator I said, "How many times has he been out of the hotel since he got here?"

"Orcutt?"

"Yes."

"I don't think he's been out any since we got here from San Francisco," Necessary said. "He was out a couple of times before that, you know, when you weren't here yet."

"I'd think he'd get cabin fever."

Necessary shook his head. "Not him. He likes playing spider king."

There were two doors to Necessary's office and both of them were busy that afternoon. Five minutes after we got there, Lt. Ferkaire came in, brimming with his sense of justice, eager to please, and proud of the University of Tennessee ring that he wore on his left hand. I think he made the chief of police nervous, although Necessary never said anything other than that he thought Ferkaire was "a nice, bright kid."

"They're bringing the first one up now, sir," Ferkaire told Necessary.

"They got their instructions like I said?"

"Yes, sir. They bring them in this door and when they come out your other one they take them back where they picked them up."

"Any trouble locating them?" Necessary said.

"No, sir. Not yet."

"You tell them all to be goddamned polite?"

"My exact words, sir. Goddamned polite. Excuse me for asking, Chief Necessary, but how important are these men?"

"To who?"

"Well, I mean how do they rank *nationally?*"

"They're major league, kid," Necessary said. "Don't worry about it, they're all pros from the majors."

"Would you like me to sit in, sir?" Ferkaire asked stiffly, but not stiff enough to keep the eagerness and hope out of his voice.

"Not this time."

327

"Thank you, sir."

"For what?" Necessary said. "I just told you you couldn't sit in."

"I just meant—" Ferkaire grew flustered and tried to think of something else to say, something pertinent, when Necessary said, "Forget it. When the first one gets up here, bring him right in. Who's first by the way?"

Ferkaire looked at a three-by-five card that he carried. "Frank Schoemeister. Chicago."

Necessary nodded. "That's all, Ferkaire."

Ferkaire said yes, sir, again and left.

"Jimmy Twoshoes," Necessary said as he moved behind his desk. "They come up with the goddamnedest nicknames. I knew one in Pittsburgh once that they used to call Billy Buster Bible because he used to carry one around and always let them kiss it before he shot them. He used to shoot them through the ear. The left one, I think." He sank back in his executive chair and looked at me. "You going to be over there by the window?"

"That's right."

"I wish to hell more light would come through it."

"There's enough to give them the idea."

"You want to go first?" he said.

"Better if you did," I said. "They may not know you, but they'll know the gold braid. I'll come in on the chorus."

Necessary looked at his watch. "It's going to be a long afternoon."

"Longer than most," I agreed.

A few minutes later Ferkaire knocked on the door, entered, and said, "Mr. Frank Schoemeister, Chief Necessary."

Then he closed the door and left Schoemeister standing there in the center of the room. Schoemeister looked at Necessary, then at me, and then back at Necessary. After that he studied the rug, the ceiling, and the two flags behind Necessary's desk. He nodded his head as if he'd reached some silent agreement with himself and put his hands in his coat pockets. Then he smiled and it came out hideous.

Necessary waved a negligent hand at him. "Sit down, Schoemeister, pick a chair. That's my special assistant over there, Mr. Dye."

Schoemeister nodded in my direction, selected a chair

328

so that he could keep me in view, and sat down. Finally, he decided to say something: "Social?"

"Social," Necessary said.

"You don't mind if I smoke then?"

Necessary waved his hand again. "You want a drink? I'm going to have one."

"A drink?" Schoemeister said. "That would be nice."

"What would you like?" I said, moving to the bar.

"Scotch and water, please."

I mixed three of them and handed Schoemeister his. He accepted it with a slim, well-cared-for hand that went with the rest of him, which was equally well tended. He was not yet forty, looked even younger, and wore dark, quiet clothes that almost made him look like a successful corporate executive whose career was a couple of years ahead of schedule. He looked like that until you noticed his shoes. And his mouth. The shoes were black alligator with large silver buckles that got encouragement from the white, brushed-suede fleurs-de-lis that decorated each toe. I had read somewhere, probably in a barber shop, that Jimmy Twoshoes had more than two hundred pairs of custom-cobbled footwear and sometimes wore as many as six different pairs in a day. But he had only one mouth, and there was nothing he could do about that, although he had tried hard enough. The twelve puckered white scars were still there where they had sewed his lips together with fishing line in 1961. The heavy mustache he wore failed to disguise the scars that twisted his mouth into a perpetual snarl. The Chicago police never did learn who had sewed Schoemeister's lips together, nor would Schoemeister tell them. During the month after he was released from the hospital funerals were held for four of Schoemeister's more prominent contemporaries. They had all died messily and none of their caskets was opened during their funerals.

"We got a nice little town here," Necessary said after he took a swallow of his drink.

"I noticed," Schoemeister said.

"Got some new industry and more on the way. Got one of the best little beaches on the Gulf. The niggers have been fairly quiet up till now. Nice big Air Force depot about fifteen miles out of town helps keep the unemployment down. Got a good, clean, local government that listens to reason. Of course, Swankerton's no Chicago, but it's a real nice little city where you can still walk the streets safe at night. You here on a vacation?"

"Vacation," Schoemeister said.

"There've been some changes here recently," Necessary said. "They put me in as chief of police and Mr. Dye's my new special assistant and it's sort of up to us to look out for law and order."

"I hear the last chief of police shot himself," Schoemeister said.

"He sure did, poor guy. Pressure, I guess. Funny you'd bring that up, but a good friend of his left town this afternoon sudden like. Name's Ramsey Lynch. Ever heard of him?"

Schoemeister nodded. He did it carefully. "I've heard of him."

"Well, he was quite prominent here in certain circles. Had a lot of interests."

"Who's looking after them for him?" Schoemeister said, and I decided that he knew what the right questions were.

"Well, that's funny, too, but it seems that me and Mr. Dye here are sort of going to have to look after things. We were talking about it just this afternoon, weren't we, Mr. Dye?"

"This very afternoon," I said. "Just before you got here."

"I see," Schoemeister said. He wasn't pushing anything.

"The trouble, Mr. Schoemeister," I said, "is that neither Chief Necessary nor I have schedules that will permit us to devote full time to the various activities that formerly were under Mr. Lynch's personal supervision. We were thinking of taking in a partner—a working partner, of course—who could devote at least a portion of his time to these various interests. Your name happened to come up, so we thought we'd arrange this meeting."

"I'm going to ask you a question," Schoemeister said.

Necessary smiled. "Go ahead."

"This place bugged?"

"You think I'd bug my own office?"

"Some do."

"Some are goddamned stupid, too."

"Okay," Schoemeister said and looked at me. "You talk awful pretty, but you don't really say anything. See if you can't make it not quite so pretty and a little more plain."

330

"All right," I said. "Lynch is out as of noon today. I'm in. So is Necessary and so are you, for a third if you can run it."

"I hear it's pretty rich," Schoemeister said.

"You hear right," Necessary said.

"I also hear that Lynch was under Luccarella."

"Luccarella's out too," I said.

"Since when?"

"Since tomorrow," Necessary said.

"What keeps him out?"

Necessary tapped the third gold button down on his uniform. "This keeps him out and gets you in, if you're interested."

Schoemeister nodded. "Like I say, I've been on vacation down here, but you know how it is, I sort of nosed around."

"We know how it is," Necessary said.

"I'd kinda heard of some trouble when I was up in Chicago."

"It gets around," I said.

Schoemeister looked at me. "When you talk about these interests, just what're you talking about?"

"Everything," I said.

"How much you figure it's worth?"

"By the month?" Necessary said.

"That'll do."

Necessary looked at me. "What did we come up with?"

"Before we reorganized the police department it grossed about two million a month. There was the usual big overhead and that knocked the net down to around two or three hundred thousand. Some months were better than others."

"How many ways is the net split?" Schoemeister said.

"Three," Necessary said. "Just three ways and each of us pays his own expenses."

"And what do you expect me to do?" Schoemeister said.

"The operation has deteriorated during the past month," I said. "Gone to hell really. We expect you to personally supervise its rebuilding. After it's functioning smoothly again, you can appoint your own supervisor. He—and whoever he hires—will be responsible to you and you will be responsible to us."

Schoemeister nodded thoughtfully. "Suppose I just moved in on my own? Suppose that happened?"

"We'd move you right out," Necessary said.

"What about Luccarella. He's tied in back east, you know."

"That bother you?" I said.

"Those guys back east don't bother me," Schoemeister said. "I don't go looking for trouble from them, but they don't bother me."

"Lucarella might get a little unfriendly," Necessary said.

"Who takes care of him?"

"You do," Necessary said. "And anybody else who starts getting pushy. There may be a couple of them or so."

"I'll have to get some people down."

"How soon?" I asked.

He shrugged. "I call 'em today; they'll be here tomorrow. How much trouble you think there might be, not counting Luccarella?"

"Two or three maybe," Necessary said.

"You got any names?"

"A couple. Tex Turango from Dallas. Nigger Jones from Miami."

Schoemeister shook his head and smiled his horrible smile. "That ain't much trouble."

"We didn't think it would be."

"One thing though."

"What?" I said.

"I'd like to go over the books. I mean you go into a business like this and invest time and money and you're a damn fool if you don't go over the books."

"Tomorrow afternoon be okay?" I said.

"Fine," Schoemeister said. "I'll have my accountant come down too."

"Good," Necessary said.

"Well," Schoemeister said, rising, "I guess that does it for now."

We shook hands all around. "I think it's going to be nice doing business with you fellows" he said.

"I think it'll work out fine all the way around," Necessary said.

"You might want to use the private entrance over here," I said and steered Schoemeister to it.

"Thanks for the drink," he said as he went out, and I told him not to mention it.

When he had gone Necessary picked up the phone and spoke to Lt. Ferkaire, who came in promptly.

"Who's next?"

"The Onealo brothers, Ralph and Roscoe. Kansas City."

"Send them in," Necessary said.

After they came in and after they were seated, Homer Necessary leaned back in his chair and said, "We got a nice little town here. Got some new industry and more on the way. Got one of the best little beaches . . ."

It went that way all afternoon. The Onealo brothers, blond, dumpy and stupid-looking, couldn't conceal their eagerness. Arturo (Tex) Turango, handsome and olive-skinned, smiled a lot with his big white teeth and said he did believe it was his kind of proposition. Edouardo (Sweet Eddie) Puranelli from Cleveland wanted to know more about how Luccarella figured in the deal and when we told him he said that he never did like the sonofabitch anyhow. Nicholas (Nick the Nigger) Jones from Miami was whiter than either Necessary or I, spoke with a clipped Jamaican accent, and thought the proposition had "fascinating possibilities" and asked if we wanted him to fly his people in that same evening and we told him that it might be a good idea.

When Jones had gone, I turned to the window and stared out at the Gulf Coast through the black-tinted glass. "How many times did we sell Swankerton this afternoon?" I said.

"Five," Necessary said. "Six if you count the Onealo brothers twice."

"The meeting with Luccarella tomorrow could get rough."

"You think he's as nutty as they say?"

"It's worse than that," I said.

"How?"

"He knows he's nutty."

Lt. Ferkaire stuck his head in the door. "That's the last of them, Chief Necessary."

"Good."

"By the way, Mr. Dye, I just got a report from the airport."

"Yes?"

"A Mr. Carmingler arrived on a Braniff flight from Washington about twenty minutes ago."

"Redheaded?"

"Yes, sir. I thought you'd want to know. Do you want us to keep him under surveillance?"

I turned back to the window and looked out at the Gulf and wished it would rain. "No. He'll get in touch with me."

"Yes, sir," Ferkaire said, and I could hear the pneumatic door close behind him.

"The hard case?" Necessary said.

"That's right."

"You need some help?"

I turned and shook my head. "Nobody stocks the kind I need anymore."

Necessary examined a hangnail. He bit it. "Maybe they never did," he said in between bites.

I turned back to the window. "You've got a point, Homer. Maybe they never did."

37

I had long admired Carmingler's ability to summarize a situation. His facts were always neatly marshaled and if a few of them needed embellishment, as they sometimes did, he supplied it with an airy phrase or two that usually began "of course" or "naturally" or "it goes without saying."

He had been talking now, and talking well, for almost fifteen minutes. We were in my room in the Sycamore, still on our first drinks, and he was near the end of his summary of things as he saw them, or wanted to see them, or as they should be, and I could only marvel at his single-mindedness.

"Of course," he said, "I don't deny that we may have made a mistake about Gerald Vicker," and with that manly confession of near fallibility he gave me a satisfied smile, as if he had just stepped on the old homestead's last termite.

"You knew he was recommending me for this thing, didn't you?"

"We'd heard."

"But you didn't mention it to me."

"It seemed harmless enough at the time. And we felt you could use the money."

"Can't you get to Simple the Wise?"

Carmingler looked pained. "We've tried."

"What's he say?"

"That we paid blackmail to get you out of jail."

"Does he know how much?"

"Yes. He got it from Vicker."

"Who did Vicker get it from?"

"From Tung, the man who interrogated you."

I grinned at him. "When you question somebody for seven hours, it's a debriefing. When they do it, it's an interrogation."

"You're quibbling."

"You want another drink?" I said.

335

"No."

"Okay, let's see if I've got it straight. The senior senator from Utah—"

"Idaho," Carmingler said.

"I just wanted to make sure you were listening. The senior senator from Idaho, Solomon Simple, will rise on the floor of the Senate a week from Friday and denounce Section Two on a couple of counts. First, that it paid some oriental despot three million dollars ransom to get three of its bungling agents out of jail and that the Secretary of State compounded the error by writing a letter of apology for the mess that his colleagues down the street were still trying to deny. All that rehash should be good for at least an hour, if he's halfway sober."

"He's quit," Carmingler said.

"Drinking?"

"Yes."

"What was it, his liver?"

"Heart."

"Well, after the first hour, during which he denounces the super-secret Section Two for groveling, with a couple of passing swipes at the State Department, he recounts how this same notorious agent, Lucifer Dye, is now deeply embroiled in the domestic politics of one of the South's fairest cities in blatant defiance of all legal safeguards. I can hear him now."

"Hear him what?" Carmingler said.

" 'Where will it all stop, Mr. President? Where will it ever end? How would you like agents of the FBI or the CIA to guide the destiny of your home town? Would you want your City Council to be elected through the machinations of ruthless, devious men who take their orders from a super-secret agency on the banks of the Potomac? Are we entering into a police state, Mr. President?' "

"You don't do imitations very well," Carmingler said.

"The essence is there," I said. "At the same time Simple is making his speech, America's favorite picture magazine will blanket the country with a sixteen-page spread on 'The Men Who are Corrupting Swankerton.' "

Carmingler almost looked startled. "Have you seen an advance copy?" he demanded.

"I just like to make things up."

"Oh."

"Why don't you get the White House to stop him?"

"They tried, but not too hard. They need his vote on the tax bill."

"What about the magazine?"

"No chance."

"You tried?"

"Yes."

"You're in a bind," I said.

"So are you."

"You could blackmail the senator. Threaten to reveal that slush fund of his."

"I said they need his vote."

"That close, huh?"

"It's that close."

"So you sent your young friend Franz Mugar down to take care of me."

"That was a mistake."

"That's two you've admitted. It must be a record."

"There won't be any more."

"Sorry I can't help."

"You won't then?"

"No."

Carmingler looked at the window and said, "If it's money—"

"It's not."

"It would only be for six months."

"I don't have six months."

He looked at me quickly. "Do you have—"

"Don't get your hopes up. I don't have aything fatal. I just don't have time to sit around in Brazil or the Canary Islands while you try to tidy things up. It's not that important to me."

"It is to us," Carmingler said.

"Why?"

Carmingler's hand darted to the Phi Beta Kappa key, which hung on the gold chain that decorated the vest of his glen plaid suit. The key didn't seem to give him as much reassurance as it usually did. For a brief moment, a very brief one, he almost looked bewildered. "What do you want, a lecture?" he said.

"I've heard them all."

"It wasn't a good question."

"That's because you don't have a good answer for it."

He shook his head. "You're wrong. I have an answer."

"I'll listen."

"You asked why it was important."

"Yes."

"It's important because it's what we do," Carmingler said with more fervor in his voice than I'd ever heard before. "We do a job, and you know what kind of job it is because you once did it. You weren't all that good at it because you never really believed in it, but most of us do, and that's something you'll never understand because you don't really believe in the importance of anything, not even yourself. If your wife had lived, you might have changed a little, but she didn't and you didn't. So you ask why it's important. It's important because form and substance are important to us and we're part of both, the important part. Without us, there'd be no form and substance—no structure. There might be another one around, but not the one that we shaped. I don't detach myself from what I do. It's an important part of me and I'm an important part of it."

"It's the job," I said.

"Yes, goddamn it, it's the job. I think the job is important."

"I remember," I said. "I remember that briefcase in Manila was important."

"It was the job."

"You had to cut off his hand to get that briefcase. You chopped it off with a machete. All part of the job."

"My job. Yes."

"And your job is to make me go away. To make me disappear as if I'd never really existed. And then I'd just be something else that the senator had found in the bottom of a bottle of Old Cabin Still."

"We'll pay you for your loss of identity," Carmingler said, losing a small battle to keep the sarcasm out of his voice.

I said no again for the same reason that I'd once said yes, which was for no reason at all other than that it seemed the thing to do at the time.

"I'll ask why one more time," Carmingler said.

"Because I don't care enough to say yes, I suppose."

"It would be easier."

"That's part of it, too."

"You don't think we're very important, do you?"

"No," I said. "Not very."

Carmingler nodded and rose. He took out his pipe, looked at it, and then replaced it in his coat pocket. He studied me for several moments as if trying to decide how to say what I knew that he had to say. "I'm sorry," he finally said and sounded as if he might really mean it, if he could ever mean anything. "I'm sorry," he said again, "but you're not very important to us either."

38

I had breakfast with Victor Orcutt the next morning. Or rather he had breakfast while I nursed a hangover, the rotten kind that makes everything taste yellow, even coffee and tomato juice.

"Breakfast is really the only hotel food that I can abide," Victor Orcutt said, and I nodded my agreement or understanding or whatever it was. I didn't yet feel like talking.

"Do you like the South, Mr. Dye? I don't think I've ever asked."

"It's all right," I said.

"There's something about it that fascinates and repels me at the same time."

"It affects a lot of people like that, I've heard."

"Really? Does it affect you that way?"

"No."

"Of course, Swankerton isn't really the South."

"It isn't?"

"Well, it's *in* the South, but it's right on the Gulf and it gets all the traffic from New Orleans and Texas and Florida and those places. No, to be in the South, the real South, you have to go about forty miles north of Swankerton."

I decided to try a cigarette.

"Swankerton is such an ugly name for a city, I think," Orcutt said, spooning some marmalade on to his toast, which still looked warm as did his link sausage and scrambled eggs. He must have had a different room waiter.

"It also has an unfortunate nickname," I said and felt as if I were prattling.

"You mean Chancre Town? Isn't that perfectly ghastly?"

"Terrible."

"They have such beautiful names down here. Natchez-under-the-hill. That's really nice. So is Pascagoula."

340

"They're in Mississippi."

"But they're still beautiful names. So is Mississippi. It's from the Chippewa and they pronounced it more like mici-zibi." He spelled it for me. "It means large river."

I put out my cigarette after the third puff.

"You sure you won't have a piece of toast?" Orcutt asked.

"No, thank you."

"I called New York and Washington yesterday," he said.

"Hmmm," I said to indicate interest.

"I learned that magazine story is definitely scheduled and that any amount of pressure has been brought to have it killed. I also learned that Senator Simon is adamant about making his speech."

"I heard the same thing."

"You're going to bear the brunt of it, you know."

"I know."

"Does it bother you? I know that's such a *personal* question."

"It's what I'm being paid for."

"I do hope Homer will bear up under it."

"He'll be all right," I said. "He did fine yesterday."

"I *heard!* He really seemed to enjoy himself. Let's see, you have your meeting with Luccarella this morning, right?"

"At ten," I said.

"I'd so like to be there."

"I'll try to give you a spicier report."

"Do. Please. Incidentally, I had a most curious call this morning."

"Who?"

"Frank Mouton, the druggist."

"Our candidate for the City Council?"

"The same. You did turn that evidence of his drug-peddling activities over to Lynch, didn't you?"

"Yes," I said.

"Well, Mouton was weeping and sobbing into the phone. He kept telling me how he had betrayed the Clean Government Association because Lynch had forced him to."

"That was the plan," I said.

"But then he stopped crying and started to shout. He
341

said that he knew what we were up to, that we were out to ruin him."

"He's right. Or at least he was."

"He really sounded disturbed, poor man. He said Lynch had told him the entire story."

"It probably was the last thing Lynch did before he left town."

"Mouton was almost hysterical."

"Did he threaten you?"

Orcutt shook his head. "No. He said that God would take care of me."

"Well, Mouton is a deacon in his church."

"That's *right*," Orcutt said. "I'd almost forgotten. The First Methodist."

At three minutes to ten Homer Necessary came by Orcutt's room for me and we rode the elevator down to the sixth floor of the hotel. We stopped in front of 622 and Necessary tugged at his new uniform. "This is gonna be interesting," he said.

"Let's hope that's all it is," I said and knocked on the door.

It was once again opened by Shorty and the baldheaded man who knew about bumblebees. "Come on in," the baldheaded man said. We went in and once again they steered from the rear.

Luccarella had a suite, not quite as large as Orcutt's, and his two human sheepdogs nudged us into the living room where Luccarella and Samuels, the lawyer, sat side by side on a couch. Two large closed briefcases rested on a low coffee table that was within handy reach of both.

Luccarella looked at his watch when we came in. "You're right on time," he said. "That's a good sign. I like doing business with people who're on time."

"This is Chief Necessary," I said. "Mr. Luccarella and Mr. Samuels who is his attorney." Necessary shook hands with both of them.

"Sit down, sit down," Luccarella said, making vague gestures toward a couple of chairs that were drawn up to the coffee table. We sat down. "You want some coffee?" he said.

"You wanta drink?"

"I'll take a drink," I said and drew a disapproving glance from Samuels, who apparently didn't think much of those who drink in the morning. I didn't feel that I could stand to care what he thought.

"How about you, Chief?" Luccarella said.

"Scotch and water," Necessary said.

"Dye?"

"That's fine."

Luccarella jerked his head at Shorty. "Fix them," he said.

After Shorty mixed and served the drinks, he moved over to help the baldheaded man lean against a wall. "Go on, beat it," Luccarella snapped at them. "And close the door behind you."

When they had gone, Luccarella leaned back on the couch and smiled with his gray teeth. "Heard a lot about you, Chief Necessary."

"That right?"

"You got a good reputation up North. Reputation of a man you can do business with."

"I like a quiet town," Necessary said. "where everything fits in place."

"You've sort of quieted this town down," Luccarella said.

"It could get even quieter."

"I think I sort of understand you," Luccarella said.

Necessary smiled. "I hope so."

Samuels cleared his throat. "Shall we go over the books?"

"We ain't got no deal yet. What do you mean go over the books? We go over the books when we got a deal." Luccarella was growing excited again.

"I just thought—"

"Don't think," Luccarella said sourly.

"Let's talk deal, Luccarella," Necessary said.

"There," Luccarella said to Samuels. "You see what I mean. We make a deal and then we look at the books." He waved a hand at Necessary. "Go ahead, Chief. I hear you like to talk for yourself."

Necessary lit one of his Camels and blew some smoke at the fourth gold button on his uniform. "Before we do, I thought I'd mention something and if it offends you, I'm sorry."

"Go ahead," Luccarella said with another wave of his hand. He was all magnanimity that morning.

"I like my privacy just like you do. So I told one of my

men to watch the door to the hall. He's my driver, Sergeant Krone."

"So we won't be interrupted, huh? I don't mind, but Shorty and Jassy'll take care of the door."

"I'm not worried about anyone coming in; it's about their going out. So if you got a bug in this room and you're thinking of taping any of this, I suggest you forget it."

"What the hell kind of creep do you think I am?" Luccarella said, not quite yelling.

"The kind who might bug a conversation like we're about to have."

Luccarella smiled suddenly. "Yeah, maybe I am at that. But there's no bug. I swear to God."

"We'll make sure later," Necessary said.

"Okay, you made a point, now make an offer."

"It's no offer," Necessary said. "It's take it or leave it. I get a third. You and Dye can fight over the rest."

An incredulous look appeared on Luccarella's squeezed-up face. "A third of what?"

"The net. On everything."

"A third. Christ, what do you mean a third? Lynch only got ten percent."

"I may as well give you the bad news now," I said. "I get a third, too."

"You're out of your fucking mind," Luccarella yelled. "You get a third, he gets a third—you know what that leaves me? You know how much?"

"A third," I said.

"Like shit it does. It leaves me just what Lynch got— ten percent. The rest goes back East."

"That's too bad," Necessary said and drained his Scotch and water. "I don't want to argue. I'll take thirty percent. Dye can talk for himself."

"Thirty's okay," I said. "That leaves you forty."

"I can't operate on forty."

"You won't operate at all unless I say so," Necessary said.

"Fifty-five, forty-five," Luccarella said.

Necessary shook his head. "It's too complicated. I can figure the easy ones like thirty percent and a third and a half and the round numbers. Figuring forty-five and fifty-five percent's too hard."

"I'll have to check back East," Luccarella said. "I'll have to explain to them what I'm up against."

"I tell you something, Luccarella," Necessary said. "Either you're in or you're out for forty percent. You can explain things later. Right now it's yes or no time."

Luccarella looked at Samuels, who refused to return his gaze. "Well, don't just sit there, dummy! Say something, for Christ's sake. That's what I pay you for."

Samuels sighed. "Under the new circumstances, perhaps Chief Necessary's proposal does have merit, particularly if the net increases over what it formerly was."

"It'll increase," Necessary said, shaking the ice in his glass. "Dye and I'll see to that, won't we?"

"Sure," I said.

"How much?" Luccarella said, a measure of greed creeping into his voice.

"Well, Dye and I've been talking about that and we thought we just might turn Swankerton wide open now that I got the department all reorganized the way I like it. From what me and Dye can figure, Lynch and that doodlebug who was his chief of police kept things running about half speed. We thought we just might edge her up a notch or two."

"What the hell's he talking about?" Luccarella said to me.

"Just what he said. We're going to exploit the town's full potential."

"Why don't you translate that into dollars and cents?"

Necessary looked at me. "Go ahead," he said.

"It means the net should go up by one hundred percent at least."

"Ah," Samuels said. "I think I see."

"In one-syllable words, just for me," Luccarella said. He was almost pleading.

"I believe what Mr. Dye is saying is that the fixed costs will remain fairly constant despite a marked increase in the volume of business." Samuels looked at me for confirmation and I nodded.

"You mean the nut's going to stay the same because the payoffs will stay the same and any new business will be just that much gravy? That's what you mean, ain't it?"

"That's it, Luccarella," Necessary said. "So your forty percent share of the new net will be equal to eighty percent of the old."

"That's better," Luccarella said softly, almost to himself. "That's a hell of a lot better. You got a deal."

"Almost," Necessary said, "Almost we got a deal."

"Now what's the matter?" Luccarella looked at me. "Now what the hell's bugging him?"

"Ask him," I said.

"All right, goddamn it, I'm asking you!" It came out a yell and this time Luccarella heard it himself. "Sorry," he said, squeezing his eyes shut. "I gotta watch that. I just get too enthusiastic. I'm impatient, you know. My analyst says that there's nothing wrong with being impatient. He said a lot of great men have been noted for their impatience. But it's gotta be channeled, he says. It's a type of energy and it's gotta be directed. Now then, Chief, I'm gonna ask you again calmly. See how calm I am? What do you mean by almost we got a deal?"

"The word got around that Lynch was slipping so some of them came down to see if it was true."

Luccarella gestured impatiently. "I heard about that. Dye here told me about it. Jimmy Twoshoes from Chicago and Sweet Eddie Puranelli out of Cleveland. Couple of others. They'll forget about it when they hear Lynch's out."

"They've heard," Necessary said.

"So they'll get out."

"They've heard something else."

"What?"

"They've heard you're slipping."

I estimated that roughly $30,000 worth of analysis was destroyed by Necessary's comment. Luccarella shot up out of his seat. "Me?" It was a scream this time, not a yell. "Who said I'm slipping? Who's the son of a bitch who said it, Necessary?" He was stalking about the room now, knocking into furniture. He picked up an ashtray and smashed it against the wall. "Slipping, huh? Who said it, goddamn it? I'll fix that sonofabitch. You think I'm slipping, Samuels? Did you tell em I'm slipping?" He rushed over and grabbed the lawyer by his shirt front and jerked him from the couch. "What are you, a goddamned spy?"

"I never said—"

Luccarella dropped the lawyer, who sank back down on the couch. He spun around to face us. "You guys—you guys told them I'm slipping. You set it all up, I can

346

tell. You guys are trying to fix me. You're trying to get everything for yourself. I can't trust nobody. I can't even—"

"Shut up, Luccarella!" It was either Necessary's harsh, slashing tone or my hangover, but it made me start. It also stopped Luccarella in mid-sentence.

"Bad, wasn't it?" he said and hung his head like a scolded child. "I know what it is, all right. My analyst explained it all to me. It's paranoia. That means that you think people are plotting against you when they're not. He said lots of great men have had it and have gone on to live real useful lives."

"It's not paranoia this time," Necessary said. "These guys think Swankerton's ripe and they think you've slipped and they're set to move in and move you out."

"You can stop them," Luccarella said.

"It's not my job when you think about it," Necessary said. "I can get my cut from them. They'll give me a deal, just like you've done. But you already know the operation and that's why I prefer to do business with you. Dye and me don't want to spend our time breaking in the new help."

"So it's up to me," Luccarella said in a quiet tone.

"That's right," Necessary said. "It's up to you. All me and Dye can give you is our unofficial support. You'll have that."

Luccarella turned to Samuels. "Get on the phone and call Ricci. Explain it. Tell him to get up here and to bring a dozen with him. If he has to import a few, tell him he can pay top dollar." He gave the instructions in a low, confident tone and for the first time I saw some reason for him to have risen as far as he had. "Now," he added, and Samuels rose and hurried to the door.

Luccarella turned to Necessary and in that same, quiet, emotionless tone said, "I want all of their names and where they're staying."

"Sure," Necessary said and told him. Luccarella didn't seem to need to write anything down.

"That's all?"

"That's all I know about, although I've heard that some of them are moving their people in."

Luccarella nodded. "I want this deal, Chief. I need it if you want to know the truth and I don't care if you do or not. I've had a little trouble lately, but I'm getting that

347

cleared up with the help of my analyst. He told me that I should trust people more. That I'm too suspicous. So I'm gonna take his advice. I'm gonna trust you and Dye. Bad things, real bad things happen to people who I trust and who then cross me. I don't want anything bad to happen to either of you."

"You take care of your end, we'll take care of ours," Necessary said.

"We'd still like to go over those books," I said.

Luccarella pointed at one of the briefcases. "There's a duplicate set in there. Take 'em with you. It's got everything—names, addresses, cash flow, everything. Lynch kept a good set of books, I'll say that for him. He didn't cross me either, so nothing bad's going to happen to him. He just made a mistake. I can take that. But I can't take being crossed by people I trust."

"You've made that clear," I said and picked up the briefcase.

Shorty stuck his head in the door. "What the hell you want?" Luccarella said.

"It's for him," he said, pointing at me. "It's some chick on the phone called Thackerty. She's all shook and says that she has to talk to him so I said I'd see."

"I'll take it," I said and crossed to the telephone and picked it up.

"What's the problem?" I said.

"It's Orcutt," she said.

"What about him?"

"You'd better get up here."

"Up where?"

"His suite."

"What about him?" I said again.

"He's dead and they took away his face."

39

Necessary hurried through the door to Orcutt's suite first, followed by Sergeant Krone who had drawn his revolver. I came last, carrying the briefcase.

Carol Thackerty stood by the window that offered a view of the Gulf of Mexico, but she wasn't looking at it. She was looking at the skinny gray-haired man who knelt by Orcutt's body. The gray-haired man rocked back and forth and crooned to himself. His hands were pressed together as if he were praying. A long-barreled revolver lay on the floor beside Orcutt. Two feet away from it was a wide-mouthed glass jar, the kind that will hold a pint of mayonnaise. I could smell the exploded gunpowder, but there was another, sharper smell that stung my nostrils. I didn't know what it was.

Necessary moved quickly over to Orcutt and lifted the towel from his face.

"I put it there," Carol said. "I came in and saw him and put the towel over his face."

"The Lord is my shepherd, I shall not want—" the gray-haired man crooned in a singsong voice and rocked back and forth some more on his knees.

Necessary beckoned to me and I went over to Orcutt's body. He lifted the towel again. Carol Thackerty had been right; something had taken away his face. The nose was almost gone, and there was some bone visible and also some blood. Only the eyes were the same, and they contained no more in death than they had in life. Necessary dropped the towel back into place.

"You know him, don't you?" he said, jerking a thumb at the kneeling man.

"Frank Mouton, candidate for the city council."

Necessary shook his head and turned to Sergeant Krone. "Call Benson at Homicide and tell him to get his crew over here." Krone hurried to a phone.

Necessary turned to Carol. "Well?" he said.

"I have my own key," she said. "You know I have my own key."

"I know," Necessary said in a patient, reassuring voice.

"I was in the hall when I heard the shots. I was still in the hall and I heard three shots."

"Take it easy, Carol," I said.

"Let her tell it," Necessary said.

"When I heard the shots I hurried and I got so frantic that I couldn't find the keys in my purse and then I found them and finally got the door open and he was kneeling over Orcutt and praying and pouring this stuff on his face." She stopped and took a deep breath. "So I called you and then got a towel and put it over his face." She turned and stared through the window at the Gulf.

Mouton must have been close to sixty. His hair was gray and sparse on top of his long slab of a head. He had closely set, dark eyes. They looked out of focus behind his rimless glasses that were cocked a little to one side about halfway down a long, thin nose that seemed to have too many veins in it. His red, wet mouth was open now, crooning something else. He rocked back and forth and then started on the Twenty-third Psalm again. He wore a tan raincoat that was buttoned up to his neck.

Homer Necessary walked round him, got down on his hands and knees and smelled the empty pint jar. He rose and stared at Mouton. "Some kind of acid," Necessary said. He walked over to the kneeling man and nudged him with his foot. "Hey, Mouton," he said.

Mouton looked up at him. "Amen," he said.

"What d'you kill him for?"

"He was a son of Satan," Mouton said. "Father, forgive them for they know not what—"

"Get up," Necessary snapped.

"I am the resurrection and the life—"

"Get your ass up," Necessary said again in a hard voice and grabbed Mouton by an elbow and jerked him to his feet.

"Whosoever believeth—"

"He's a deacon in his church," I said.

"I remember," Necessary said. "Take off your raincoat, Deacon."

Mouton looked coy and suddenly went into a pose that resembled September Morn. "Not in front of you," he said.

"Jesus," Necessary said.

Mouton looked wildly around the room. He saw Carol Thackerty and smiled and I couldn't find much sanity in that smile. "I'll show *her!*" he said.

"All right," Necessary said, "show her."

Carol turned from the window as Mouton moved over to her. "You're very pretty," he said, unbuttoning his raincoat. "I like pretty girls. I'm going to show you something nice." He held his raincoat open.

Carol looked at him and then turned back to the window. "He's naked underneath the coat," she said in a dull tone. "He's got the legs of his trousers belted to his thighs somehow, but the rest of him's naked." She paused. "He's ugly."

Mouton spun around and held his raincoat wide open so that we could all take a look. He was ugly all right. "Button that up, mister!" Sergeant Krone snapped, and Mouton pouted before he re-buttoned the coat up to his neck.

Mouton looked down at Orcutt's body. "It's all so confusing. First, I was Judas and he was the Savior and then he was Judas and I was—I was—" He stopped, looked at me, and then in a calm, rational voice said, "I'm a professional man, you know."

"I know."

"I'm a pharmacist," he said, a little desperately this time.

"I know," I said again.

"Why d'you kill him, Mouton?" Necessary asked.

"Why?"

"That's right. Why?"

"Because, you miserable fuckhead, God told me to!" With that, he walked over to a chair and sat down. He closed his eyes and refused to say anything else. The homicide cops finally took him away not long after Orcutt's body was carted off to the morgue where they found three bullets in it.

Carol Thackerty answered the phone when it rang in Orcutt's bedroom-office where the three of us sat. The homicide crew was still busy in the living room. Forty minutes had passed since they had taken Mouton away.

"It's Channing d'Arcy Phetwick the third," Carol said.

351

"He wants to talk to whoever's in charge of Victor Orcutt Associates."

I made no move toward the phone and neither did Necessary. Finally, he said, "Take it, Dye."

I took the phone and said, "Lucifer Dye."

Old man Phetwick's voice was dry and gritty as emery dust. "I am grieved to learn of Mr. Orcutt's death," he said.

"Yes. All of us are."

"So is Dr. Colfax, who is on the line with me."

"I was sorry to hear about it," Colfax said.

"Yes," I said.

"Poor Mouton, too," Phetwick said. "Is he really mad?"

"I'm no doctor," I said, "but he looked crazy to me."

"Orcutt's death changes things," Colfax said, all business now that condolence time was over.

"Especially for Orcutt," I said.

"With the Lynch person gone and with the police department reorganized by Mr. Necessary, I think our main objectives have been accomplished," Phetwick said. "In view of Mr. Orcutt's death, we have decided that we can dispense with the services of his firm. This is no reflection on you, Mr. Dye, and we expect to offer a generous cancellation settlement."

"You want us to pack up and leave then?" I said, more for the benefit of Necessary and Carol than for my own clarification. I understood what he wanted.

"Well, yes, if you insist on putting it that way," Phetwick said.

Dr. Colfax chimed in. "You did your job, Dye, and a damned good one. Now we don't need you anymore, so we'll pay you off and everybody's happy."

I decided to go formal. "Would you hold on please while I confer with my colleagues for a moment?"

"Sure," Colfax said.

I turned to Necessary and Carol. "They want us to bug out," I said. "They'll make a cash settlement."

Necessary frowned and carefully removed a piece of lint from the sleeve of his blue uniform. He looked at Carol. "Had Orcutt told them about what Dye and I have got set up with Luccarella and the out-of-town guys?" he said.

"No," she said. "He was going to tell them today."

352

"He tell them about the senator and the magazine?"

She nodded. "He told them about that. Phetwick's already got the counter-attack written."

"They're trying to cool it off," Necessary said.

"So it seems," I said and took my hand from the mouthpiece of the phone. "It'll only be a few seconds," I said.

"Take your time," Colfax said and chuckled to demonstrate that he understood how people might scurry about when they suddenly found themselves out of their jobs.

"Well?" I said.

Necessary looked down at his blue left sleeve again, stroked it gently with his right hand, smiled to himself, and then looked up at me. "I think," he said softly, "I think they're going to have to fire themselves a chief of police."

I nodded. "Carol?"

"I'd like to see if he gets the girl in the last reel."

I took my hand from the phone. I looked at the mouthpiece rather than at Carol and Necessary. I felt their eyes on me. I took a deep breath. "I explained things to them," I said.

Phetwick's voice was dry and remote. "I knew that they would be reason—"

"Our answer is no," I said and hung up.

40

I wasn't asleep when Necessary called at six-thirty Friday morning. I was lying in Carol's bed, staring at the ceiling, and thinking about Victor Orcutt. He seemed far more attractive in death than he had in life, but there must be a great many persons who seem that way.

"It's started," Necessary said.

"When?"

"Just before dawn. Luccarella and his friends went calling."

"On who?" I asked.

"On all of them."

"What happened?"

"The next flight out of here is a direct one to Minneapolis and St. Paul. It leaves in fifteen minutes. Tex Turango's on it."

"He's from Dallas," I said.

"The Onealo brothers are from Kansas City, but they're on it, too," Necessary said.

"Anyone else?" I said.

"Sweet Eddie Puranelli. All he could get was economy class."

"But he took it."

"Uh-huh," Necessary said. "And glad to get it. Lt. Ferkaire says Puranelli doesn't look too well. There're some teeth missing, Ferkaire says, and one eye's closed, and something's wrong with his nose. Looks busted, Ferkaire says."

"He'll feel better back in Cleveland," I said. "What about Nigger Jones and Jimmy Schoemeister?"

"That's why I'm calling you."

"Where are you?" I said.

"In the lobby."

"I'll be down in fifteen minutes."

"Make it ten," Necessary said and hung up.

Carol rolled over in the bed and propped herself up on an elbow. "Necessary?" she said.

"He said it's started."

"You want some coffee?"

"No time."

"I can use the immersion unit."

"Okay," I said and started to dress. She had the instant coffee ready by the time I came out of the bathroom. I drank two sips and lit a cigarette. I used to smoke Pall Malls then.

"He say anything else?" she asked.

"Some are leaving town; some aren't." I drank more of the coffee and then handed her the cup.

"I never knew what life could be, captain," she said, "until you came here to Pago Pago."

I kissed her. "I'm riding with them, Alma," I said. "Sodbusters've got rights too."

Necessary was pacing the lobby when I stepped out of the elevator. His eyes looked tired and bloodshot and it gave them a peculiar three-toned look, or four, if you counted their whites.

"You took long enough," he said in the grumpy voice of a man who's been up most of the night.

"I had to rinse out a few things," I said and followed him to the long black Imperial which waited in front with Sergeant Krone at the wheel.

Once we were rolling I asked Necessary about Nigger Jones and Jimmy Twoshoes. He shook his head as if trying to clear it. "They won't budge," he said. "Their people came in last night. Schoemeister's got about a dozen; Nigger Jones's got about the same."

"What's Luccarella got now?"

"About ten from New Orleans and maybe a dozen more from back East. Ferkaire's keeping score out at the airport."

"Anyone prominent?" I asked.

He shook his head again. "Run of the mill guys; nobodies."

"So it's a three-way race now," I said.

"Three-way," Necessary agreed and stared out the window. "You know something," he said.

"What?"

"The little fellah would have liked all this."

"Orcutt?"

"Yeah. He'd of wanted us to report in with color Polaroid shots of all of them. Then he'd of started plotting and figuring what to do next."

"You miss him, don't you?" I said.

He nodded again. "Sort of. Don't you?"

"Sure," I said and then tried to determine whether I'd lied. I decided I hadn't.

"He had a head on him," Necessary said. "You got to give him that."

"I don't think it's hard to figure out what he'd do now," I said.

Necessary turned to me and I'm sure he was totally unaware of the look of relief that spread across his face. He needed a new Orcutt and he thought he'd found him in me, but he was wrong, of course. I was intuitive where Orcutt had been coldly logical. I made it up as I went along while Orcutt already had the next two paragraphs polished in his mind. Orcutt had been a genius and I was just barely smart enough to knot my own tie. I didn't want to play Orcutt for Necessary. I wanted to tag along and now and then say, "That's right, Chief."

"What do you think old Orcutt would do?" Necessary said.

"Where's Nick the Nigger?" I said.

"In a private home over in Niggertown."

I sighed. "I think that Orcutt might remind Schoemeister of that, in case he didn't already know."

Necessary stared at me for several moments. He shook his head slowly and then smiled, but there was nothing pleasant in it. "Orcutt never would've said that."

"No?"

"No," Necessary said. "He was damn cold-blooded, all right, but never that cold-blooded."

We went calling on Frank (Jimmy Twoshoes) Schoemeister in his four-room suite on the top floor of the Lee-Davis Hotel, which was in a ho-hum race with the Sycamore for the title of "Swankerton's Finest." We had to go through three of the suite's rooms before we were ushered into the one that Schoemeister occupied. He was alone, but the three rooms that we passed through had contained young and middle-aged men in quiet suits. They had looked at us with flat, expressionless stares and then gone back to whatever it was they had been doing, cleaning their Thompsons, I suppose.

Schoemeister smiled at us with his ruin of a mouth and

I checked the morning's shoes. They were made of soft-looking brown mottled leather and when Schoemeister caught my glance he said, "Ostrich," and I said, "They're nice."

He turned then to Necessary and said, "Out early this morning, aren't you, Chief?"

Necessary nodded as he gratefully accepted a cup of coffee that was brought in and silently served by a slim, fit-looking man in his late twenties. "Not as early as some," Necessary said, after a sip. "Not as early as Luccarella."

"A real early riser," Schoemeister agreed, watching the young man pour my coffee. After serving it, he sat in a chair in the farthest corner of the room. Necessary looked at him and Schoemeister said, "Don't let Marvin bother you. He's my nephew. My oldest sister's kid."

"What've you got in those other three rooms?" Necessary said. "Cousins?"

Schoemeister smiled terribly again. "Just some friends."

"I counted eleven of them."

"That's about right."

"Did Luccarella count them?"

"I don't know," Schoemeister said. "He didn't stay very long."

"What'd he want?" Necessary said.

"He wanted me to catch a plane."

"To St. Paul?"

"That's right. He seemed to get a little upset when I told him that I didn't know anybody in St. Paul. Not even in Minneapolis."

"The Onealo brothers do," I said.

"Is that a fact?" Schoemeister said, trying to make it sound as if he were actually interested, and succeeding fairly well.

"They caught that plane," I said. "So did Tex Turango and Puranelli."

Schoemeister nodded at the information. "What about Nick the Nigger?"

"He doesn't know anybody in Minneapolis either," Necessary said. "Or St. Paul."

"Nick's still here, huh?" Schoemeister asked, trying to make it casual, and again almost bringing it off.

"He's staying with friends," Necessary said. "About

twelve of them over on seventeen thirty-eight Marshall in Niggertown."

Schoemeister glanced at his nephew who nodded. "I always liked Nick," he said, "but that Luccarella's something else. He's buggy. I wonder if they still call him Joe Lucky?"

"I think the newspapers do," I said.

Schoemeister locked his hands behind his head and gazed up at the ceiling. "Somehow," he said softly, "I don't think they will any more."

When we were in the Imperial again. Necessary stared at me and I saw that the chill was back in his eyes. "Okay," he said, "you're calling it. Now what?"

"We pay another social call."

"On who?"

"On Nick the Nigger."

"Yeah," Necessary said softly and smiled a little. "Orcutt would have done that, too."

41

Sergeant Krone parked the car on 47th Street, around the corner from 1738 Marshall. We were in the heart of the upper middle-cleass section of what everyone called Niggertown—even its residents—and it looked very much like its white counterpart across the tracks, except that the blacks' lawns seemed to be a shade better tended, if that were possible. They also used more imagination when it came to trimming their shrubbery. I spotted a dog, a cat, and what must have been a giraffe that were all carved or trimmed out of thick, hedge-like plants.

Krone stayed with the car and the sports page as Necessary and I walked to the house at 1738 Marshall. It was a large gray brick rambler with a graveled roof and a picture window that boasted the inevitable decorator lamp with a scarlet shade and a yellow ceramic base. The house belonged to William Morze, a plump, sixtyish Negro with gray hair, a number of young girl friends, and a fondness for yellow Cadillacs. He had two of them parked in his garage, a convertible and a sedan.

Morze, sometimes referred to as Saint Billy, ran the black section of Swankerton and had done so since the end of World War II. He distributed what little political patronage there was, operated his own charity, oversaw the flourishing numbers business, conducted a profitable loanshark operation more or less as a sideline, ran a thriving burial, life and auto insurance agency, and contributed steadily, if not heavily, to the Democratic party. It was Morze who opened the door to Necessary's knock. There was a bell, but I'd never known Necessary to use one when he could pound on a door.

The black man wore a yellow silk dressing gown, maroon pajamas, and fur-lined leather slippers. His brown eyes flicked over Necessary and me and registered dislike, even contempt, before the big white smile split his face and he slipped into his Southern Darkie role. He did it well enough.

"Why, I do b'lieve it's Chief Necessary and Mr. Dye," Morze said, mushing it all up. "You gentlemen's out early this fine mawnin."

"We're looking for Nick Jones," Necessary said.

"Nick *Jones*," Morze said thoughtfully, as if he might have known someone by that name a long time ago, but wasn't quite sure. Then he gave us his brilliant smile again. It was also brilliantly meaningless. "Now I do b'lieve Mistah Jones is up and receivin. Come right on in."

Nick the Nigger could have passed if he'd wanted to. In fact, he had at one time when, fresh from Jamaica, he had used his English accent and tall, lithe blond good looks to hustle rich widows along Miami Beach. They could be of the grass or sod variety, and they could be thirty or sixty; it didn't matter to Nick as long as they could pay his stud fee which, some said, ran as high as a thousand a week.

Jones, a living embodiment of at least one American dream, saved his money and when he thought he had enough he deserted the glitter of Miami Beach for the squalor of Miami's black ghetto. He shot his way into the rackets against competition as bitter and ruthless as could be found anywhere. He also invented his nickname, insisted that it be used, and if it wasn't when his picture appeared in the Miami papers, which it did often enough, he'd call up the city desk and raise hell. I remember somebody once telling me that the Jamaican had even considered changing his name legally to Nick the Nigger Jones but, for one reason or other, never got around to it.

Jones waved at us lazily from the far end of Morze's thirty-five-foot living room which could have been copied from a 1954 edition of *House Beautiful*. It was that kind of furniture and that kind of taste. He was sprawled on a green divan, dressed in a cream polo shirt, fawn slacks and brown loafers. He wore no socks.

"Help yourself to some coffee, Chief," Jones said, not rising. "You look as if you could use it. You too, Dye."

"Thanks," I said, "I will." I poured two cups from an electric percolator and handed one to Necessary who sipped it noisily. Nobody asked us to sit down so we stood in front of the picture window.

"How was Luccarella?" Necessary asked Jones.

"Luccarella," Jones said softly and then said it again.

"Pretty name, don't you think?" He turned to Morze who sat slumped in a green easy chair that faced the large window. "Do we know a chap called Luccarella, Bill?"

Morze grinned and this time looked happy about it. "I b'lieves he was with the gentlemens who came callin earlier this mawnin," he said, still talking mushmouth.

"Ah," Jones said. "*That* Luccarella." He was silent for a moment and then gazed directly at Necessary. "He's quite insane, you know."

"So I hear," Necessary said and sipped some more coffee.

"He kept raving about some plane or other that was scheduled to leave at six-forty-five this morning or some such ghastly hour. He even seemed to think that I should be on it."

"He thought a lot of people should be on it," Necessary said. "Some of them agreed with him."

"Really?" Jones said. "Who?"

"Puranelli's on it," Necessary said. "He's a little busted up, but he's on it. So are the Onealo brothers. Tex Turango caught it, too."

Jones nodded thoughtfully. "I think," he said after a moment, "that it may be far more interesting to learn who's not on it."

"Schoemeister," Necessary said. "He's not on it."

Jones once again nodded his tanned face with its cap of tight golden curls. His eyes, I noticed, were dark brown with long thick lashes. He had a thin, straight nose and a broad mouth that smiled easily above a neat chin. Nick the Nigger was almost pretty.

As he picked up his cup and headed toward the percolator, I turned toward the window and saw them. There were two of them, two Ford Galaxie sedans, and they came much too fast down Marshall Street. I shoved Necessary hard and he went reeling away and crashed into a small table some fifteen feet from the window. Jones turned quickly, holding his cup in his left hand and the percolator in his right. I dived at him and the hot coffee spilled over my neck as we tumbled and twisted down behind the far end of the green divan. I could see Morze start to rise from the green easy chair that matched the divan. He was halfway out of it before the picture window shattered and one of the bullets slammed him back in the chair. It seemed to press him deep into its cushions. There was another burst from the submachine gun, or they could have had two of them, but the second burst hit nothing other than three framed prints of some Degas dancers who were dressed in pink and white.

I could hear one of the cars roaring off and I wondered how deep its rear wheels churned into Morze's finically kept lawn. I stared at Morze who leaned forward now, his mouth open as he tried to gasp big gulps of air. My peripheral vision saw the first one as it arched through the broken picture window. I tightened up quickly into a ball as the grenade's explosion blasted through the living room. I didn't see the second one; I had my eyes squeezed shut, but it sounded louder than the first and underneath me Jones screamed and jerked violently.

The grind and roar of the second car as it dug its wheels into Morze's lawn was all I could hear for several moments after the second blast and I couldn't hear that too well because I seemed to be partially deaf. Then there was nothing, only that godawful silence that I'd heard once, a long time before, if you can hear a silence, on Shanghai's Nanking Road.

I opened my eyes and rose carefully. The room was a mess and William Morze huddled in the remains of the green chair, whimpering, a blinded mass of black flesh that was covered with strips of torn yellow silk and patches of dark red blood. Nick Jones writhed on the floor and screamed once more. I bent down and saw that the left leg of his fawn slacks was soaked with blood just below the knee. I ripped the slacks open and looked at his calf. It was beeding all right, but it wasn't serious. I tapped him on the shoulder. "You'll live," I said.

"It feels like the goddamned thing is gone," he said and managed to sit up. I turned and looked at the opposite end of the room. Necessary was already on the phone, talking into it from around one of his Camels. He hung up and moved toward us.

Suddenly the room seemed full of tall, broad-shouldered blacks who poured into the living room from the rear of the house. Some of them held revolvers. They advanced on me threateningly until Jones waved them away. He sat on the torn and shredded divan and stared at his bleeding leg. Then he looked up at the blacks and said, "One of you motherfuckers go see if the bathroom's got anything to bandage this with." A chunky tan man hurried away and then they all began talking at once.

Necessary was bending over Morze. When he got up, he shook his head. "Dead?" Jones asked.

"He's alive, but I think he's blind," Necessary said. "If the ambulance ever gets here, they might keep him alive. Maybe. He's a mess." He turned to me. "You all right?"

"I'm okay."

Morze was whimpering again in the remains of the green chair. Jones stared at him. "He was a very good old man," he said softly. The six or seven Negroes were quiet now, looking at Morze with a kind of horrified fascination. The chunky tan man returned with a roll of gauze and knelt down by Jones and started to bandage his bleeding calf. He wasn't very good at first aid.

Necessary drew close to me. "You saw them," he said.

"Just two cars. Two Fords. That's all I saw."

"You couldn't tell who it was." Necessary wasn't asking questions; he was merely stating the facts as he understood them.

"They were too far away," I said.

Necessary nodded and then looked at me with his brown and blue eyes. "Thanks for—" He never did finish thanking me for whatever favor he thought I'd done him, probably the hard shove that had sent him reeling down the living room, because the siren screamed outside. We looked through the shattered window and it was Sergeant Krone and the Imperial. Krone was out of the car now and running toward the house, his .38 revolver drawn. He kept swinging the revolver from left to right and back again and the crowd of blacks opened and then closed behind him. There must have been five hundred of them and they stared at Krone and at the house and at its shattered window.

"Where the Christ did they come from?" Necessary asked.

One of the blacks opened the door for Krone and he bounded through, waving his .38 around. "Will you put that goddamned thing away," Necessary snapped. Krone gazed around wildly before he put the revolver back in its holster.

"What happened?" he asked. "They called me on the radio with an OIT here."

"Well, they were right," Necessary said. "An officer

363

was in trouble, but he's not now so you can take all these people into the rear of the house and get their names and find out if they saw anything."

Just as Krone was herding the last of the blacks through the door that led to the rear of the house, we heard another siren. A red-and-white ambulance edged its angry way through the black crowd and two white attendants got out and started rolling a stretcher toward the house. Two squad cars, their sirens also moaning, arrived just after the ambulance. Four white cops spilled out of the cars, took a look at the sullen crowd which must have grown to 750 by then, and started edging toward the house, their hands on their holstered gun butts. Necessary, watching, shook his head in disgust. "Christ," he said, "all we need is for one of those rednecks to shoot some nigger."

I let the ambulance attendants in and they frowned when they saw what was left of Morze who still whimpered and squirmed in the green chair. The older of the two looked at me and grimaced. "I reckon we'll have to take him all the way down to Charity emergency," he said and frowned again as if he didn't much care for long rides.

Necessary tapped the attendant on the shoulder. "What's the closest hospital?" he demanded.

"I suppose the Colfax Clinic is, but—shit—we can't take a nigger there."

Necessary shot out his right hand, grasped the attendant's shirt front, and jerked him close. Their faces were no more than six inches apart. "You're going to take two niggers to the Colfax Clinic," he said softly, "and they're going to get the best treatment there is by the best doctors there are. You understand?"

The attendant nodded—a little vigorously, I thought.

"And if you get any static from anyone at the Colfax Clinic, you tell them that unless these two niggers get the best treatment there is, then Chief Necessary's gonna get whatever kind of court order he needs to close that place down tight by six o'clock tonight. Now you got that?"

The attendant nodded again, even more vigorously than before. "Yessir," he said. "I understand."

Quickly, the two attendants loaded the whimpering Morze onto the wheeled stretcher. I moved over to Jones and helped him up. "You'd better go with him," I said.

364

Jones nodded and grimaced at the pain as he stood on his wounded leg.

"Here," I said, and took his left arm and draped it around my shoulder. We moved slowly out of the house, past the four cops, and into the crowd which by now numbered at least a thousand. It was a sullen, too quiet crowd. They pressed in close to the wheeled stretcher and there were some gasps and oh mys when those near enough caught sight of Morze's bloody, blinded face. I helped Jones limp close behind the stretcher.

Morze suddenly popped upright and screamed: "Nick! I can't see, Nick! Where's Nick?" Then he collapsed on the stretcher as I helped Jones to kneel down by him.

"I'm here, Bill," Jones said softly. The man on the stretcher nodded and stared wildly about with his sightless eyes. "You gotta do something, Nick, you gotta do something for me." He said that loudly enough for those who pressed close to hear it.

"Come here," Morze said, "come here, Nick."

I helped Jones go closer. "You gotta do it, Nick."

"Whatever you say, Bill."

Then he whispered his dying request and there were only two who heard it, Nick the Nigger and me. "Burn it, Nick, burn the fucking place down." Then William Morze whimpered once more and died.

I helped Jones rise. He looked at the crowd of dark faces that encircled him. "What he say, Nick?" one large black man demanded. "What Saint Billy tell you t'do?"

The word spread quickly through the crowd—Saint Billy done told Nick what to do. Other voices near the stretcher started demanding the instructions. Nick the Nigger looked around carefully at the encircling black faces. Then he looked at me and smiled faintly. "This one's for you, Dye."

"Don't do me any favors," I said.

"Help me over to that one," he said, indicating the large black who had first asked what Morze's final request had been. I helped him over. He looked at the man for several moments. The man stared back patiently.

"You want to know what Bill said?"

"We gotta know," the man said.

Nick the Nigger nodded several times, not taking his gaze from the man's face. "Bill said cool it. That's all. Just cool it."

I helped Jones limp the rest of the way to the ambulance. The word had already flashed through the crowd and it was beginning to disperse by the time I helped him into the rear of the ambulance where he sat next to the dead William Morze.

"We're even now, Dye," Jones, just before they closed the doors.

"We always were," I said.

42

By three o'clock that Friday afternoon Mayor Pierre (Pete) Robineaux was pounding on Necessary's desk and demanding that Swankerton's police force be withdrawn from Niggertown. "They got the First National for fifty thousand," Robineaux yelled and slammed his fist down on the desk for the ninth time in forty seconds. "Fifty thousand!" he yelled, "and it was forty-eight goddamned minutes before a cop showed up. Forty-eight minutes!"

Necessary leaned back in his chair with his feet propped up on the desk. He nodded at the Mayor. "The FBI's looking into it," he said. "They're pretty good at bank robberies. I think they catch about half of them." He looked at me. "Or is it a third?"

"I think it's half," I said.

The mayor sputtered and pounded the desk again. "You got a crime wave going on, Necessary! A goddamned crime wave!" Boo Robineaux, the mayor's son, looked up from his copy of *The Berkeley Barb* and smiled at his father. A little contemptuously, I thought.

Necessary took his feet down from the desk and leaned forward in his chair. "Now you can take your pick, Mayor," he said coldly. "You can have yourself a full scale race riot that can wreck this town or you can put up with a few extra holdups."

"A few!" Robineaux yelled, his face taking on an apoplectic shade of red. "You call eighty-nine armed holdups a few?"

"Better than watching the whole town burn," Necessary said and put his feet back on the desk.

"Listen to me, Necessary. Listen to me now! If you don't get those men out of Niggertown within the hour and back to protecting life and property over here, you won't be wearing that badge by sundown." The mayor pounded his fist on the desk again. "I'll have your ass, by Christ, I will!"

"Who you working for now, Boo?" I said.

367

The mayor's son jerked a thumb at his father. "It," he said.

"Well, now, mayor, just calm down a little," Necessary said. "As soon as the feelings about old man Morze's death sort of simmer down over in Niggertown, I'll call the men back."

"Goddamn it, Necessary," the mayor yelled, "there ain't no trouble in Niggertown! The trouble's all over here."

"I'm exercising my professional judgment, Mayor Robineaux," Necessary said coldly. "Law and order is *my* business—not yours."

Robineaux pranced over to the black tinted window and waved at it. "Look out there! They're robbing the fucking city blind and you sit there and call it law and order!"

The idea had come to Necessary on our way back from Morze's house. When he was through explaining it to me, I turned to him and said: "Homer, Orcutt would have been proud of you." I'd never seen Necessary look happier.

At nine o'clock that morning he canceled all leaves and ordered ninety-five percent of the Swankerton police force into Niggertown. They patrolled it—every square block of it—on foot and in cars. By eleven o'clock they had made two arrests. Doris Emerson, twenty-three, was booked for soliciting. Miles Camerstone, thirty-seven, was taken in for drunk and disorderly.

On a normal day the white section of Swankerton experienced between two and three armed robberies. By eleven o'clock that Friday morning, forty-six had been reported—not including the First National Bank which had been hit by a lone white gunman with a stocking mask over his face.

In Niggertown, the citizens strolled along the sidewalk and goodmawnined and lifted their hats to the patrolling police. And then they smiled broadly and used their hands to stifle their giggles. By noon, the frustrated cops were looking for jaywalkers without much luck. Niggertown had cooled it.

Necessary yawned when Robineaux, his eyes bulging, once more crashed his fist down on the desk and screamed: "You're fired, goddammit!"

"Pete, you know you can't fire me," Necessary said

calmly. "The city council's got to do that—a majority. And I understand that most of them are partying over in New Orleans."

"Throw him out," I said. "You're wasting your breath."

"By God, I think you're right." Necessary buzzed for Lieutenant Ferkaire who popped in looking harassed and a little forlorn. "Show the mayor out, Lieutenant," Necessary said.

"I'm not going," Robineaux said and took a tight grip on the edge of Necessary's desk.

"The mayor, sir?"

"Throw him out."

"The mayor."

"The press is out there, Chief."

"Fine. He can make a statement on his way out."

Ferkaire approached the mayor and tentatively put a hand on his arm. "If you'll just step this way, sir."

"I said throw him out, Ferkaire. You're a cop, not a goddamned wedding usher."

Ferkaire looked first at the mayor who still clung to the desk, then at Necessary who glowered at him, and then at me. "Throw him out," I said.

There was a brief struggle, but not much of one. Ferkaire got a hammerlock on the mayor and marched him across the room. "I'll get your ass for this, Necessary," Robineaux yelled. "I'll get both of you for this!"

"Get the door for your father, will you, Boo?" I said.

"My pleasure," Boo said, opened the door, and made a low sweeping bow as his father was frog-marched from the room.

"Thanks," Boo said to me.

"Don't mention it," I said. And then, because I'd promised myself that I would, I said: "How'd you get those scars on your face?"

Boo nodded his head at the closed door. "Him. He did it to me when I was twelve. With an old piece of chain."

"For what?"

"For what do you think? For jerking off in the bathroom, what else?"

"What else," I said as he closed the door behind him.

Ferkaire popped back into the office and stared around, a little panicky, I felt. "You got any coffee out there?" Necessary asked him.

"He's making a statement to them," Ferkaire said. "They

got pictures of me throwing him out and now he's making a statement to them."

"I think I'll have a drink instead," Necessary said.

"I'll join you," I said.

"What'll I do with them?" Ferkaire asked.

Necessary poured Scotch into two glasses before he answered. "Send them in here about five minutes from now," he said. "I'll have a statement." Ferkaire nodded and went out quickly.

Necessary walked over and handed me a drink. "I can't keep them out there in Niggertown much longer," he said.

"You probably won't have to."

"When do you think Schoemeister will try it?"

"It could be any time now."

"You think it was Luccarella who got Nick and old man Morze?"

I shrugged. "Luccarella or Schoemeister. Does it matter?"

"I guess not," Necessary said. "I thought he'd stay in the hotel though. He'd've been smarter to stay in the hotel."

"You mean Luccarella?"

"Yeah. Luccarella."

"No back way out," I said. "That's why he moved to that old house of Lynch's."

Necessary took a long swallow of his drink and smiled. "Well," he said, "we found what we were looking for anyway."

"What?"

"Something to stir it up with."

"You mean the long enough spoon?"

"Uh-huh."

"There's only one thing wrong with it," I said.

"What?"

"It's a little longer than I'd counted on."

There was no reason to be polite to the press anymore and Necessary wasn't. A dozen reporters crowded into the office and we ignored them until the television cameras were ready.

"This live?" Necessary asked.

"That's right."

"I got a statement to make."

"We want to ask you some questions, chief. Why did you throw Mayor Robineaux out of your office?"

"What's your name, sonny?" Necessary asked his questioner, a prominent local TV personality. It hurt his feelings. "Campbell," he said. "Don Campbell."

"Well, Don Campbell, if you don't shut up, I'm going to throw you out just like I did the mayor."

Two newspapermen and a wire-service reporter tittered.

Campbell whirled quickly to his camera and sound men. "You get all that? Did that go out?"

"We're getting you right now, stupid," the cameraman said.

Necessary stood up behind his desk. "I have a statement. It's not prepared, but I'll make it and then you can ask some questions." He cleared his throat and stared into the lens of the nearest camera. "Through the efforts of the men of this police department, the city of Swankerton has been spared the horror of a serious riot. The brutal murder of William Morze could have provoked a tragic disturbance—the kind they have up North. It didn't. And we can thank the good common sense of our colored population—and the efforts of Swankerton's policemen—that it didn't. I would like to announce that we know who the killers of William Morze are. They will be arrested within a few hours. In the meantime, law and order will prevail in Swankerton." Necessary started to sit back down, but instead came back to the microphone, said "Thank you," and then he sat down.

"Why did you throw the mayor out of your office?" Campbell asked.

"The mayor is ill. He was helped out of my office."

"He said that he was going to have you fired."

"Like I said, the mayor is ill and isn't responsible for what he says. Next question."

"How long have you known who killed William Morze?"

"Not long."

"Can you reveal their identity?"

"No."

"How many armed robberies have been committed in the white section of Swankerton today?"

"More than usual."

"How many?"

"The last figure we had was one hundred three."

"Jesus Christ!" a wire-service man said.

371

"Would you call that a crime wave, chief?"

"I would, but I'd rather have a crime wave than a race riot and that was the choice we had to make."

"What's been the total take so far?"

Necessary looked at me. "Close to a quarter of a million," I said.

The wire-service man said Jesus Christ again.

"The mayor says you're more interested in protecting blacks than you are in protecting whites and their property."

"The mayor's sick," Necessary said.

"What's wrong with him?"

"Ask his psychiatrist."

"Has he got one?"

"If he doesn't, he should."

"He says he's going to call the National Guard in."

Necessary smiled and circled his ear with a finger. I watched the cameras zoom in on that for a close-up and then I rose and said, "That's it, gentlemen. The press conference is over."

"Hey, Dye," a wire-service man called to me. "You think the mayor's nutty?"

"As peanut brittle."

"Can I use that?"

"I hope you do," I said.

It was nearly 5 P.M. before the call came from our man who was watching the Lee-Davis Hotel. "They're coming out now," he said, his voice tinny over Necessary's desk telephone speaker.

"How many?" Necessary asked.

"I counted thirteen."

"Schoemeister with them?" Necessary said.

"He's in the first car. They got three cars."

"Okay," Necessary said.

"You want me to follow them?"

"No," Necssary said. "We know where they're going."

He switched off the speaker and looked at me. "How long's it take to get from the Lee-Davis to that old house of Lynch's?"

"Fifteen minutes," I said. "Maybe sixteen."

He nodded. "You'd better tell Ferkaire that I want every ambulance in town there in forty-five minutes."

"When'll we get there?" I said.

"When do you think?"

"In about forty-five minutes," I said.

Carol Thackerty came in a quarter of an hour later and told me: "I didn't know any place else to go." She looked at Necessary. "I saw you on television, Homer. You came over well."

"I know," Necessary said. "Sincere."

"Extremely," she said.

"I wonder if it'll go network?" he asked.

"Why?" I said.

"Well, I'd just sort of like the wife to see it."

The second call came from a plainclothes detective that we'd stationed in a house across the street from the Victorian one that Ramsey Lynch had once occupied. It was now home for Giuseppe Luccarella and nearly two dozen assorted friends.

Necessary turned on his desk telephone speaker again. "Okay, Matthews," he said. "We just want you to tell us what you see—not what you guess. I'm not going to interrupt with any questions except this one: you know what Schoemeister looks like?"

"He's the one with the mustache and the funny looking lips."

"That's right. It's all yours now."

"Well, there's not a hell of a lot to see. Sometimes one of them will come out on the porch and look around and then go back inside. I figure that there're maybe a couple of dozen of them in there—at least that's what I counted since I've been here and that's been since ten this morning. Luccarella got here about noon, I guess. I haven't seen him since. Wait a minute. There're some cars coming down the street now—three of them. They've stopped in front of the house now. About four guys in each car—maybe five in the back one.

"It looks like Schoemeister in the front car getting out on my side. Two guys are getting out with him. One of them's got what looks like a pillowcase. He's waving it around and he seems to be yelling something at the house. Let me get the window open and maybe I can hear what he's yelling."

We could hear Matthews' grunts over the phone speaker

as he tried to open what must have been a stubborn window.

"I got it," he said. "He's yelling for Luccarella to come out. That they want to talk. The pillowcase must be some kind of truce flag or something. Anyway, they're still waving it. Now somebody's coming out of the house—a baldheaded guy. He's carrying some kind of white handkerchief or something. He's yelling something about halfway—that they'll meet halfway.

"I guess that's okay with everybody. The door to the house is opening and it looks like Luccarella—let me get the glasses on him. Yeah, it's Luccarella. Schoemeister's moving around his car now—the two guys with him. One of them's carrying the pillowcase. They're on the sidewalk now and Luccarella's at the porch's screen door."

We heard it then. It was the long crack of a submachine gun. "Oh Jesus Christ Goddamn sonofabitch!" Matthews moaned over the speaker. "Jesus Christ! Oh, God!"

"Quit praying and tell it!" Necessary snapped.

"They shot em. They shot all three of them. Luccarella dove back through the door and they used a submachine gun and they got all three of them. I mean Schoemeister and the guy with the pillowcase and the other one. Schoemeister's guys are firing at the house now and a couple of them are dragging Schoemeister back to the car. The one with the pillowcase is crawling back. They shot the baldheaded one on the steps. He was one of Luccarella's. I think he's dead. I know goddamned well Schoemeister is. They're dragging him into the car and still firing at the house. Aw, Christ."

Necessary didn't seem to be listening any more. He was busy strapping on an open holster that held a .38 caliber revolver. When he was through with that, he reached into his desk drawer, brought something out and offered it to me. I just looked at it. "It's a gun," he said. "A Chief's Special."

"I know what it is," I said.

"You may need it." He gazed at me curiously. "You know how to use it."

"I know."

"Then take it, for Christ sake, and let's go."

My hand moved toward the gun and an hour or so

later I was holding it and when I looked at it, that was all that it was, a gun. I dropped it into my coat pocket.

"Just you and me?" I said.

"That's right, Dye, just you and me."

43

By the time we got to the old Victorian house eleven ambulances jammed the street and their white-coated attendants were wandering around looking for someone to cart off to a hospital—or the morgue. A crowd of around two hundred or two hundred and fifty persons had formed and they were all telling each other what had happened. One of the ambulance attendants spotted Necessary and pushed through the crowd toward him.

"I can't find anything or anybody, Chief," he complained in a whining, nasal tone. "Everybody says they heard a lot of shots and there's sure as hell a lot of blood on the sidewalk, but there's nobody dead. There's not even anybody sick."

"Must have been a false alarm," Necessary said.

"With all that blood?"

"That's right," Necessary said, "with all that blood. Now tell the rest of those ambulances to get on out of here."

The attendant shrugged and disappeared into the crowd. We pushed through it and made our way up the walk, skirting the bloody spot where Schoemeister must have died. I wondered if the man with the white pillowcase had been his oldest sister's kid, Marvin.

I let Necessary do the pounding on the door. It was opened cautiously by the man called Shorty. He grinned when he saw who it was and opened the door wide. "Worked out real nice, didn't it?"

"What worked out nice, friend?" Necessary asked.

"Yeah. Well, come on in—he's expecting you."

We followed him into the stiff parlor where the man from New Orleans with the squeezed-together face wore the broadest smile he could manage. There was a magnum of champagne on the coffee table. Samuels, the lawyer, was fiddling with its cork.

"Just in time," Luccarella said happily. "You just made it for the celebration." He nudged Necessary in the ribs. "The way you got rid of the cops out in Niggertown. That was something, Chief, really something, let me tell you."

"There could have been a riot," Necessary said.

Luccarella snuffled. "A riot," he said. "I thought it was a real riot when I saw old Schoemeister's face. You should've seen it—it was really something." He turned to Samuels. "Give the Chief a glass of champagne. We're gonna celebrate, by God, because it all worked out so nice. It worked out so nice that I even sent all the boys back home except what you see right here."

There were six of us in the room now. Necessary, Luccarella, Samuels, the man called Shorty, and another one whom I didn't know and didn't particularly want to meet. He leaned against the wall across from me and smiled pleasantly at everything.

"I haven't got time for champagne, Mr. Luccarella," Necessary said.

"What do you mean, you haven't got time? And what's this mister shit? You don't have to call me mister. I don't like it that you should call me that."

"You're under arrest for the murder of William Morze, Mr. Luccarella," Necessary said just as Samuels popped the cork out of the champagne bottle. The lawyer looked up quickly. The man across the room from me stopped smiling. Luccarella's face colored—a bit purplish, I decided. Necessary raised a small, typed card that he'd palmed and started to read Luccarella all about his rights. Then he looked at Samuels and said, "Does Mr. Luccarella understand these rights?"

Samuels nodded slowly. "He understands them."

"Let's go, Mr. Luccarella," Necessary said, reaching for the man's arm. Luccarella danced away, his mouth working furiously, but making no sound.

Finally he stopped dancing around and pointed a finger at Necessary. "You crossed me, you sonofabitch!" he yelled. "You swore you wouldn't and you crossed me. I didn't have nothing to do with killing any Morse or whatever his name is. You goddamned well know I didn't. You're putting the frame on me, Necessary, you and that slick buddy of yours."

Necessary turned to Samuels again. "Maybe as his lawyer you should inform him of his rights and make sure that he understands them."

"I don't think—" Samuels made a helpless gesture with his hands and moved away from the champagne bottle and toward the door to the hall. He looked around once frantically and then darted through it.

"Let's go, Luccarella," Necessary said again.

"No, by God! It's a frame. I got friends—I got friends just like anybody else." He hurried over to a small desk and yanked open a drawer. He pawed through it and almost got the revolver out, but Necessary moved over quickly and slammed the drawer on his hand. Luccarella screamed and sank to the floor, clutching his injured hand. Necessary reached down, got hold of an arm, and yanked him to his feet. Luccarella squirmed loose again and danced over to the man by the wall, the one that I kept watching.

"Shoot him, goddamn you! Kill him!" Luccarella was screaming now. "You saw what he done to me!" The man looked at Luccarella and then at Shorty who stood near the door. They nodded at each other. The man against the wall came up with his gun and I shot him twice and then turned and shot Shorty once. Then I looked at the gun for what seemed to be a long time and laid it carefully on a table. Necessary had his revolver out now and was looking around, as if for someone to shoot. He aimed it at Luccarella.

The thin man's face contorted and his mouth worked and he screamed again. No words, just sounds. His analyst wouldn't have liked those sounds. Luccarella jerked open his coat and held it wide from his chest as he stumbled toward Necessary, still screaming. Necessary slapped him hard across the face and it stopped screaming and lost its distortion. It just looked old and crumpled now. "You shoulda shot me," he muttered. "You shoulda killed me."

Necessary turned to me. "You all right?"

"Sure."

"You didn't bring any cuffs along, did you? I forgot to bring any."

"You shoulda shot me, you sonofabitch," Luccarella said. He was whimpering now and I thought he sounded very much like William Morze.

"No," I said, "I didn't bring any cuffs."

"Christ," Necessary said, "I wish I'd thought to bring some cuffs."

The crowd outside the Victorian house had grown by another hundred persons or so when we came out the front door and walked down the steps that led from the screened-in porch. I pushed my way through the crowd and Necessary followed, his left hand clamped on Luccarella's right arm. Necessary had his gun out and clasped firmly in his right hand. Someone in the crowd wanted to know who the guy in front was and somebody replied that he was with the FBI and then someone else wanted to know why the FBI man didn't have no gun like the chief of police had.

We were halfway to the Imperial when Necessary yelled: "Look out, Dye!" I turned just in time to see him. He was coming at me fast, the familiar triangular-bladed knife held in the acceptable style and I remember thinking that he knew all the tricks that I knew, and then some, and that there wasn't one goddamned thing I could do about it but watch. So I did and, fascinated, heard the sound of the two shots and watched the twin holes appear in his vest. Just above the Phi Beta Kappa key. It was Carmingler. The one they sent when they sent their very best.

He stumbled backwards and dropped the knife and looked down curiously at the two holes in his vest. He didn't touch them. He looked at me and there was surprise and, I suppose, sorrow in his face. I remember thinking that he looked like a sorrowful horse. His mouth worked a little, but no words came out. He lurched toward me then and there was nothing else to do but try to catch him before he fell.

I caught him, but he was dead weight, and I knew I couldn't hold him up for long. He looked at me again, his face no more than a few inches from mine. The sorrow in his gaze seemed to have been replaced by contempt, but you can never really tell. It may have been just pain. His lips worked and finally he got it out, what he very much wanted to tell me.

"You still aren't very important to us, Dye," he said. I nodded, but he didn't see it because he could no longer see anything. I lowered him to the sidewalk gently, but it didn't matter any more how I did it because he was already dead.

Necessary, still clutching Luccarella, yelled at the crowd to move back. He picked out somebody and told them to call an ambulance. "Call three of them," he added.

He and Luccarella moved up to me as I stood there

379

staring down at Carmingler. "The hard case?" Necessary said.

"As hard as they come," I said.

"That was a goddamned fool thing of me to do in a crowd like this," he said. "I could have shot somebody."

"You did," I said.

"I mean somebody else."

"It doesn't matter now," I said. "You shot him."

"If it doesn't matter, then what the hell are you crying for?"

"I didn't know that I was," I said.

44

Three things happened Saturday, the day after the crime wave. First, as a special favor to the Swankerton Police Department, the First National Bank let me visit my safe-deposit box. They may have felt that it could help them get their stolen $50,000 back. It didn't.

The second thing happened after I left the bank. I called a private number at Police Headquarters and said: "I'm all done." Five minutes later Swankerton's chief of police submitted his resignation.

The third thing was the telegram that I got from New York. It read: "I died by my own hand last night. Just thought you might like to know. Regards. Gorman." A postscript read: "Mr. Smalldane left instructions insisting on the wording of this telegram." The postscript was signed by Gorman Smalldane Associates, Inc., and I wondered who they were.

45

I sometimes still take out a rather crumpled copy of that Sunday's edition of *The Swankerton News-Calliope*. Because it never published on Saturday, it was full of news that Sunday. There was the one-day crime wave, of course, and six or seven shootings and killings to recount and speculate about. There was also the resignation of the chief of police to announce. But in the center of the front page was a large three-column picture of a rather puzzled looking man and underneath it in very black, very bold forty-eight point type is a headline which asks the question:

WHO IS THIS MAN?

I sometimes read the story over because it's quite long and it goes into great detail about someone called Lucifer Dye. According to the story, Lucifer Dye was the man who corrupted Swankerton. All by himself. He was, if one were to believe the story, a onetime spy, a hired gun, a crooked cop, a confidence man, a crime czar, and an agent provocateur for some unnamed foreign power. He was also a long list of other things, none of them fashionable, and *The News-Calliope* hated the man and urged its readers to hate him and to undo the evil that he had done by going to the polls in November and electing good men to office. If they didn't, the newspaper implied in an editorial signed by Channing d'Arcy Phetwick III, they were fools. The editorial then thoughtfully listed a number of men who, it said, deserved the votes of all those citizens of Swankerton who weren't absolute fools.

I like to reread the long article about Lucifer Dye because it promises to tell who he really is, but it never does. I keep hoping that it will. Clipped to the fading newsprint is a shorter article, only a couple of inches long, that was torn from a copy of the international edition of *Time*. It's about how the citizens of Swankerton elected a last-minute, write-in slate to fill all of the major municipal offices. It has a kicker, of course, or *Time* wouldn't have printed it. The kicker is that one of the new city councilmen is Buford Robineaux, only son of the city's defeated mayor.

I live in Mexico now and I've quit smoking and I run a store in a seaport-resort town that sells books in English about Mexico to tourists who can't read Spanish. There seem to be a lot of them. It doesn't cost much to live in Mexico and the bookstore earns enough to support my wife and me. My wife's name is Carol and her best friend is a twenty-three-year-old stunner from the midwest whose husband runs a boat marina. Sometimes her husband and I go to a local cantina and drink beer with a redheaded Mexican who's the chief of police. The Mexican feels that there's nothing unusual about his hair, but he thinks that my friend has rare eyes because one is blue and one is brown.

We sit there and drink beer in the afternoon and talk about crime in far off places. We never talk about a place called Swankerton.

ALLEN DRURY
THE PROMISE OF JOY

Allen Drury gives a chilling look into an all-too-possible tomorrow in this engrossing saga, the last in Drury's magnificent series of novels about American politics which began with the Pulitzer Prize-winning ADVISE AND CONSENT.

Orrin Knox, the Senator from Illinois, has been elected President after a savage assassination attempt that killed his wife and running mate. In the face of brutal personal tragedy and brutal opposition from America's enemies, both within and without, he must stop the almost certain world destruction when Russia and China turn on each other with atomic weapons!

 AVON 27128 $1.95

POJ 2-76